To
Louie + Reggie

Margaret Mosci
"Maggie"

Longing for Wickhaven

MARGARET MASCI

authorHOUSE®

AuthorHouse™
1663 Liberty Drive
Bloomington, IN 47403
www.authorhouse.com
Phone: 1-800-839-8640

All characters appearing in this work are fictitious.
Any resemblance to real persons, living or dead, is purely coincidental.

First published by AuthorHouse 8/18/2009

ISBN: 978-1-4490-0750-8 (e)
ISBN: 978-1-4490-0748-5 (sc)
ISBN: 978-1-4490-0749-2 (hc)

Library of Congress Control Number: 2009907157

Printed in the United States of America
Bloomington, Indiana

This book is printed on acid-free paper.

This book is dedicated to my mom-in-law, Christine, the true definition of a muse and an inspiration to me for many years.

To Sherri, I miss you. Your enthusiasm and editing skills kept me hopeful. Both of these women have shared with me an appreciation for peace, nature, blessings, and love.

I am thankful for my husband, Nello, my son, Michael and my daughter, Michelle for their support and for backing me up with every cockeyed plan I come up with.

Chapter 1

The year was 1996 and the intensive care unit in Cleveland Heights Medical Center was abuzz with activity. The pungent odor of rubbing alcohol and freshly waxed floors hung heavily in the air. Nearing 7:00 AM, the ever-increasing *ping* of patient's call buttons alerted the staff that patients were awake and in dire need of pain medication and bedpans. What probably appeared chaotic was actually a rather organized shift change as the early morning staff arrived for a new workday. Nurses checked charts for new instructions, exchanged friendly chitchat along with the usual hospital gossip, while slow-moving, bleary-eyed cafeteria staff arrived with carts stacked high with breakfast trays.

Doctor Frank Candafini, a young surgeon that specialized in colon care, was standing at the nurse's station. He was leaning heavily on the counter, obviously exhausted, and his expression was pensive as he flipped through the pages of one of the many charts splayed before him. A stethoscope was draped around his neck, along with his loosened paisley tie, and he let out a frustrated sigh while running his fingers through a thick tuft of dark, wavy hair. He was tall and lean with sharp, handsome features, and his amber-colored eyes were bloodshot and heavy with fatigue.

"Who's assigned to Mr. Preste today?" he asked, of no one in particular. An impatient, strained smile crossed his lips as he looked from one nurse to the other.

"Right here, Doctor Candafini," answered Lily. She was a first-year nurse with a childlike voice, and deep dimples that dented her lightly rouged cheeks. She raised her hand, the rubber soles of her clogs squeaking as she approached him. Her freshly highlighted hair was pulled back into a ponytail that swayed from side to side as she crossed over to where he stood with a medical chart in his outstretched hand.

"Oh, your name's Lily, right?" He managed a cordial smile. "Mornin'." He finished writing in the chart and gave her a quick glance. His voice was low and raspy, and in a serious tone said, "Take a look at this chart please, and tell me if you can read my writing."

She took the chart from him, and smiled. "I'm sure I won't have a problem, I've had to decipher your chicken scratch before, Doc." She was suddenly aware of the strain on his face that told her he was in no mood to joke. She thought she saw his hand shake as he handed her the chart. "Sorry," she said, quietly and cleared her throat. Looking down at the chart, she gave the first page a quick read-through. She observed Doctor Candafini again. "You look like you could use some sleep, Doctor." When he didn't answer, she flipped to the next page. "Did you pull an all-nighter?"

"Yeah," he answered absently. He glanced at his watch, then over his shoulder. "What?" His attention turned back to her. "An all-nighter? Yeah, you could say that."

"Huh..." Lily looked puzzled. "You were here till late last night, weren't you? You never went home? I didn't think you were on call."

"No...uh, Lily is it?" He spoke with obvious irritation. "I left for a while, and I *did* get called in. Is that okay with you?" he asked, sarcastically. He dropped his head and mumbled. He took a deep breath and looked up at her, and quickly corrected his tone. He smiled apologetically. "Sorry...didn't mean to bark. Guess my mood is a little sour after a twenty-two hour shift. Mr. Preste had some major trouble last night."

"I can see that," she said, keeping her eyes on the chart in hopes to hide her hurt expression. She continued to read. "Wow." Lines of concern formed between her brows and she chewed at her lower lip. "That's a shame. He was doing so well. I'll keep an eye on him, doctor." She closed the chart with a 'clap'. "So, why don't you get outta here while you can? I'll call you if there's a problem."

"Please don't," he teased, seeming more relaxed. "Just kidding...call me if there's any change. I don't think there will be though, he's on the respirator for now...comatose..." He added, almost as an afterthought. He stood silent for a few seconds, shook his head, and took a deep breath. "I'll be back later to speak with the family." He slipped off his lab coat and hiked up his pants. "I'm outta here." He stretched his arms back, yawned and gave her a wink. "Thanks, Lily, and...uh sorry 'bout the mood.

"S'okay."

"Talk to ya later." He turned toward the double doors that led out of the unit, into the corridor, toward the main lobby.

*

The weather was unusually cold for early October, raining for the third day in a row. Dominic Preste was lying in a hospital bed, his head slightly elevated. He was in room #3 toward the back of the intensive care unit. An intricate entanglement of tubes and wires were attached to him, and plugged into various beeping machines. The drone of a respirator pulsated as it pumped artificial life into his chest, and his eyes were slightly open but fixed and devoid of life.

Dominic Preste's eldest son, Phillip got a call from his younger brother the previous night, and was shocked when told their father was in critical condition. The following morning Phillip and his wife, Bethany boarded a flight from Steamboat Springs, Colorado to Ohio. They rented a car at the airport, and drove through the small town where they were once high school sweethearts, and now headed to Cleveland Heights Medical where Phillip's father lay dying.

"Phillip?" Bethany said, quietly as he maneuvered the car into the hospital parking lot. She sat with her head leaning back on the seat, her hands resting in her lap.

"Hm?" Phillip glanced at her as he drove up and down the aisles of the crowded parking lot, looking for an open space.

"Can you believe that the last time we were at this hospital was more than twenty years ago, when Caroline was born?"

"Oh my gosh...that's right. Twenty years." His expression softened as he thought of Caroline and Andrew, now grown, and off on their own. Phillip pulled into an empty spot, turned off the wipers and ignition, and peered through the windshield at the familiar sight of the hospital where they had been so many times before. Both kids were born at Cleveland Heights Medical, and Andrew, as an active tot got his first stitches there. Beth's grandfather died in a room on the fourth floor. "Seems like a lifetime ago, doesn't it?"

"Sure does." She reached over and rubbed the back of his neck.

He let his head ease back into her hand, turned and gave her a slow smile. "Well," he sucked in a deep breath of air, held it, and slowly blew it out through puckered lips. "I guess we'd better get in there."

"Are you okay?"

"We'll see," he said, with a forced laugh.

Phillip felt secure with Beth at his side. He had grown to depend on her to the point that he never made a decision without her. He admired her ability to feel at peace in any situation, and wished he could find that peace one day, but doubted he ever would. Every time he looked at her, and seriously studied her face and her expressions, he was reminded of why he fell in love with her thirty-five years before. Her eyes were crystal blue, clear and sparkling with mischief. She had a wicked sense of humor that Phillip found hysterically funny, and at the age of fifty, she still had a childlike face, framed with straight blonde hair that she kept trimmed short and casual. She was comfortable in her less than slender body, and it seemed that her only aspiration in life was to make sure everyone was happy.

"Well, if you're sure you're ready, let's go." Beth hoped that the concern written on her face masked her own uneasiness at the prospect of being with his family again. It had been a long time. There were memories that still haunted her, even though she, Phillip and the kids had moved away years before.

*

Phillip was twenty-one when he married eighteen-year old Beth, and his father had never really accepted her into the family, and took great pains to make sure she knew it. His main complaint was that she wasn't Italian, but to further Dominic's anger, Beth and Phillip moved away from Cleveland Heights, and he blamed Beth for taking his son away from him. He refused to admit that his oldest son's marriage was a success, and that their children didn't turn out to be juvenile delinquents, as he predicted. He actually seemed disappointed that he was wrong. Dominic didn't like being wrong. He smirked whenever anyone mentioned that Phillip had built one of the most successful public relations firms in Steamboat Springs. He was jealous of his son, and Phillip found it hurtful and pathetic.

*

Phillip stepped out of the car, opened his umbrella, and walked around to the other side, and opened the door for Beth. "Stay under the umbrella, hon." He wrapped his arm around her waist and like a well-choreographed ballet; they sidestepped puddles of rain that filled the potholes in the parking lot. Finally reaching the overhang in front of the hospital's main entrance, he closed the umbrella and tapped it on the ground. Beth leaned over and brushed droplets of rain from her hair.

Phillip felt his face flush with apprehension. His stomach was in knots, and his thoughts were a jumble of questions. What was about to happen? Was his father actually going to die? A wave of guilt gripped him as he tried to wipe a brief sense of relief from his thoughts. Was it wrong for him to want his mother to finally have some peace?

As the automatic doors swung open, Beth linked her arm with Phillip's as they walked into the main lobby. After being directed to the ICU, Phillip went directly to his father's room, and Beth decided to give him some privacy and went to find the waiting room.

Phillip located room #3, and closed his eyes before entering. He took a deep breath and rubbed the back of his aching neck as he slowly approached his father's bedside. "My God," he whispered upon seeing the man he'd feared his entire life. He picked up the old man's lifeless hand, and was horrified to see that his father's usually ruddy complexion had turned a pasty shade of gray. His chest had taken on a grotesque shape as it rose up and down, responding to the pulse of the respirator.

Phillip was unaware that his younger brother, Vito was leaning up against the wall behind the open door. With his arms folded, he stared down at the floor, and only looked up when he heard Phillip enter the room. "Hey, Phil," Vito said, casually.

"Vito, holy sh..." Phillip put his hand to his chest, and snapped his head in the direction of his brother. "I didn't even see you there." He gently laid his father's hand on top of the white sheet that was covering him from the waist down, and walked over to where his brother now stood at the foot of the bed. The two men embraced, and gave each other a friendly thump on the back. "Hey listen, thanks for calling me yesterday," Phillip said.

"No problem. Mom didn't want me to, but I saw Dad like this..."

"Yeah," Phillip looked back at his father. "God, he looks awful."

The two brothers stood quietly as they watched and listened to the respirator.

*

Even though Phillip was ten years older than Vito, the resemblance between the two brothers was striking and both looked like their father. Phillip was middle-aged, and of average height and slight of build. He had dark, thinning hair that curled at the nape of his neck. His complexion was olive-colored, like his mother's but furrowed with deep lines in his cheeks and forehead that, for some reason Beth found 'dreamy'. His eyes were like his father's; deep blue-green and intense, hooded in a way that made them appear sad. His smile was warm and captivating. Years removed from the dysfunction of his youth, he was sensitive and thoughtful, with an attractive sophistication that one acquires when re-raised by the people you meet in adulthood.

Vito was a head taller than Phillip, with a solid, stocky build. What little hair he had was fine and straight. He had a dimpled grin, and hazel-colored eyes, with thick, dark lashes. He, like Phillip was financially successful, working his way up to an executive position with the local phone company, and strangely enough, unlike the way Dominic was jealous of Phillip, he was proud of Vito.

Vito laughed at his own jokes, and was rarely serious, but like his father, was quick tempered and possessed an over-sized ego. He was married with two sons that Phillip had only seen a handful of times over the years, and with little contact between the two brothers, this current reunion was pleasant but awkward for both.

"Go 'head...go 'head." Vito gestured to Phillip to go back to their father's bedside. "I've been with him all night. Hey...uh, did Beth come with ya?"

"Yeah, she went to a waiting room. I guess she'll find Mom." Phillip turned back to Vito. "She's here, right...Mom's here?"

"Oh yeah, are you kidding? She wouldn't leave if ya dragged her. You know...the whole guilt thing. Dad had her running like a maniac... before this happened."

Vito resumed his position behind the door. He leaned back, crossed his arms and bent his knee and placed the sole of his brown, wing-tipped shoe against the wall. It had never occurred to him that their father's minor surgery would soon be followed by a massive heart attack. He thought about the day before when Doctor Candafini assured him and his mother that the surgery went well, and that Dominic would be fine.

Phillip stared at his father's face for a remote sign of life, then turned to Vito, "It was only a cyst on his colon, for God's sake. What happened, Vito? Did the doctor explain anything to you?"

"No...I don't know, Phil," he responded, shrugging his shoulders. "They said he was doin' okay, and then all of a sudden...I don't know... they said it was a heart attack. When I got here last night, he was in a lot of pain...I mean really bad pain, and he was panicking. Hey," he said, raising his eyebrows, "you know how Dad is. He was goin' nuts and throwing things around the room. Holy shit...I didn't know what to do." Vito's head bounced up and down as he laughed nervously. "So, the doctor gave him some kind of a shot to calm him down, I went home to get Ma, and when we got back...well, this is how we found him; on this respirator thing and all these tubes and shit...I don't know," he said, shaking his head.

Phillip turned back to his father and took his hand again, and Dominic, seeming to sense his oldest son's presence, weakly squeezed his hand. "Damn," Phillip said under his breath. A wisp of a smile crossed Phillip's lips, as it occurred to him that this was the first time that he could remember a sign of affection between father and son. He mostly remembered the pain of his father's fists, and the biting humiliation of his ridicule. It was strange now, at this moment, feeling compassion for the man, but this was the first time Phillip had ever seen his father weak and vulnerable.

*

Phillip's mother, Connie was sitting quietly in a waiting room down the hall from the ICU. The room was cold and smelled of cleaning fluid and stale coffee, and she was shivering even though her shoulders were wrapped in a thin, scratchy blanket a nurse had given her earlier that morning.

Her mind was like a tape recorder, playing and replaying the events of the previous day. She thought about Dominic being brought to his room from recovery. He looked good, seemed comfortable in the cheerful room on the second floor. When he was settled in the bed, she had nervously fussed over him, fed him ice chips, wiped his face with a cool rag, and made sure he was warm enough. She had smoothed his covers, and arranged his pillows all the while crying that she was sorry this happened to him.

"Connie? What the hell are ya doin'?" Dominic had asked irritably. "Would ya sit down and stop fussin'? And what're sorry about, for Christ's sake...you didn't give me a cyst!" His voice was raspy from the tube that had been inserted in his throat during surgery.

Connie obeyed, sat, folded her hands and stared at him until he drifted off to sleep. She got up, tip-toed to the foot of his bed, and rearranged the water pitcher, a tube of lotion, a tissue box...

"Connie! My God, would you stop?"

"Oh! Did I wake you?" She put her hand over her mouth.

"Yeah, how'm I supposed to sleep with you movin' stuff around there?" He whined. When he noticed she was about to cry again, he waved a hand at her. "Ah...don't worry 'bout it, Connie. You can't help it that you do stuff like that. Listen, I want you to do me a favor."

"What is it, Dominic?" She rushed to his side.

"I want you to go home and get a couple things for me."

"What's that?"

"I need my comb and toothbrush. Oh, and bring me some clean pajamas. I hate this shit'n thing they got on me now," he said, tugging at the neckline of the hospital gown that was draped over him and tied around his neck.

"Okay," she said, wringing her hands and nodding anxiously.

"Come right back though, ya hear?"

"Oh sure Dominic. Are you sure it's okay for me to leave? Can I get you anything before I go? "

"No, go ahead. Jesus...you're drivin' me nuts.

"Sorry Dominic."

"Just hurry up, and calm the hell down, would ya? My God...ya make me a nervous wreck."

"Sorry."

"And stop sayin' you're sorry!" He barked, and grabbed his stomach. "Maybe on your way out, you could ask the nurse if I could get some more stuff for pain." He sucked in air and winced as he shifted his position in the bed. "Sonofabitch! Ow!"

"You're having pain?"

"That's why I need the pain stuff, Connie," he said, sarcastically through clenched teeth.

"Okay, okay, don't get upset." She patted the mound under the blanket that was his foot and adjusted his covers again. She leaned over and kissed him on the cheek before leaving the room.

After making sure Dominic would get more pain medication, she inhaled a breath of cool, damp air as she walked out of the hospital. She let the rain mist her face for a few seconds, covered her head with her purse, and ran through the parking lot to Dominic's pumpkin-colored Cadillac. It was crookedly parked in the last row of the lot, looking like an over-sized cabin cruiser. She slid in the driver's side, wrapped her fingers tightly around the wheel, and closed her eyes.

"Sweet Jesus, give me strength," she pled, in a high-pitched cry. When she felt steady enough to drive, she started the car, and craned her neck to peer over the top of the steering wheel, and drove the few minutes home.

She climbed the two steps onto the tiny back porch, reached her hand under the mat and retrieved the back door key, and let herself into the house. After putting the things that Dominic asked for in one of Vito's old gym bags, she perked a pot of strong coffee, poured herself a cup, and sat down at the table. She placed her hands over her face. Her eyes felt gritty, and swollen as she rubbed them with her fingers. She smoothed her honey-colored hair that now had at least two inches of dark roots, streaked with gray.

Connie looked as tired as she felt. She had been tired for years. She survived on black coffee and ice cream, and accepted the fact that she hadn't mattered for a long time. Only Dominic mattered.

She looked down at herself, and realized she was wearing the same brown, polyester slacks, and pink and white striped pullover she had worn the day before. After taking Dominic to the hospital the previous day, she came home, and ended up sleeping in her clothes, on the sofa in the den. She had spent many nights on the sofa, since it became her habit to start her day at two or three o'clock in the morning. Sleep did not come easily to Connie. Years of worry scored her face with deep lines and creases, and darkness surrounded her eyes; eyes that were once warm, and a rich brown, now looked haunted, tired and red-rimmed.

She took a sip of the hot, black coffee and savored the bitterness on her tongue, feeling herself relax. The house was uncommonly quiet. She wondered what it would be like to live like this all the time. Quiet, just sitting, or eating ice cream and listening to Sinatra on the radio. She jumped when the phone rang, rudely interrupting the precious silence. She reached for the phone on the wall just above her head, and grabbed the receiver.

"Yes?" she asked tentatively.

"Ma, it's me." It was Vito. "I gotta come over and get you, and bring you back to the hospital."

"Coming back to get me…why? What happened? I was going back in a little while." Connie was suddenly aware of a sour feeling in her stomach.

"It's Dad, Ma. I don't know what's happening. I'm comin' to pick you up, so wait there for me. I don't want you to drive in this rain."

Something was terribly wrong. Hanging up the phone, she went to the kitchen sink, splashed water on her face, and dried it with a dishtowel. She grabbed the gym bag, and waited by the kitchen door, nervously tapping her one long fingernail on the doorframe while she watched for Vito's car.

He arrived within minutes, and gave the horn one quick blast. Connie stepped out the back door, paying no attention to the rain that was soaking through her sneakers and socks as she ran to the car. Vito leaned across the seat and opened the passenger side door for her.

"What happened, Vito? I just left him." A stream of rain dripped from the top of the car door into her hair. She quickly pulled the door shut.

"I dunno, Ma. I got there right after you left, and when I went to Dad's room, they told me they brought him to intensive care."

"What the hell…" Connie covered her mouth with her hands.

Vito shivered and turned up the heat. "And Ma," he said, with hesitation, "I called Phillip. He's on his way."

"Oh, Jesus, Joseph and Mary, it's that bad?" she gasped, making the sign of the cross. They rode the rest of the way in silence. Connie stared out the window, her lips moving in prayer as Vito drove through the driving rain the short distance back to the hospital.

I'm glad I called Phil. Vito angrily told himself. *Why am I the only one to have to deal with all this shit?* The car's tires cut through deep gullies of rain. Waves of water splashed over the sidewalk as he pulled into the driveway in front of the hospital's main entrance.

Connie jumped out of the car and ran inside to the front desk, and after getting directions to ICU, got on the elevator without waiting for Vito. It seemed to take forever for the elevator to come to a stop and when the doors finally opened, Connie approached the nurses station, and breathlessly asked, "I'm Mrs. Preste, where's my husband?"

"Mrs. Preste?" A nurse named Francine smiled, and noticing Connie's panic, gently took her by the arm. "Let me take you to your husband but first, we'll see Doctor Candafini, okay?"

"Oh, yes...the doctor…" Connie mumbled with confusion. "Can *you* tell me what happened?"

"Oh, there's Doctor Candafini, just down the hall." Francine guided Connie by holding her elbow. The two women approached the doctor, who was leaning up against the wall, writing in a chart. When he saw Connie, he placed the chart in the holder on the door. He reached out his hand as he walked toward her. Before speaking, he looked at her, his eyes warm and sympathetic.

"What happened Doctor? What's going on?" Connie asked.

"Well, to be honest with you, we didn't expect *anything* to go wrong, Mrs. Preste. Your husband was doing fine, then he got very agitated, and after trying to calm him…well, he went into cardiac arrest. We were able to stabilize his breathing with a respirator, but I'm afraid there's been too much damage." He waited for her to respond. "He's on life support, Mrs. Preste…not breathing on his own," he added.

"Oh, my God." Connie felt her legs go weak. "What do I do? Is it my fault?"

"What? Your fault?" He cocked his head and gave her a confused look. "What happened to your husband couldn't be helped, Mrs. Preste. We're doing all we can right now."

"Can I see him?"

"Of course. Francine, would you take her please?"

"Sure, come with me Mrs. Preste." As they walked, Francine said, "There are some other family members here."

"What? Oh, you mean my son?"

"No, not your son. I think your husband's sisters…I'm not sure."

"Oh, dear Jesus…" Connie grimaced. "Just what I need right now."

They continued toward ICU. Connie took a deep breath when she spotted Dominic's two sisters standing in the hall outside the unit doors. She felt her face flush as she approached them, and swallowed the acrid saliva that had suddenly collected in her throat.

"Conchetta," Gia snarled through her thin, brightly painted lips. Her voice was guttural as she spoke with a pronounced Italian accent. She was in her sixties, well dressed with a heavily lacquered hairdo that covered her head like a helmet. Her tone was icy, as usual, and she pronounced Connie's name as though it left a sour taste in her mouth. She eyed Connie with repugnance. "They won't let us in, for God's sake! We're his family," she growled indignantly. "We're here…where have *you* been?" She asked with an accusatory tone. "Maybe if you had been here, this would not have happened to our brother. You leave him here alone? What's wrong with you?"

"Gia, for God's sake. I just went home to get a few things he asked for," Connie shot back, defensively.

Annette, the younger of the two sisters, was bracing herself against the wall. Also in her sixties, she wore a dress that hugged her less than slim body, with a neckline low enough to reveal a wrinkled cleavage. Overly dramatic but less caustic than her sister, she held a tissue to her nose, and sobbed. "Oh dear God…Dominic…he's dying, I just know it. Mother of God, Connie, what did you do to our brother?"

"Jesus Christ," Connie hissed under her breath. "Get out of the way. I have to go in and see my husband." She pushed past them, and walked through the doors of the ICU.

*

After shifting to another chair in the waiting room, Connie folded her arms and laid her head back against the wall as she thought about the night before, recalling walking into Dominic's room. She found him laying flat on his back; arms down to his sides, stiff, like a soldier at attention. She had held her breath, and put her fingers to her lips when she saw the thick rubber tubing that was placed in his mouth, and secured with surgical tape. She couldn't help but feel the urge to gag. She swallowed hard, placing her hand to her throat. His chest was heaving mechanically, and his eyes were slightly open but vacant. Her eyes locked on his face, and a whimper escaped her throat. Tears stung her eyes as she thought about the many times she had wished him dead. Her stomach felt like ice.

"God forgive me. Please, please, please," she had begged, her eyes gazing heavenward. "Is this my fault?"

She had taken his hand and sat by his bedside that night. Not until dawn did she let a nurse escort her to the room where she still sat and waited, for what...she didn't know.

*

"Mom," Beth whispered, as she peered around the corner of the waiting room's doorway.

Connie looked up and started to cry when she heard Bethany's voice. She stayed seated but stretched out her arms, beckoning her daughter-in-law to come to her. Beth warmly embraced her, and kissed her on the cheek.

"Beth, oh my God" Connie said, with a quiet sob. "I'm so glad you're here." She dabbed a balled up tissue to her eyes. "Where's Phillip?" She glanced over Beth's shoulder toward the empty doorway.

"He went in to see his father. He'll be here in a while," Beth said, gently placing her hand on Connie's cheek. "Are you okay, Mom?" Connie grabbed hold of Bethany's hand and pulled her into the chair next to her. Beth glanced up at a television that was hanging from the ceiling, providing the only light in the room. The sound was turned off. "Mom, I'm so sorry." Beth shifted in the chair to face Connie.

"I know, I know," Connie lamented. She closed her eyes and nodded slowly. "I don't know what happened. He was doing fine...then all of a sudden..." her voice trailed off, "I'm so glad you're here. Was your flight okay? Are you hungry?" She rambled but before letting Beth answer, sat back and asked, "Let's just sit quiet for a while, huh?"

"Okay Ma, but can I get you anything? Have you had anything to eat?"

"No Bethany, come on...you know I can't eat." She looked at Beth as though she had said something stupid.

"Sorry...I was just wondering." Beth quieted and looked down at her lap.

Connie leaned her head back, closed her eyes, and moved her mouth silently, in prayer.

The two women sat side by side. Connie was still quiet but Beth fidgeted, first crossing her right leg over her left, then her left over her right. She squinted at the silent television; the screen filled with a map covered with raindrops across the mid-west. She yawned, her eyes tearing and burning.

Later that morning, Phillip's sister, Luci walked into the waiting room. Connie lifted her head with a jerk. Beth smiled and silently mouthed the word, hi.

Luci was dressed in jeans, a pink hooded sweatshirt, and sneakers. She wreaked of cigarette smoke and hairspray, and with her car keys in one hand, she juggled a Dunkin Donut's coffee in the other. Beth was shocked to see how her sister-in-law had aged. Luci was a year younger than Bethany but her face was sallow and wrinkled, with dark purplish circles under her eyes. She was forty-nine years old, with frosted hair that she wore in the same style she wore in high school, and for whatever reason she only wore the upper part of false teeth, causing her lower lip to sink in.

Luci lived only minutes from her parents, as did Vinnie who was the youngest of the four Preste kids. Vito lived an hour north, with his wife, Barbara and their two young sons, Nicky and DJ, short for Dominic James.

Luci, like her brothers was born and raised in Cleveland Heights, and fresh out of high school married a dropout who soon became the town drunk. They had three sons, and lived a life of dysfunction for thirty some-odd years, which seemed to suit them just fine. She now seemed mildly pleased to see Bethany, and casually gave her a quick hug, as though they had seen each other the day before. She leaned down and kissed her mother on the cheek.

"Hi, Ma…how ya doin'?" she asked, in a deep whiskey voice that made Bethany wince. Connie didn't speak but pointed to a chair across the room, and Luci obediently sat. "How *you* doin', Beth?" Luci asked. Her tone was cool and flat. "Ya look good."

"Thanks, Luci. You look good, too," Bethany lied.

"Christ…I haven't seen you in what…three years?"

"Has it really been three years?" Beth responded, raising her eyebrows for emphasis.

"Time flies, huh?" Luci joked. Her attempt at a laugh was more like a grunt. "How was your flight? Were you scared? God, I hate flying… scares me to death. If I can't drive, I won't go nowhere, know what I mean?"

"Well, I'm not scared of flying, Luci," Beth said, trying to disguise her irritation. She turned her head and rolled her eyes. She didn't know why, but it irritated her that Luci, along with the rest of the Preste family focused on fear and negativity. But it was just one of those things that set Beth's teeth on edge. She felt her jaw tense. "Nothing to be afraid of," she added.

"You're braver than me then," Luci grunted again. Placing her coffee cup on the chair beside her, she folded her arms and looked up at the television.

"So, how are *you* holding up, Luci?" Beth asked, breaking an uncomfortable silence.

"Okay, I guess. This is nuts though, ain't it? Christ, ya never know what's gonna happen." She nervously brushed her hand on the lap of her jeans as though wiping away crumbs that were not there. "Yup… this is crazy, all right. Life's a bitch, as they say." She grunted again and seemed edgy. She looked over at her mother again. "You okay, Ma? Can I gitcha anything?"

Connie sat with her head still resting on the wall behind her. Her eyes were closed, and when she didn't answer, Luci looked at Beth and with an uneasy grin, shrugged.

"And the boys…how are they?" Bethany changed the subject.

"Oh Jesus, they're okay, I guess," she said, jerking her head in order to flip the hair from her eyes. "Little Ray, he's in community college, and Kevin's in junior high. Can you believe it?" She looked up and gave Beth a cock-eyed smile when she thought about her middle son. "Craig's okay, I guess. He's workin' at a gas station...he's, ya know... tryin'... he's got a lot a problems...but, ya know...he's in counseling, and he's got one of them big brother guys...takes'm out and stuff. He's doin' better, I guess. Doesn't really mean the shit that he does." She paused and smiled. "My ol' man won't let him come back home, though." She was rambling again, wringing her hands. "Shit...I could use a cigarette," she said, twisting in her chair as though there was going to be a place she could go light up. "So...Ma? Is there anything new about Dad?" She settled back in her chair and quickly changed the subject.

Connie was leaning forward now, with her elbows on her knees, and her face resting in her hands. Once again, there was no response.

"We haven't heard anything new, Luci," Beth volunteered. "Phil's in with your father now."

"Oh, I guess I should go see him. I would 'a been here sooner," Luci said, defensively, "but I had to take Kevin to his soccer practice, and then stop at the store for cigarettes." Another grunt. "Kids, they drive ya crazy, don't they?"

"Yeah, sometimes they do," Beth politely agreed.

"And my ol' man...God, forget about it. What a pain in my ass! The bastard took my car away from me again. Did I tell you that, Ma?" She looked toward her mother, who was still sitting with her head in her hands. "Bastard," she repeated. "But I told him, 'hey, my dad's in the hospital, for Christ's sake. I need the car! And I don't need your shit neither', I said."

"Lucinda, please..." Connie finally broke her silence, with an exasperated cry. "Not now, for God's sake! Don't mention that sonofabitch in front of me!"

"Oh...sorry, Ma," Luci said, with an embarrassed expression. She looked at Beth and grimaced. "I guess she don't wanna hear it."

"That's okay," Beth said. "I think she just wants quiet right now." *Oh my God...get me outta here!* The words screamed in Beth's head.

"So...where's Vinnie, Ma? Did anybody call him to tell him about Dad?" Luci asked, dismissing Beth's suggestion to be quiet.

"No." Connie sighed, tilted her head and gave Luci an icy stare. "Luci, come here," she ordered.

"What? What do you want, Ma?" Luci looked confused.

"I said…come here," Connie repeated sternly. She pointed an arthritic finger at the floor. Luci got up and walked to her mother and stood, obediently in the spot that her mother had indicated. Connie reached into the bottom of her purse, pulled out a handful of crumpled-up hundred-dollar bills and thrust them at Luci.

"What's that for?" Luci asked, curiously.

"Go down to city hall and bail out your jack-ass brother."

"Oh, God…what'd he do now?" Luci shifted her weight to one foot, put her hand on her hip, and rolled her eyes.

"Just you never mind. Go get him but tell that sonofabitch not to come here! I don't want him at the hospital. He's an embarrassment to this family. Tell him to go home to his house, and wait for me to call. Do not come to the hospital! Do you hear me, Luci?"

"I hear ya, Ma. Jesus…take it easy, will ya?" She said, indignantly. "What're ya mad at me for?"

"Just do as I tell you."

Luci took the money from her mother, and stuffed it into the pocket of her jeans. "I'll be back later I guess," she mumbled, and walked toward the door. "Hey, say hi to Phil for me, will ya, Beth? Tell him I'll see him later."

"I will."

Once again, the two women were alone. Connie was tense and chewed at her bottom lip. "May God forgive me," she blurted, pounding her fists on her thighs. "I'm embarrassed to say Vinnie is my son. That bastard is gonna kill me yet!"

"Oh geez, Mom," Beth responded looking alarmed. "I'm sorry you're going through all this. Listen, don't worry about Vinnie right now, okay?" Beth felt helpless, and hesitantly patted Connie on the arm.

Hours dwindled. Connie was in constant motion, flexing her hands, tapping her heels on the tile floor, every few minutes a quiet moan.

Beth struggled to keep her eyes open. *Where the heck is Phil?* She wondered. *I wish I were home in bed, with the electric blanket turned on high.* She suddenly felt selfish. *God, how I dread seeing Vinnie*, she thought to herself. He gave her the creeps. A shiver ran down her spine just thinking about him. He had always made her feel uncomfortable, and she could only imagine what he'd been arrested for this time. He was a drunk and a "druggie", as his parents called him. He'd been arrested so many times that there were probably several arrests that she and Phil didn't know about. Beth and Phillip heard about how many jobs he was fired from; how much money he owed to drug pushers, and about the times he had been beaten up. His parents bought him a house that was now trashed, and being shared with fellow drug users and ex-convicts. Phillip had gotten to the point where he didn't want to know anything more about his youngest brother. It was too embarrassing and too painful.

Luci never came back to the hospital that day. Connie, feeling tired and disgusted angrily grumbled that Luci had probably bailed Vinnie out of jail, and with whatever money was left over, was probably used to get drunk at some bar over on Cedar Road.

" Oh my gosh...do ya think?" Beth wasn't really surprised. She actually felt a sense of satisfaction that her mother-in-law finally realized what her grown children were really like. Beth knew all along but Connie was in denial for years and always made excuses for Vinnie and Luci. When Connie finally calmed, Beth yawned, stretched and briefly closed her eyes.

Connie suddenly sat up straight. "I can't do it, Beth!" She proclaimed, her voice high-pitched. She wrapped her fingers tightly around Beth's arm.

Opening her eyes wide, Beth was startled. She looked around the room to see what had happened. "Do what, Ma?"

"I can't tell them to pull that plug!" She said, with a desperate cry. "God will have to make that decision because I can't do it! I just can't!"

"The plug...oh," Beth nodded. "The life support thing." When she gathered her thoughts, she realized what her mother-in-law was stressing over. "Mom, listen," she said, wrapping her arm around Connie's quivering shoulders. "I'm sure you won't have to make a decision like that. Please, don't worry." She held her tightly but Connie pulled away. "Let's calm down, Mom, okay? Let's not worry about that right now." '*Oh God, Phillip...where the hell are you?*'

Connie shuddered, and rested her head on Beth's shoulder, which took Beth by surprise. She reached over and tentatively patted her mother-in-law's arm. Not that Connie was cold, but she always seemed uncomfortable with signs of affection. Hugs were usually quick and unemotional. Dominic didn't like seeing Connie touched by anyone; not even her own children.

Quiet again, both women sat staring at the silent television screen. Beth's lips curled into a sleepy grin as she watched Elmer Fudd, wearing a red hunter's hat chase Bugs Bunny through the forest, his rifle shots just missing the awnry rabbit's tailend.

Craning her neck to the left, Beth discovered that she was able to see the small corner of a window across the hall from where they sat. The rain had stopped, and she was surprised to see that it was already getting dark. *Gosh, how long have we been sitting here?* She thought. Her lower back was aching, and her stomach growled, reminding her that she hadn't eaten since dawn that morning. She remembered she had a package of peanut butter crackers, and deftly scrambled for them in the bottom of her purse. She offered one to Connie but not surprisingly, she waved refusal.

Connie turned to face Beth, and placed her hand on Beth's arm again, more gently this time. "Beth," she said, calmly. A bewildered but relaxed smile crossed her lips. "I feel happy. Why in the world would I feel happy right now? Am I going crazy or something? Why do I feel such…I don't know, relief all of a sudden?"

"What do you mean, Ma?"

"I'm serious. I feel happy."

"Maybe you dozed off and were having a dream or something."

Before Connie could speak again, Doctor Candafini walked into the waiting room. His expression was somber.

"Mrs. Preste? I'm awfully sorry. We did everything we could, but your husband just passed away."

Chapter 2

It was the late 1800's when Angelina Luccio was born in the province of Avellino in Compania, Italy. Vincenzo Borzanna, the son of a cheese maker was a young boy raised in Naples. Their fathers were longtime friends and had discussed the marriage of their two oldest children well before the boy and girl learned how to walk. The two played together as children, and when they became of proper age, they obediently did as their fathers had planned, and married with a traditional Italian wedding that lasted for days, with dancing in the streets, gallons of homemade wine flowing, and tables full of delicious dishes prepared by neighbors and relatives.

The two were well suited for each other, and because they were childhood friends, were used to each other's likes and dislikes. They understood each other's sense of humor, and Angelina was looking forward to being Vincenzo's wife. She was a head taller than Vincenzo but had a way of looking at him that made him feel taller. She respected him, trusted his judgment and admired his courage. He was her protector, and she liked that.

Vincenzo walked with pride and confidence. He held his head high, and his back straight. Always impeccably dressed, he seemed dignified and determined. He was not particularly handsome, but more boyish-looking, with jet-black hair, parted on the side, and a feathery mustache that covered his upper lip. His skin was smooth and olive-colored, his eyes, dark and serious.

Angelina, a pudgy child was now a young woman of seventeen carrying enough weight to be considered buxom. Her hair was dark and silky, parted in the middle and pinned under, just below her ears. Her face was youthful and vivacious, with warm brown eyes and a classically shaped, Italian nose that Vincenzo humorously liked to tweak when she was mad. Her crooked smile thrilled him, and he loved the way her eyes warmed when she looked at him. She was shy, but opinionated when asked. Her mother had made sure her young daughter was domestically trained, prepared to be obedient but demanding of respect.

Much to their parents' surprise and disappointment, Vincenzo and Angelina decided they wanted to move to America to live and raise a family. After the wedding, Vincenzo continued to work in his father's cheese shop near the coast of Naples while Angelina stayed with her parents. He saved his pay and along with a substantial amount of money they'd received as wedding gifts, they decided they had enough to make the trip to America.

Vincenzo finally bid his family goodbye, traveled to Angelina's home and stayed with them until it was time to leave on their trip across the ocean.

They sat on the edge of Angelina's bed each night, repeatedly counting the money they'd saved. They stacked it neatly one last time, placing it in a cigar box that Angelina got from her father. She tied the box securely with string, and placed it under the bed that she now shared with her young husband, and they excitedly anticipated the day they would leave for America. That day came two months later. Mrs. Luccio wept as she helped them pack. She made sausage and pepper sandwiches, wrapped them in brown paper, and put them in a sack for them to eat during their ride to the coast, where they would board a ship called the *Carmania.*

Vincenzo retrieved the cigar box from under the bed, buried it in the bottom of Angelina's travel satchel, and instructed her to never let it out of her sight. She held it tightly under one arm as she embraced her father, mother, brothers, several aunts and uncles and finally her Grandmother Violetta before letting Vincenzo pull her into the back of a two-wheeled cart owned by their neighbor, Constantine. Angelina wept and buried her face in Vincenzo's shoulder as they drove off.

A lumbering, sway-backed horse called Poco neighed as he labored to pull the cart, heavy with bags of clothes and hand-crocheted linens. Mrs. Luccio stood in the doorway of the house, holding a white lace handkerchief in her hand, waving it in the air. She held another handkerchief over her mouth to stifle her cries. Mr. Luccio stood stoically, his arm wrapped around his wife's waist, and as he watched the cart slowly disappear, a single tear trickling from the corner of his eye.

*

The sky was a deep azure blue, and dappled with puffy clouds above the Bay of Naples. Vincenzo and Angelina stepped from Constantine's wagon, and were rendered speechless as they took in the sight of the *Carmania* docked before them.

"*Mamma mia*!" Constantine marveled, his eyes traveling from one end of the ship to the other. "*La barca e' molto grande!*" He lifted the bags from the wagon and set them at the young couple's feet, never taking his eyes from the ship.

"*Si, grande,*" Vincenzo agreed, his youthful eyes filled with wonder. Turning, he took Constantine's hand and pumped it vigorously with gratitude for the ride. "*Grazie, Signor Constantine.*"

"*E' piaceremio. Non c'e-niente che io non favei per la madre di Angeline e perie pepe',*" Constantine responded, explaining that he would do anything for Angelina's parents. Vincenzo gathered up the bags, took Angelina by the arm, and led the way toward the multitude of passengers congregating at the edge of the pier. Placing his hand above his brow to shield his eyes from the sun, he looked up at the massive body of the ship, and turned to Angelina and gave her a reassuring smile.

Many Italians boarding the ship were called *birds of passage*, working as migrant laborers in America for a year or two, and bringing their hard-earned money back to Italy. Vincenzo planned on staying in America for good.

It was the twelfth of May, in the year 1912. Stepping foot on the main deck of the ship after a slow progression up the gang plank, Vincenzo handed over their two tickets and he and Angelina were led to a stairway that took them below to steerage, where they would stay for the remainder of the trip. What they hadn't realized was that steerage was actually the bowel of the ship. Rows of narrow, metal bunks crowded the area. Frenzy erupted, as passengers made their way down the stairs, snatching up the first bunk they came to. Vincenzo flung his satchel on an upper bunk that was tucked behind the stairwell, and Angelina claimed the bunk below. She looked up at Vincenzo with a triumphant grin, and bounced on the thin, horsehair mattress.

"*Il letto e' giusto,*" she said, giving her approval.

"*Si,* is okay," he agreed. His smile was not as convincing as hers.

She ran her hand over the coarse, brown blanket that covered the bed, and looked up at Vincenzo again, this time forcing a smile.

Every bunk was now taken. Mother's, fathers, grandparents and children scrambled to get situated. The din of noise grew as they stashed their belongings under their bunks. Two and three children huddled on single cots, and mothers, with confusion and worry in their eyes, held tightly to their babies, and waited to see what was to happen next.

A uniformed officer came halfway down the stairs, rang a large brass bell and read from a clipboard he held in his right hand. Without waiting for everyone's attention, he began to shout the rules for anyone who may have been listening, then turned and ascended the stairs, slamming the door behind him.

Vincenzo understood that they were only allowed to go one deck above twice a day for food, and to wait for the sound of the bell before doing so. Angelina was horrified when she realized there were only two bathrooms to be used by more than three hundred people, the smell of which was already making her stomach turn.

Later that evening, they discovered that the food provided to them was nearly inedible, and reeking of stale fish. They had to peel away green mold from hunks of bread, and the water tasted salty, and smelled of sulpher.

Vincenzo and Angelina realized they were in for a hellish experience. It was stifling hot, and soon after leaving port, the nauseating stench of sweat and vomit permeated the air. Children cried through the night, and quieted only in the wee hours of the morning when their small bodies were too sick or too tired to cry anymore. Many people were seasick, and most were dehydrated. The younger, healthier ones tended to the sick or the babies whose mothers were desperate for sleep.

Vincenzo and Angelina lay in their bunks most of the time, he staring at the framework of iron pipes just six or seven feet above his bunk; she staring at the springs of Vincenzo's bunk above her. Angelina often crocheted while Vincenzo played chess with a teenaged boy who was traveling with his grandparents.

The third night of the journey, Angelina tossed restlessly in her bunk. Vincenzo was wide awake, worried that Angelina was not getting enough to eat or drink, and he feared she would get sick like the others.

He sat on the edge of his bunk, his legs dangling over the side. He clasped his fingers together and rested his elbows on his knees. Angelina was finally asleep. He lifted his head, sat back and took a deep breath when he noticed an old man sitting on the side of his own bunk just a few yards away. He crooked his finger, urging Vincenzo to join him.

"Psst, psst, *venire*." The old man motioned again for Vincenzo to come to him. He put his finger to his lips warning Vincenzo to be quiet.

Vincenzo raised his eyebrows, pointed to himself, silently asking the man if he meant *him*. The old man nodded, and Vincenzo hopped down from his bunk, and walked over to where the man was sitting.

"I am Luciano," he whispered when Vincenzo sat down next to him. He extended his hand.

"*Piacere di cohoscerla. Sono Vincenzo. Cosa valeva lei?*" Vincenzo said, introducing himself and asking what the old man wanted.

"I see you wife. You worry 'bout her, *si*?"

"Everyone worry, *signor*," Vincenzo nodded in agreement.

"I hep you, eh?" His eyes closed when he smiled. "You see da steps?" He waited while Vincenzo looked.

"*Si*, I see da steps."

"You go up-a...notta one, but *due*." He spoke slowly and held up two fingers for emphasis. "*Dove mangia la prima classe*." He twisted his cheek, indicating that that was where the best food was.

"*Si*? But why you tell me dis?"

"Ahh," the old man said, sounding secretive and looking over his shoulder. "Dere are cans where dey put-a da food...big cans." He gestured with his arms. "Dey take-a food from da tables. Good food, *si*? Some-a time, nobody eben touch!" He smiled, and opened his jacket and showed Vincenzo how to fill his pockets. "You go…seet and wait. I tell you when to go, eh? Den, you wife…she eat, eh?"

"You have done dis?" Vincenzo asked.

"*Si, si,* many, many time. And you no see me do, right?" He seemed amused.

"No."

"I tell you dis cause-a I see you wife cry. She need to eat."

Vincenzo looked over at his sleeping wife and nodded. "*Grazie, Signor Luciano.*"

He went back and stood by Angelina's cot. She was curled up, looking like a child. He took his handkerchief from his pocket, and wiped beads of sweat from her forehead, then pulled himself up onto his own bunk and lay down on his side. He stayed awake until late that evening, and kept watch on Luciano to give him the signal to start up the stairs.

When Luciano got Vincenzo's attention and gave him a nod and a wink, Vincenzo removed his shoes, and discreetly climbed the metal stairs in his stocking feet. Few people noticed, and those who did, didn't seem to care. It was quiet; no crew members. He quickly climbed the second flight of steps until he reached the upper deck where the door of the kitchen loomed directly in front of him.

Creeping across the deck, he climbed over the side of a dinghy and hid under a tarp while he waited for the last of the food to be discarded. He stepped out of the dinghy, and crept over to one of the large metal trash bins. He filled his handkerchief with the discarded food, as well as his buttoned-up jacket.

When he could carry no more, Vincenzo tiptoed back down the two flights of stairs, passed by Luciano, who raised his fist in victory, and sat on the side of Angelina's bunk.

She sat up and with a sleepy grin crossing her lips, looked at Vincenzo. "Where you go Vincenzo?" She asked.

He snuggled up close to her and reached inside his jacket, pulling out a chicken leg. He smiled mischievously, and raised his eyebrows.

"Where you get dat?" She looked at him curiously.

He proceeded to empty bits of baked potatoes and baking powder biscuits onto the bed and they ate quietly until they were full.

"I be right back, Angelina." Vincenzo walked over to Luciano, and emptied one of his pockets into the old man's hands.

"*Grazi, l'amico,*" Luciano said.

"No, I t'ank you, Luciano." Vincenzo nodded and went back to his wife.

Vincenzo continued to make the late-night trips to the upper deck, and did the best he could to bring back enough food to share with some of the children, and older folks. Sometimes even half-full, bottles of milk were discarded, but were priceless gifts for the children.

*

The trip was fourteen days along when Vincenzo was awakened from a deep sleep by a sudden quiet. The ship's engines had come to a stop. The silence was broken when a thumping emanated from the deck above. Angelina was already sitting on the edge of her bunk, listening. Vincenzo shook the sleep from his head, looked around, and finding several empty bunks, detected a different feeling in the air. *Where had everybody gone*? The sound grew louder and more frequent, and Vincenzo took Angelina by the hand and pulled her toward the stairs. The hatch was open, and they were overwhelmed with emotion when they realized the sound they heard was that of hundreds of immigrants falling to their knees, awestruck with respect and reverence at the sight of the Statue of Liberty. When Angelina later related the story, she swore she heard angels singing that day.

The ship floated lazily in New York Harbor off the New Jersey coast, and off in the distance they could see the indication of a tall, red brick building with four majestic bronze cupolas. As the Statue of Liberty welcomed the immigrants to the new land, the American flag flapped furiously and proudly in the sea air.

A ferry neared, and suddenly bumped the side of the big ship with the screeching sound of wood against wood. The crew on the ferry tossed thick ropes onto the deck of the Carmania, and they steadied the massive boat in preparation for transporting several hundred immigrants onto the ferry. Vincenzo and Angelina rushed below to gather up their belongings, then back up to the crowd of people gathering on the deck, waiting to be next in line to debark.

As they continued their long and uncertain journey, they found themselves being shuffled along with the next group of several hundred to be shipped off to Ellis Island. They were tightly huddled with other immigrants, but the thrill of being one step closer to their destination much outweighed the discomfort of being pushed and shoved while enduring the deafening thrum of the engines.

Finally reaching Ellis Island, they took their place at the end of a line that had formed in front of the red brick structure called the *main building.* High arches loomed above, with ornately trimmed windows covering the span of the building from one side to the other. A steep staircase led to the main doors.

It was a humbling sight to see thousands of immigrants lined up in front of this place. Excited, frightened, apprehensive; clothing tattered, wrinkled and covered with dust and stained with food. Mothers carried their babies in scarves slung over their necks in order to free up their hands to carry bags. Some children rode on their father's shoulders. Strangers helped the sick and old along.

Uniformed guards barked orders in English to folks who didn't speak a word of any other language but their own.

At the top of the stairs, guards carefully scrutinized the people. They were picking out those that were having trouble walking and those who looked sickly. A chalk mark was swiped across their shoulders.

Vincenzo and Angelina looked young and healthy and had no problem walking but many around them were struggling. Everyone was confused by the chalk mark, later finding out that it indicated to the doctors inside the building that these folks needed further examination.

The examination was brief but some immigrants were sent back to the ship after showing signs of trachoma, favus or trouble with their eyes. As they were escorted back to the ship, they howled with fear and grief, terror written in their eyes. They were being torn away from their loved ones who were being forced to go ahead without them and realizing they would probably never see them again. Angelina covered her ears to block out the painful wails of panic.

Vincenzo was ordered to place their bags in a room for inspection; he obeyed. They spoke little English, but enough to understand what they were being ordered to do. They both waited anxiously for the satchel with the cigar box to be returned to them, and when it was handed to Vincenzo, he checked the box, relieved to find all of their savings in tact. Tags, noting where they were from were placed around their wrists. When their bags were cleared, Vincenzo and Angelina stood in line and waited for a custom's officer. There were hundreds of immigrants in line before them and all had their paperwork at the ready. The officers' stood behind metal cages, and heavy metal chains separated the lines of people. They were finally in the *great hall*, and waited another five hours before reaching a cage where an officer stood with his hand outstretched, waiting for Vincenzo to hand over their papers. The young man standing behind Vincenzo spoke to him in Italian, telling him that he would have to prove that he and Angelina each had at least twenty dollars before they would be allowed to leave the building with their papers. Angelina dug into the cigar box and produced the proper amount of *i soldi* to be exchanged for forty dollars, and the officer, with a quick nod stamped their papers and sent them on their way.

Before exiting, Vincenzo approached two men sitting on a wooden bench by the doors that led outside the building. He simply smiled and waved his hand from side to side, requesting they move; they obliged, leaving a spot for Angelina to sit. He gestured for her to stay while he stepped into another line that was waiting to exchange their money for American dollars.

With the cigar box tucked under his arm, Vincenzo handed over his money, and in return was given a stack of American dollars. He placed it in the cigar box and walked back to where Angelina waited patiently.

"*Sei pronto? Andiamo?*" He smiled and asked if she was ready to go.

Before walking out into the sunlight, they watched with fascination as several people gathered around a central pillar located just outside the main registration room. People were greeted with hugs and kisses from their relatives, eager to take their loved ones home. The pillar was later called the *kissing post*.

When exiting the building, Vincenzo spotted Luciano. He remembered that during one of their late night chats, the old man had mentioned that he had a brother living in a place called Wickhaven, Pennsylvania. He spoke of the coalmines and that they hired a lot of

Italians. Vincenzo, with Angelina struggling with two satchels and walking behind her husband, walked over and tapped Luciano on the shoulder.

Luciano spun around, a jubilant and toothless grin spreading across his face. "Eh, Vincenzo! We here in America!" Gray-haired and round-shouldered, he shouted with excitement. "*Buone fortune a te e allatue spose*," he said, wishing them good luck.

"*Grazie, Signor Luciano. Ettu.*" Vincenzo smiled, and patted the old man on the back. "*Mi scuzi, Signor*?"

"*Si?* Wha' you wan', my boy?"

"Can you tell me your brother's name…in dat place you tol' me about? How you say…Pen…se…vania?" Vincenzo asked, struggling with such a strange sounding place. "You go dere?"

"No, no, I go to live wit' my sister, Apalonia, in New York…in Brooklyn," he added proudly.

"Das nice for you," Vincenzo said. "Me and Angelina…*noi non abbiamo famiglie*," explaining they had no family in America.

"Ah, das too bad but you and you wife…you be okay," he nodded with assurance. "Dis America!" He threw up his hands and laughed. "Eh…I tell you how to get to my brudder, no?"

"*Si, si,* please."

"See da boat?" He turned and pointed toward the edge of the harbor where a small ferry was docked, and boarding the last group of passengers. "Das da ferry to New Jersey. *Sbrigati!*" Luciano warned that they had better hurry.

Vincenzo's eyes followed to where Luciano pointed.

"You ask-a somma body how to get to Wickhaven. You find my brudder, Roberto Morelli…he's a nice man…he help you. Please-a, tell him his brudder say *ciao*!" He handed Vincenzo a slip of paper with his brother's address, and Vincenzo shoved it into the pocket of his jacket.

"*Grazie, Signor Luciano*," Vincenzo said, taking hold of Luciano's hand and giving it a quick shake. He grabbed Angelina by the arm and rushed off toward the ferry that was beginning to pull up the passenger ramp.

"*Aspetta, aspetta…stiamo venendo!*" Vincenzo shouted and waved his arms for the crew to wait for them. Out of breath and laughing,

Vincenzo and Angelina stepped onto the ferry, and thanked them for waiting. They held onto the railing as the ferry blasted its horn and slowly pulled away from the dock and into the harbor.

Vincenzo was wearing the same brown suit that his father had given him for his wedding day, but it was now wrinkled and stained from many days of travel, as well as smelling of sweat. He wore a brown fedora with a red feather tucked into a cream-colored satin hatband. His face was unshaven and peppered with stubble.

Angelina's shoulders were draped in the black shawl that her mother crocheted and gave to her as a wedding gift. A white scarf was tied around her head, and the hem of her blue-flowered dress just touched the tops of her sturdy, thick-heeled shoes. It was her favorite dress, and featured tiny pearl buttons that ran from the bottom of her skirts to the top of the neckline. The collar was of white cotton and fanned out over her shoulders. Her hair, stringy and oily from lack of washing, was pulled back and wrapped into a knot at the back of her neck.

The ferry ride to New Jersey was brief, and decidedly more pleasant than what they experienced on the *Carmania*. Rolling waves billowed from the sides of the boat as it cut briskly through the choppy water leaving a trail of foam in its wake. The air was cool and moist as it whipped their faces, and the smell of saltwater filled their nostrils. The drone of the engines harmonized with the shriek of hungry seagulls that circled overhead.

*

Once in New Jersey, Vincenzo and Angelina found their way to the train station, where Vincenzo, after asking how to get to Wickhaven purchased two tickets to Philadelphia. They found a bench on the platform where Vincenzo laid his head in Angelina's lap and immediately fell asleep. She watched for the train and soon heard the whistle before she caught sight of the engine approaching at the far end of the track. Vincenzo stirred when the train came to a stop in front of them with a hiss of steam, and another blast from the whistle. He ran his hand over his face, yawned and stretched, and Angelina giggled at the silliness of his sleepy grin. They grabbed their belongings, and climbed the steps into the first car that stopped in front of them.

Vincenzo picked two seats at the back of the car, Angelina by a window, and Vincenzo on the aisle. They placed their bags between their feet, and when the train slowly made its way out of the station, Angelina rested her head on the back of the seat, and scanned the few people sitting around them. Across from them was a pretty young girl with a head full of long, chestnut brown ringlets who was giggling along with her moonfaced baby. The child was cooing as his mother tickled his ample chin, and with his pudgy thumb plunged into his mouth, he drooled as he screeched with delight. She looked older than Angelina, twenty or so, and when she noticed Vincenzo and Angelina admiring the baby, she beamed at them with a proud smile. Vincenzo tipped his hat, and Angelina wiggled her fingers at the baby.

"*Tu hai un bambino bellissimo*," Angelina said, commenting on how beautiful the baby was.

"*Grazie,"* the girl said.

"Ah, Italiano?" Vincenzo mused.

"*Si*. This is Alesandro." When she spoke English, her accent was slight. She ruffled the baby's mop of blonde, curly hair. "My name is Antoinette."

"Nice to meet you, Antoinette. I am Angelina." She placed her hand on her chest then pointed to Vincenzo. "*Lui e' Vincenzo, mio marito*."

Antionette smiled and nodded. "How d'ya do? Are you going to Philadelphia?"

"*Si,* we go to…how you say? Week-a-haven," Vincenzo said, slowly. "You know of dis place?"

"I think so. You mean Wickhaven, yes?"

Vincenzo nodded.

Antionette looked up and pondered. "Maybe in the upstate."

"Upstate," Vincenzo repeated. He looked at Angelina with a quizzical expression. "You from dere, *Signora Antionette*?"

"No, we live with my sister and her husband in Harrisburg," she said. "My husband is there too. He had to work and couldn't go with us to visit my aunt in Jersey," she went on. "So now we go back." She looked at Alesandro, puckered her lips and spoke baby talk.

"It is nice, you have family." Vincenzo closed his eyes and smiled.

"Is this your first time to America?" Antionette asked.

"*Si*," They answered her in unison.

"Ah...I know how scary it is when you don't know your way around. I came from Milan three years ago. That's when I met my husband, Joe."

"Mmm." Vincenzo nodded, feeling sleepy again.

"How are you getting to Wickhaven? Is someone taking you?"

"No," Angelina said.

"You are nice people. Alesandro likes you too. See? He's smiling at you!" She giggled and playfully chucked him under the chin again. "I can help you, if you like. My sister's husband, Augie is picking us up when we get off the train in Philadelphia. He has a car," she announced proudly. "I'm sure he would take you to Wickhaven. He knows where it is. He is very smart."

"Oh, so nice." Vincenzo looked at Angelina, and shrugged. Looking back at Antoinette he said, "you sure ees okay?"

"Yes, yes...Augie is a very nice man, you'll see." The train slowed as it approached the station, then came to a stop with a sudden jerk. "This is our stop," Antoinette said, grunting as she lifted the baby into her arms.

"Come, come...we go, Angelina." Vincenzo helped her to her feet, picked up the bags that were tucked under the seat, and followed Antoinette off the train where she led them toward the east end of the platform.

They walked out of the terminal, into the sunlight and onto the corner of a bustling intersection, and sat on a wooden bench by the side of the road. Cars chugged as they sped by, weaving in and out of traffic, honking at slow moving horse drawn carriages. Streetcars bobbled along tracks that traveled down the middle of cobblestone streets. Vincenzo and Angelina's eyes were wide with wonder as they watched the constant rush of people passing by, crossing streets, in and out of stores but stopping briefly at sidewalk vendors for a hotdog or pretzel.

While they waited for Augie, Alesandro entertained them by clapping his hands, and blowing bubbles. Angelina covered her mouth, and giggled when a bubble popped and sent drool dribbling down his dimpled chin.

Antoinette suddenly jumped to her feet, and stood on her tiptoes when she caught sight of a familiar car. She balanced Alesandro on her left hip, and waved vigorously as the car approached. The young man driving the car spotted her, smiled and flipped his hand back and forth out the driver's side window. He pulled up to the curb, jumped out of the handsome, green car, and enveloped his sister-in-law and baby in his long, slender arms.

"*Eh,como sta, surelia*!" he said, with a hearty laugh that eminated from his belly. He took Alesandro from her and flung him playfully in the air. Alesandro laughed wildly, his arms and legs flailing in the air, and after a few more tosses, Augie handed the baby back to Antionette. He looked over at Vincenzo. "Hello," he said, cordially.

"Augie, this is Vincenzo and Angelina, they just got married!"

"Congratulations." He continued to smile but looked at Antionette curiously.

"They just got here from Italy, and they're going to a place called Wickhaven. Do you know where that is?"

"Sure, it's upstate. I've been there once or twice. Coal country." He looked from Antionette to Vincenzo. "That's where you're going?"

"*Si*...yes. We go dere."

"Can we give them a ride, Augie? Would you mind?" Antionette asked, with an earnest look in her eyes.

"I can take them, yes." He turned to Vincenzo and repeated, "I can take you."

"*Grazie, mio amico*," Vincenzo said, taking the man's hand.

"Everybody ready?" Augie gestured toward the car. "Let's pile in."

Vincenzo and Angelina shared the backseat, while Antoinette sat in front, her arms wrapped around the baby's middle as he bounced happily on her lap. Augie managed to squeeze their bags into the tiny trunk of the car but Angelina held her satchel on her lap.

"Dis a nice auto, *Signor* Augie," Vincenzo said, loud enough to be heard over the growl of the motor. The windows were open wide, and warm air billowed into the back of the car. Angelina held her scarf tightly under her chin.

"Thanks Vincenzo, it's one of the new Ford Model T's," he boasted. "When we get outta the city, I can get this thing up to forty-five miles an hour!"

"Ah nice, eh Angelina? We get one of dese, how you say, model t."

She nodded and smiled. Her eyes blinked as the cool, spring air blew in her face, and her ample bosom bounced jauntily as they bumped along the road, heading north, out of the city.

*

Wickhaven was a small town called a *coal patch.* The towns were built by the owners of the coal companies for the purpose of making it easier for the workers to get to the mines. Within the town were small homes called *doubles,* usually occupied by two families, called *patch families,* and the rent was about four dollars a month. Miners worked for their twenty-five cents an hour while their wives stayed home and tended to the children.

Augie pulled over onto the shoulder of the road, and turned his head to look at Vincenzo and Angelina. "Here we are...Wickhaven." He pointed to a small wooden sign that was shoved in the ground a few paces before them.

"Ah...*si,* Wickhaven," Vincenzo said, as he craned his neck to look down the narrow road dotted with tiny houses. He and Angelina hesitated, seeming reluctant to get out of the car.

"You want me to drive into town?" Augie asked, noticing their uneasiness.

"No, no, Augie, dis is good, very good. *Grazie, grazie.*"

Augie twisted further in his seat so he could face them. His arm was draped over the back of the seat. "I can take you if you like," he offered again.

"No, no, we be fine. You are good people, and we are happy to know you." Vincenzo covered his heart to express his gratitude.

Antoinette got out of the car, and laid her sleeping baby on the front seat. She embraced Angelina and turned to Vincenzo. "If you come to Harrisburg, come and see us, okay? Augie and Lena Costanza...you look up the name...okay? Joe and I will be there too."

"*Grazie,* Antionette. God bless you." Vincenzo reached into his pocket, and shoved a handful of money toward Augie, who was leaning both arms on his open window.

"No, no, please...happy to do it." He waved his hand, refusing Vincenzo's offer. "Let's go, Nettie, Lena's waiting for us."

Angelina and Vincenzo stood on the shoulder of the road with their bags in hand, and watched Augie's car fade away, its tires spattering mud over the back bumper. They turned, and looked curiously at the rows of houses before them, and started walking carefully to avoid deep mud-filled ruts left by wagon wheels and horses hooves. Nearing the first group of houses, they stepped onto narrow planks of wood that were placed end to end as a makeshift sidewalk. The gray, wooden houses with flat roofs were small, but neatly kept. A group of children were taking turns swinging on a rubber tire that was hanging from a frayed rope dangling from the branch of an oak tree. An old woman was tending a patch of garden on the side of her house, while her husband rocked on the front porch, a newspaper covering his face.

"Look nice, eh Angelina?" Vincenzo seemed pleased with what he saw. She was a little more apprehensive and stayed close to Vincenzo as they made their way along the wooden planks. She modestly lifted her skirts, but her sturdy shoes and black stockings were flecked with mud.

A small girl, sitting on wooden steps in front of her house was talking to a rag doll she had cradled in her arms. She looked up and waved at them as they passed by. Angelina smiled and waved back. A young mother stopped sweeping dirt out the front door long enough to scold her son who was jumping in and out of a mud puddle. He stopped and waited for her to close the door, then proceeded to jump back into the puddle. Another boy called out to him as he passed by, rolling an old tire down a narrow alley between the houses.

It was a gentle climb to the part of town where they saw a general store, a mine office, and a saloon called D'Amo's. They stopped in front of a horse stable where an elderly gentleman was sitting in a chair that was tilted back and resting on the wall behind him. His feet dangled as he lazily sipped from a tin mug. A large black dog with a white face slept contentedly at the man's feet.

Vincenzo held up his finger, telling Angelina to wait. He walked toward the man who suddenly let the chair fall forward as he watched Vincenzo approaching. The dog lazily looked up, seemed disinterested and lowered his head back to where his chin rested on his front paws.

"Hallow?" Vincenzo said, in broken English. He smiled and tipped his hat.

The man squinted into the sunlight as he looked up at Vincenzo. His face was thick with snow-white stubble, and his slow smile revealed a mouthful of crooked, tobacco-stained teeth. "*Scuzi*?" He responded, in a gravelly voice.

"*Italiano*?" Vincenzo sounded pleased.

"*Si…Italiano…*but I speak-a *Englese* too," he said, almost defensively.

"*Ah…va bene.* My English not so good but I will learn," Vincenzo said, returning a pleasant smile. "I am Vincenzo. Vincenzo Borzanna." He extended his hand toward the man.

The man put down his mug, stood up, wiped his hand on the back of his pants and took Vincenzo's hand. His skin felt rough and callused. "Ernesto Siambre."

"*Signor Siambre,*" Vincenzo nodded. "She's-a my wife," he said, pointing toward Angelina, who was waiting patiently by the side of the road. Vincenzo pulled a piece of paper from his pocket and handed it to the man. "Do you know dis name?"

Ernesto took the paper. "*Si,* I know Roberto. Roberto Morelli," he said, with a grin. "He live by da company store." He pointed toward the next group of buildings perched at the crest of an embankment, within sight but probably a twenty-minute walk. "Just across the railroad tracks…at P.L.& E. Railroad station, on Route 51," he said, slowly to make sure Vincenzo understood. "When you find his house, bang loud or he no hear, *capice?*"

"*Grazie, Signor Siambre,*" Vincenzo said, turning to walk back to Angelina. "Maybe we meet again, eh?" He shouted over his shoulder.

"Maybe." The man sat back down, picked up his mug and leaned back against the building again.

They followed the man's directions, and came to a sign that read *Star Junction.* Crossing the railroad tracks on Route 51, they passed the Company Store, and Vincenzo rechecked the piece of paper in his pocket.

"Dunlap Street," he read aloud. "We look for number fourteen, Angelina." He looked at the paper, then at the street sign in front of them. "*Si,* dis ees da street, Angelina," he said, placing the heavy satchels on the ground. He pulled a handkerchief from his pocket, wiped his brow and rested his hands on his hips.

They rounded the corner, and came to a row of simply constructed, wood frame houses with address numbers hand-painted on scraps of wood, and nailed by the front doors. Halfway down the block, they found Mr. Morelli's house, and once again, Vincenzo instructed Angelina to wait by the side of the road while he approached the front door. The wood of the door was gray and cracked with age, and a rusted doorknob hung loosely by one screw. Clay pots with plants bulging with small green tomatoes sat on the windowsills. Vincenzo knocked on the door, and remembered to knock hard.

"Who ees?" A thin, weak voice asked.

"*Un amico di suoi fratelli, Signor Morelli.*" Vincenzo put his face close to the crack in the door.

The door opened slowly, its hinges groaning. A wizened man with wisps of white hair in a tousled mass on the sides of his head peered out the door. His back was curved and frail looking. A pair of wire-rimmed glasses rested on the end of his nose, and he looked up with difficulty, a pleasant smile crossing his face. "You know my brudder?"

"*Si*...Luciano. We meet on da boat from *Italia*."

"Ah," he nodded. "Den you know Apalonia too?"

"No, *signor,* just Luciano."

"How ees my brudder?"

"Oh, *bene, bene.* A nice man, he is."

"*Si,* I miss heem." He closed his eyes and nodded seeming to reminisce about a time long ago. "How can I help you?"

"He tol' me to ask you 'bout a job in the coal mines...here in Wickhaven."

"*Si*, my son-in-law, he da big boss at Washington Coal and Coke Company. You go see heem at the mine office...over by D'Amo's Saloon. Say Papa Morelli send you, *si*?"

"*Grazie, Signor Morelli.* I go see him."

"You just get here?"

"*Si,* jus' today. Das my wife." He turned, and made a scooping motion in Angelina's direction. She smiled shyly, and raised her hand to say hello.

Lifting his head, the old man peered over Vincenzo's shoulder. His spectacles shifted as he squinted and wrinkled his nose. He smiled with approval. "*Molte bene...bella espouso.* You take-a you wife, and go to da Star Boarding House. Das t'ree blocks from the mine office, eh? You ask-a for Gertie Belamy...she run da place. You will like her. She make-a da spaghetti for me some time...eh?" He laughed, and poked Vincenzo playfully in the arm.

Vincenzo looked at the man curiously, and responded with a courteous laugh. He thanked him for his help, joined Angelina, and started walking back down the dirt road toward the corner of Dunlap Street. Reaching Route 51, they found the Star Boarding House half way down the block, next to the public square.

It was a three-story frame house painted white, its front steps standing just a few feet from the edge of the road. Several lofty maple trees dominated the side yard, and a wooden sign, propped by the porch steps read *Rooms for rent.*

Vincenzo and Angelina stepped up onto the porch, and entered a small parlor, sparsely but tastefully furnished with a burgundy-brocade settee, and two brown fabric-covered chairs. A brick fireplace, with fresh logs on an iron grate graced the corner of the room, and the sun peeked through yellowed, lace curtains covering a window that looked out over the street.

Vincenzo stood next to a chest-high desk that was, at the moment unattended. He tapped a tarnished, brass bell that sat next to a guest registry, and soon after, an elderly woman barreled through a swinging door that led from the kitchen. She wore a blue, flowered apron over her full-skirted dress, and after wiping her hands on the hem of the apron; she untied it and flung it over the edge of a chair.

"Hello!" She sang out cheerfully. "Kin I hep ya?" Her smile was warm and natural, her accent thick with a southern twang. The woman was short and stout, and she walked with a pronounced limp that made her swing her arms as she approached them.

"We wan a room, *signora*," Vincenzo said. "Roberto Morelli tell us-a to come see you." Vincenzo politely tipped his hat.

"Oh, my little friend Roberto...now, ain't he a hoot? Likes my macaroni dinners, bless his heart." She shook her head and laughed. "Alrighty." She wiped her hands again and walked past them. "Let's see what we got here." She stepped behind the desk, and breathed heavily as she ran her finger over the register. "I got room four available...it's on the second floor. How's that?"

"Is good, *signora*." .

"Can I gittcha to sign here, darlin'?" She asked, spinning the register toward Vincenzo.

When he finished signing, she turned the register again, and glanced at the name. She looked up at them and smiled. "It's so nice to have y'all stay with us, Mr. and Mrs.... Borzanna, is it?"

Vincenzo nodded.

"We don't really have that many guests here right now. It's mostly the coalminers that ain't married yet." She clucked with a good-humored laugh. "Yeah, they sleep here, and sometimes eat here...over there in the dinin' room...see? Mostly when I make fried chicken." She laughed again. "Right through them doors over there." She pointed toward a room leading from the parlor. A long, oak table with two wooden benches on either side took up most of the room. "Sometimes they eat at the Star Diner, right next door." She paused, took a deep breath, and wiped a droplet of sweat from her forehead. "Well, that'll be seventy-five cents fer tonight."

"I pay for a week...ees okay?"

"Suit yourself, son."

Angelina opened the cigar box and Vincenzo scooped out a handful of coins, and placed them on the desktop.

"That'll be just fine and dandy." She dropped the coins into the pocket of her dress. "I think we're all set." She grabbed a room key from the wall, and handed it to Vincenzo. "Now, if you need anythin', just give me a holler. I'm Mrs. Belamy...I know we're in northern territory, but I believe in good ol' southern hospitality!" She hooted, and clapped Vincenzo on the back. "Where're you kids from, anyways? What's that accent you got there?"

"We from *Italia, Signora Belamy,*" Angelina said, shyly.

"E-tal-ya...E-tal-ya..." she said slowly, looking puzzled.

"*Si,* uh...Italy," Vincenzo pronounced it *eetaly.*

"Oh, you mean It-ly!"

"*Si,* Italy," Angelina said, covering her mouth to stifle a giggle.

"Well, my stars! You youngins' sure did come a long way, now didn't ya?"

"*Si,* uh...yes-a. We travel a long way."Vincenzo put his arm around Angelina's shoulders.

"Well, ya look kinda tuckered. You two best get some rest, ya hear? There ya go, right up them stairs. Now listen...see out that back door there?" She pointed to a door adjacent to the dining room entrance.

"There's a wash house halfway down the road where ya can get cleaned up, and get fresh water. I put a bucket a fresh water, though at the end of the hall every mornin', so suit yourself. Don't forget…call me if ya need anything!"

"*Grazie, Signora Belamy.*"

"Ain't that a hoot?" Mrs. Belamy put her hands on her hips, leaned back and laughed. "That's some darlin' accent ya got goin' there, sweetie!" She continued laughing as she turned and walked back into the kitchen.

Vincenzo picked up the bags, and started up the stairs with Angelina close behind.

They climbed two flights to room four, unlocked the door, and dropped their bags on the floor. It was a small room, but appeared clean and neat. They eyed the iron-framed bed greedily. It was covered with a blue Chenille spread that was neatly tucked under two thin pillows. There was a tall walnut dresser with six drawers, and an electric light bulb dangled, uncovered, from the ceiling. A freshly swept, frayed carpet covered the hardwood floor, and a small, round table sat in one corner of the room by a tall window that overlooked the alley below. The table was covered with a lace doily, and a Cain-backed chair sat next to it.

Suddenly aware of their extreme exhaustion, Vincenzo and Angelina decided to leave the unpacking until later. They slipped off their shoes, layed down, and immediately fell into a deep sleep.

*

Early the next morning, Vincenzo was the first to awaken. He squinted as a beam of sunlight shone through a tear in the shade that hung in the window across the room. He grinned when he looked at Angelina, still asleep, on her side, and in the same clothes she had been wearing for days. He was still in his wrinkled suit, and his favorite fedora was crushed between his head and the pillow. He reached over and playfully pinched her bottom. She stirred and slowly opening her eyes, turned to face him.

"*Cio ha doluto*," she pouted. She reached back and rubbed her bottom.

"Don be a baby…dat no hurt you," he laughed, and gave her a peck on the cheek.

"Uh-mm," she moaned, snuggling closer to him.

"Eh, Angelina…*sbrigati*! Time to get up!" He sat up straight, this time swatting her on the backside.

"Vincenzo!" She scolded, and slowly rolled out of bed. She started to empty the bags, placing their clothes in the dresser drawers before sitting back down on the bed. She stretched and yawned.

"You sit…I wash first," Vincenzo said, laying a hand on her shoulder.

He filled a basin with fresh water that he scooped from a bucket at the end of the hall. He stripped down to his underwear, splashed cool water over his face, and under his arms, while Angelina laid out his pants and jacket, draping a white cotton shirt on the back of the Cain-backed chair. He reached for a towel that was neatly folded next to the basin, dried his face and got dressed. He stepped into the hall so Angelina could wash and dress, and after several minutes, she called him back into the room. She was wearing a simple, tiny-checked dress with a high collar, and full skirt that touched the tops of her shoes. Her hair was neatly brushed, and clasped at the back of her head with a mother-of-pearl comb.

"Let's walk outside, Angelina."

She followed him downstairs, and out onto the dirt road. It was a dazzling, spring day, and the mud-filled roads were dry once again. Horse drawn wagons passed by, crowded with coal miners, dressed in overalls and helmets. They sat stooped, and somber-looking, cigarettes dangling from their lips.

"Dey go to da mines, amma t'ink," Vincenzo said, quietly as he stood watching them pass. His eyes followed the wagons as they bumped their way out of town.

"You wan' to do dis mining, Vincenzo?" Angelina asked with concern.

"No but maybe I do for a leetle while, Angelina," he shrugged.

They continued walking in the town square. Vincenzo pointed out a two-story building, with a sign that read, Star Supply Co. Limited. Just past that building, was a church with a tall steeple, and wooden steps leading to a double set of weathered mahogany doors.

"*Vincenzo, ho fame.*" Angelina rubbed her stomach.

"I hungry too," he agreed. "We go back, *si*?"

They turned back, and walked toward the boarding house. The Star Diner was set back from the road, and two elderly gentlemen sat on a bench under a window, one picking his teeth with a matchbook, the other drawing deeply on a hand-rolled cigarette.

As Vincenzo and Angelina walked through the swinging doors into the diner, the two elderly men nodded in their direction. Vincenzo tipped his fedora.

The aroma of freshly brewed coffee, and baking powder biscuits filled their nostrils. The sound of flatware chinking against plates intermingled with the buzz of lazy conversation, and an occasional laugh between men as a joke was passed around the table.

The room was filled with miners waiting for the next wagon pickup. With their helmets and work tools at their feet, they hungrily scooped gravy-covered biscuits and pinto beans into their mouths.

Vincenzo found a table against the wall toward the back of the room, and he and Angelina sat down. Shortly after, a waitress came to them, pulled a pencil from behind her ear, licked the tip, and held it to a pad of paper. She wore a uniform of dark blue cotton, and a food-stained white apron was tied around her slender waist.

Angelina was fascinated with the woman's orange-colored hair that she wore swept up into a Gibson-girl style. Curly tendrils fell casually on the sides of her long, high cheek-boned face. The fronts of her oversized teeth were smeared with the same bright red lipstick that was swiped across her thin lips.

"Mornin'," she said, without looking at them. "What can I gitcha?" She slapped playfully at a man sitting at the table behind her. He was poking her in the hip with his elbow.

"Yes…uh, hallo lady," Vincenzo said. "What do you have?"

"Well, we got biscuits and gravy, with pinto beans on the side. That's 'bout it, toots. Two orders?"

"Yes-a. T'ank you, *signora*, and *caffé,* please-a."

"You got it, toots!" she said, turning to walk away. "That means two coffees, right?" She said, over her shoulder.

"*Si*, please-a," Vincenzo nodded.

She rushed off toward the end of a zinc-covered counter where customers were sitting, perched on wooden stools, hunched over their meals.

A barrel-shaped man with a face-full of dark stubble was cooking on a cast iron stove behind the counter. He wore a grease-stained undershirt, and whistled while ladling gravy over puffy, golden biscuits.

"*Che cosa significa, toots*?" Vincenzo asked, looking curiously at Angelina.

She shrugged her shoulders. "Toots," she mused. "I don' know what dis mean. Maybe she like-a you," she smiled sheepishly.

"Here ya go, toots." The waitress quickly returned, and placed platters of hot food in front of them and said, "Pay up front, and have a nice day."

Vincenzo and Angelina sniffed the aroma of fresh biscuits. They ate hungrily, and when Vincenzo savored the last bite of pinto beans, the waitress stopped by their table again.

"You kids is new here, ain't cha?"

Vincenzo nodded.

"Well, how 'bout that? Just married?" She guessed.

"Two mont'." Vincenzo smiled, and held up two fingers.

"Ain't that cute?" She looked at Angelina, then back at Vincenzo. "Where ya from?"

"Italy."

"Italy! We got lots of *I*talians here…most work in the mines. You a coal miner, toots?"

"I gon' try," Vincenzo responded.

"It's hard work, ya know?" she said, raising her eyebrows. "My husband works in them mines, and I'll tell ya what, it don't pay much money, toots. Heck, it don't pay *no* money!" She laughed, and a few men looked over, and laughed with her. "Ya get paid with a scrip. You heard of a scrip, toots?"

"No…what ees…how you say, screep?"

"Well, here's the thing with scrips. That's what they give ya instead of money, and it's only good at the company store…you know, for food and stuff."

"Ah," Vincenzo replied, looking bewildered.

"Oh yeah, they git ya comin' and goin', toots. Ain't that right Jubel?" She turned to speak to the man that was teasing her earlier.

He looked up, wiped his mouth on his sleeve, and nodded.

She turned back to Vincenzo, and lowered her voice. "Everything in Star Junction is owned by Washington Coal and Coke, and I'll tell ya what; when ya only get paid what's worth about forty cents for every five tons of coal ya mine, it ain't much of a pay envelope at the end of the week."

"*Mamma mia.*" Vincenzo thought for a moment, and said, "I work harder, den."

The waitress threw back her head and laughed. "That's right, I guess. Just dig more coal. Why didn't you chumps think of that?" She said to a group of men preparing to get up from their table. "Oh, that's a good one, toots. I like you. You too, sweetie," she added, nudging Angelina with her hip.

"Vincenzo," Angelina said, worry written in her eyes.

"Don' worry Angelina, we be fine." He reached across the table, and touched her hand. "I work da mines a leetle while, den I get good job. You see, don' you worry. You Vincenzo ees a boss...no worker."

"Hey, it's not that bad," the waitress interjected. She had realized she had probably said too much. "I didn't mean to upset ya, sweetie. You two'll be fine, really."

"Hey, Clara!" the cook yelled from behind the counter. "Ya gonna come pick up these plates, or what?"

"Keep yer pants on, Charlie!" she shouted over her shoulder. "Gotta go. You two kids'll be just fine, you'll see." She winked, and walked toward the counter to pick up more platters of biscuits and beans.

"I pay now, Angelina," Vincenzo said.

She pulled the cigar box out of her satchel and handed it to him, and he scooped out a handful of coins. He stood by the cash register and placed a handful of coins on the counter, giving the young cashier a hopeful smile. "Ees enough?"

She put her index finger on top of each coin needed to add up to twenty-two cents.

"Twenty-one, twenty-two, there ya go," she said, giving him a warm smile. "You can take the rest back." She pushed the remaining coins toward him.

"*Vincenzo, guarole le gette di pane*," Angelina nudged him, and pointed behind the counter. There was a shelf stacked with loaves of fresh bread, and balls of wax-covered cheese on the counter below. Vincenzo put the change back on the counter. "Please-a, take what ees for bread and cheese, t'ank you."

The girl took the money, shoved the bread into a paper sack, and cut a large wedge of cheese. She wrapped it in brown paper, and placed it in the paper sack with the bread.

"T'ank you," he repeated, and tipped his hat.

They left the diner and walked to the boarding house and, after making sure Angelina was safely tucked away in their room, Vincenzo left to go find the mining office.

Angelina finished emptying their suitcases, and placed Vincenzo's belongings into the first three drawers of the dresser, and her own things in the bottom three drawers. She found her crochet hook and yarn, and sat in the Cain-backed chair by the window, and crocheted until Vincenzo came back later that day.

He walked in the door, grinned, and gave Angelina a kiss on the forehead. "I have-a som'tin' for you," he said, pulling a package from behind his back. He set a container of chocolate ice cream on the table.

"*Cosa stiamo festiggiando*?" she asked, wondering if something had happened to call for celebration.

"You Vincenzo getta job!" he said, his chest puffed with pride. He was sure to point out, though, "Dis job is jus' for now, you see… until I find better, eh, Angelina?"

"What job you get, Vincenzo?"

"I work in da mines, Angelina…but jus' for now, see?" He repeated. "I gonna do good here, Angelina. You will see."

Vincenzo had found the mining office that morning, and after speaking with Mr. Morelli's son-in-law, he was now an employee of The Washington Coal and Coke Co.

"I need tools, Angelina."

"Ees okay, Vincenzo," she assured him. "We buy."

Vincenzo sat on the edge of the bed and stretched. "Ah, watta day, eh Angelina?" He put his head down and thought. "You know what?

I wan' to look for a house-a for us, Angelina. Den we hav-a lotta baby, no?"

"A house? Vincenzo, we haf money for a house?" She asked, surprised by the idea.

"I t'ink so, Angelina. Mr. Morelli's son-in-law, his name is Eddie…" he said, excitedly. "He tell me we can rent for two dollar a mont' but we can *buy* a house-a for maybe nine hundred dollar! I tink' we got dat, Angelina! American money, we got dat, no?" He lowered his voice, and looked toward the door hoping no one heard him speak of money. "When I walk here," he said in a hushed voice, "I see a sign on a nice-a leetle house-a, jus' down da road. You wan' go see? Come, come, come, we go see." Vincenzo hurried his wife as she slipped on her shoes. "We go before da sun go down."

Angelina reached into the dresser drawer and pulled out the cigar box. She put it into her satchel, followed Vincenzo down the stairs, and out of the boarding house. They walked briskly to a narrow, dirt road called Hazel Street, and Angelina smiled when she saw the tree-lined street crowded with tiny wooden houses.

They stepped up to the front door of a house in the middle of the block, and Vincenzo pointed to a handwritten *for sale* sign propped against a maple tree in the front yard. White paint was peeling from the wood of the house, and the trim around the windows and eaves was once pale yellow but now weathered enough to show mostly bare wood. A line of rose bushes, with leaves growing through the openings of a wire fence surrounded the small yard. Angelina was thrilled. "Ees so nice, Vincenzo," Angelina said.

Vincenzo knocked, and an elderly woman opened the door. Her old eyes sparkled and with a pleasant smile, she invited them in.

"*Allo.* We come-a to see you houzza." Vincenzo tipped his hat and nodded. The woman was thin and fragile-looking in her print housedress, and her snow-white hair was held in place with black hairpins. They stepped into a living room that smelled of mothballs but appeared tidy and quaint.

Her name was Mrs. Dilworth, and she explained that she couldn't afford to keep the house since her husband had passed on. She further explained that she was moving to Uniontown to be with her daughter and grandchildren. She was gracious and kind, and held onto Angelina's arm as they walked through the kitchen and dining room. Pointing out the back door, she directed their attention to the corner of the yard where an outhouse sat hidden within a group of juniper shrubs. There was no indoor plumbing but Vincenzo and Angelina were already familiar with outhouses back in Italy. Mrs. Dilworth took them upstairs to see three small but brightly lit bedrooms, then back downstairs to a door that led to the basement. In one corner of the cool, musty smelling underbelly of the house, Vincenzo noticed a pile of tools sitting on the dirt floor.

"Mine tools?" Vincenzo asked.

"Oh yes, Frank, that's my late husband, was a miner. That's what killed my Frank, you know." She shook her head slowly, her eyes clouding with remembrance. "They call it black lung disease."

"*Oh, la mia bonta',*" Angelina said, putting her hand over her mouth.

"A horrible sickness it is." Mrs. Dilworth looked away, and took a deep breath but soon a gentle smile returned to her lips when she made eye contact with Vincenzo. "I'm leaving the tools here, so if you buy the house, they're yours if you want...the furniture too."

Vincenzo attempted to contain his excitement. "If Angelina like-a, den we buy." He turned to Angelina, and she nodded her approval.

"*Quanto lo fa e' costato, signora*?" In his eagerness, he forgot to speak English.

The woman looked at him with confusion. "I'm sorry, my dear..."

"Oh, so sorry... eh, how much do you wan'?"

"Oh my gracious," she laughed. "I thought that's what you meant. I hope it's not too much for you...you're such a nice young couple." She hesitated and thought. "I would like five hundred dollars."

"Das a lotta money," Vincenzo shook his head. "I don' know...what you t'ink, Angelina?"

"If that's too much..." Mrs. Dilworth quickly added.

"No, don' be ashamed, lady." He pulled Angelina aside and Mrs. Dilworth, respecting their privacy stepped over to the base of the stairs.

"Angelina? *Quanti soldi abbiamo?*"

She took the box from her satchel, and counted out four hundred and twenty-five dollars, and shrugged as she handed it to Vincenzo.

"Das all I got, *Signora Dilwort'*. You take?" Vincenzo shoved the neatly stacked pile of bills toward her.

She placed a thin, delicate hand to the side of her face and smiled sweetly. "Of course, that'll do." She took the money and her eyes glistened with tears. She led the way back up the stairs, told them she would have her things out of the house within a few days, and expressed how pleased she was that the house was going to such a nice young couple. Vincenzo and Angelina walked back to the boarding house, hand-in-hand.

Chapter 3

Conchetta Marie was born to Angelina and Vincenzo in 1923. She arrived just before dawn, at home on Easter Sunday. Mabel Korzinski was the neighborhood midwife, and Vincenzo had run to her house the night before, rapping frantically on her front door.

"*Eh, Signora Korzinski*! Ees time, ees time!" Vincenzo shouted.

She opened the door, and with her black, leather medical bag already clutched in her hand, she gave Vincenzo a reassuring grin, and quickly followed him out the door.

She was short and round, with a sweet face, sparkling blue eyes, and a jolly smile. She was still in her nightgown but it was covered with a long white apron that was tied at the back. A white scarf was wrapped around her head and her rosy, apple-shaped cheeks jiggled as she walked briskly by Vincenzo's side. She was about to bring the fourth Borzanna baby into the world.

Mabel found Angelina groaning in mid-contraction when she walked into the dimly lit bedroom. She gently wiped Angelina's face with a warm, damp cloth she took from a white porcelain basin of water Vincenzo had placed at his wife's bedside. Mabel took hold of Angelina's hands, and braced herself for her tightening grip as the pain intensified.

"Il bambio ste venendo!" Angelina groaned, gritting her teeth as she pushed. Within minutes, the top of the baby's head appeared, and soon to follow was a pink face with puffy eyes, and a mouth open wide,

prepared to wail. Angelina took a deep breath, squeezed her eyes tight, clenched her teeth and gave one final push. The baby girl practically leapt into Mabel's waiting arms, and Angelina fell back on her pillow, her face glistening with sweat. She smiled as Mabel laid the tiny girl on her chest.

Mabel pulled a pair of scissors from her bag, cut the umbilical cord with one quick snip, and took the tiny bundle from Angelina. She gave the infant her first bath, humming as she gently rubbed the palm of her hand over the baby's head. She wrapped her in a soft white blanket, and handed her to Vincenzo, who proudly presented her to her three sisters, Violet, Giordana and Philomena. The girls had been sitting obediently on the floor outside their parents' bedroom, anxiously waiting for the birth of the new baby. When they found out it was another sister, they held hands, jumped up and down and squealed with delight.

"Shh," Vincenzo scolded, though still beaming with pride. "You mama and me…we name her Conchetta," Vincenzo told them.

They looked at each other, giggled and whispered, "Conchetta? That's pretty Papa but can we call her Connie, for short?"

"*Si,* Connie ees okay," Vincenzo mused as he looked down at his newest daughter.

Over the next few years, four more girls were born to Angelina and Vincenzo; Carmella, Maria, Bettina and Lourdes, and after eight girls, Angelina was relieved when Vincenzo suggested they stop trying for a boy.

*

The year was 1931, and the Borzanna girls lived a carefree life in a typical Italian household. Their mother doted on them, and their father diciplined them. When the girls were little, Vincenzo was still working in the mines. There was little money but the girls never knew it.

Vincenzo eventually followed through on his promise to Angelina to find a better way of making money, and simply walked away from the mines one day. He decided to take advantage of Prohibition and worked his way into an underground organization that kept saloons supplied in bootlegged liquor. He was "small time" compared to the New Jersey and Chicago gangs but in Wickhaven, he was called *Maestro*. He was feared but respected and ruled over clandestine meetings with old, and trusted friends in the backroom of D'Amo's Saloon where they divided money and distributed bottles of gin and whiskey. Once a week, Vincenzo, alone met with the New Jersey men who supplied him with cases of whiskey that he brought home and stored in the cellar of his house until it was time to deliver to clients from Wickhaven to Uniontown. After handing over the money he collected to the Jersey bosses, he was given his cut along with a fresh supply of whiskey. To Vincenzo, it was easy money and his lungs were free of coal dust.

Against Angelina's wishes, Vincenzo brought sixteen-year old Philomena into the bootlegging business. She was tough and arrogant, and acted as a cover for her father, expertly maneuvering his old Dodge through town, in the dark of night to deliver liquor and collect money. She was the most like her father, proud and fearless, and he treated her like the son he never had. Vincenzo also taught her how to stay one step in front of the law.

The other Borzanna girls were sometimes embarrassed by their father's reputation as a tough man, who was known to carry a six-shooter in the waistband of his pants. Teenaged boys interested in any of the Borzanna girls cowered in fear at the thought of talking to the girls, let alone asking for a date.

Later that year, Vincenzo and the New Jersey bootleggers got word that they were being watched. Even meeting at D'Amo's Saloon had become risky. Local police and federal agents had them under surveillance, and the big bosses in Chicago convinced Vincenzo to hold the meetings in the privacy of his home. Angelina relunctantly agreed but gave strict instructions to her daughters to remain upstairs in their rooms until the meetings were over. They obeyed, and happily occupied themselves with homework, curling their hair, or gossiping about boys while their parents entertained a group of threatening looking thugs in dark suits and black fedoras. The men sat around Angelina's dining room table devouring spaghetti, attentively listening while a fat, beady-eyed, cigar-chewing character named Mr. Capone barked out orders.

Philomena pleaded with her father to allow her to sit in on the meetings. She found it exciting, and felt she was entitled to be part of the business since she risked her life repeatedly, delivering whiskey all over town. To Angelina's horror, Vincenzo allowed Philomena to come downstairs but Angelina insisted she stay in the kitchen with her.

"Mama, please," she pleaded. "Papa needs me in there with him."

"Stop whining, Philomena," Angelina scolded. "Papa no need you."

Philomena pouted, wishing she could sit at the table with the men; maybe even smoke a cigar and say cuss words but her mother wasn't having it.

When the table was cleared, Capone and his men lit up fat stogies, counted money and gave Vincenzo his cut. He nodded with gratitude, and walked Capone and his men to the back door.

"Thanks for the meal, Mrs. Borzanna," Capone growled, before leaving. "And tell the kid we said t'anks." They left quickly and quietly, piling into a black Oldsmobile sedan that was parked discreetly in the grass behind Vincenzo's garage. Philomena cupped the sides of her face as she peered through the front window watching the car disappear down the street.

"He called me the kid," Philomena said. "Is that good, Papa? Does that mean Mr. Capone likes me?"

Vincenzo sighed. He was tired, and second guessing his decision to allow Philomena to be involved in such dangerous business. "Go to bed, Philomena. Mr. Capone...he no like nobody."

*

An unscrupulous character named Melio Garibaldi was a saloon owner, jealous of Vincenzo's business relationship with Lucky D'Amo. He had been trying for months to get Vincenzo to leave D'Amo's Saloon and have his meetings in *his* bar. He knew it would be financially beneficial to him, getting liquor at cut-rate prices. To Vincenzo's annoyance, Melio cornered him several times, promising to keep it a secret that Vincenzo was involved with Capone and his bootlegging operation. It concerned Vincenzo that Melio knew about his business with Capone, and it angered him that Melio seemed to use the information as a threat but Vincenzo was loyal to Lucky. Once again, he turned Melio down.

Non capisco, Signor Borzanna," Melio objected in anger. "I give you good drinks...just like Lucky...and I give you protection. Nobody bother you. I don' never ask no questions, ya know what I mean?"

"*Melio, per favore*." Vincenzo held out his hands, and shrugged. "Why you always beggin'? It don' look good...I tol' you, we happy at D'Amo's. Maybe one day...but, not now, c*apice*?"

Melio scowled and nodded his head slowly as Vincenzo turned his back and walked away. "I show you," Melio growled under his breath. "*Maestro*, huh! Amma show you who *Maestro* is." His lips curled into a sinister snarl, and his eyes glared as Vincenzo got into his car. The following day, Melio went to the authorities.

*

It was a steamy July night, and the girls were about to fall asleep when a thunderous pounding jolted them from their beds. One by one they huddled together at the top of the stairs. They could hear muffled voices and heavy footsteps rushing down the basement stairs.

Giordana went to the window that overlooked the back of the house. "Oh my God, there're police cars in the back yard!"

"What?" Violet ran up alongside her sister, thrusting her head out the window.

"Yeah, look." Giordana pointed. "They're shining their headlights into the woods. What's goin' on, Vi? I'm scared."

"Goddamnit!" Philomena pushed them both out of the way, and looked out the window. "Shit!" She quickly headed for the steps. "I have to go help Papa."

"Are you crazy?" Violet said, grabbing her arm. "You stay right here! Mama and Papa can handle this."

"You don't understand. Papa's in trouble!" Philomena cried. "The bottles…the whiskey's out there…in the woods!"

"Ma and Papa will handle it, I said," Violet repeated, sharply. They froze in their tracks when they heard the horrific sound of glass shattering as bottles were being thrown to the cellar floor. The shelves holding their mother's jarred tomatoes and peppers were being torn down along with the whiskey. In the woods, the sound of breaking glass continued for more than a half hour, and when it stopped, footsteps thundered through the house, out the front door.

The girls scurried from the top of the stairs to the window in their parents' bedroom, where the view was of the front stoop below. What they saw terrified them. Their father was standing there in his long johns, handcuffs on his wrists, about to be shoved into the back of a police car. Their mother stood helplessly by his side. She ran her hand through her hair in frustration, and her eyes were dark with rage.

"Where you take my husband?" She screamed.

"Don't worry, maam, he'll be fine. We're taking him to lockup at the courthouse in Uniontown," a young policeman said, as he paused before getting into the passenger side of one of the police cars. His expression was sympathetic. "But ya know maam, ya can't sell booze like that. You people know that, don't ya?"

"When can I see him?" Angelina asked, ignoring the officer's question.

"You can see him tomorrow, I'm sure." He held up his hand. "Goodnight, maam…and sorry 'bout the mess."

Another officer loaded sledgehammers into the trunk of his car, and Angelina could see Vincenzo in the backseat, his hands behind his back. He turned to look out the window. When their eyes met, he gave her a reassuring wink.

The girls crept down the stairs, and when their mother came back into the house, she ordered them back to their beds.

"But, Ma…" Violet protested.

'Per favore figlie. Domani," Angelina demanded. She assured them they would talk the next day.

They obeyed but were unable to sleep that night as they lay in bed holding onto each other for comfort.

Philomena snuck into their parent's bedroom, reached under the mattress and pulled out her father's gun. She brought it into the room she shared with Connie and Carmella, and placed it under the mattress.

Connie watched out of the corner of her eye. "What are you doing?" She asked, in a whisper.

Philomena stood with her feet spread apart, and her hands on her hips. "Well, it's up to me now to protect this family. Just go to sleep, Connie. Anybody messes with us now, I'll blow their damned heads off!" She leaned over and patted the side of the mattress where the gun was stashed.

"Oh, good Lord," Connie groaned, turning on her side, squeezing her eyes shut.

*

The next morning, the girls came downstairs expecting to find their mother looking miserable from the previous night's events but she was surprisingly cheerful. She gave them their usual good morning kiss and was preparing a picnic lunch. She was wearing her Sunday dress and her hair was brushed and neatly pinned back from her face. "We go see you papa today, eh? No worry…everythin' be fine."

"See him where, Mama?" Lourdes asked, innocently.

"Don' you worry, Lourdes, just go get ready," Angelina answered, gently. She continued filling a wicker basket with a loaf of bread, a block of cheese, purple grapes and sugarcoated cookies. She covered the basket with a checkered dishtowel, and smiled as she sat in a chair by the front door, the basket resting on her lap.

The girls lined up in front of Angelina, and after nodding her approval, she walked out the front door with her eight girls trailing behind her. They were headed to the courthouse in Uniontown. Angelina had selflessly and lovingly turned a scary situation into an exciting excursion. They held hands as they walked to the corner of Hazel Street and Lemmings Avenue to board the streetcar. Angelina dropped a handful of coins into the conductor's opened hand and found seats for the girls. They sat two by two, Lourdes sitting with her mother, nestling her head on her mother's shoulder. It took them nearly an hour to get to East Main Street in Uniontown, and the streetcar came to a screeching halt a block south of the courthouse.

They walked, single-file to the courthouse. It loomed in front of them, bigger than any building they had ever seen before. It was constructed of gray stone, with a clock tower that seemed to touch the sky. They went inside to the main desk, and a clerk referred to a list attached to a clipboard that hung from the wall, and after finding Vincenzo's name, told them to go to the back of the building where lockup was located.

A chain-link fence topped with barbed wire surrounded a yard of grass that was sparse and burned brown by the sun. Wooden tables and benches were already occupied with men in gray overalls, casually chatting and smoking cigarettes, some sitting across from women that Angelina assumed were their wives. Children played nearby. It seemed oddly festive.

"This isn't so scary, Mama," Lourdes said, still clinging to her mother. "Is this where Papa is?"

"*Si*, you papa is here…hush now," Angelina said, placing a gentle hand on her youngest daughter's cheek. A tall, muscular guard stood outside the door of a gatehouse, and eyed the girl's curiously.

"Hello sir," Philomena said, in an authoritative tone. Angelina smiled as she watched her daughter take charge. "This is my mother, Mrs. Vincenzo Borzanna, and these are my sisters. We've come to see our father."

The guard looked the girls up and down as they lined up behind their mother, opened the iron gate, and pointed in the direction of the side yard. "Over there," he said, without expression.

"Thank you." They approached the yard slowly, and quickly spotted their father exiting a door to the left of them. He stood with his hands on his hips, squinting as he looked up at the sun.

"Papa!" They yelled, running toward him.

He waved and held out his arms. The girls surrounded him, showering him with kisses. He laughed, hugged them back and looked over at Angelina, who was smiling, and shaking her head.

"*Vieni qua, vieni qua*," he ordered them to a table with two long benches shoved underneath. He assured the girls they had nothing to worry about, that he would be home at the end of summer, and everything would be back to normal.

"Don't worry about us, Papa. I'm lookin' out for everybody while you're here," Philomena told him. "Anybody come near the house…well, I'll blow their brains out!"

"Philomena!" Angelina gasped. "The t'ings you say…"

"Sorry Mama, I just mean I'll watch out for all of us. I'm tough, like Papa. Right, Papa?" She looked at her father. He nodded and winked.

"Is it terrible here, Papa?" Carmella asked.

"No, ees not too bad," he said, shaking his head. "You Papa is strong…like Philomena!" He raised his arms and flexed his muscles.

They all laughed with him. Philomena put her shoulders back and raised her head, looking proud.

"Hey Angelina, you know who is here wit' me?" Vincenzo asked.

"No, who?"

"Lucky D'Amo."

"No! Why? Why dey arrest him?" she asked, with surprise.

"I t'ink we must ask Melio Garibaldi dat very same question," Vincenzo said, looking at her with a sly, sideways glance. "Ees strange how da police wen' to his saloon the same night dey come to our house, eh?" Vincenzo squinted his eyes and nodded slowly. "I hear dat Melio rat on me…and Lucky too. Mr. C no gonna like dat."

"*Oh, la mia bonta.*" Angelina made the sign of the cross. "Dis not good, Vincenzo."

"No, ees no good," he agreed.

"Mama? Can we eat now?" Maria asked, seeming nervous as she listened to her parent's conversation.

"Yes Mama, can we see what's in the basket?" Bettina echoed her sister.

"Yes, we eat now." Angelina emptied the basket onto the table and they ate and laughed, while Vincenzo tore off a hunk of bread and covered it with a thick slice of cheese.

Every weekend, during that summer, and until Vincenzo was released from jail, a representative of Mr. Capone's made a visit to Vincenzo's house and handed Angelina an envelope of money in appreciation for Vincenzo's sacrifice. Capone, later that summer went to prison for tax evasion, but his men continued doing business with Vincenzo. Lucky reopened D'Amo's and Melio Garibaldi disappeared, never to be heard from again.

Chapter 4

The girls were as close as sisters could be, but the older ones were busy with their own group of friends while the younger ones stayed close to their mother. Like most sisters, they fought, but the reasons why were soon forgotten.

By 1938, the girls ranged in age from eleven to twenty. Lourdes was the youngest, and Violet the oldest. They obediently followed their parent's household rules, one of which was to start their day early. When Vincenzo got up in the morning, everyone got up. And whether it was a school day or a weekend, when their father got up from his chair at the end of the day and headed up to his room, lights were turned off, doors were locked, and everyone went to bed. *Vi rispettiamo mamma e pepe'*," the girls said, pledging their respect to their parents as they climbed the stairs to their rooms.

The little wooden house on Hazel Street had one bedroom for Vincenzo and Angelina and two bedrooms for the girls to share. There was one bathroom where Vincenzo had recently had a bathtub installed, considered quite the luxury, especially one with running water. A toilet would have to wait. A trip to the outhouse was still the only way to relieve oneself in the Borzanna house. It was located at the back corner of the yard about forty paces from the kitchen door. Vincenzo had placed narrow wooden planks, end to end from the back door to the outhouse, and in the middle of winter, when it was fifteen degrees below zero, the walk to the little wooden house with the creaky door was torture. The girls laughed, hysterically every time they told the story of Philomena's bottom freezing and sticking to the slab of wood with the hole in it, or how Connie always clipped a clothespin over her nose, and held her breath before entering the outhouse.

Vincenzo was a patient father and seemingly unfretted by his houseful of females. He rarely lost his temper, but when he did, he didn't need to say a word. His eyes spoke for him.

Prohibition was over in 1933 and Vincenzo found himself out of a job. Bootlegging was no longer necessary, and he needed to make money, so he went back to work for the coalmine as a *buggie runner.* He transported the loads of coal from the mine to the distributor and stayed on the job long enough to get insurance for his family.

Angelina breathed a little easier now that Vincenzo and Philomena were out of the bootlegging business and she was perfectly content to have less money coming into the house, as long as it meant her family was safe.

D'Amo's remained a second home to Vincenzo, and the back room was still made available to him and his cronies. Good wine was stocked for them, and Lucky never forgot that Vincenzo was the reason he was able to stay in business during prohibition, and why he was able to make money when everyone else went broke. Lucky and his staff still referred to Vincenzo as *Maestro*, which always made Angelina laugh. He was simply Vincenzo to her, and Papa to her girls. He was the one she would shake her finger at when he'd come home, more than a bit tipsy, with a tub of chocolate ice cream tucked under his arm. "*Maestro*," she scoffed, as he stumbled up the stairs to fall into bed.

*

Vincenzo woke to the aroma of fresh-brewed coffee. Sitting on the edge of the bed, he contemplated his day, and after pulling his pants up over his long johns, and stretching his suspenders over his shoulders, he slid his feet into his slippers, and shuffled toward the stairs. Walking by the closed doors of his daughters' bedrooms, he rapped loudly, and headed down the stairs where Angelina was moving thick slices of ham around in a cast iron pan.

"*Buon giorno, caro,*" he mumbled in Angelina's direction.

"*Lei he dormito bene?*" Angelina replied, asking if he slept well.

"*Si,*" he answered, and headed out the backdoor toward the outhouse.

With Violet in the lead, the girls marched down the stairs two by two, and waited by the kitchen door for their father to return. Starting with the youngest, they took turns making the trip to the outhouse.

Angelina packed lunches, made stacks of toast in the wood stove, and hummed contentedly while listening to her girls' giggle and prattle.

As he did every morning, Vincenzo poked a hole in the small end of an eggshell, and sucked out the egg before going to sit at the dining room table. He sipped coffee from his favorite mug, while looking toward a window expertly draped with lace that was hand-crocheted by Angelina. He squinted as the early morning sun beamed brightly through the curtains, sending warm rays across the room. Vincenzo was oblivious to the din around him. He sat quietly, his hands resting on the linen table cover.

Angelina brought him a glass of wine, a large chunk of bread that she had baked the night before, a thick slice of ham, and a bowl of fat, purple grapes. The girls came to the table, plates in hand, some with eggs, some with fruit.

Breakfast was brief but hectic, and as the younger ones gathered up schoolbooks, sweaters, and lunch bags, they kissed their parents before hurrying out the door to join their friends for the walk to school.

Philomena and Giordana stayed home to help their mother, while Violet set off to her job working behind the counter at the Star Company Store.

By four o'clock in the afternoon, the girls were home again, eagerly waiting for the supper their mother had been preparing for most of the day. Macaroni was served everyday, and Vincenzo's favorite was bucatini, a long noodle with a hole in the middle.

"Oh Papa," the girls would hold their stomachs and howl, "you're so funny," they said, as he slurped loudly, puckering his lips, sucking a strand of bucatini into his mouth. It slapped the sides of his face, leaving splashes of tomato sauce that he wiped away with the back of his hand.

"*Vincenzo, lei e' cose' sciocco,*" Angelina laughed, telling him how silly he was.

Vincenzo savored a couple of glasses of his homemade wine each night. He kept bottles in the cellar along with long chains of homemade sausages that were wrapped around clothesline strung from one end of the cellar to the other. Lined up on wooden shelves along the walls were jars of roasted peppers, tomato sauce and green beans soaking in olive oil and garlic. Large wheels of aged cheese hung from the ceiling's rafters, and the girls complained about the smell, dreading the times their mother ordered them to the cellar to retrieve cheese or sausages.

They often sat at the table in their mother's kitchen, watching her make ricotta cheese from milk that boiled in a large pot on the wood-burning stove. Taking her big slotted spoon, and scooping the curd that rose to the top, Angelina placed it in a bowl, covered it with a plate and stored it in the icebox. She used the cheese for ravioli or their favorite cheese and spinach pie. She jarred fresh vegetables from Vincenzo's garden, and stored them in the basement to be used in the winter. Vincenzo grew enormous red tomatoes, green and red peppers, green beans, lettuce, cucumbers, Swiss chard, watermelons, and a variety of herbs. The garden took up most of the backyard, and Vincenzo always said it was the best soil outside of Italy, and to the girls' horror, he believed that the outhouse made it even more fertile.

Angelina was older now and what some might call a handsome woman. She was delightfully soft and round, with a mischievous smile and sparkling brown eyes. Her hair was still dark but now streaked with gray. She kept it long, parted in the middle, and pulled back in a bun. An expert seamstress, she almost always wore housedresses she made herself out of remnant material she purchased at the company store. She owned two pairs of shoes, one pair for church, weddings and funerals, the other for every day. She wore black stockings, rolled above her knees in the winter and down around her ankles in the summer.

She cuddled her daughters no matter what age they were, and her embraces were firm and heartfelt. She smelled of vanilla and garlic, depending on what time of day it was, and her girls could always count on her to make them feel better when they had a problem. Life was good for Angelina's girls.

*

Violet was tall and thin with coal black hair and intense green eyes. She was mature for her age; confident and charming and whenever her parents were not around, she took it upon herself to be in charge of her sisters. Giordana and Philomena were the closest in age and looked like twins. They were both short and stocky, with pretty faces and smooth, dark-olive skin. With deep brown eyes and prominent noses, they most resembled their mother and where Giordana was quiet and sweet, Philomena was independent and outspoken.

Carmella was thin, and pretty like her older sister, Violet. Her hair was straight and the color of mahogany. She was the most mischievous of all the sisters. She had a long, expressive face with a toothy grin that creased her cheeks with deep dimples, and she seemed to find almost everything amusing, which drove Philomena crazy.

"That's not funny, Carmella!" Philomena would rage. "Mama, make her stop!"

But Carmella couldn't help herself. Along with her fits of laughter, she was a shameless flirt, and her light-hearted attitude seemed to prevent her from taking anything or anyone too seriously.

Bettina and Maria were just beginning to blossom into young ladies. They were best friends and looked up to their older sisters for advice but were perfectly content spending time with each other in their own little world of dolls and tea parties. Lourdes was the baby and spent most of her time with her mother, in the kitchen or doing chores around the house. She had brown eyes, flecked with gold and as big as saucers. She was always able to melt her father's heart. She was delicate and shy and would often curl up next to her father, squeezing into his favorite chair with him. Like a little lady, she'd draw up her knees and wrap her long skirts around her legs. She had a habit of nervously twisting her long curly hair around her finger while she told her father stories about her day. He would listen, nod and laugh at her silly jokes.

Connie was petite and fairskinned, with honey-blonde hair that she pains-takingly wrapped in pincurls every night before bed. She had a sweet personality and loved to sing and was obsessed with dancing. She was drawn to anyone who shared her love of music and dancing, and she and her sisters spent most weekends listening to the Philco radio they kept in their bedroom. Connie was fifteen, and along with her love of dance, was also a skilled roller-skater. She was full of energy and curiosity, with a complex personality, sometimes comical and other times shy and sensitive. She admired Violet, feared Philomena, and was amused by Carmella. She was closest to Giordana. She fussed over Maria, Bettina and Lourdes and often helped her mother by babysitting her younger sisters.

The older girls had lots of friends in Star Junction, and they were all very active with roller-skating and bicycling. Weekends were busy at the Regal Oak Skating Rink, and the girls met with their friends every Friday. One particular night though, was a night that would change Connie's life.

*

It started out like any Friday night at the Regal Oak, packed with teenagers from the girls' school. Some of Connie's friends were already at the rink, skating to the music coming from the organ, and Connie and Carmella were just finishing up lacing their skates. Giordana and Philomena were already on the floor happily gliding along with the other skaters. They were making their first lap around the rink when the organist started playing *Stardust.*

"Oh, listen Carmella!" Connie said, excitedly. "They're playing *Stardust*! I love that song! Come on, come on, lets go…skate with me." Connie grabbed Carmella by the arm, and together they skated toward an opening in the railing and waited for the right moment to jump in and join the other skaters passing by. With halting steps, they worked their way onto the rink floor.

They took smooth strides in an effort to get into the rhythm of the music, and though they were both good skaters, they held hands for support. Connie, now fifteen was a year older than Carmella, and much to Connie's dismay, her younger sister had embarrassed her more than once when it came to flirting. Deep down, Connie was curious about boys, but would rather have died, than let a boy know she was interested. Her sisters laughed at her and imitated the way she put her nose in the air and gave the cold shoulder to any boy who got a little too familiar.

The second time around the rink, Carmella spotted a group of young men standing by the snack bar. She didn't recognize them, and they looked too old to be in high school. Curiosity got the better of her when her eyes were drawn to one particular boy standing in the group. His hair was dark, slick and shiny. He clenched a cigarette in his teeth, his blue-green eyes smoldering from the smoke. He was slight of build, and had a cocky smile that was movie star handsome. A freshly pressed, white shirt was neatly tucked into the waistband of his Italian cut, gray slacks, and Carmella practically swooned.

"Gosh, look at that cute guy over there, Connie. I think I'll go over and see if he wants to skate with me."

"No, Carmella!" Connie was horrified. She held onto the sleeve of her sister's sweater. "You should be ashamed of yourself." Connie glanced over to where her sister had pointed, and the boys were now gathered in a huddle. "Carmella, please don't do that. What are they gonna to think of you?" She asked, desperately holding onto the sleeve of her sister's sweater.

"Connie! For goodness sake; don't be such a fuddy-duddy!" Carmella pulled away and weaved her way between other skaters until she found her way out of the rink. Connie rolled her eyes in frustration and sped up her pace to catch up with Giordana and Violet. When she told her sisters what Carmella was up to, they just laughed, and told her to stop worrying.

"She would be in so much trouble if Papa and Mama knew what she was doing!" Connie protested.

"She's harmless, Connie. For goodness sakes, Carmella's all talk, you know that. Anyway, I've got my eye on her, and I'll wallop her good if she goes too far."

Violet, being the oldest and engaged to be married was very much the mother hen. Her fiancé was in the Italian army, stationed in Foggia, Italy. She had met him only once. It was still a tradition in some Italian families to choose mates for their daughters, and the plan was for her fiancé, Pasqual Siamento, to finish his military obligation, come to America, marry Violet, and become an American citizen. Pasqual's father, Pietro Siamento, was an old friend of Vincenzo's, from the old country and Vincenzo considered him an honorable man who raised his son to be hardworking and trustworthy. Apparently, Violet was most pleased when she met Pasqual, two years before when he and his parents came to America to visit. He was a tall, handsome teenager, with thick, curly hair and a hearty laugh that Violet found contagious and wonderful. She loved a good sense of humor, and Pasqual seemed to fit the bill. After she balked at the idea of her father finding a husband for her, she changed her mind after meeting Pasqual, and the prospect of marrying him now excited her, and she looked forward to having children one day.

*

Carmella, acting coy approached the group of young men standing together toward the back of the skating rink next to the snack bar. They were speaking Italian to each other and paid no attention to her at first, so she took a deep breath, fluffed her freshly curled hair, and gently bumped one of the boys as she skated by. "Oops…scuze me," Carmella cooed, and fluttered her eyelashes.

They turned to look at her. One said something in Italian, and they all laughed.

"I speak Italian too, ya know…so ya better be careful," she scolded.

"Look at the skinny little chicken who's looking for a rooster!" one of them said, pointing and laughing.

Carmella pouted and squinted her eyes. She put her hands on her hips. "Well! That was rude."

The boys turned and resumed their conversation. She cleared her throat, fluffed her hair and tried again. "Haven't seen you boys here before."

When there was still no response other than laughter, Carmella turned in frustration and skated over to the snack bar. "Gimme a pop, will ya Irlene?" Carmella asked.

Irlene was a tall, gangly girl with buckteeth, freckles and red hair that she wore in long braids. She was in the eighth grade at Carmella's school, and she knew most of the Borzanna sisters. Irlene worked part time at the rink serving up soda pop and hot dogs, and was a pretty good source to go to if you needed to know the latest gossip.

"So…how ya doin', Carmie?" Irlene asked, snapping the gum she was vigorously chewing. She popped the cap off of a bottle of pop.

"I'm fine, but…" Carmella covered her mouth with her hand and whispered, "Do you know these guys…especially the one in the white shirt?"

Irlene glanced in their direction. The boys were busy making wolf whistles at girls that were passing by.

"No, not really but one of them got kinda fresh with me, and I told 'em to hit the pike," she said with a smirk. "I heard them say they drove over here from Uniontown. I think they're all brothers, or something... I'm not sure. They look like a bunch of wise guys, if you ask me. Why do you want to know?"

"I don't know," Carmella shrugged. "I thought that one guy was kinda cute." She giggled and a dimple dented her cheek. "But they won't pay any attention to me."

"These guys are too old for you, Carm."

"Say's who?" Carmella protested. She pinched her cheeks until they stung with pinkness. She checked her image in the napkin dispenser and seeming satisfied, started toward the boys again.

"Hey, do your sisters know what you're doing'?" Irlene called after her.

"I don't need my sisters to tell me what to do!" She said, indignantly. "And you're asking' too many questions, Irlene." She continued to sip on the paper straw that was poking out of her pop bottle and approached the boys again. "Hello, again." She wriggled her way between them, until she was standing in the middle of their circle. "I hear you boys are here from Uniontown."

"Yeah, so?" The tallest one said, giving her an amused look.

"No reason, just curious." Carmella turned to face the boy in the white shirt. "What's *your* name?" she asked.

He was busy watching the skaters in the rink, and it took a few seconds before he realized Carmella was talking to him. The guy next to him elbowed him in the ribs and, cocking his head, gestured toward Carmella.

"What? Oh, my name? Dominic Preste." He spoke with a slight Italian accent.

"Well, Mister Dominic Preste...how's about a skate?" Carmella cooed.

Ignoring her flirtatious tone, his attention was still on the rink. "No, not now, *Bella*," he said, absently. "Hey...uh, who was the girl you were skating with before? What's *her* name?" Dominic asked.

Carmella was crushed. "That's Connie...why?"

"Just wondering," he said, turning and skating off toward the rink.

Carmella stood frozen, a look of shock making her mouth fly open. She crossed her arms in defiance. The other three boys resumed their conversation as Carmella watched Dominic catch up with her Connie. "Of all the nerve," she said, and skated off toward the girl's room.

"What's the matter, Carm? Did they throw ya back, like a baby fish?" Irlene teased as Carmella sped past the snack bar.

"Shut up Irlene! The guy is a jerk, and ya know what? He can't even skate!"

Dominic sidled alongside Connie, and struggled to get in step with her. He awkwardly bounced to the rhythm of the music, and nearly fell over backward. She looked surprised, and she couldn't help but giggle as he tried to get his balance.

"'Hello Connie," he said, panting from the exertion to stay upright.

She looked at him curiously. "How do you know my name? I don't know you." She raised her voice in order to be heard over the organist's music.

"I asked your girlfriend what your name was…and she told me," Dominic said, shrugging his shoulders. "Simple, eh?"

"What girlfriend?"

"The one you were skating around with. See? Over there," he said, pointing to where Carmella had returned to the snack bar. She was talking with Irlene, her hands flailing about, obviously upset about something.

"Uh-oh, that's my sister. What did she do?"

"No, nothin'…cute kid."

"Yes, she is. So, what do you want?"

"Wanted to meet you. Want to have a pop with me?" He added.

"I don't even know you." Connie felt her face flush red.

"Okay…I can fix that. My name is Dominic! There, now you know me. Want to get a pop?" he asked again.

She looked at him with amused skepticism.

"That's better," he said, still struggling to keep in step with her. "Hey, ya think you could slow down a little? I'm about to break my neck here."

Connie laughed and slowed her pace. "You're asking' *me* to have a pop with you?" She seemed surprised he would choose her over Carmella.

"Yeah."

"Well okay, but just for a couple a minutes."

Dominic took her by the hand and they skated out of the rink together and headed for the snack bar. There were metal tables and benches nearby and Dominic gestured for Connie to go and sit, while he got two bottles of pop. While she waited, she looked for Carmella and finally saw her, back in the rink, skating with a school chum, seeming happy.

Connie snuck a peek at Dominic as he stood at the counter waiting for Irlene to hand him the bottles of pop. He was short, and very thin but she found his face interesting. He seemed confident, maybe too confident, bordering on arrogance. His skin was smooth and tanned, and he had a way of cocking his head ever so slightly as he spoke. His smile was slow and easy, and Connie almost laughed out loud when she saw Irlene giggle and turn red when he reached for the pop bottles, accidentally touching her hand. He laughed too, like he understood why she was flustered. He seemed used to the reaction.

Connie quickly looked away when he turned in her direction. He was skating toward the table, and after handing her one of the bottles, sat down opposite her. He took a cigarette out of his shirt pocket, deftly flipped it into his mouth, and lit it with a wooden match he had tucked behind one ear.

"So Connie, where're you from?"

"Right here, Wickhaven," she answered, feeling uncomfortable as he looked at her with his head cocked in that way she had noticed earlier. His eyes were bluer than they were green and seemed to look right through her. She found it disturbing, yet it took her breath away.

He nodded, and cleared his throat. "So, that's your sister…the skinny one?" he finally said, with a slight Italian accent.

"Mm-hm, that's my little sister. She's a little…I don't know, crazy sometimes," she laughed. "Can I ask you something, Dominic?"

"What?"

"Did she tell you to come and ask me to skate?"

"What? No…she was just being friendly, I think. I asked her who you were…ya know…I wanted to skate with you."

"Oh, great," Connie grimaced, feeling bad for Carmella but flattered for herself.

"What? What's wrong with that?"

"Well, she thought you were cute, and she was coming over to get you to skate with her."

"*Oh, non ho saputo*! I didn't know!" He smacked his forehead with the palm of his hand. "I mean she's so young…like a little girl. I'm almost twenty, ya know? I feel bad. Do ya think she's mad?"

"It's okay, she's not mad," Connie said. *Oh dear sweet Jesus! He's twenty?* Connie said to herself. *Papa would kill me!*

"I get that a lot, you know?" he said, while smoothing his hair, and raising his eyebrows.

"What? You get what a lot?" Connie eyed him curiously.

"Girls…ya know…wantin' to meet me. Think I'm cute…you know?"

Oh my God, is this guy serious? She looked away, and rolled her eyes. "Don't worry about it, I'm sure she's forgotten about you already," Connie laughed. "Carmella's that way. Flirts with ya one minute… forgets ya, the next." She was surprised when he seemed offended. "Oh, come on, I was just kidding."

"Oh yeah, well I knew that." He forced a laugh. "So, what do *you* think?"

"Think about what?"

"You think I'm good lookin'?"

"Oh brother, you're joking, right?" Connie smacked the table with her hand and laughed, choking back a mouthful of pop. Realizing he wasn't joking, she quickly added, "Well yeah, I guess I think you're cute." She felt her face redden with embarrassment, never having said anything like that to a boy before.

Seeming pleased, Dominic sniffed as he slid his hand along the side of his well-oiled hair.

"Do you always make sure all the girls you meet think you're cute?" Connie asked.

"No, I was just askin', that's all."

"Uh-huh." Connie paused, then turned to him. "Well, aren't you gonna say anything about me?"

"What about you? Oh…ya mean, about how you look?"

"Well, we've established that you're cute…what about me?" Connie said, feeling the conversation had turned quite silly.

"Yeah, well…" he started. He looked her up and down and finally said, "You look nice."

"Nice," she repeated. "Nice?"

"Yeah, nice. I'll tell ya what, you look like you eat pretty good," he teased, and made an hourglass shape with his hands. His shoulders moved up and down as he laughed.

Connie didn't know whether to slap him or run away. She sat up straight and glared at him. "You're fresh, Dominic!"

"Wha…what's the matter?" he asked, holding out his hands and shrugging. He got up and moved to the other side of the table and sat next to her. "You asked me and I tol' ya. I happen to like girls with a little meat on 'em."

She stood up and started to step over the bench.

"Sit down, sit down," he said, taking hold of her arm, pulling her back down onto the bench. She sat with a thump but refused to look at him.

"Those are all my brothers, ya know?" Dominic said, changing the subject, seeming unfazed by her anger. He pointed in the direction of the group of young men still standing in a huddle by the snack bar. They were smoking and sipping bottles of pop.

"So?" Connie said, glumly. She was resting her chin in her hands; her elbows perched on the table.

"Just thought you'd be interested, that's all. That's my brother Vittorio," he pointed, "he's learning to be a stonemason, and my brother Antonio? He's only sixteen but he's workin' in the mines with my oldest brother, Sergio. He's the one with the green sweater. When we lived in Italy, I used to go in the mountains with my father and herd the sheep." His expression turned serious. "He died when I was ten." He suddenly quieted, and lowered his head.

"You okay?" Connie asked.

"What?" His thoughts seemed to have drifted away. "Oh yeah… I'm fine. Anyway, when me and my brothers come here from Italy, I was in the sixth grade, but I never went back to school. I got a job at the shipyard and started makin' pretty good money, so I didn't need school."

Connie watched him as he spoke. She was surprised, yet touched that he felt comfortable enough with her to tell her everything about himself.

"My mother," he continued, "she's still in Rome with my sisters, Gia and Annette. When me and my brothers make more money, we're gonna bring 'em here to live one day." He finally paused, looked at her and gave her a nervous smile. "Papa died when I was ten. Did I tell you that?"

"Yeah, you did. I'm sorry about your father." Connie's mood softened.

"Yeah so, my mother raised all us kids herself. She was tough, too. Huh," he laughed and shook his head. "I'll tell you what…" he quieted again.

"My, you have quite a family," Connie said.

"Huh? Oh, yeah," he said, absently.

"I have quite a family too," Connie continued. "I have seven…"

"Hey! What's that song?" he interrupted her. "I like that one," he said, looking up at the ceiling, concentrating on the sound of the organ. He pushed his body up close to hers, and she wrinkled her nose. She detected cologne, but it was overpowered by the smell of cigarettes and garlic. When he put his arm around her shoulders, she stiffened.

"I'm probably gonna be gettin' a car pretty soon. What d'ya think about that?"

"That's nice."

He lit another cigarette, and swayed back and forth to the music. "Ya like to dance?" he asked. He snapped his fingers and bopped his head up and down.

"I love to dance," Connie suddenly looked intrigued and excited. "And you?"

"Oh, I love to dance. I'm good too." He took her hand and motioned like he was twirling her. "We'll go dancing sometime, yeah?"

"Maybe, I mean…I guess so," Connie shrugged. She looked over her shoulder when she heard her name called.

Giordana was standing by the main doors. "Connie! Come on… lets go! Papa will be waiting for us."

"Oh my gosh, how long have we been sitting here? I have to go, Dominic. My father's waiting outside," she said, jumping up, stepping over the side of the bench. Dominic grabbed Connie by the arm and pulled her back behind the snack bar. It was dark and musty smelling. The wheels of their skates made a *thwacking* sound as they rolled on the sticky floor, and before Connie could resist, Dominic took her by the shoulders and kissed her, hard on the lips. With her arms down to her sides, she stood motionless and struggled to catch her breath.

Dominic buried his face in her hair, and with his lips touching her ear, whispered, "Be here on Friday, *capice*?"

"*Capice*." The word drifted from her lips in a choked whisper.

Dominic skated back to his brothers, and Connie, finally able to move, sat on the bench, removed her skates, retrieved her shoes from a locker and walked toward the exit as though in a trance. She jumped into the backseat of her father's car and sat between Violet and Giordana. Carmella sat in front between their father and Maria. Carmella had long since gotten over the cute boy who snubbed her, and started to playfully tease Connie. "Connie's got a boyfriend…Connie's got a boyfriend," she chanted.

"Shhh!" Violet shushed her. She tapped Carmella on the back of the head. "You're gonna get Connie in trouble," she warned.

They rode the rest of the way in silence except for some giggling at Connie's expense. She was still reeling from what was her first kiss, and she placed her hand over her stomach in an attempt to calm the butterflies.

*

Connie, an average eighth-grader at Wickhaven School was popular with her classmates; always friendly and cheerful but today she was quiet. She spent the day daydreaming. She sat at her desk in her last class of the day and stared at the clock, willing its hands to turn to three o'clock. It was only Monday, and she was counting the days until Friday would come again. She felt a strange stirring in her stomach when she thought about seeing Dominic again. When the bell rang, Connie gathered her books, and without waiting for her sisters, started to walk home alone. She stepped outside and sniffed, filling her lungs with the crisp, cool air of early spring. She started down Bolton Street, and made a right on Andrews Avenue that would eventually take her to her house on Hazel Street.

The sidewalks were broken and bumpy from years of tree roots pushing their way up through the concrete. The trees were old and now thick with tender, pale green leaves. Puffs of unmelted snow still clung to the grass on the side of the road, yet the honeysuckle was starting to bloom and filled the air with its sweet perfume. Mrs. McNally, the school librarian lived on Bolton Street, and Connie stopped to admire a row of purple crocuses poking through the dirt on the side of her house.

"Connie…Connie!" She heard someone call. Giordana was running toward her. "Wait for me," she shouted.

Connie waved, and when Giordana finally caught up with her, she was out of breath. "What did you do, leave school early?"

"No, I don't know why but I couldn't wait to get out of school today. Could be the spring air, I don't know. I love spring, don't you? "

"I do."

The two sisters were close and often confided in each other. Connie envied Giordana's wide, toothy grin and warm, deep-set eyes. Giordana made her laugh too, and Connie liked being around her. They walked quietly arm in arm for a while, their books held together with leather straps and slung over their shoulders. They stopped to pick some honeysuckle blossoms and giggled as they gently pulled out the little green stems, licking the tiny droplet of honey that clung to the tip.

"So…what's wrong, Connie? You've been so quiet. After church yesterday, you went right up to your room when we got home. Are you okay?"

"I'm fine, Giordi."

Giordana gave her sister a sideways glance.

"No, really I am. It's nothing."

Giordana smiled. She knew that Connie couldn't keep a secret. They continued to walk toward home when Connie suddenly blurted, "Okay, I'll tell you!"

Giordana amused, shook her head. "Tell me what."

"Did you see the guy I met at the skating rink Friday night?" Connie asked.

"I think so. What about him?"

Connie paused, stopped and spun Giordana around to face her. "He kissed me!" Connie squealed.

Giordana laughed. "That's it? That's what you're so excited about? That's not such a big thing. Unless..." she added, mysteriously.

"Unless, what?"

"Unless, he did that French kiss thing."

"French kiss? What's that?"

"I heard some girls talkin' about it in the girls' room at school," Giordana said, in a whisper. "Sounded disgusting."

"Well, what is it?"

"Something about touching tongues."

"E-eww...Giordy, please! That's not funny...that sounds horrible!" Connie gave her sister a playful shove, and they both hooted with laughter. "Anyway," Connie continued, "There's something about this guy. I mean, he was a smart-alecky kind of guy...I didn't even think I liked him at first. He didn't pay much attention to me. He mainly talked about himself."

"Gosh, sounds like a real dreamboat!" Giordana smirked.

"Come on Giordana, I'm being serious. Listen, you're older than me; didn't you ever meet a guy who was nothing like what you imagined you would like?"

"Huh?"

"You know, but then you couldn't help it, and you got this strange feeling inside? Like, I think I like this guy kind of feeling, but I don't know why?" Connie rambled on.

"I don't even know what you just asked me! And just for the record, I'm only a year older than you. And...no, I've never felt that way about a boy."

"Oh, well that's how I'm feeling, you know...kind of confused."

"Why don't you ask Violet, she's the one with experience? I mean, she's engaged and all." They walked a while in silence, pondering Connie's situation. "So, what's the big deal about a kiss? It's not like you're gonna marry the guy or something."

Connie looked at her sister and rolled her eyes. "I know that but he wants me to meet him again on Friday night. Should I? Would you, if you were me?"

They rounded the corner of Hazel Street, and their house came into view. Giordana didn't answer because their father was by the curb in front of the house, washing his car.

"Hello, Papa!" They called out.

Vincenzo looked up and waved the wet, soapy rag he had clutched in his hand. He went back to washing the car, and the girls went into the house where they found their mother in the kitchen, rolling out gnocchi for dinner. Using her thumb, she sliced off dumplings the size of marbles, placed them on the kitchen table and covered them with a dishtowel. A pot of tomato sauce bubbled on the stove, and fresh bread and garlic perfumed every room of the house.

"*Come state figlie mie*?" Angelina asked, wiping sweat from her face. She planted a noisy kiss on their foreheads. "*Vai a prendere La biancheria de guori,"* she said, ordering the girls to bring in the clothes from the line out back. Connie and Giordana piled their schoolbooks on the table in the living room and went outside to get the laundry. When they closed the backdoor, and were sure they were out of their mother's hearing range, Giordana continued their earlier conversation.

"Meeting him where, Connie?" Giordana asked, quietly.

"The Regal Oak." Connie glanced toward the kitchen door. "Are you going Friday night? You'll go, right? Please, please, please?" She begged. "Violet and Carmella…I'm sure they'll be there too. I won't feel nervous if you're all there with me."

"Sure, I'll go," Giordana assured her. "Gee whiz, Connie…sometimes you're scared of your own shadow! And listen, you'd better be careful because if Papa gets wind of this, he'll box your ears but good!"

"Gets wind of what?" Connie asked, sheepishly.

"You know what I'm talking about," Giordana scolded. "You're going on a date with a guy who Papa hasn't met or approved of, that's what!"

"Shh," Connie said, putting her finger to her lips, warning her to be quiet. She took a crisp white sheet from the clothesline, handed one end to Giordana and held onto the other, folded it neatly and placed it in the basket. "Mmm, I love the smell of sheets just off the line, don't you?" Connie took a whiff from a handful of a sheet that was still hanging on the line.

"Me too Connie, but don't change the subject," Giordana said, still looking concerned.

They continued to fold the sheets, placing them into a tattered wicker basket sitting in the grass. The towels were old and frayed, stiff like cardboard from the lye soap their mother used to launder with. When everything was off the line and neatly folded, Connie and Giordana lifted the basket and carried it into the kitchen, where Carmella and Philomena were arriving home from school.

With everyone home, a happy chatter continued while the girls helped their mother with the cooking and the setting of the table. Vincenzo came into the house and put the bucket and rags in the cellar before settling in the living room for a quick nap. Peeking around the corner of the kitchen door, he sniffed the aroma of garlic and bread, and retreated to the quiet of the living room. He lit up one of the hand-twisted stogies he kept in a wooden box tucked away in the middle drawer of the sideboard, and nestled back in his easy chair. He laid his hand on the lace doily that covered the arm of the chair, and encircled the cigar with his fingers. He drew deeply on the cigar, blowing a thin stream of smoke through puckered lips. His eyes closed as he savored the bitter taste on his tongue, and after a few minutes, nodded off with the cigar clenched in his teeth.

"You need any help, Mama?" Connie asked, even though it wasn't her turn.

"No, no…you go, Conchetta," Angelina said, waving her arm in the direction of the living room. "Carmella will do for me."

Connie glanced at Carmella, who waited for their mother to turn her back before sticking out her tongue. Laughing, Connie sashayed into the living room, where she found her father contentedly snoring. He was holding his cigar loosely between his fingers, and Connie, noticing a chunk of ash about to fall, gently took the cigar and placed it in an ashtray. Gathering her books, she climbed the stairs to her room.

After tossing her books on the bed, Connie fell backwards onto the mattress, crossed her legs and put her hands behind her head. She was enjoying a rare moment of quiet but knew it wouldn't last long. The room she shared with three of her sisters was comfortable though cramped with two double beds that were covered with patchwork quilts. A tall dresser stood by the window, and a large, antique mirror was propped against the wall in the corner of the room. In winter, Angelina kept heavy blankets folded neatly at the foot of each bed but as spring approached, the blankets were stored in the hall closet.

Connie liked the heat of summer but when the house was too warm for sleeping, all eight girls slept in one room, stripped down to their panties and undershirts in front of the fan their mother had set up behind a bowl of ice.

Connie rested a while, daydreaming, and fighting off the butterflies that continued to plague her stomach. Deciding to change her clothes, she slipped off her skirt and blouse, and after rummaging through the closet, put on a cotton housedress. She kicked off her shoes and socks and wiggled her toes feeling the coolness of the wood floor beneath her feet. Dropping back on the bed but this ttime on her stomach, Connie propped her schoolbook on a pillow in front of her but her thoughts were not about arithmetic; they were about Dominic.

*

It was Friday afternoon and Vincenzo drove to town to meet with his friends at D'Amo's. As they had for years, the men gathered at the same time, every day in the backroom, drank Chianti and ate hardboiled eggs. They reminisced about the "old country" until it was time to go home for dinner. Vincenzo was still considered the boss, and was always the first to get up from his chair to head for home. "I see you tomorrow, eh?" His fedora was cocked to one side, keeping the right side of his face in shadow. He let the last drop of wine trickle down his throat before placing the glass on the table. After leaving through a back entrance, he decided to drive home by way of Bolton Street, past his daughters' school. He spotted Connie, Carmella and Giordana as they crossed the road. He pulled up to the curb and tooted the horn. The girls waved while running toward the car and after piling in, each gave their father a kiss on the cheek as he stepped on the gas pedal and headed for home.

The girls giggled and talked about their day at school, except for Connie. She sat quietly, biting her lip, and wringing her hands. It was Friday. She was going to see Dominic, which thrilled her but also terrified her. She had a lot to do to prepare for her first date. What to wear was most important to her, and of course her hair had to be perfect. She knew Carmella, Giordana, and Violet would help her, and knowing they would be with her that night, gave her courage.

"Can I borrow your pink sweater tonight, Carmella…the one Ma knit for you?" Connie asked, as Vincenzo pulled the car up to the curb in front of the house.

"Hmm, let me see," Carmella teased. She rubbed her chin and looked up, as though it was a big decision. "*Should* I let you borrow my sweater?"

"Come on, Carmella…stop fooling around," Connie pled, giving her sister a playful shove. "Can I? And your pink lipstick too?" She added.

"Eh!" Vincenzo barked. "Wadda you talkin'?" He asked, suspiciously. "Wadda ya gettin' all fancy for, Conchetta? I don' wan' you fool 'round wit' no boys, you hear me?" He shook his fist in the air.

Connie grimaced and glanced at Carmella, who was covering her mouth to keep from giggling. "Sorry, Papa," Carmella apologized.

Connie was never able to lie to her father and feared he would ask her what they were planning at the skating rink that night. He would surely forbid her to go if he knew she was meeting a boy there, let alone a boy that was almost twenty.

When they walked into the house, the girls went about their daily chores but Connie was edgy and distracted. Dinner was on the table, and Vincenzo to Connie's relief seemed to forget about the incident in the car. She was pushing the food around on her plate, not noticing that her mother was eyeing her suspiciously. After dinner, it was Connie's turn to dry the dishes, and she was drying them faster than Giordana could wash them, placing them on the shelf with a crash.

"Conchetta!" Angelina scolded. "Eh, what're you in so hurry for? You gonna break my deeshes!"

"Sorry, Mama." Connie's face reddened. She finished the last dish, hung up the wet towel and tore up the steps two at a time, slamming the bedroom door.

"Watta matter wit dat' girl?" Angelina questioned.

Giordana and Philomena looked at their mother and shrugged which she returned with a look of warning.

Connie dampened her hair, and with a towel covering her head, sat on the floor in front of the antique mirror. She wrapped pieces of her honey colored hair around her finger and secured the curls with hairpins, then shimmied over by the open window and spent a few minutes drying the damp curls in a warm breeze that was gently drifting over the sill. Connie slipped into a robe and found Carmella's pink sweater, holding it up to three different skirts before deciding on a slim, gray skirt with a kick pleat. After getting dressed, she examined her image in the mirror. Satisfied with her outfit, she practiced her smile before putting on white socks and brown loafers.

"Ooh, don't you look nice?" Giordana commented, as she came into the bedroom. "I'm just grabbing a sweater for Carm and me."

"Okay, I'll be ready in a minute." Connie dabbed her lips and cheeks with a pale pink lipstick.

"Ya better hurry, Papa's already getting everybody in the car."

Connie pulled the pins from her hair, brushed it vigorously and fluffed it with her fingers. As she took one last look at herself, she heard her father's voice at the bottom of the stairs.

"Conchetta!" He bellowed. "*Sbrigati*! We in da car."

She bounced down the stairs, past her father, hoping he wouldn't notice her pink lips and cheeks but to her dismay, he did.

"Conchetta, *vieni qua*," he stopped her, ordering her to come closer. He studied her face.

"What, Papa? What's wrong?" Connie asked in an attempt to sound bewildered by her father's questioning look.

He took a handkerchief from his vest pocket, spit on a small corner of the cloth, and handed it to her. She knew what he wanted her to do, so she took the handkerchief and wiped her lips and cheeks, and with shame on her face, handed it back to him.

"No daughter of a mine ees looka like *prostituta*!" Vincenzo said, pounding his fist into the palm of his hand.

"Sorry, Papa," Connie said, choking back tears. She didn't know what made her feel worse... her father being angry at her, or the fact that she had to meet Dominic with her plain old face.

"Go...get in da car," Vincenzo said, shaking his head, his tone softening. He knew Connie was a good girl but he had to protect the reputation of all of his daughters. He refused to have any of his daughters painted up like loose women.

Giordana, Violet, Carmella, Philomena and Connie squeezed into their father's car, with Carmella sitting on Violet's lap and Connie wedged between Giordana and Philomena. Vincenzo slid into the driver's seat. Maria, Bettina and Lourdes peered out the living room window as the car disappeared down the street. Vincenzo dropped the girls at the skating rink and warned them to be careful, and not to make him wait when he came to pick them up at eight o'clock. They assured him they would be on time, and one by one, they pried themselves from the car and quickly rushed inside.

"Come on girls, let's go," Violet said, impatiently as she laced up her skates. "You're such slow-pokes."

"We're coming," Giordana and Philomena whined in unison. "Are you coming Connie?"

"Not yet. I'll be there in a minute," she said, her eyes scanning the room hoping to spot Dominic.

"Suit yourself," Violet said, taking Giordana by the hand, pulling her toward the rink. They made one lap around, and came back to where Connie was still sitting on the bench.

"Are you okay, Connie?" Giordana asked. "Do you want us to stay with you? We don't have to skate right now."

"No...I'll be fine. I'll just wait for Dominic over there by the snack bar. I'm sure he'll show up soon. You go ahead." Connie waved them on. She went over to the snack bar and saw Irlene behind the counter. "Hi, Irlene. How are you?"

"Hey, Connie. Wow, you look great...I love your hair."

"Oh, thanks." Connie playfully fluffed her curls. Her eyes sparkled, and her cheeks were flushed with anticipation. "Irlene? Do you remember the guy I was sitting with last week? His name was Dominic."

"Yeah...what about him?" Irlene asked while she flipped the cap off a pop bottle.

"Have you seen him tonight? He asked me to meet him here for a date," she added, feeling her face flush red just saying the words.

"Oh...he did, did he?" She smirked. "I've seen him, alright." She looked toward the side entrance. "Isn't that him over there?"

Connie looked in the direction that Irlene indicated, and it *was* Dominic. He was standing with a girl whom Connie didn't recognize, and they were leaning up against the wall, their faces close together. Connie thought they were about to kiss. Dominic was touching the girl's hair, and she had one hand on Dominic's chest as she coyly twisted a blond-curl with the other. He leaned in to kiss her, and she eagerly obliged. Connie stood with clenched fists, her fingernails digging into the palms of her hands. Her mouth went dry, and she didn't know if she was going to scream or cry. She was embarrassed by her own stupidity, thinking that Dominic thought she was someone special.

"Jerk." Irlene muttered, feeling sorry for Connie. "Can I get ya something, Con? You wanna pop or…?"

"No!" Connie said, looking away from Dominic. "Oh, I…I mean… no thanks, Irlene. I don't want anything…I gotta go." She went to find Giordana.

"Oh, Connie...I'm sorry," Giordana said, after Connie told her what she had seen. "Are you okay? Do you want to go home?"

"No, I'm okay. I'm just so blame mad. What a creep!" Connie pounded her fists on her sides. "How could I be so dumb?"

Giordana wrapped her arm around Connie, and listened sympathetically. Connie took a deep breath, and composed herself. "No," she said defiantly, "I don't want to go home. I'm staying, and I'm going to forget about him, and I'm going to have fun! Yes, that's it," she emphatically determined. "I'm going to have a good time!"

"Good girl, Connie!" Giordana said, giving her sister a supportive grin. "Come on, let's go find Violet."

Connie spent the remainder of the evening skating with her sisters but also continued to look for Dominic. She didn't know what she would say if she ran into him, or if she would even bother to speak to him at all, but one thing she knew for sure; she was swearing off boys.

Chapter 5

The school year came to a close, and Connie had barely eked her way into the ninth grade. When she got home that last day of school, she handed her report card to her mother, as did her sisters. Everyone had passed, and that seemed to satisfy Angelina and Vincenzo.

Dominic's image flashed into Connie's thoughts from time to time; she'd wince and place her hand over her knotted stomach and the feeling quickly passed. She needed something to occupy her time, so she asked her father to help her find a summer job. He called his friend, Mr. Leone. He owned Leone's Italian Bakery on Beech Street, and as a favor to Vincenzo, hired Connie. She worked in the back of the store, where the ovens were located, and helped Mrs. Leone bake breads and cookies. Mrs. Leone was kind and patient while she taught Connie how to make dough for the pastries, how to decorate cookies and bake a variety of breads. She spoke with a slight Italian accent, had a natural pink glow to her cheeks and penciled her eyebrows so that she always looked surprised. Connie loved her.

Mr. Leone was a grandfatherly type, friendly and jovial, with a hearty laugh and a soft spot for customers who were down on their luck. He gave away more loaves of bread than he sold. He knew how difficult it was for the families of coalminers.

*

One afternoon, Connie was stacking fresh butter cookies on the display shelf in the front window of the store. She made them herself and was proud that they would be on display for everyone to see. When she finished, she stood back, admired her work and swiped at a smudge of flour that dusted the tip of her nose. The sun was causing a glare on the window glass but the image of someone standing on the other side of the pane caught her eye. She cupped her hands on the sides of her head, looked through the window and groaned when she realized it was Dominic Preste. He was admiring the baked goods when a look of recognition turned his curious expression to a broad grin. Connie quickly scampered back to the kitchen in hopes that he would go away but the tinkle of the bell that hung in the front door stopped her in her tracks. Muffled voices brought nausea to her stomach. She peered through the small window at the top of the kitchen door and saw Dominic looking in her direction.

With one hand on her stomach and one hand on her forehead, she groaned, "Oh no."

"Conchetta, dear? There's someone to see you...says his name is Dominic," Mrs. Leone said, poking her head in the door.

"Please, please, Mrs. Leone," she begged, "tell him I'm not here."

"But I already told him you *are* here, dear," Mrs. Leone replied, with a puzzled look on her face. "He looks like a nice young man. Come, come Conchetta, say hello to him." She took Connie by the hand and pulled her through the door. "Here she is, young man." She smiled and winked at Connie, leaving them standing alone. Mr. Leone occupied himself with cleaning the counter tops but clearly had his eye on them.

Dominic was standing a few feet in front of her. She looked up when he cleared his throat. He was standing next to a large barrel of apples, and was filling a brown paper bag while he watched her. Connie's voice was quiet but cold. "You wanted to see me?"

"Yeah, I wanted to see how you were doin'...uh..."

"Connie...my name is Connie." She rolled her eyes and crossed her arms. *"My God...he doesn't even remember my name."*

"Oh yeah, that's right. Sorry," he said, with a chuckle. "Stupid." He tapped his forehead with the palm of his hand.

"Listen, I've got work to do," Connie said, turning away from him.

"Nno, don't go." He took a step toward her and reached out his hand, then quickly drew it back. "Listen, I'm sorry I forgot your name. I mean, gimme a break! It's been a long time," he said, defensively. "So don't be mad." He took a deep breath, smiled and dropped his hand down to his side. "I just remember you being the prettiest girl at the skating rink."

Connie gave him a skeptical look.

"Come on, you can't be mad at me," he teased. "Remember, you thought I was cute?"

A half smile curled her lips.

"That's better," Dominic said. "You should see how nice you look when you smile."

"You were supposed to meet me that night at the Regal Oak, Dominic. You made a date with me, remember? When I got there, you were kissing some girl. You made a fool of me. So, I should smile for you now? I don't think so," she said, defiantly.

He cringed. "I did that? I must be crazy to do that to you." He stepped toward her and put his hand under her chin. He lifted her head, encouraging her to look at him. "Hey Connie, like I said, I made a mistake," he said softly. "I get carried away sometimes…with the girls, I guess," he added. "I didn't mean to hurt you like that." He stood back and studied her face. "I got a good idea. Why don't we start over? You and me, we'll make another date."

Connie huffed out a laugh, and backed away from him.

"I'll tell you what," he said, ignoring her anger. "There's a dance Saturday night at the Uniontown firehouse, just outside of town, and they got a big band and everything. Go with me. You said you like to dance," he suddenly remembered.

"Oh, no you don't! I'm not going through that again," Connie said, waving her hand and shaking her head. "I'd probably get there and you'd be smooching it up with some girl on the dance floor. No…no thanks," she repeated, turning her back to him.

"Connie, wait. Listen, I'll…I'll come pick you up at your house, like a real date. Okay? And I'm not takin' *no* for an answer," he added.

She closed her eyes, took a deep breath and turned to face him. When she opened her eyes, her expression was one of warning. "Oh…I must be crazy but okay…I'll go," she moaned. "But only cause I like to dance," she warned.

"Don't sound so excited," Dominic responded, sarcastically. "Hey listen, once you see me on the dance floor, you'll be glad you came."

"Zat so?"

"No really, I'm a good dancer."

"We'll see," Connie smirked. "Listen, my father will never let me go out with you alone, so I have to bring some of my sisters with us."

"How many sisters?" He frowned, giving her a questioning look.

"I have seven, remember?"

"Dear God…seven sisters…"

"Just a couple of them will come with me, so don't panic."

"Okay. Hey, it'll be fun. I'll bring my brothers!"

Connie wrote her address on the side of the paper bag containing the apples he was purchasing.

"So, I'll see you Saturday?" He placed fifteen cents on the counter for the apples. "Seven o'clock okay?"

"Seven o'clock," Connie agreed.

Dominic left the store, and Connie pressed her nose to the window and watched as he walked down the street.

"Eh, Conchetta…you workin' or wha'?" Mr. Leone asked, half teasing.

"Sorry, Mr. Leone!" She turned and hurried through the kitchen door.

*

When dinner was over that night, Connie spoke with Giordana and Philomena about the dance in Uniontown, and they agreed that it would be fun. The three girls went to their mother to ask for permission, and also asked for her help in convincing their father to let them go. Since they assured her that the young man in question was coming to the house, like a gentleman should, she agreed to speak with their father.

Connie waited impatiently in the kitchen, and jumped when her father suddenly appeared in the doorway.

"Who ees dis boy, Conchetta? I don't know dat name…what name you say? Dominic who?"

"Preste, Papa. His name is Dominic Preste."

"I no like-a dat name!" he said, shaking his head and waving his arms. "He go to you school?"

"No Papa, he has a job. He works at the shipyard in Uniontown. And Papa? Giordana and Philomena are going too! Did Mama tell you that? So ya see, it's not really a date…just a group of friends going to a dance," Connie said, trying to sound casual. Shifting her weight from one leg to the other, she impatiently waited for his answer.

"*Ame nonpiece cose sta succedendo*," Vincenzo said, expressing his displeasure but knowing he would eventually give in. "He's coming here…to our home? I wan' to look to him, eh? Wit' my own eyes!"

"Yes, yes Papa. He's coming here to pick us up. Then we're taking the streetcar to the firehouse. It's very safe, Papa…we'll all be together. Please don't worry." Connie put her hands together as though she were praying.

"Ach!" Vincenzo finally conceded. He grunted with disgust and slapped at the air with a wave of his hand.

"Thank you, Papa," Connie said, lunging at him, placing a quick kiss on his cheek.

Vincenzo walked back into the living room, sat down heavily in his chair, and exhaled a sigh of frustration. Angelina soon followed carrying a small bowl of fruit she had cut into bite-sized pieces. She placed it on the table beside his chair and gently touched his hand. She had a strong faith in God and trusted her girls but it was hard for Vincenzo to see his girls growing up. Like most wives, Angelina had secrets that she found necessary to keep from her husband, for his own good, of course.

Angelina sat in her chair next to Vincenzo and smiled as she thought about a night when Violet and Giordana were barely teenagers. It was a school night, and they had sneaked out of their bedroom window, climbed down a trellis and run to the end of the block to meet with a boy from school. Their judgment had apparently been impaired by the intoxicating idea of going for a ride in his new twenty-five dollar car. One of Vincenzo's rules was to be in the house by eight o'clock but late that evening, something told Angelina to check on the girls before going to bed. Giordana and Violet were nowhere to be found. Everyone was asleep, except Lourdes. She was only seven at the time, and when she saw her mother come into the bedroom, she began to cry. She didn't want to tell on her sisters but she could never lie to her mother.

Angelina took Lourdes in her arms and comforted her. "Lourdes *caro*, why you cry? You know where is Giordi and Violet?" she asked, feeling the breeze coming from the opened window.

"I don't want them to get mad at me, Mama."

"*Va bene, piccolo mio*," she comforted her. "Dey no get mad at you. Please tell you mama, where dey go?" she asked again while caressing Lourdes' cheek.

Lourdes didn't know where her sisters were going, but she had seen them sneak out the window. Angelina dried Lourdes' tears, tucked her back into bed, and kissed her on the forehead. She left the room and quietly sat at the top of the stairs hoping not to wake Vincenzo. She waited patiently.

An hour went by. With her arms folded and her head leaning back against the banister, Angelina heard the faint creak of the floorboards at the base of the window in the girls' bedroom. She quietly got up and stood in the doorway. When Giordana and Violet got back into their room, they were whispering and softly giggling.

Violet was the first to see the ominous figure of their mother standing in the doorway and she tapped Giordana on the shoulder. Giordana turned and looked toward the door, and unable to speak, they stared, wide-eyed, mouths agape. Angelina simply crooked her finger and gestured for them to follow her downstairs. She couldn't help but smile as they each blamed each other.

"I told you we shouldn't go!" Violet said.

"You did not, Vi!" Giordana objected, in a choked whisper.

"I did too! I remember saying to you, 'we shouldn't go, Giordana!'

"Did not!"

"Did too!

Angelina got to the bottom of the steps, turned and put a finger to her lips. "Shhh, *stai zitto*!" telling them to be quiet.

Their mouths snapped shut and their eyes were locked on their mother's face. Angelina walked across the room and sat in her chair, while the girls stood in front of her, looking terrified and ashamed. The room fell silent. Angelina glared. She finally asked, "What you hafa to say?"

"Mama, we're so sorry," they both cried. "We'll never do it again. We promise."

"I'm very sad by bot' of you, and I don' know if I can trust you ever again."

"Oh, Mama, yes you can, yes you can," Violet cried.

"*Chetare*!" Angelina snapped. "Now, you go to bed and say you prayers and ask God to forgive you for *mancanza di rispetto*. It would break you papa's heart if he knew what you did. He didn't raise his daughters to act like *prostituta*."

Giordana and Violet gasped. Their mother had said they were like prostitutes! They both started to sob, and Angelina showed them no mercy.

"Mama, please," Giordana pleaded. "Please don't tell Papa. We'll never do anything like that again. We promise."

"I no tell you papa but I be watching you, you hear?"

"Yes Mama, we hear. Thank you, thank you," they said, breathlessly.

"Now, go to bed. And stay in bed!"

Neither slept that night, and 6 A.M. came quickly. Angelina had no sympathy for them. She prepared their breakfast, handed them their books and lunch bags, and shooed them out the door.

"Why dey so tired?" Vincenzo asked, casually.

"Oh, I don' know," Angelina lied. "Maybe too many schoolwork."

*

Connie, Giordana, and Philomena were in their room getting ready for the dance. Bettina and Lourdes were putting away the last of the dinner dishes, and Carmella and Maria were at the library in town. Violet lay in her bed nursing a cold. Their mother was in the kitchen preparing the bread dough for the following day. She smiled and shook her head as she listened to the racket coming from the floor above. The girls were laughing and trying on different outfits, borrowing each other's shoes and putting the final touches on their hair.

Angelina stood at the bottom of the stairs and yelled, "Hey, you quiet down or da *honey dipper* come take you away!" The girls quieted but giggled when their mother teased them about the *honey dipper*. He was a tall, skinny Negro man who lived in Uniontown by the trolley station in "dark town", a place the girls were curious about but were never allowed to go to. His real name was John Lincoln Towser, and his job was cleaning outhouses. He wore overalls, a porkpie hat, and rubber boots that came to the top of his long, skinny thighs. He never spoke but when seeing the girls watching him from the kitchen window, he always gave them a shy smile. The girls would giggle and quickly duck away from the window.

Vincenzo sat in his easy chair seeming relaxed, but staring at the front door. He was waiting for this suitor of Conchetta's to arrive. He had made up his mind that he was not going to like him but for Conchetta's sake, he didn't want to frighten the boy too much. He did, however want to make sure this Dominic person knew that if he harmed Conchetta in any way, he would see to it that he never harmed anyone again.

"Eh, Conchetta!" Vincenzo yelled up the stairs. "Where dis boy… he late! You notta goin', *capice*?"

"Papa, it's only a quarter to seven. He's picking us up at seven. If he came to the door now, he'd be fifteen minutes early," she protested.

"Don' you backtalk me!" Vincenzo warned.

"Sorry, Papa.

"Ach." He waved angrily, went back to the living room, flopping in his chair.

Lourdes was sitting on the living room floor, playing jacks. She sensed that her father was troubled, and squeezed in along side of him, laying her head on his chest. She affectionately patted his stubbled cheek. "S'kay, Papa," she assured him.

"You Papa's leetle angel, eh?" Vincenzo said, stroking her long, dark ponytail. "You no grow up too fast, eh? You be a good girl and stay wit' you Mama and Papa, *capice*?"

"I will, Papa. I promise." Lourdes placed her rosy cheek against her father's, and for a moment he calmed. Tension gripped him once again when he heard a firm knocking at the front door. Lourdes slid off the arm of the chair, and watched as he walked with a menacing gate toward the door. Angelina came from the kitchen and followed close behind. She was still wearing her apron and drying her hands on a dishtowel as she stood a few feet behind her husband. Vincenzo opened the door and stared icily at Dominic, who was leaning up against the porch column with one foot crossed over the other. He was casually running a comb through his freshly oiled hair. He clenched a cigarette between his teeth, and upon seeing Angelina and Vincenzo, took the cigarette between his forefinger and thumb and flicked it into the front yard.

"Hello, my name is Dominic, I'm here to pick up Connie." He placed the comb in his breast pocket, wiped the palms of his hands on the sides of his jacket, and thrust his hand toward Vincenzo.

Angelina gave Vincenzo's elbow a light tap, urging him to shake the young man's hand, which he reluctantly grabbed and quickly released. He grunted and gestured for Dominic to come inside, then turned and glared at Angelina.

She frowned, whispering, "*Fai il bravo,*" telling him to be nice.

Dominic sauntered into the living room, looked around, and gave Angelina a friendly smile. He stood in the middle of the room with his hands shoved into the pockets of his gray, pinstriped suit. A bowtie was clipped to the collar of his blue cotton shirt.

"My daughters will be down soon," Angelina said, politely.

"*Grazie, Signora.*"

"*Lei parla l'italiano.*" Angelina responded, pleased that he spoke Italian. She looked at Vincenzo and raised her eyebrows. Vincenzo was not impressed and looked away.

"Can I get you a drink? Water? Or maybe you like coffee?" Angelina asked.

"No thank you," Dominic answered.

"So...you live near?" Angelina asked, taking a seat on the sofa.

"I live near Uniontown…not too far. I took the bus to Fernwood, then picked up the streetcar to the south end of Hazel Street." He cleared his throat. "I plan on getting a car soon," he added, hoping to impress them.

"Where you take-a my daughters?" Vincenzo asked.

"Oh, uh… there's a dance over in Mercer, near Uniontown…in the firehouse. It's a nice firehouse," he rambled, pausing to wipe beads of perspiration that suddenly appeared above his brow. He was irritated that this old man was making him feel uncomfortable. "There'll be a band," he continued, "The Paul Bixler band? You heard of them?" When they didn't respond, he lowered his head and mumbled, "Didn't think so." He squirmed in the chair, letting out a sigh of relief when he heard Connie and her sisters coming down the stairs. He felt sweat trickle down the middle of his back.

Connie was wearing a blue, pleated skirt that clung to her narrow hips and stopped just below her knees. A white sweater with pink rosettes was topped with a silk scarf tied loosely around her neck. Her hair bounced in loose curls that just touched her shoulders. Giordana wore a dark blue, flowered dress, cinched at the waist with a leather belt, her hair, smooth in a pageboy. Philomena, dressed in a gray skirt and white cotton blouse, stood back looking bored and uninterested.

"Hello Connie, you look nice," Dominic said.

"Hello, Dominic," Connie said shyly. "Thanks. I see you've met my parents."

"Yes, yes...you have a nice family." Dominic glanced in Vincenzo's direction and tried to smile but could only manage an awkward grin that made his upper lip quiver.

"These are my sisters, Giordana and Philomena," Connie said, suddenly aware that Dominic was showing signs of panic.

"We never really met but I remember seeing them at the rink." He gave them a casual salute. "How ya doin'?"

"Hello." Giordana smiled, and cutely wrinkled her nose.

Philomena simply nodded, remembering how badly Dominic had hurt Connie. She only agreed to join them in case Connie needed protecting.

"Dominic, where are your brothers? Didn't they come with you?" Connie asked.

"No...I asked them but they couldn't come, so I...well, I just came alone. I hope that's okay."

"Sure it's fine with me as long as you don't mind escorting three girls," Connie giggled.

"Nah...I don't mind. Well, what do you say, girls...are we ready to go?" He asked, clapping his hands together.

The girls grabbed their sweaters and took turns kissing their parents goodnight. Dominic turned and extended his hand toward Vincenzo, and once again Angelina gave Vincenzo's elbow a shove. He reluctantly took Dominic's hand, tightened his grip and pulled him close enough to whisper in his ear. "You do one tin' to harm a hair on da head of my daughters, *io ti ammazzo*!" Vincenzo threatened.

Dominic pulled back and stared with disbelief. Vincenzo had just threatened to kill him if he harmed one of his daughters. *This man is crazy,* Dominic thought. His eyes locked on Vincenzo's lips as they slowly curled into a sinister smile. Dominic flinched when Vincenzo suddenly winked at him.

"Goodnight, Papa. *Memme e pepe – ie vi respetto.*" Connie said, as she opened the front door.

"Nine o'clock!" Vincenzo barked.

Connie turned and looked at her father with shock. "Nine o'clock?" She cried. "But Papa, it's seven o'clock now. By the time we get there… well…we'll have to turn around and come right back!"

"Nine o'clock! Or you stay home!" Vincenzo commanded, raising his finger for emphasis. He was being unreasonable but Connie knew there was no arguing with him. Angelina shooed them out the door, and whispered to the girls, "Go, go…have fun. Don' worry, I fix."

*

They walked to the corner of Hazel Street and 14th Avenue, where the streetcar was due at quarter past the hour. It was a chilly evening for early June, and the usual patches of dirty, slush that seemed to stay collected on the sidewalks had finally melted away.

"Good, we're just in time," Dominic said, spotting the approaching streetcar. It was gliding along the smooth iron rails, sparks spitting into the dusk sky. The car pulled up, and screeched to a stop. The door swung open, and the four of them stepped inside the car, dropped their fare into the slot and turned toward two rows of empty seats. The streetcar started with a sudden jolt that nearly knocked them off their feet, sending the girls into fits of laughter as they steadied themselves. Connie and Dominic sat together, and Giordana and Philomena sat behind them. They rode in silence, deciding not to compete with the clamor of the wheels bouncing over the tracks, but when they stopped at the next station to pick up passengers, Dominic leaned toward Connie and said, "Your father threatened to kill me." He looked at her with the expression of a frightened child, and cast his eyes down at his lap where his hands were clasped between his knees.

"What?" Connie looked as him with surprise. "What are you talking about?"

"He said if I hurt one of his daughters, he'd kill me."

Connie smiled. "Oh Dominic, come on. He didn't really mean that."

"Sounded like he meant it," he insisted.

"Dominic, that's just how my father talks." Connie looked away, biting her lip to keep from laughing.

Dominic pouted.

"He's very protective of us girls."

"Yeah…I can see that."

"Don't worry about Papa…he's harmless."

"I don't know 'bout that."

"No really, he is. I'll talk to him, okay? I'll tell him to stop scarin' ya."

"He doesn't scare me!" Dominic protested.

After several minutes of riding in silence, Connie decided to change the subject. "You look nice in your suit. Is it Italian?"

"Yeah." He looked down and brushed his hand over his lapel. "You look nice too."

"Thanks."

"So, was your father serious when he said you had to be home by nine o'clock?"

"No, not really. My mother said she would handle things with Papa but we can't get home too late."

"N'kay," he said, somberly and stared out the window. Connie turned and waved at her sisters. Giordana waved back, Philomena scowled.

Finally arriving at the firehouse, Connie ignored Dominic's complaints that it was already past seven-thirty. The room was full of young men and women, some dressed in military uniforms. The band was playing *Alexander's Ragtime Band*, which was obviously a crowd favorite since the dance floor was full. Dominic and Connie, with Giordana and Philomena close behind, walked around the room looking for an available table. They came to a large table already occupied by two couples, but large enough for four more. Dominic gestured toward the empty chairs. "Mind if we sit here?" he asked the couple sitting at the far end of the table. They stopped gazing into each other's eyes long enough for the young man to nod approval. Philomena and Giordana sat together on one side of the table, while Dominic and Connie sat across from them. The room was steamy hot but it didn't seem to bother anyone. Connie was thrilled by the music, tapping her feet and clapping her hands as she sat on the edge of her chair. Dominic stood up, took her by the hand, and pulled her out onto the dance floor.

"Well, would you look at that?" Giordana exclaimed, as she elbowed Philomena in the arm. "They really dance great together, don't ya think?"

"I guess but I still don't trust that guy." Philomena watched as Dominic twirled Connie so fast that her skirt fanned out baring her short, slender legs.

"He seems like a nice enough guy, Phil."

"I guess."

The music reached a fevered pitch as Connie and Dominic danced to one song after another. A crowd formed a circle around them, cheering and clapping their hands, and when the song was over, Dominic and Connie ran back to their table. She was laughing and clutching her chest as she tried to catch her breath.

Connie sat down next to Dominic, and smiled as she watched her sisters dance with two young sailors. Dominic took off his jacket, and placed it on the back of his chair. He opened his shirt collar and swiped at his face with a handkerchief. Connie lifted her hair and fanned herself. She was having fun and feeling more comfortable with Dominic when he took her by surprise and dabbed the perspiration from the back of her neck with the same handkerchief. With a sudden move, he placed his hand on the back of her head and pulled her close, kissing her greedily on the mouth. When he finished, he pulled away, sighed and sat back. He stretched his legs in front of him and slid down into the chair, clasping his hands behind his head. He looked at Connie, and with a satisfied grin, winked.

Connie returned an uncomfortable smile and quickly looked away. She discreetly wiped her mouth with the back of her hand.

When the music stopped, Giordana bounded toward them. "Hey, you two really cut a rug," she said. Dominic looked up and gave her a slow grin, still licking his lips. Philomena was close behind Giordana, dragging the two sailors with her.

Giordana sounded almost giddy. "I want you to meet George and Benjamin." She squealed and took a little hop in the air as she pushed the two young men forward. "Aren't they cute? They're sailors," she added.

"I think they can see that, Giordana," Philomena scolded. "Stop actin' silly."

Connie smiled at the two sailors, and Dominic, clearing his throat looked up as he leaned forward in his chair.

George was a tall, lanky young man, and the trousers of his white navy uniform hugged endlessly long, lean legs. His hair was fiery red and kinky, his face long and freckled. A shy smile revealed two front teeth that hung over his bottom lip, and Philomena stared at him as though he was a Greek God. She was obviously completely smitten. Connie couldn't help but laugh.

Benjamin was shorter and quite stocky. Connie stared at his bulging arms. His complexion was ruddy but flawless, and he spoke with a lisp that Giordana found adorable.

"How do you do?" George asked, with a booming voice that almost sounded operatic. He extended a boney-fingered hand toward Dominic.

"Nice to meet ya," Dominic said, accepting the young sailor's grip.

"*Ith* a pleasure," Benjamin said, waiting his turn to shake Dominic's hand.

Connie stepped forward and extended *her* hand but Dominic, with a sudden move, firmly grabbed the back of her arm, digging his fingers into her skin. She snapped her head to look at him, but he continued to smile, never taking his eyes from the two sailors. When he released his grip, she rubbed at the soreness that lingered on her arm.

The band started up, and Philomena and Giordana rushed onto the floor, pulling George and Benjamin behind them. Dominic took Connie by the hand and urged her toward the dance floor, and she reluctantly followed. After several more dances, Philomena signaled everyone to the table and suggested they head for home. After saying goodnight to George and Benjamin, the girls gathered up their purses and sweaters, and followed Dominic toward the exit. Giordana quickly slipped a piece of paper to George that had her address scribbled on it, fluttered her eyelashes, and followed Dominic and her sisters out of the firehouse.

The girls giggled as they walked to the corner to catch the streetcar but Connie's mood was subdued. Giordana squealed and playfully slapped at Dominic as he teased her about her sailor. He ignored Connie's silence, and she was beginning to think she was over-reacting.

"Gosh, Dominic," Giordana said. "You're a great dancer. You should be in the moving picture shows."

"Yeah? Ya like the way I dance?"

"Uh-huh, and Connie's a good dancer too, right Phil?"

"Sure is," Philomena agreed, absently as she brushed her hair.

Dominic turned to Connie. "Yeah, I guess we did pretty good together, right Connie?"

She gave him a conciliatory smile.

"What're *you* so quiet about?" His expression was more annoyed than concerned.

"Nothin'."

Turning back to Connie's sisters, he continued. "I'll teach her a few steps, and maybe she'll be as good as me one day."

"You don't need to teach her nothin'," Philomena snapped. "She's a good dancer with ya or without ya!"

"Holy God, I was just kiddin'," Dominic sat back, looking surprised.

"Yeah, well...you'd better be kiddin', right Connie?"

Connie looked tired. She wanted the evening to end, and when they finally arrived home, their mother was sitting in the living room, with a ball of yarn resting in her lap. Connie was the last to step inside the door when Dominic reached for her hand and pulled her back onto the porch. He leaned in and kissed her on the cheek.

"I don't know 'bout you but I had a good time, Connie." His voice was low and smooth. His eyes seemed to look right through her, and caused her stomach to flutter.

Connie smiled and nodded. "Sorry if I got a little quiet."

"I was wonderin'...but that's okay." He winked and gently squeezed her hand. "Night," he said, leaning in to kiss her again.

Angelina suddenly appeared in the doorway and smiled at Dominic. "T'ank you for bringing my girls home, Mr. Preste." She gently placed her hand behind Connie's back and urged her into the house. Dominic nodded, and when the door closed, he walked back to the sidewalk in the direction of the streetcar stop.

*

"I'm goin' up to bed, Mama," Philomena said, sounding irritable.

"Y'okay, Phil?" Giordana asked, giving her a curious look.

"I'm okay, just tired." As she started up the stairs, she continued to mumble, "Don't like that guy...who's he think he is anyway..."

Angelina cocked her head and gave Giordana an inquisitive look.

"She's all right Ma...she just thinks it's her job to protect us all the time."

"Why she need to protect, as you say?" She turned to Connie. "He hurt you, Conchetta?"

"No, Mama...it's nothing. We had a really good time."

Giordana changed the subject. "I met this really cute sailor. His name is George and we danced all night." She clasped her hands and held them to her heart and rolled her eyes. "He's dreamy, isn't he Connie?"

"Mm, dreamy," Connie repeated, looking at her mother, giving her a sheepish grin.

"Das nice, Giordy. You go up to bed...we talk about you' sailor tomorrow, yes?"

"Night, Mama," Giordiana kissed her mother on the cheek. "You comin', Connie?"

"You go ahead...Connie will be up soon," Angelina interjected.

Without questioning her mother, Giordana went upstairs. Connie sat on the arm of her mother's chair. "What is it, Mama?"

"Dis boy...Dominic, he nice...treat you like a lady?" Angelina asked, unable to hide the concern in her voice. She affectionately stroked Connie's arm.

"Oh yes, Mama, he does treat me nice. Really, I like him a lot, and he's such a good dancer. You shoulda seen us, Ma." Her eyes sparkled. "People were cheerin' and clappin'." She had convinced herself that

Dominic meant no harm by grabbing her arm. Maybe he was protective too, like her father. She liked that.

"Dat's good, Conchetta." Angelina seemed satisfied with her daughter's answer. "You tell me everytin', *si*?"

"Yes, Mama."

"*Promettete*?"

"I promise." Connie took her forefinger and crossed her heart.

Angelina looked deep into Connie's eyes and smiled at the innocence she found there. She sighed, made the sign of the cross, and took Connie by the shoulders, giving her several noisy kisses on the forehead before shooing her up to bed. Angelina stayed downstairs for a while; the room now dark and quiet. She nestled back into the softness of her favorite chair, and prayed until she fell asleep.

Connie crawled into bed and lay staring at the light of the moon as it spread across the ceiling. Waiting for sleep to take her, she watched the eerie dance of shadows on the wall as the curtains flapped in the cool breeze. The window by her side of the bed was open, and she closed her eyes letting the night air wash over her face. She turned on her side, clutching the sheet to her chin and listened to Giordana snore contentedly. Connie heard the faint sound of a voice coming from outside her window. *What was that?* She thought. She stiffened and raised herself up onto her elbows. Her eyes darted back and forth while she listened. This time, the sharp *ping* of pebbles hitting the glass quickly brought Connie to a sitting position, the sheet falling to her lap. Someone was in the alley on the side of the house.

"Connie…Connie?" She heard someone call in a whisper.

She slipped out of bed and went to the window, squinting into the darkness. She saw Dominic standing amongst the trashcans that sat in the shadow of the garage. "Dominic! What are you doing down there?" She whispered.

"Connie…good, you're still up. I didn't get to say goodnight! I wanted to kiss you goodnight, but…."

"Shh, are you crazy?" She put her finger to her lips. "Wait there." She bit her lower lip as she closed the window, hoping that its rumbling wouldn't wake anyone. She looked to make sure her sisters were still sleeping, grabbed her robe and tiptoed, barefoot out of the room. She crept past the bedroom where the other girls were sleeping, and by her parent's room, where she knew her mother would be asleep by now. She avoided the steps that creaked, and made her way to the bottom, through the living room, into the kitchen and out the back door. When she opened the door, Dominic was waiting for her at the base of the tiny porch. He took her into his arms.

"Let's get off the porch, Dominic. The light is shining on us," Connie said, taking him by the hand, leading him to a spot next to her father's vegetable garden. "What are you doing here?" she asked, breathlessly. He wrapped his arms around her again, and Connie felt her knees weaken.

"I didn't get a chance to kiss you goodnight." His voice sounded strange, breathy and husky. He leaned his head forward and kissed her full on the lips, hard and hungrily. His mouth felt hot. His hands drifted to the small of her back, then clutched at the youthful roundness of her buttocks.

Confused and embarrassed, Connie stood with her arms hanging at her sides. She took a quick breath of air through her nostrils, and placing her hands on his chest, pushed him hard enough to make him stumble into a patch of lettuce heads. "Dominic, stop. I…I can't. Please…I… you have to go." He was reaching for her again but she ran to the back door and left him standing alone.

"Connie, wait!" He whispered. When she turned to look at him, he asked, "You belong to me now, right?"

Without answering, she stepped inside the door, closed it behind her, and ran through the house, up the stairs to her bed. She pulled the covers up over her nose and shivered. A slight smile crossed her lips. She ran through the house so quickly, she hadn't noticed her mother standing by the window in the darkened kitchen.

"*I no like dis one, Lord,"* Angelina said, putting her hands together in prayer. "*Ha gli occhi del diavolo,"* declaring that Dominic had the eyes of the devil.

Chapter 6

Summer came upon Wickhaven with swiftness. It seemed that one day the thermometer read ten degrees, and the next day was in the nineties. Connie was working at the bakery full time. She was happy and full of energy because she loved her job, and Dominic was her beau. She was also excited about Violet's upcoming wedding in August. The whole family was making plans. The wedding was going to be at St. Mark's Church on Hanover Street, where the girls were all baptized, and where they attended church with their mother. An outdoor reception was planned at the Borzanna home.

Connie walked into the living room where her mother was working on Violet's wedding dress. "Oh, Vi...you look so beautiful! You look like a princess."

Violet wrinkled her nose and giggled. "Thanks, Connie."

Their mother was kneeling on a pillow on the floor, putting the last straight pin into the hem of Violet's puffy, white satin skirt. She had already completed six bridesmaids' dresses for the girls, and a matching dress for Lourdes, who was going to be the flower girl.

"You know what? I happen to *feel* like a princess," Violet beamed, and then picked up her skirts to curtsy.

"Eh, be still!" Angelina scolded. She slipped the last pin into place. "*Interamente fatto,*" she said, with a satisfied smile. Connie helped her mother to her feet. Angelina looked at Violet and clapped her hands. "*Cosi' bello,*" Angelina said, her eyes glistening with tears.

Violet looked at herself in a mirror that was propped against the dining room table. She drew in her breath. "Oh, Mama…how can I ever thank you? I do look beautiful!" Violet grabbed her mother and sister and the three danced in a circle.

"Is enough, enough," Angelina said, holding her stomach, gasping for air. "If you tear da gown, I whollop you, eh?" She looked at Violet with pride. "Conchetta, you help Violet, eh? Take off da dress and hang it up, *si?*" She handed the girls a cloth bag and a wooden hanger. "I finish tonight, but now…I make supper." She rubbed her lower back as she headed into the kitchen.

Connie undid the tiny satin buttons that ran down the back of the gown. She held it open while Violet gingerly stepped out of it, then hung it on the hanger and covered it with the bag. They carried the dress to their room and placed it neatly in the closet. Connie lay down on her bed next to Philomena, who was curled up on her side reading a book.

"Wha'cha doin'?" Connie asked.

"I'm readin', what'dya think I'm doin'?" Philomena snapped, without lifting her eyes from the book.

"Geez." Connie recoiled, and lay back on a pillow. "Grouch," she responded. She waited a few minutes before trying to talk to her again. "We're going to the firehouse dance again. Wanna go?"

"No," Philomena said, flatly.

"Why not?"

Philomena put her book down and looked curiously at Connie. "What's the matter with you lately, Connie? You seem…I don't know, different."

"What'dya mean?"

"When you're with us girls, you're fun but when you're with Dominic, let's face it…you're different. You change. You get all quiet." She paused, laid the book on her chest and flopped back on her pillow. "I hate it."

Connie looked confused. She turned on her side, and looked at Philomena. "Really? I don't think I act different. I'm fine. I just…well, I guess maybe it seems like I'm a little different around Dominic cause… ya know…I don't wanna do anything to make him mad."

"Ugh, see? That's what I hate. That's crazy, Connie! God, that kind of talk makes me sick. Any guy that ever wants to be with me, better like me jus' the way I am, cause I ain't changin' for nobody!"

"Don't get mad Phil, please. I like Dominic a lot and it's just that he doesn't like it when I'm too giggly and stuff. He likes when I'm…oh, I don't know, more quiet. And he's a really a good dancer and we dance great together. He likes to show me off. What's so wrong with that?"

Philomena stared at Connie with disgust.

Connie looked bewildered. "What? What are you looking at me like that for? You know we dance good together! You said so yourself, Phil!"

"Oh, my God," Philomena laughed. She wrapped her arms around her knees and gazed up at the ceiling. "What a stupid reason to like a guy! Good dancer," she smirked.

Connie folded her arms defiantly, and frowned. "Stop it, Philomena. Come on…that's not fair. It's not just the dancing…he can be sweet sometimes." She paused, and thought for a minute. "I guess I have to admit he *does* get jealous.

"No, really?" Philomena responded, sarcastically.

"I don't understand," Connie continued, "I mean, I don't *do* anything to make him jealous, do I, Phil? I mean, do you think I do anything to make him jealous?"

"God, you are so naïve." Philomena sat up abruptly, and faced Connie. "That's exactly my point, Connie. You don't do anything wrong, but he still acts like a jerk, if you want my opinion. I think you're too good for him!"

Connie laughed and playfully slapped at Philomena's arm. "No, I'm not. You see how all the girls like him. I'm lucky to have *him*."

"God Connie, listen to yourself. You're such a fool!"

"Why do you say that?" Connie asked, obviously hurt by Philomena's comments. "You don't know Dominic the way I do."

"Huh!" Philomena scoffed. "I know him well enough, and all I can tell you is, I know what I see, and I don't like it! He gives you that evil eye thing, like he's warning you or something…who is he to do that? I see the way you get nervous and start wringing your hands, it's disgusting! I'm tellin' ya, you're different around him." Philomena glared at Connie.

"Just...oh I don't know...get the cobwebs outta your head, for God's sake!" She slid off the bed and stomped out of the room.

"What in world was that about?" Violet asked, as Philomena brushed past her.

Connie waved her hand. "Oh, I don't know. I don't think she likes Dominic.

Violet looked at Connie and raised her eyebrows.

Connie was surprised. "What? You don't like him either?"

"I dunno, Connie. Maybe there's something about him you're just not seeing."

Connie sighed, and lay back on her pillow. *No one knows Dominic the way I do. What's the big deal if I act a certain way around him? At least he wants to be with me.*

*

Mrs. Strobel, the church organist was pounding out a dramatic rendition of *Ava Maria.* Connie and her sisters were in the back of the church waiting for their cue. Vincenzo was last in line, looking handsome and proud with Violet towering over him, and holding tightly to his arm. She was a vision in white lace and tulle. Her veil was delicately draped over her face but couldn't hide her luminous smile as she waited to walk down the aisle toward Pasqual. She was beaming, and tears glistened in the corners of her hazel eyes.

Connie was fourth in line behind her older sisters, while the three younger ones stood behind her. Their pink taffeta skirts swished and rustled as Mrs. Wetzel, the head of the church's women's club, urged the girls to line up straight. Connie glanced back and caught her father's eye. He smiled and gave her a wink.

Mrs. Wetzel stood alongside the girls, making a sweeping motion with her hand, signaling them to start walking down the aisle. "Slowly, slowly, girls," she whispered urgently. "We're not running to a fire," she added.

Giordana turned to look at Connie and rolled her eyes. "We're not running to a fire," she mocked.

Connie laughed nervously, and fell into step behind Giordana. *One step together, two step together,* she counted to herself. Her eyes stayed focused on Giordana's back but when she briefly shifted her eyes toward the congregation, she spotted Dominic on the bride's side of the church. She gave him a shy smile and he smiled back.

The mass was long, and Connie felt lightheaded. The church was hot, the air filled with the heady scent of carnations and incense. Finally, Father Lorenzo beamed and uttered the words, "*I now pronounce you man and wife.*" Pasqual lifted Violet's veil and kissed her gently on the lips as the organist attacked the organ with such gusto that Connie jumped and grabbed hold of Giordana's arm for support. Violet and Pasqual kissed again and turned to face the crowd of relatives and friends that were anxiously waiting to see the faces of the new Mr. and Mrs. Pasqual Siamento.

They started down the aisle, arm and arm, toward the back of the church. Violet's sisters, along with the groomsmen followed. Connie took the arm of Pasqual's youngest brother, Rudolpho. He was a handsome young man with smooth olive skin, dark hair, thick with waves, and a smile glowing with pearl-white teeth. He placed his hand over hers and gave her a timid but charming smile, and when they finally reached the back of the church, Mrs. Wetzel began pushing and shoving everyone into place for the receiving line. Guests started to filter out of the church, dabbing their eyes as they greeted the wedding party.

Connie smiled sweetly, and accepted kisses from friends and family. She spotted Dominic a short way down the line. She was eager to talk with him, and hoped he liked the way she looked in her dress. He was neat and handsome in a blue suit and yellow striped tie. His hair was oiled and swept into a Pompador, and Connie felt a familiar flutter in her stomach as he neared. She couldn't help herself; she liked his swagger. There was something dangerous about the way he looked and that excited her. Finally in front of her, he took her hand, smiled cordially and leaned in for what Connie thought would be a kiss on the cheek. Instead, he squeezed her hand until her knuckles seared with pain, and put his lips close to her ear. He whispered, "Don't ever touch that guy again or I'll beat the shit outta you." He stood back, continued to smile and tightly grip her hand. His eyes held hers as he said, "*capice?*"

A chill went through her as she ripped her hand from his. She stared at him, confusion and anger filling her eyes. "What…what man? What are you talking about?" She swallowed hard, choking back tears.

His eyes darted back and forth to the two sisters standing on either side of her. He continued to smile. He leaned in again, "I can smell him on you," he said. He forced a fake laugh as though she had said something funny. He winked, and calmly moved forward to greet the rest of the family. His smile never changed. Connie stood stunned, her feet unable to move. She rubbed her throbbing knuckles, and when the pain subsided, she greeted the remaining guests with a smile that she now wore like a mask. As the minutes passed, the angrier she got, wanting to end things with Dominic as quickly as possible.

Guests walked the block and a half to the Borzanna house. Two of Vincenzo's friends, Louie Palmentaro and Pietro Sangio, were playing mandolin and violin. They stood at the curb and played their instruments in front of the house as the guests arrived. Three long tables were set up in a u-shape, overflowing with traditional Italian dishes that Angelina and her daughters prepared. Two ladies from the women's club volunteered to arrange the tables, and when Angelina and Vincenzo arrived home, they were delighted with the display of food. Connie, Maria, and Lourdes had decorated the chairs with crepe paper carnations and covered the tables with white lace clothes. Folks congregated in the street, and with their glasses held high, cheered and toasted the bride and groom. Guests greeted each other with hearty laughs and good-natured slaps on the back, and the buffet table was already crowded with people hungrily filling their plates with ravioli, roast beef, sausages, gnocchi, pastries and homemade bread. Chianti flowed and the atmosphere was festive as the musicians played Italian songs.

Connie, along with Giordana and Lourdes walked toward the house. Lourdes was holding onto her skirt, swinging it playfully back and forth; feeling fancy in her taffeta gown and high- heeled shoes. Angelina even allowed her to wear lipstick and rouge that day, and she was feeling quite grown up. Connie was quiet. She forced a smile as she listened to her sisters excitedly recall the wedding ceremony. When they got close to the house, Connie looked for Dominic. She was going to have to get to the bottom of what his problem was, and why he was so needlessly jealous. When she realized he wasn't there, she decided to put the ugliness of his behavior out of her mind and enjoy her sister's wedding day.

Violet and Pasqual were surrounded, and Connie had to work her way through the crowd to get to them. "*Mi scuzi, mi scuzi,*" she said, as she gently pushed people aside. "Whew! There you are!"

"Hi Connie," Violet said, excitedly.

"I'm so happy for you Violet, and you look so beautiful. And you, Pasqual...my, my you look so handsome. I always wanted a brother!" She teased. "Come here...let me hug you both!"

Violet wrapped her arms around Connie and held tight. "Thank you, Connie...isn't this exciting? Mama and Papa made us such a beautiful wedding. And you girls...just look at the decorations you did. Thank you so much."

Connie lovingly wiped tears from her sister's eyes. The rush of high-heeled shoes approaching warned them that the rest of the Borzanna sisters were bounding toward them. Philomena, Carmella, Lourdes, Maria, Giordana and Bettina threw their arms over each other's shoulders and formed a huddle, with a very embarrassed Pasqual stuck in the middle. He laughed and shrugged his shoulders as they danced around him. Angelina and Vincenzo stood by, smiling with pride.

Vincenzo clapped his hands and shouted, "*mangi, mangi ognuno,*" urging everyone to eat.

The celebration was in high gear when evening fell upon them, and Connie gave up on hopes that Dominic would make an appearance. She went to sit on the top step of the front porch. She thought she had gone unnoticed until her mother sat down next to her.

"You having a good time, Conchetta?" She asked, stroking the back of Connie's hair.

"Mm-hum," Connie answered glumly. She sat with her arms wrapped around her legs, her chin resting on her knees.

"Where is Mr. Dominic Preste? I have not seen him."

"I don't know, Mama...I think he had to go somewhere. I...I'm not sure."

Angelina reached an arm around Connie and rested her cheek on the top of Connie's head. "Connie, go join our guests and have a good time," she urged, gently. "Everything will be okay, yes?"

Connie took a deep breath, straighted her back and slapped her hands to her knees. "Okay but only for you, Mama." She walked over to where Philomena and Giordana sat, balancing platters of food on their laps. Connie placed two nut-filled cookies on a plate and pulled a chair next to Giordana. "Hi," she said, and took a bite of cookie.

"Hey Connie, havin' fun?" A drop of tomato sauce clung to Giordana's chin and Connie took a napkin and wiped it away. "Oops, thanks," Giordana said, her mouth filled with ravioli. She swallowed, wiped her mouth and placed the empty plate on the ground beside her. "Oh my God, I'm stuffed," she said, slouching in the chair, rubbing her bloated stomach. "Hey, where's Dominic…haven't seen him all night. I figured you two would be dancin' up a storm by now."

Before Connie had a chance to answer, Carmella ran toward them, pulled Giordana from her chair and led her out into the street to dance the Tarantella.

"Come on, Connie!" Carmella shouted over her shoulder.

"I'll be there in a minute." She turned, and ambled through the freshly mowed grass, and found a folding chair by a fig tree. She sat and gazed at the streetlights, mesmerized by the halo that surrounded each light bulb. She suddenly felt the warmth of tears flowing down her cheeks. A tap on the shoulder made her jump. She quickly wiped her face dry, and turned in her chair.

"Hey Connie, what'cha doin?" Dominic asked, casually.

She looked up at him, and fought the urge to slap his face. "Dominic," she said, unable to keep anger from her voice. "I don't want to talk to you." She turned her back and folded her arms.

"That's not very nice."

She spun around to face him again. "Not very nice? I don't understand you. Why did you get so mad at me after the ceremony? What did I do? You were so…so mean!" She stood up, suddenly feeling brave enough to confront him.

"Calm down, will ya?" He was laughing at her.

"It's not funny, Dominic. And where did you go after the wedding? I can't believe you just left. Everybody's been asking about you and I didn't know what to say. I don't understand! You hurt me, Dominic! You really hurt me!"

"Hey…stop!" He seemed amused by her anger. He raised his eyebrows and held out his hands. "I don't like it when you touch other guys, ya know what I mean? And you were holding onto that guy like you were in love with him or something."

"What guy?" Connie looked completely baffled.

"You know, the guy you were holding onto when you walked outta the church…holdin' hands and shit."

Connie's eyes widened, her mouth dropping open. "Oh my God, are you serious?"

"I was mad Connie, real mad…so, I went for a walk," he said.

His pouting disgusted her. Connie looked down at the ground and breathed heavily, trying to compose herself. "For three hours?" She placed her hands on her hips. "It was my sister's wedding, for God's sake. Do you know how upset you made me? I couldn't even enjoy my own sister's wedding! And for your information, I *had* to hold that guy's arm. It's how it's done at weddings!" *You moron*, she thought to herself. "It doesn't mean anything! I don't even *know* him." She was tapping her foot in frustration. "I met him one time when my parents invited Pasqual's family to our house for dinner. I mean… it *is* normal to meet the family of your sister's husband, isn't it?" She asked, sarcastically.

"Yeah, well…" He looked away in an attempt to hide his guilt. "Ya don't need to get so mad. Can we just forget about it?" He took her hands and pulled her close, her forehead resting on his chin. "Come on…" he said, "let's go have fun."

"No!" Connie said, defiantly, and suddenly pulled away from him.

"Oh come on Connie, you can't be mad at *me*." He reached for her again, and held her so she couldn't pull away. He slowly rubbed the smoothness of his cheek against hers. The faint scent of his cologne filled her nostrils, and feeling intoxicated, she closed her eyes. "Let me show you what a good guy I can be."

Taking her by the hand, he led her toward the street where the cry of the violin filled the air with a lilting melody. He wrapped his arm around her tiny waist and held her tightly as he hummed softly in her ear. He smiled when he felt her body weaken. "You belong to *me*, Connie," he whispered.

*

The party was winding down when the newlyweds stole away, changed their clothes, and started their drive to Atlantic City for a short honeymoon. It was after midnight when the last of the guests left for home. Angelina and Vincenzo were happy but exhausted. They shared a glass of wine together before falling into bed for a much-needed rest. Angelina laid awake thinking about Connie and Dominic. She made the sign of the cross, and fell asleep.

*

Violet and Pasqual moved into the back of a double house that was owned by Heinz Beidermier, an old friend of Vincenzo's from his coal mining days. The house was a block away, and Heinz, recently widowed only charged the young couple eight dollars a month.

Violet often invited Connie and Dominic for dinner. Dominic liked Pasqual, and they talked for hours about Italy, and Connie loved the two couples spending time together.

One Sunday evening after dinner, Connie was helping Violet in the kitchen while Dominic and Pasqual retired to the living room. The girls washed dishes while the boys relaxed, sipping Sambucca and smoking cigarettes.

"Dat was good, eh Dominic?" Pasqual said proudly, his English improving over the months.

"Oh yeah," Dominic agreed, and patted his stomach.

"*Si*, ees good," Pasqual repeated. He stretched and yawned. "I like-a be married, Dominic," he said, with a boyish grin. "She's a good girl, my Violetta." He put his hands behind his head and lifted his feet to the coffee table, crossing his ankles. "Conchetta...she's a good girl too, yes?"

"Yeah, yeah sure she's a good girl. The best."

Poking her head around the corner of the kitchen door, Violet asked, "What are you two talking about in there?"

"Talkin' 'bout you." Pasqual winked at her.

Violet giggled, and went back into the kitchen.

Dominic leaned forward and spoke softly. "You know, Pasqual, you treat her too nice."

"What?" Pasqual gave Dominic a sideways glance. "Too nice? What-a you mean, Dominic?"

"Yeah, I watch you. You treat her too good, and ya know what? She's gonna walk all over you one day, you'll see."

"Ach," Pasqual said, waving his hand to dismiss Dominic's comment. "Das crazy."

"Ah," Dominic said, waving his finger, "you'll see."

"We'll be done in a minute, save us a seat," Violet shouted from the kitchen.

Connie dried the last dish and placed it in a cabinet above the sink.

"Come, Violet!" Pasqual called to her. He tapped his hand on the sofa cushion next to him. "Come and sit.... you cook-a all day...ees enough."

"We're almost finished, honey," Violet called back.

"You two are so cute together, Vi," Connie beamed. She draped the wet dishtowel over a wire rack.

"Thanks, Connie. He makes me happy."

"I mean it Vi, Pasqual really loves you and respects you... I like that." Connie's bottom lip began to quiver, and she turned away.

"What's the matter, Connie?" Violet asked. She took Connie by the shoulders and turned her so she could see her face. "Connie, come on... what's going on?"

"Nothing Vi, really. I guess," she spoke hesitantly, "I mean I hope I have that respect from Dominic one day."

"What do you mean, Connie? He respects you, doesn't he? I know you two have had your problems in the past but everything's okay, right?" She was suddenly concerned. "Is there something you're not telling me?"

"No, no...everything's fine. Forget I said anything." Connie took a deep breath and wiped her eyes on her apron. "Please Vi...I can't let him see me crying," she said, looking anxiously toward the kitchen door.

"Okay, if you're sure. Listen, you can talk to me anytime Connie, you know that, right?"

"I know, and thanks." She wrapped her arms around Violet and held her tight.

"Feel better?"

"Yes, I'm fine," Connie forced a smile, and followed Violet into the living room.

Violet flopped down next to Pasqual, and snuggled into his arms. Connie sat on a pillow, on the floor by Dominic's feet.

"*Buon pranzo, bella.*" Pasqual said, kissing the tips of his fingers to show his appreciation for the meal his wife made.

"*Grazie il mio amore.*" Violet patted her husband's contented belly.

Connie watched them, and smiled with admiration.

"How come you don't talk to me in Italian?" Dominic asked.

"What?" Connie was surprised by his question.

"How come you don't say things to me in Italian?"

"I don't know…you never asked me too. Anyway, I don't speak as well as Vi."

He turned away. "Stupid," he mumbled.

"What did you say?" Connie's head snapped in his direction.

"Nothin'." His mood suddenly turned dark.

Connie had been resting her elbow on Dominic's knee but now, feeling dejected, drew her knees up, and wrapped her arms around her legs.

"So, how long have you two been dating now?" Violet asked, noticing a chill between Connie and Dominic.

"Oh...I don't know." Connie looked up and asked, "What's it been Dominic, about eight months now?"

"Yeah, I think so. Eight months…that sounds about right."

"You two are quite a team. How many dance contests have you won now?"

"Oh gosh, I've lost count. Last Friday we won second place at the church dance. Little trophy…cute…" her voice trailed off.

"We're gonna win a lot more too," Dominic said.

"Maybe you get married, eh?" Pasqual blurted.

"Pasqual!" Connie gasped, waving a hand at him. "Stop that!" She glanced up at Dominic. A strange smile appeared on his face.

"Pasqual," Violet scolded, "Connie is just a baby."

"I'm young Violet but I'm not a baby!" Connie protested.

"No, she's *no* baby," Dominic teased. He looked down at Connie whose face had turned bright red. "Maybe we *should* get married…you and me, Connie. What'dya think?" He raised his eyebrows, and waited for her response.

"What? What are you saying…that you wanna get married?"

"Yeah…why not?" He shrugged.

"Oh, Connie," Violet said. "Papa and Mama would kill you."

"Gosh…I don't think…" Connie stopped short, afraid of making Dominic mad. "Well, let's talk about it later, Dominic."

Dominic cocked his head, and smiled at her. "That sounds like a yes to me!" He stood up and raised a fruit juice glass of red wine.

Connie sat up and looked at Violet. She felt panicked.

Violet went to Connie and knelt down next to her. She embraced her and whispered, "It'll be okay…you'll talk later."

"Well, how 'bout dat, eh?" Pasqual said, looking at Violet.

Connie still didn't know what to say. She wasn't even sure she loved him. He had never even told her he loved her. *Shouldn't that happen first?* She thought. While Dominic shook hands with Pasqual, Connie got up from the floor. She stood next to Dominic and smoothed her skirt. "Gosh, I…I'm really surprised, Dominic," she said, quietly. "I didn't even know you were thinking about getting married."

"Well, I wasn't…'til now." He placed his hands on her shoulders and kissed her on one cheek, then the other. Violet hugged them both, and Pasqual took Connie's face in his hands and gave her a gentle kiss on the forehead. Connie stiffened, her eyes shifted nervously from Pasqual to Dominic as she pulled away. She stepped back and stood by Dominic's side, and slipped her hand in his.

Pasqual poured more wine and proposed a toast. *"Cin cin e cento anni oli felicita."* He wished them to always be happy.

"Connie," Violet said, looking at the clock on the wall. "You'd better get home, it's nine o'clock and Mama and Papa will be waiting for you." She went into the bedroom to get their coats.

"Nine o'clock! Is it really?" Connie said, taking Dominic by the arm. "Dominic, come on, I need to get home."

"Ooh, nine o'clock," he mocked. "I'm so scared of your father."

"Dominic, please don't make fun of me…I'm just respecting my parents."

Violet returned to the living room with their coats, and walked them to the door.

"Thanks, Violet. Dinner was wonderful," she said, hugging her. "I'll brag to Mama what a good cook you are." Pasqual leaned in to give Connie a hug but hesitated when she suddenly extended her hand instead. He looked puzzled, and awkwardly shook her hand.

Connie and Dominic started on the short walk back to her parent's house. The moon was hiding behind thick, gray clouds that made the night seem darker than usual. The temperature had dropped considerably, and Connie pulled her coat tight around her neck, wishing she had worn a hat to cover her ears. Dominic was walking a few paces behind her with his head down. Puffs of steam billowed from his mouth as his warm breath hit the cold air.

"Dominic? I can't believe you want to get married," Connie said, turning around to see where he was. "Shouldn't we talk about it?" He was silent, and Connie stopped to look at him. "Dominic? Why aren't you walking with me? Did you hear me when I asked you about getting married?" When he didn't answer, she rolled her eyes and continued walking ahead of him. *What now?* She thought.

Suddenly, and without warning, Dominic grabbed her by the back of the hair, yanking her head so hard that she almost fell over backwards. She cried out in pain and grabbed hold of a wire fence that was along the sidewalk. She reached for his hand, digging her nails into his clenched fingers but his grip was too tight.

"What are you doing? Dominic, please…" she cried, and continued to claw at his hand.

"How dare you put me down in front of them…like I'm a child. And what… are you fucking Pasqual now? Huh? You want him to fuck you? I saw how you looked at him."

She peered up at him, and managed to catch a glimpse at his face. His eyes were red with rage, a stream of saliva trickled from the corner of his mouth.

"Maybe you don't wanna marry *me*…but maybe you wanna to marry him, huh?"

"What are you talking about? Let go of my hair, Dominic!" Her fear turned to rage. "I said…let go!" She demanded. Taking a deep breath, she thrust her head forward, breaking free from his grip. She quickly stepped back, out of his reach. Panting and wheezing, her mouth hung open with disbelief as she rubbed the back of her throbbing head.

He stared back at her, looking dazed. "Whore," he growled. "You're like a whore! That's all you ever do is humiliate me, hanging all over every man you see!"

"Are you crazy? I don't even know what you're talking about? What did I do?"

"I saw the way you were looking at Pasqual…and kissing and hugging…ach! You make me sick! I don't want no woman like that! You disrespect me!"

Connie stared at him as if he had just dropped from another planet. "He's crazy!" She shouted, looking up toward the heavens. "You're crazy!" She repeated, this time turning to look at him as she walked toward home. She left him standing in the same spot. She angrily took a swipe at her disheveled hair, sniffed her runny nose, and continued walking. She glanced back at him. He was still not moving. He was breathing hard, his hands clenched into tight fists and down at his sides. His stance was wide, as if he needed to steady himself. As Connie got further away, she heard the *thwang* of the wire fence as Dominic kicked it, like a child having a tantrum.

When she reached the front door of her house, she paused, took a deep breath, held it briefly, and let it out with an audible moan. She composed herself before opening the door, and shook her head clear. She forced a smile and walked into the living room where her mother was sitting in her chair. The floor lamp that stood beside her provided the only light in the room as she crocheted a yellow and white blanket. She looked up when Connie came in.

"Hi Mama," Connie said, as cheerfully as she was able to at the moment. "Where's Papa?" She couldn't help that her voice was quivering.

"He went to bed, Conchetta," Angelina said, peering at Connie over the top of her glasses.

"Oh, that's good. Well, goodnight, Mama." She stretched and yawned before leaning in to give her mother a kiss on the cheek. She felt the intensity of her mother's piercing eyes. Connie smiled and touched her mother's forehead, gently moving a strand of her graying hair.

"Did you have a good time, *bella*?" Her mother asked.

"Oh, yes. Violet cooks almost as good as you do, Mama," Connie teased.

"*E' La verita'?*" Angelina smiled and asked if this was true. She nodded with approval. "So, how is Mr. Dominic Preste?"

"Oh, he's fine Mama." Connie looked away. "Gosh, I'm awful tired Ma, how 'bout you? You ready for bed?" Connie yawned again, and held her breath as she walked to the stairs.

"Mm-hm." Angelina watched as Connie climbed the stairs. "I go to bed soon, don' worry 'bout me."

"Goodnight, Mama." Connie blew her a kiss. She went into the bedroom, took off her skirt and blouse and hung them in the closet. Philomena was in bed with a book lying open on her chest, and by the steady drone of her breathing, Connie assumed she was in a sound sleep. She kicked off her shoes, and placed them in the closet, pulled her pink flannel nightgown over her head and climbed into bed. She buried her face in her pillow, gently rubbed the back of her throbbing head, and wept silently until she fell sleep.

*

The following morning, Connie went to work, though nausea from a migraine headache had her stomach tied in knots. Mr. Leone depended on her and since Mrs. Leone had taught Connie well, she often worked in the back of the store alone.

"Mornin' Mr. L." Connie said, cringing at sound of the tiny bell above the door. It sounded more like a gong to her throbbing head.

"Eh, Conchetta!" He greeted her. He was always happy to see her. "How ees you Mama and Papa? Everybody well?"

"Everybody's fine," Connie answered. She reached for the apron she kept on a hook by the kitchen door, and walked over to the counter where Mr. Leone was stacking pizzels that his wife had made the night before.

"Mm, they smell great." Connie closed her eyes and sniffed the sweet scent of anisette. "No matter how much I bake, I'll never be able to make pizzels as good as Mrs. L."

"Ah…I don' know, Conchetta…you gettin' pretty good," he chimed. His smile turned to a frown when he noticed something different. "Hey…*venuto qui*." He placed his hand under her chin, and looked closely at her face. "What's a matter wit' you? You gotta puffy eyes… you been cryin', girl?"

"Nno, I'm fine. Really, I got up with a little headache."

"Uh-huh," he said, looking intently at her red-rimmed eyes. He took his hand from under her chin. "Okay…if you say so. You know, if you gotta problem, you tell me, *capice*?"

"*Capice*." She stood on her tiptoes and gave his whiskered chin a kiss. "You're like my mother, you worry too much," she teased. She turned and walked through the kitchen door and started mixing the ingredients for butter cookies. She patted oval shaped loaves of bread dough into metal pans, placing them by the warm oven to start rising for the next day's supply of bread. Fat loaves of risen dough were already in the oven for today's customers. She felt better when she worked.

*

Two weeks had passed, and Connie hadn't heard from Dominic. She was relieved that her parents didn't seem to notice. She wasn't in the mood to explain. She did however confide in Carmella who, out of all her sisters was the least judgmental.

"Gosh that's horrible, Connie. Are you going to see him again? Maybe he didn't mean to hurt you. I don't know Connie…what do *you* think? He's Italian, right?"

"Right…but what's that have to do with anything?" Connie looked at her curiously.

"Well nothing really, I just mean…that's the way they are sometimes, aren't they? I know Papa's not like that but… "

"That's no excuse Carm. Nobody should act like that." Connie shook her head. "No, nobody should do that to another person," she repeated.

*

Connie walked into the house just as Violet was leaving. Their mother was draping a sweater over Violet's shoulders.

"Connie…hi," Violet said. She tied a bandana around her head, and gave her sister a quick hug. "I'd love to stay and talk to you but I have some errands to run."

"That's okay, maybe I'll stop by your place a little later," Connie said.

"That'll be fine…oh, and did you tell Ma…about you and Dominic?"

"Tell her what?" Connie asked, and suddenly realized that the last time she saw Violet was when Dominic mentioned marriage. A wave of panic came over her. "Uh…I don't know what you mean. Didn't you say you had to go?" Connie's eyes widened with warning as she stared at Violet.

"Oops, sorry," Violet gulped, and gave her sister an apologetic grin. "Gotta go."

Connie let Violet out the door. "Thanks a lot, Vi," she said, sharply.

"I said I was sorry."

Connie closed the door and turned to face her mother, who was standing with her arms crossed.

"Did you tell me what, Conchetta?" Angelina asked.

"What? Oh…you mean…" Connie laughed nervously. "I don't know what she's talking about. You know Violet, always kidding around."

"Mm-hm. Yes, she do…how you say… keed around but I t'ink you know what she was talkin' about, Conchetta."

Connie paused and looked down at the floor. "Okay," she sighed heavily. "Come, sit with me Mama."

Angelina sat down in Vincenzo's chair. Connie sat on a footstool and placed her hands on her mother's knees. "Remember a couple of weeks ago when Dominic and I went to dinner at Violet's?"

Angelina nodded. "I remember."

"Well, we had a fun evening, we really did, and when we were talking," Connie shrugged and raised her hands, her eyes wide to show surprise, "out of nowhere, Dominic said he wanted for us to get married!"

Angelina stared at Connie and spoke slowly, "I see…go on."

"Well, it was all so crazy. I didn't know what to say and before I knew it, Violet and Pasqual were congratulating us and…I don't know... that's about it…except that on our way home, Dominic and me...well, we had a fight."

"About what?"

"Nothing...it was stupid." She sat back and waved off the question.

"Marry..." Angelina turned her head and swallowed hard, as though the word stuck in her throat. "What you say to him? You said *no* to him, yes?" Angelina rarely raised her voice, and quickly corrected her tone. "You're just a little girl, Conchetta. You're only sixteen years old."

"I know Mama, but I didn't really get to tell him anything. Violet and Pasqual got all excited, and Dominic...well, I didn't say anything to him, so...I don't know...listen, after the fight we had, he may not even come around again. Who knows..." her voice drifted off, and she lowered her head. She slowly raised her eyes to look at her mother. "It was a terrible fight, Ma."

"But if he come back...what you do?"

"It doesn't matter Ma, I think it's over."

"What if he come back?" She pressed for an answer.

Connie looked away. "I don't know," she said, quietly.

"You take him back?" Angelina looked alarmed.

"No, how could I? I mean...I'm not sure, Mama." She felt ashamed, unable to look her mother in the eye. "I was angry for a while but now, I don't know, I guess I kinda miss him. He's not a bad guy, Mama. Just...I don't know... troubled I guess. I know there's good in him somewhere." She sat up straight and threw her head back. "Ah God, what's wrong with me?"

Angelina pulled her daughter into her arms. *Dear God,* Angelina prayed, *my Conchetta love dis man who has the eyes of the devil.* "Connie please, listen to me. Don' let no man disrespect you, eh...and if he do, you walk away, you hear?" Angelina's eyes turned sad. Like a slow-moving fog, the heaviness of worry clouded her thoughts. "Maybe you right, Connie...maybe he no come back, eh?" She paused again. "Den everyt'ing be okay." She put her hands on her knees and pushed herself to her feet. "I know what," she said, "Why you no go out wit' other boys? Go out and have fun...wit' boys you own age, eh? What you t'ink?"

Connie smiled at her mother. "Maybe Mama, we'll see," she appeased her mother. "Thank you, Mama."

"Don' be silly...for what you t'ank me?" Angelina scoffed. "I no do nothin'. I am you mama.

*

When Connie arrived at the bakery early Monday morning, the door was locked; a sign that read, *CLOSED DUE TO ILLNESS* was in the corner of the window. Connie was alarmed. She immediately started walking in the direction of Mr. and Mrs. Leone's house, a few blocks south on Riverside Avenue. She turned the corner and saw their yellow bungalow, walked up to the porch and noticed the front door ajar. She peered through the screen and saw Mr. Leone sitting quietly in a chair, his elbows on his knees, his head in his hands.

Connie knocked softly. "Mr. Leone? It's me, Connie…are you okay?"

Mr. Leone slowly lifted his head and appeared disoriented. Finally recognizing her voice, he beckoned to her, "Oh, Connie, please come in." He rose and ran his fingers through his uncombed hair. After unlatching the screen door, he let her into the house.

She sat on the sofa across from him. "What's happened, Mr. Leone?"

"It's the Mrs., she had a stroke," he answered, with a catch in his voice.

"Oh my goodness, is she all right?"

He looked across the room at her, his eyes tired. "No dear, she's in the hospital but…I don't know, Connie. It don' look too good."

"I'm so sorry." Connie got up, walked over and knelt by his chair. She touched his arm but didn't know what to say.

"She's paralyzed on her left side," he continued. "And she can't speak. I see the fear in her eyes Connie, and it breaks my heart."

"Is there anything I can do? I mean I'd do anything for you and Mrs. L…you know that."

"Yes, Conchetta but there's really nothing anyone can do right now."

Connie wanted to ask about the bakery but didn't want it to sound like she was worried about her job.

Mr. Leone sat back and looked down at her, a sudden idea coming to him. "Conchetta, you know what? You *can* help me, now that I think about it."

"Anything, Mr. Leone."

"Do you think you could run the bakery? I can't afford to keep it closed."

"Sure, I can."

"There's gonna be medical bills and if I don't open the bakery..." his voice trailed off, he buried his face in his hands again.

Connie felt a lump in her throat. "I'm sure she'll be okay." She awkwardly patted his arm. "Please don't worry. I can open the bakery and I'll be fine. You take as much time as you need with Mrs. Leone, and don't worry 'bout a thing."

He took his hands from his face, swiped at tears under his eyes, and rested his hands on his knees. He looked at her and sniffed, "Connie, you're such a wonderful girl and you're a fine little baker but you can't do it alone, you're just a little girl." He affectionately pinched her cheek.

"Right," Connie said, slowly. *Why does everybody keep calling me a little girl?* "I know what!" Connie said, "I'll ask my sister Violet. She's been looking for part-time work, and you don't have to worry about the extra pay, because I'll share my pay with her."

"Oh, no, no, no," he protested. "I can't ask you to do that."

"No, it'll be fine, I don't mind. Really I don't."

He placed his large, callused hands on the sides of her head, and kissed her on the forehead. "How can I ever thank you?"

"You don't have to thank me. I'm happy to do it for you…I mean, you and Mrs. Leone have been so good to me, and you've taught me so much."

"All right, I trust you to do a fine job." He went into the kitchen and plucked a set of keys from a hook on the wall next to the icebox. He walked back into the living room, with the keys dangling from his index finger, and held them up for her to see. "This is the only set of keys I have Connie, so you must be very careful not to lose them. This one is for the front door and this one is for the back door. The smaller key is for the cash drawer, behind the counter." He placed the keys in the palm of her hand and, wrapping his hand around hers, closed it into fist. He walked into the dining room, opened the top drawer of a sideboard, and pulled out a small, gray pouch with a drawstring. "This is the money to put in the drawer, Connie," he told her. "That'll get you started for the day…you know, to make change." He handed her the bag, and she slipped it into her pocketbook along with the keys. "Now, if you have any problems, you send someone to come and get me at Holy Cross Hospital, but never leave the bakery unattended."

"Oh no, Mr. Leone, I would never do that."

"And remember, when the widow Rumininski comes in, she gets a loaf of bread for free."

"Okay."

"And officer Dobbins…I let him take apples for him and his partner."

"Yes, I remember," she said, as she walked toward the front door. "I'm going to go talk to my sister right now. Please give Mrs. Leone my love. I'll pray for her."

"Thank you, Connie. Go, go…make me proud."

"Oh, I will…*ciao*."

She walked down the sidewalk, and turned toward Violet's house. When she knocked, she could hear Violet's muffled voice. "Coming," she shouted. Her face lit up when she saw Connie standing there. "Connie, hi! What're you doing here? Aren't you working today?"

Connie stepped inside, sat down at the kitchen table and explained what had happened to Mrs. Leone, and added, "Mr. Leone asked if I could run the bakery…if I could get some help, so I thought of you."

"Gosh, I'm so sorry to hear about Mrs. Leone, is she going to be okay?"

"I don't know. Mr. Leone said she's pretty sick."

"That's a shame…such a nice lady," Violet said, shaking her head. "Well, gee Connie…I'd be happy to help you. I told Pasqual I wanted to get a part-time job, so it would be fun working together. How long do you think you'll need me?"

"Don't know."

"Okay. Well, what do I do…I don't bake like you do, that's for sure," she laughed.

Connie smiled. "Can you go with me now?"

"Sure." Violet threw a sweater over her shoulders.

"We'll talk on the way."

"Just let me leave a note for Pasqual in case he comes home before me." She wrote the note, placed it on the kitchen table, and followed Connie out the back door.

*

Violet was a quick study, always listening intently to her younger sister's instructions. She taught her everything from keeping the display cases stocked to how to make change. They were a good team, and worked well together for more than two months. Customers frequented the store just to enjoy the girls' sunny personalities but never left without a bagful of baked goods. At the end of each day, Connie stopped by Mr. Leone's to give him the day's receipts and he was so impressed with the increase in sales that he started paying both of them a salary.

*

Connie was alone in the shop one morning. She was sliding a tray of lemon tarts in the display case, when she heard the *tinkle* of the doorbell. She looked up to see a tall, handsome young man with a pleasant smile on a very youthful but familiar face. She stood up, flipped the hair from her eyes, and returned his smile. "Can I help you?"

"Connie? Hi, remember me? We went to elementary school together."

She tilted her head, squinted and studied his face.

"It's me…Elmer. Elmer Friedmont," he said, putting his hand on his chest.

"Oh, my gosh. Yes…Elmer. Of course! How are you?" She remembered him as a skinny, shy boy with curly blonde hair and bad allergies, always sneezing and wiping his runny nose on the sleeve of his shirt. She also remembered that his parents were wealthy, and lived on the outskirts of Star Junction in Yeager County. His father was the owner of two coal companies, one of which her father had been employed for many years. "Did you move away? I haven't seen you since…gosh, what…since fifth grade?"

"Has it really been that long?" He shook his head and paused. "My parents sent me to Huffington. It's a private school in Johnstown but we still live out in Yeager County."

Connie smiled. His liquid-blue eyes, and sharp jaw line intrigued her. "How 'bout that?" She caught herself staring, cleared her throat and asked, "So, how have you been? What's new? I mean, look at you now. You sure have grown," she commented, awkwardly.

"Yeah, a little, I guess," he laughed. "I'm on spring break, right now."

"Oh, spring break. You mean for Easter?"

"Yeah." He leaned over and casually peered through the glass of the display case. "Oh, by the way, I ran into your sister Philomena at the Company Store. I can't believe she remembered me." His smile was charming, friendly. "I asked how *you* were doing and she told me you worked at Leone's, so I thought I'd stop in and say hi."

"Well, that was nice of you Elmer."

"You look really good, Connie. I always remembered you and how much fun we had when we were kids. You were always so nice to me. I don't know if you remember but I was kinda shy."

"I remember," she nodded.

"Yeah, well…I just wanted to say hello. I better get goin'." He looked away and ran his fingers through his hair. "The streetcar is due in a couple a minutes and I gotta take the stuff I got at the Company Store home to my mom." He picked up the paper sack he had placed on the floor, turned toward the door then stopped, "Hey listen Connie, I don't know if you have a boyfriend or what, but how bout' you and me goin' to my spring dance."

"Spring dance?" Connie repeated. "Well…I don't know." She had never dated anyone other than Dominic.

"Oh," he said, sounding disappointed. "You have a boyfriend."

"No…I don't," Connie said, quickly. "I mean I did, but we're not together anymore."

"Oh, well then…you can go, right?"

"Well sure, why not?"

"Great!"

"When is it?"

"The twenty-first of April."

"Twenty-first, it is." She nodded. "What do I wear?"

"It's pretty formal. I have to wear a suit and all that stuff," he shrugged. "I think the girls are all wearing long dresses. Is that okay?"

"Sounds wonderful."

"I'm not much of a dancer but we'll have fun."

"I'm sure you dance just fine, Elmer."

"So, I'll pick you up, okay? My dad said I could use his car…I drive now," he added proudly.

"Do you know where I live?"

"Of course, still Hazel Street, right?"

"Right."

"I'll pick you up at six-thirty…what kind of flowers do you like?"

"Oh my gosh…flowers too?" she raised her eyebrows and giggled. "Let me think." She placed her finger on her chin and thought. "I like roses."

"Roses it is."

"Thanks, Elmer." She crossed her arms and smiled at him as he opened the door. "It was really nice seeing you."

"You too, Connie." He took long-legged strides out the door and carried the paper sack of groceries under his arm. He peered in the front window as he started down the sidewalk and smiled at her again, giving her a quick salute. She watched until he was out of sight.

Connie went home that day, in a better mood than she'd been in a long time. She was anxious to tell her mother about Elmer, and was sure her mother would be pleased. She had always liked Elmer and his father was always good to Vincenzo.

"Ma! I'm home," she hollered. "Are you in the kitchen?"

"*Si*, Conchetta, *vieni qua*!" Angelina shouted back.

Connie sidled next to her mother, tore a piece of bread from a fresh loaf that was cooling on the table and dipped it into the pot of tomato sauce that was bubbling on the stove. "Ma, you'll never guess who came into the bakery today," she said, with a mouthful of bread.

"Who?"

Connie swallowed and wiped her mouth on a towel. "Do you remember Elmer…from elementary school? His dad owned the mines."

"Elmer…you mean little Elmer…" she closed her eyes to think. "What was his papa's name?"

"Friedmont, remember Ma? But Elmer's not so little anymore. He's tall and good lookin' and so, so nice," Connie said, while flopping in a chair, cupping her face in her hands. "He's downright dreamy."

Angelina laughed. "See, you mama say you gonna meet a nice-a boy."

"I know, I know, you're always right, Ma," Connie playfully poked her mother in the arm. "He asked me to his spring dance…at his private school."

"Sounds very fancy, Conchetta."

"I think it'll be fun. He asked me what kind of flowers I wanted and everything!" She paused, sat up and leaned back in the chair. "Gosh, I can't believe he wants to take *me*. I mean, you would think he'd wanna take one of those beautiful rich girls from his school, you know?"

"Eh, I no wanna hear dat kinda talk!" Angelina scolded, waving a finger in the air. "Nobody ees more beautiful den my girls, you hear me? Rich! Phew!" She made a spitting sound into the air. "Means nothin'!"

"Oh, Ma…you're so funny." Connie went over and kissed her mother on the cheek. "I gotta go tell Philomena about seeing Elmer at the shop." She ran up the stairs and before reaching the bedroom, called out, "Phil, guess who I saw today?" She flopped down on the floor next to her.

Philomena, with her knees drawn up was leaning against the wall, sewing a button on a sweater. "Ah, let me see…" she teased, "Elmer Friedmont?"

"Oh my God, isn't he handsome?" Connie pinched Philomena's arm.

"Ouch, and yes, he *is* good lookin' and by the way, *you're* welcome."

"Oh, right…thank you, Philomena, for telling him where to find me. Well, anyway, he asked me to go to his spring dance with him."

"Spring dance? What spring dance is that?"

"Some fancy dance they have for Easter, I guess. It's at his private school."

"What're ya gonna wear?" Philomena asked, as she bit the end of the thread and admired her handiwork.

"I'm gonna talk to Ma about that." Connie got up from the floor and smoothed the back of her skirt. "It's gotta be something special."

*

Philomena, along with two school chums, attended the opening night of a local carnival that had just set up camp in the baseball field of their high school. After her third ride on the Ferris wheel, she exited the ride through a gate when she spotted Dominic Preste standing with his brothers by the bumping cars. They were laughing and sipping on bottles of pop. She tried to avoid him but he spotted her just as she ducked around the corner of a ticket booth.

"Hey! Philomena," he called out, and started walking in her direction.

"Damn it..." she said, under her breath, "Dominic...how ya doin'?" She asked, forcing a smile.

He walked with a swagger that Philomena loathed. He stood in front of her with his hands shoved into the pockets of his jacket. "Good, good," he said, nodding his head. "Hey...uh...how's Connie doin'?"

"She's fine, Dominic," she said, looking down at the ground.

"Does she talk about me?"

Philomena looked up at him and smirked. "No. As a matter of fact, she's dating someone. She's going to a dance with a rich guy that goes to school up at Huffington." Philomena was hoping to make him jealous.

"Oh, yeah?" He was suddenly edgy.

"Yeah, he's taking her to his spring dance and everything." She had said too much but she couldn't help herself. She wanted him to feel like a fool, and also to know that Connie was getting along fine without him.

"Huffington, huh?" Dominic was visably shaken. He turned away and mumbled something under his breath.

Philomena cleared her throat, adjusted her purse strap and looked off in the distance. "Hey, wait up you guys," she called to her friends. "Well, I gotta go, Dominic." She turned and walked away feeling guilty but satisfied.

*

Angelina stood back, placed her hand on the side of her face and studied Connie as she posed in front of her mother. Connie was wearing the bridesmaid's dress she wore for Violet's wedding, and Angelina seemed satisfied with the changes she had made. "Um-hmm, um-hmm, *si,* I like," Angelina said, after a few minutes. "I like very much." She had made a cape out of extra material, and a satin sash that she tied in a bow around Connie's waist.

Connie smiled, and said to her mother, "Did I tell you that Elmer has come in the bakery at least three times just to make sure I'm still going to the dance with him?"

"Das nice," Angelina said, focusing on her work.

"Isn't that cute?"

"*Si,* ees cute," she repeated. She stood back and studied the dress again. "It look good, Conchetta. Go change you clothes and hang da dress in you room, eh?"

"Yes Mama, and thank you, the dress is really pretty." She ran upstairs, changed into slacks and a white cotton blouse, went back downstairs and sat on the back porch with a cast iron pot between her knees, snapping the ends from a pile of green beans her father had just picked from his garden.

"Connie, Connie!" Carmella shouted, running into the kitchen.

"She's out back, Carmella," her mother told her.

"Thanks, Mama." She went out the back door. "Connie…there you are," she said, breathlessly, and sat down next to her. "You're not gonna believe this."

"What?"

"I was at the store today buying flour for Ma, and I was talking to Phil…"

"Catch your breath, Carmella."

"I will, I will…just listen. This cute guy came in and we get to talkin', and he says his name is Rizzo. And wait 'til you hear this. He goes to Huffington!"

"No!" Connie stopped snapping the beans and looked at Carmella. "What're the chances?"

"I know! Anyway, I mentioned that spring dance you told me about…kinda casual like, ya know? I told him that my sister was goin', and then he said he didn't have a date for the dance yet, and he asked me to go! Isn't that crazy?"

"Are you kidding?" Connie said, almost giddy over the coincidence of them both being asked to the same dance.

"Yes, can you imagine?" Carmella squealed with excitement.

"No, I can't." Connie placed her hand on Carmella's arm. "Uh-oh."

"What?"

"What're you gonna wear? Cause I'm wearing the dress I wore to Violet's wedding, and we can't wear the same thing."

"I already thought about that. I'm wearing Violet's dress; you know the one Ma made for her graduation party, the blue one with the skinny straps? I'm sure Ma can take in some of the seams and it'll be fine."

"Ooh, that's perfect!" Connie put the pot of green beans aside, and hugged her legs, resting her chin on her knees. "What'd you say this guy's name was?"

"Rizzo...something. I forget his last name."

"Rizzo? That's a funny name. How come we don't know him?"

"I don't know, maybe 'cause he goes to Huffington. We don't know anybody from that school, 'cept for Elmer. But, he's kinda cute, Connie. Anyway, he asked me to go have a soda pop with him. We talked for a while, and then he asked me to the dance. Just like that! Isn't that cute, Connie? Funny thing though, he doesn't look like the type to go to Huffington, ya know? He sort of looked...gee, I don't know. Not rich lookin', like Elmer." She waved her hand. "Oh, it doesn't matter...I'm goin' and we're gonna have a fine time, right? "

"Yeah," Connie said, her thoughts elsewhere.

"Yoo-hoo," Carmella sang. "Connie?" Carmella bumped Connie's knee.

Connie jumped. "What?"

"Holy cow...where'd you go?"

"Nowhere...I was just thinkin' about something. So, what did you say this guy's last name was?"

"I'm not sure, Figli or Figalo...oh, I don't know, something like that."

"Oh, Carm...you're a stitch, ya know that?" Connie laughed and shook her head.

*

Elmer arrived at the Borzanna house five minutes before seven and was greeted by Angelina and Vincenzo. When Connie came downstairs, he complimented her appearance and presented her with a corsage of white roses that he slipped onto her wrist. He wore a dark blue suit and a bright red tie that was perfectly knotted around the neck of his stiffly starched white shirt. He smelled of soap and Aqua Velva, and Connie blushed when he wrapped her cape around her shoulders.

Previously that evening, Rizzo had arrived earlier than expected, and when Carmella's mother called for her, she quickly brushed her hair and dabbed pink lipstick on her lips and cheeks before running down the stairs. She had wanted to wait for Connie but when Rizzo mumbled something about his cousin waiting in the car, she shrugged, kissed her parents and followed Rizzo out the door. Angelina looked concerned as she watched her daughter get into the backseat of a car, and Vincenzo stood at the window shaking his head, grumbling something in Italian. He didn't like the way Rizzo looked when he came into the house. The boy simply grunted hello and stared at the floor until Carmella came downstairs. He was short and thin, with black hair that was oiled and hanging, like string over his eyes. He wore a suit that was obviously borrowed. The shirtsleeves covered his knuckles, and the cuff of the pants lay draped over the tops of his scuffed, brown shoes. A clip-on bowtie hung crookedly under the points of the shirt collar. He stuck his finger into the neck of the collar as though he was on the verge of choking, and Angelina didn't want to judge but she thought he looked more like a hoodlum than a private school student. Vincenzo's only comment was that he looked like a bum.

*

When Connie and Elmer arrived at the dance, Carmella and her date were standing in the foyer by the school gym.

"Connie!" Carmella called, jumping up and down, excitedly. She grabbed Rizzo's hand and dragged him to where Connie and Elmer were standing. "Connie, this is Rizzo. Remember, I told you about him?"

"I remember." Connie turned to him. "Hi, Rizzo," She smiled and shook his hand. "Nice to meet you. This is Elmer."

"How ya doin'?" Rizzo mumbled, looking uncomfortable and out of place.

"It's nice to meet you, Rizzo." Elmer bowed slightly and took the boy's hand. "Connie said you go to Huffington?"

"Yeah, well…"

"I'm surprised we never met. I know pretty much everybody in the school."

"Well I, er…" he stammered. "I don't really *go* to the school. I know this guy, and he…uh… got me a ticket to the dance, so I thought…" He looked down as he drew a circle on the floor with his foot.

"You told me you went to Huffington," Carmella said, looking confused.

"No, I didn't," he answered, defensively. "I said I have a ticket and asked you if you wanted to go."

"Oh," Carmella looked embarrassment. "Well, it doesn't make any difference. We'll still have a good time."

Elmer cleared his throat and suggested they go into the gym. "After you, girls," he said, gently placing his hand on the small of Connie's back.

As the evening progressed, Connie could see that Elmer was a perfect gentleman. He was charming and polite. She was flattered that he had taken dance lessons just for her, and it was nice being treated with respect. He seemed genuinely interested in what she had to say. She wanted to like him but couldn't help wishing Dominic was on the dance floor with her.

Connie noticed that Rizzo paid more attention to her and Elmer, than he did Carmella. When they sat down, Rizzo dragged Carmella off the dance floor and sat down next to them. When Elmer went for punch, Rizzo followed him.

"What do you think is with this guy, Connie?" Carmella asked. "I'm feeling kind of hurt, ya know? I don't think he even knows I'm here. I mean he's watching you and Elmer all the time. What gives?"

"I have no idea. It's weird," Connie agreed, taking her sister's hand. "I'm sorry, Carm. Are you having a bad time?"

"No, I'm sorta having a good time…it's just that…I don't know, I wish he'd pay more attention to *me*. I'm surprised he even remembers to take me with him onto the dance floor!"

"Aw Carmella, I'm sorry." Connie said.

"I see you…you're laughing at me."

"No, I'm not. You're just so funny."

Carmella smiled too. "He's a pretty pathetic date, isn't he?"

"Mm-hm."

"Shh, here they come." Elmer, with Rizzo by his side walked toward the girls. They each held two cups of punch. Carmella sat up straight, fluffed her hair and pinched her cheeks while Rizzo set a glass of punch in front of her. "Thank you, Rizzo," she said, sweetly.

"Huh? Oh yeah, s'okay."

Elmer handed a cup to Connie, and after she took a sip, he gently took her hand and led her out onto the dance floor. Rizzo stood up then decided to sit back down.

"Did you wanna dance?" Carmella asked.

"Nah, I'm kinda tired." He slouched in his chair and stretched his legs under the table. Carmella rolled her eyes when he yawned.

When the last song ended, Connie hugged Carmella and told her she would see her at home. Elmer collected Connie's cape, and wrapped it around her shoulders, and said goodnight to Carmella and Rizzo.

Rizzo stood up, stretched and hiked up his pants. He snorted loudly and took the palm of his hand, smoothing the side of his hair before heading for the door. Carmella walked behind him. Rizzo's cousin, Sammy was waiting for them in front of the school. "You kids have a good time?" He asked. He stood by the car, leaning on the roof, took a drag on a cigarette then cleverly flicked it into the street.

"Yeah, it was okay," Rizzo mumbled.

"It was a very nice dance," Carmella responded. "Thanks for driving us here and picking us up."

"No problem. Was my cousin a gentleman?" He playfully slapped Rizzo on the back of the head, sending his hair flying over his eyes. "Did he treat you like a lady? Or was he the jerk?"

"Cut it out, Sammy," Rizzo said, irritably.

Carmella smiled, and stole a look at Rizzo out of the corner of her eye. "He was fine." During the ride home, Carmella and Rizzo sat quietly in the backseat while Sammy rambled on about his evening at his girlfriend's house in Uniontown. They fought about his laziness. When they pulled up in front of the Carmella's house, Sammy shoved Rizzo out of the car, "Stop being a slob and walk her to the door, moron."

"All right! Gimme a chance, will ya?" He trailed behind Carmella. He shoved his hands in his pockets, and when they reached the edge of the porch, he lowered his head and muttered, "Well…uh…night."

"What?"

"I said g'night…see ya 'round."

"Sure." Carmella reached for the doorknob. "Thanks for taking me to the dance."

"Huh? Oh, yeah…no problem."

*

When Elmer brought Connie home, he kissed her on the cheek and said he'd hoped she had a good time. Connie thanked him and went into the house and as usual, her mother was waiting up. They went upstairs together and said goodnight, and when Connie saw Carmella climbing into bed, she said, "Oh, Carm…I'm glad you're still up. Are you okay?"

"Oh yeah, I'm fine. Rizzo just wasn't my knight in shining armor, I guess."

They lay in bed talking about their evening, and Carmella, with her usual sense of humor made fun of the situation. Connie was still talking about Elmer when she realized Carmella had fallen asleep. She pulled the covers up to Carmella's chin, lay back with her hands behind her head and closed her eyes. "Good night, Dominic," she whispered, before drifting off to sleep.

*

Violet was relieved when Mr. Leone came back to the bakery. She was three months pregnant, and nausea was keeping her in bed most mornings.

Connie was excited about Violet's baby and pleased to have Mr. Leone back to work. She was able to return to the kitchen and do what she loved most, which was baking. She happily made breads, lemon cookies, cannolli, cheesecake and a variety of big puffy muffins, and she now realized that it was her dream to have her own bakery one day. She was actually building the courage to ask her parents if she could leave school and work full time.

It was six o'clock on Friday evening and Elmer had wanted to take Connie to the movies. It would be their last date for a while since he was leaving for a late summer vacation with his parents. To his dismay,

Connie turned him down because it just happened to be that particular night that she had planned on talking to her parents about school.

At the end of the day, she placed cookie dough in the icebox, cleaned her workspace and hung up her apron. Mr. Leone had gone home early, so Connie emptied the cash drawer, jotted the amount on a piece of paper and left it in the drawer. She placed the money in the pouch and was about to lock the door to the safe when she heard the tinkle of the bell. She smiled, assuming it was Elmer coming to convince her to go to the movies. "I'll be out in a sec," she hollered. She gave the safe handle a jerk to make sure it was locked, and went to the front of the store.

Dominic Preste was standing at the counter, grinning and wiping cookie crumbs from his chin. "Mm, good cookies, Connie." He tossed another into his mouth.

"Dominic," she said, softly. "What're you doing here?"

"Well, it's the funniest thing...my brother asked if we was still goin' together, and I wasn't sure if we were or not, so I thought I'd come ask ya."

"Still goin' together?" Connie looked confused. "Uh, I don't think so," she responded, unable to keep sarcasm from her tone. "I don't take kindly to people beating me up."

"I didn't beat you up! When did I beat you up?"

"Listen, just forget it. If you don't remember the night we were at my sister's..."

"Oh, that," he said, looking down at the floor.

"Yeah...that."

"You didn't tell your parents, did ya?"

"Some of it, not all of it. Anyway, what do you care?"

"Hey, I care! What did ya tell them?"

"I talked to my mother, not my father. I told her we had a fight, that's all. I didn't tell her that you practically pulled the hair out of my head. Oh...and yeah...that's right...something about getting married. Did you think I would tell her you were gonna beat me up that night, for no reason? Would I be that stupid? Oh, and by the way, if I had told my father, your legs would be broken by now!"

"What?" He smirked. "Are you threatening me now?" He shook his head and laughed. "God, you're just like your father."

"Where have you been, Dominic? One minute you wanna get married, and the next minute you're beating me! Then I don't see you for months!"

He rolled his eyes and groaned. "Here we go..."

"Ugh, ya know what Dominic? I think I want you to leave," she said, pointing to the door.

"Okay, okay, I know I messed up again, all right? Come on...can't we just drop it now and start over?"

"Start over?" She laughed. "No."

"Why? Because of that Elmer guy?"

Connie turned and looked at him, her eyes squinting with suspicion. "How do you know...?"

"Never you mind how I know, I just know, that's all."

"Elmer is none of your business," Connie stated.

"Oh, he's my business all right."

Connie walked away from him, and went behind the counter.

Dominic followed and when he spoke again, his tone was smoother. "Listen, how 'bout you forget about that guy and you start thinkin' bout me again, huh?"

"Dominic, please. Just leave me alone."

"You don't mean that." He was close to her now, and she could feel his breath on the back of her neck.

"Don't touch me Dominic, I mean it."

"I'm not gonna touch you. I'm just trying to be nice, that's all. I thought maybe we could get back together."

She turned to face him. "Why should I take you back?"

"Because you love me, that's why."

"Oh yeah? What makes you think that?"

"Connie come on, I said I was sorry."

"No, you didn't."

He wrapped his arms around her waist. "Let me show you how sorry I am."

"Stop it Dominic," she warned, and pushed him away.

"For Christ's sake, Connie...you know us *degos*. We get a little rough sometimes but it don't mean nothin', you know that. You belong to me."

"Well, you're not gonna get rough with me anymore."

He made a fist and chucked her playfully under the chin. "Come on, Connie. You know me and you should be together." He lowered his voice and looked away. "Not you and that dumb lookin' Elmer guy."

"He's not dumb lookin', and I still wanna know how you know about him."

"I have my ways."

"I don't like that, Dominic! What are you, having me followed?"

"All right, all right. Don't get mad…I'm just teasin'. I just heard around, you know. People talk."

"People talk, huh?"

"Look Connie, I'll treat ya better from now on, okay? Would that make you happy?"

"Yes, it would make me happy but I don't know, Dominic…you really hurt me."

"I won't do that no more…I promise." He took his finger and marked an "x" over his heart.

"See to it that you don't."

"Hey, don't get cute with me, hear?" Catching himself, he raised his hand in a silent apology.

Connie cocked her head and glared at him with raised eyebrows. "Gee, that was quick. That's all it takes to make you mad? Forget it, Dominic."

"That's just me Connie, I don't mean nothin' when I say shit like that."

"Well, it meant something to me," she pouted. She watched as he casually leaned against the display case.

He reached for another cookie and tossed it into his mouth, closing his eyes savoring the buttery taste. "These are pretty good…you make 'em?"

"Yeah," she answered, quietly. She busied herself cleaning the counter.

"Hey, forgot to tell ya…I got news!"

"What news?"

"I moved outta Uniontown. Livin' here now!"

"So?"

"So…so…" he mocked. "I'm bunkin' up with my brother, Vittorio."

"That's nice." Connie straightened the lid of an apple barrel.

"When Vittorio got married, they moved to Wickhaven and said I could stay with them for a while. I start working for a construction company on Monday...pretty good money, too."

"That's nice." Connie took an apple from the barrel, wiped it on her skirt and took a bite. "Your brother got married?" She asked, wiping juice from her chin. "I didn't even know he had a girlfriend."

"He didn't, 'til he got a letter from our mother. She told him she was sending this girl over to the states. She lives in the same town as my mother, and her parents owed my mother a favor, so they offered their daughter for Vittorio."

"Offered her, for what?"

"For marriage," he said, seeming surprised by her question.

"Oh."

"Anyway, her name's Tessa Faretti and when Vittorio read the letter that she was comin', he said, '*eh, why not*? *I'm tired of takin' care of myself, anyway*!' So, he takes the train to New York, goes to the boat dock, and starts askin' around for a girl named Tessa Faretti." Dominic started laughing.

"What's so funny?"

"Well, he sees this ugly girl; I mean *brutta faccia*! He looks around at the people standing by the dock and sees this girl and thinks '*that can't be her; Ma would never pick somebody that looks like that!*' He waits, and she's still standin' there, holding onto a suitcase! Anyway, he says, '*Come si chiama lei*? And she says, '*Tessa Faretti.*' Vittorio looks her up and down and says, '*Okay, let's go home!*' Dominic clutched his stomach and laughed so hard, he nearly fell off the counter. "That Vittorio, he's so Goddamned funny."

Connie folded her arms and tapped her foot impatiently. "I think that's awful, Dominic. That poor girl, in a strange place and getting married to someone she doesn't even know. And even worse; he thinks she's ugly and just wants her to cook and clean for him." Connie shook her head. "That's disgusting."

"What's the big deal? Isn't that what wives do? Listen, she's lucky to be here but I tell ya what, I wrote my mother and told her not to send no girl for me...I'm spoken for!"

Connie looked at him with amusement. "You are, huh? Well, who would that be?"

"You!"

"Me?" Connie threw up her hands, turned and walked behind the counter.

"Yeah you. We're still gettin' married, right?"

"Oh Jesus, Joseph and Mary, you *are* crazy."

"Well, you're not getting any younger, ya know. What are you now, 'bout thirty or forty?"

"Very funny," she smirked. "Goodbye, Dominic." She shoved him from behind and he slid from the counter, his feet landing on the floor. "It's time for me to lock up, so you have to go and I'm tired and wanna get home. Plus, I don't like being stuck in here with a crazy person."

"Wait, I wanted to ask you something."

"Ask me what?"

"There's a carnival at the high school."

"I know."

"You wanna go?"

"No."

"Come on," he whined.

"No, I can't. Not tonight. I'm tired and I have to get home. I have some important things to talk to my parents about."

"Is it about me?"

"Don't flatter yourself."

"Well then, tomorrow night. How 'bout that? Ask your sisters too. Vittorio, Sergio and Antonio are going. So we'll have fun."

"What about Vittorio's wife?" Connie asked.

"What about her?"

"Well, he's married now. Doesn't he take her with him?"

"God, no!"

"No? Well, why not?"

"She stays at home…I don't think she likes to go out," he shrugged.

"That's too bad. I feel sorry for her."

"Nah, she's okay."

"Ya know, Dominic, I don't think my parents would let me go out with you, anyway."

"Come on, Connie. Your parents don't have to know. It's just for a good time."

"I can't lie to my parents, Dominic…any more than I already have," she added.

"What are you, a saint or somethin'?" He asked, sarcastically.

"No, I just don't like to lie to my parents."

"It's just a carnival, Connie…God…"

"Well…we'll see. Stop by the bakery tomorrow and I'll let you know."

*

During the walk home, Connie felt the twinge of a migraine starting to throb between her eyes. It was probably guilt, she thought. She couldn't imagine explaining to her parents that not only did she want to quit school but that she was thinking of seeing Dominic again.

When she arrived home, her mother immediately saw that her daughter was troubled. *"Tutto sta bene?"* Angelina asked, wanting to know if everything was okay.

"Everything's all right, Ma," Connie assured her. "But I did want to talk to you and Papa about something."

"First we eat, eh?"

Connie sat between Lourdes and Carmella. Vincenzo, sitting across the table eyed Connie while sipping a glass of red wine.

"What's going on, Connie? What'dya wanna to talk to Ma and Papa about?"

"Nothing that concerns you, Lourdes!" Connie snapped.

"*Conchetta, chetare!"* Vincenzo scolded. Everyone jumped when he pounded his fist on the table with a heavy thud.

"Sorry." Connie felt ashamed and turned to her sister. "I'm sorry, Lourdes. I'm just a little tired and I have a lot on my mind."

"S'okay, Connie," Lourdes said, smiling sweetly.

Connie seemed unable to swallow her food. Her head was pounding. The sound of everyone chewing was about to send her screaming from the room but she remained poised. Her father was the first to finish his dinner. He left the table and went into the living room while Angelina cleared dishes from the table.

"Is everything all right, Connie?" Philomena whispered.

Connie wiped her mouth with a napkin, and pushed away from the table. "Everything's fine, why?"

"Well, something seems to be going on. You seem so grumpy."

Connie lowered her voice. "Everything's fine, I said. I'll talk to you later."

"I heard Dominic was back in town," Philomena said, suddenly. She waited for Connie's reaction.

Connie looked at Philomena but said nothing.

Philomena gasped. "But you already know that, don't you?"

"Yes."

"You saw him?"

"What are you two whispering about," Carmella asked.

"Shut up, Carmella," Philomena snapped, and turned back to Connie.

"Well, how rude!" Carmella countered, and left the room.

"Yes…I saw him," Connie whispered, "and will you please keep your voice down? He stopped in the bakery…big deal. We just talked. He wanted to tell me he moved in with his brother."

"Mm, really?" Philomena spoke with sarcasm. "Well, that's just great. I hope you're not thinking of seeing him again."

"Maybe, I don't know." Connie wanted the conversation to end.

"Connie, come on! Are you crazy?"

She regretted telling Philomena about that last night with Dominic. "Phil…please, I know what I'm doing.

"I don't think so."

"Can we talk about this later, please? I need to talk with Mama and Papa."

Carmella came back into the dining room, stuck her tongue out at Philomena and looked at Connie. "Don't worry Con, whatever you two are fighting about, I'm on *your* side."

"God, you're such an idiot," Philomena said, taking Carmella by the hand, forcing her to follow her upstairs.

Connie went into the living room where her father was seated in his chair. He was holding a match to the end of a cigar, and looked up when Connie approached. Smoke seeped from the corner of his mouth in a steady stream, and Connie waited for him to invite her to sit. When

Angelina joined them, Vincenzo nodded toward Connie, and she sat Indian-style on the floor between them.

"Mama…Papa…" she said, slowly.

"Yes, Concetta. What dis about?" Vincenzo asked.

"You know how much I like working at the bakery."

"*Si,* go on."

"Well, Mr. Leone has given me a lot of responsibility at the bakery, and I've been thinking...I'd like to work fulltime…so…what I'm asking you…or telling you is…I don't wanna to go back to school in the fall. "

"You wan' to quit school, Conchetta?" Vincenzo asked.

"*Uno momento,* Papa," Angelina interjected. She gently touched Vincenzo's hand. She studied Connie's upturned face. "Conchetta? You *need* to go to school. Don' you t'ink is good for you to go to school?"

"Yes I do, Mama but running the bakery is what I love to do, and I'm learning so much from Mr. L that I would never learn in school. I really want to do this, Mama…I really do. I'm good at what I do, just ask Mr. L."

"Ach! Meesta L!" Vincenzo said, irritably. "Listen how you young people talk! *Mancanza di rispetto*! You must call a man by his name!"

"I'm sorry, Papa. I meant no disrespect. Mr. Leone likes when I call him Mr. L."

"Vincenzo, please. Dat is not da problem here," Angelina said. "She wan' to quit school, don' you see?"

"I see," he said, leaning back in his chair. "What you t'ink, Angelina?"

Connie looked up at her mother, her eyes wide with anticipation.

"We will talk, Conchetta…Papa and I. Okay? Okay," she said, with finality. With a groan, she pushed herself to a standing position. "You go now, Conchetta." A wan smile crossed her lips but Connie saw the disappointment in her eyes.

"Thank you, Mama." She hugged her mother, and kissed her father, and ran upstairs to talk with a very angry Philomena.

*

"Oh no, oh-ho-ho, no!" Philomena protested, at the thought of helping Connie sneak a date with Dominic.

Connie looked toward the door and flapped her hands. "Shh… please, keep your voice down!"

Lowering her voice, Philomena warned Connie. "I'm not going to help you get back with that, that bastard! You know I can't stand him, Connie. I think you're crazy to have anything to do with him! God…I can't believe you even talked to him!"

"Philomena, please listen to me. I would do it for you."

"Well, you'll never have to, cause no guy is ever gonna treat me the way he treats you!"

"He's apologized to me like crazy and he means it this time, Phil. He really does, and ya know what? I made him swear that he would treat me good from now on."

Philomena sat stone-faced, with her arms folded.

"Phil, come on…even you have to admit he's a great dancer, and you know how important that is to me."

Philomena turned and looked at Connie with shock on her face. "Oh my God, Connie…a great dancer? That's what you think is so great about him?"

"Well…yeah. I mean, nobody else dances with me the way he does. We have fun. Most of the time," she mumbled. "And look how many dance contests we've won! Heck, nobody else dances with me, or even pays any attention to me."

"What are you talking about? What about Elmer?"

"Elmer." Connie smiled, shrugging her shoulders. "He's sweet but he's too fancy for me. I'm nothin' like the girls he's used to at that fancy school. I mean, come on Phil…look at me."

"Yeah, what? I'm lookin' attcha. What's wrong with ya?"

"Well, nothin' I guess but what if Dominic's the only guy that wants me?"

"For God's sake, Connie, you're only sixteen years old!"

"I know but, listen Phil, I'm just gonna give this one more try, ya know? I think I should give him a chance." Connie cocked her head, and looked at Philomena with pleading eyes.

"Oh, for God's sake! All right…just this once!"

"Come with me to the carnival and you can see for yourself that he's changed."

Philomena put her hands over her face. "I know I'll regret this."

"Thank you, Phil. I owe you big time."

"You're pathetic, you know that?"

Philomena rejected Connie's hug and asked, "Are you gonna tell Mama and Papa that you're seeing him?"

"I'll tell them…just not yet."

"Oh God," Philomena groaned. "You're not gonna tell them, are you?"

*

Connie had planned to go to the carnival with just Philomena but as the days passed, Carmella, Bettina and Giordana decided to join them. That was fine with Connie as long as they agreed not to tattle about Dominic. The evening was cool and breezy when the girls arrived at the carnival. Bettina and Giordana wanted to see the sideshow, and Connie, Philomena and Carmella wanted to go on the rides.

"Hey, you two…be back in this spot by eight-thirty, ya hear!" Philomena warned.

"We will!"

Connie and Carmella followed Philomena to a booth where they purchased twenty-five cents worth of tickets. Carmella bought a cotton candy and shared it with them while they watched the rollercoaster roar above their heads. Teenaged boys raised their arms in the air as their girlfriends screamed with delighted terror. The air was thick with the aroma of fresh, roasted peanuts and popcorn, and the girls giggled as a man on stilts, dressed like Uncle Sam towered over them.

"Hey Connie, look," Carmella pointed. "Isn't that Dominic Preste over there? Yoo-hoo, Dominick…" she called out.

He was leaning against a wooden post by the bumping cars, smoking a cigarette, and chatting with another young man. He turned, smiled with recognition and waved. After drawing a final toke on the cigarette, he tossed it over a fence and sauntered toward them. His eyes locked on Connie's. "Hey Connie…I knew you'd come".

"Hello Dominic." Connie felt a familiar stirring in her stomach when he took hold of her hand.

"E-hem." Philomena cleared her throat.

"Oh, Phil…Carmella, how ya doin'?"

"Dominic," Philomena said, cooly.

"Isn't this fun…the rides and sideshow and everything?" Carmella gushed. "Gee, we didn't know you'd be here, Dominic."

"Humph," Philomena grunted.

Dominic's attention went back to Connie, and Carmella took Philomena by the hand and dragged her toward the bumping cars.

"Hey, wait for us," Connie called after them. She and Dominic followed and handed their tickets to a pimply-faced boy that was in charge of the ride. Connie and Dominic hopped into a bright red car behind a yellow car where Carmella was holding tight to the metal bar in front of her. Philomena sat next to her and took the wheel. Her foot was poised above the gas pedal. When they started to move, Carmella closed her eyes and screamed while Dominic chased them, causing them to run into the row of rubber tires that lined the rink. Sparks flew from the metal rods that scraped along the ceiling, and Connie threw back her head and laughed as the car glided around the rink.

When the ride was over, Carmella begged to go again but Philomena had already exited the car. Carmella followed, and suddenly noticed a familiar face. It was Rizzo. He was standing in line and turned when he heard his name.

"Rizzo?" Carmella said, with surprise.

"Oh hi," he said, casually.

"Who're you here with?"

"Just some guys…Dominic…and some of the gang."

" Oh." Carmella looked confused. "You know Dominic?"

"Well…uh, yeah. We're cousins. Didn't I tell you that?"

"No."

"Huh, thought I did. Anyway, Dominic told me you was gonna be here, so I came along for the ride. Thought it might be neat to see ya again…I dunno."

Connie walked toward them. "Rizzo?"

"Hey, how ya doin'?" He pulled a comb from his pocket and ran it though his hair.

Carmella turned to Connie and asked, "Did you know Rizzo and Dominic are cousins?"

"Cousins?" She turned to Rizzo. "Dominic is your cousin?"

Dominic suddenly appeared behind Connie and took her by the hand. "Connie, come here, I wanna talk to you." He pulled her aside and paused before speaking. "Okay, okay," he said, in an appeasing tone. "I know what you're thinkin', so let me explain."

"I'm waiting." Connie crossed her arms and tapped her foot impatiently.

"I heard you were goin' to a dance with that Elmer guy and I...well, I wanted to know what was going on, so I got a ticket to the dance from my supervisor's kid. I gave it to Rizzo, okay? No big deal! I told Rizzo to get to know your sister and then ask her to the dance. I wanted him to keep an eye on ya."

"Oh my God, Dominic! You were spying on me?"

"Okay, I was but I didn't like you going out with that guy, Connie. You belong to me."

"I can't believe you, Dominic...and what about Carmella? She had a horrible time that night." She looked over at Rizzo, lowered her voice and covered her mouth. "Your cousin's a jerk, ya know?"

"I know, I heard about it." Dominic smiled, and looked down at the ground. "Rizzo's not exactly known for his charm."

"Oh, this is funny to you?"

"Gimme a break, will ya?"

"Oh, for God's sake, Dominic. What you did was wrong." Placing her hands on her hips, she turned and left him standing alone. She walked back to Philomena, who looked disgusted. "Where's Carmella?" Connie asked her. Philomena pointed toward the bumping cars, where Carmella was snuggled up against Rizzo. "Oh my God," Connie threw up her hands. "I give up."

Dominic came up behind her and held up his hands and shrugged. "See, everybody's good, right?"

Chapter 7

In 1941, war broke out in Europe. The United States was getting involved, and many young men from Wickhaven were receiving their draft notices. Two of Dominic's brothers had been ordered to report to Fort Dix, in New Jersey and were waiting for orders to be shipped overseas. Vittorio was exempt because he was married, and Dominic had not yet been called. He feared it would be soon, though.

Connie and Dominic were together again. Months had passed and her time with him had become more of a habit than a relationship, dysfunctional but comfortable. She pacified his dark moods and often blamed herself for making him angry, and found herself constantly apologizing for things she knew nothing about. Dominic controlled her, and liked her weakness. He was glad she was not a fighter, like Philomena. Connie was obedient and quiet and he liked that. That was the kind of woman he wanted to marry.

*

One evening, midsummer and just before sundown Dominic and Connie were standing on the corner of Hazel Street after walking home from a visit with Violet and Pasqual. Dominic leaned against a street light, smoking a cigarette, seeming troubled.

"You okay, Dominic?" Connie asked.

"I'm gonna get drafted soon, Connie. You probably want me to go away to war."

"No, I don't," she said, defensively. "Why do you say that?"

"Well if I go, it'll be your fault, Connie! Just cause you don't wanna get married..."

He glanced at her out of the corner of his eye.

"Dominic, please...that's not fair."

"I gotta good job now, Connie. I can get us an apartment, or maybe even a house. You don't hafta worry 'bout nothin'."

"I don't know Dominic."

"Now look, Connie, would you rather me go in the army and get myself killed?"

"No, I don't want that," she answered, suddenly feeling guilty.

"Well, then..."

"Just give me a little time to think about it, Dominic. Right now my parents are still getting over me quitting school, so I wanna wait a little while, okay?"

"Yeah, yeah," he grumbled. "But don't take too long, hear?"

"I won't."

*

It had been a good week for Connie and Dominic; no fights, just laughter, a Friday night dance and leisure Saturday. It was a hot, sticky night and after a bikeride to Bickman's Ice-cream Parlor for a cone, they stopped in front of Connie's house. Earlier that evening, they sat by Muggins Lake with Carmella and Rizzo and cooled their feet in the lake while sharing slices of watermelon. Connie was more relaxed than she'd been in a long time and finally felt confident that Dominic was putting forth an effort to change.

Sitting on the front porch steps, Dominic popped the last of his cone into his mouth and with the back of his hand, wiped a drop of ice cream from the corner of his mouth. "Connie?"

"Mm-hm?" she answered lazily. She stretched her suntanned legs in front of her, and leaned back, her elbows resting on the step.

"So...uh, are you ready to get married?"

Connie turned to look at him. "Is that your proposal?"

"Yeah, I guess so."

"Not very romantic," she teased.

He frowned. "Don't be stupid, Connie. We've talked about it a million times already."

Connie took a deep breath, swallowed the last of her ice cream cone and wiped her hands on her shorts. "Okay," she said, casually.

"What? Is that a *yes*?" Dominic stood up in front of her, and looked down at her upturned face.

"Yeah, I guess."

"Oh well, when do you wanna…you know, do it?" He asked, stupidly. He was surprised by her sudden change of heart.

"I don't know," she shrugged. "When do you want to?"

"How 'bout next month…I don't know."

"Oh my gosh, why so quick?"

"Well, why not? I mean, we want to be together, right?"

"Yeah," she agreed. She thought for a second and said, "Well, I guess next month would be okay."

Dominic sat down next to her, and they spent the next few minutes lost in their own thoughts. Connie put her head back, and stared up at the moonlight while Dominic lit up a cigarette.

"You know you have to talk to my father, don't you?"

Dominic sat up. "What? What for?"

"You have to ask for my hand in marriage, even *you* know that."

"Shit. I know I do," he responded, irritably.

"Tonight."

"Tonight? Oh, Connie, I don't know if I'm ready for your father!" Dominic jumped to his feet and started to pace. "He's so mean."

"He is not mean! Why do you say that, Dominic?"

"Well…I've heard things," he said. "And every time he looks at me, he makes faces at me."

"Oh, he does not." She couldn't help but laugh. "I don't even wanna know what you heard about my father, so if you wanna marry me, you will have to talk to him tonight."

"But he hates me!"

"No, he doesn't! He just doesn't like anyone that he didn't personally choose for his daughters. He's old fashioned like that. But he knows how I feel about you, so it'll be fine…I promise."

"Damn it!" He knew she was right and that frustrated him. He clenched his fist and punched the post he was leaning against. "Okay." His expression was pained and he took a deep breath as he hiked up his trousers. "Come on, let's get it over with."

Connie stood up and took him by the hand, and pulled him through the front door, into the house. Angelina and Vincenzo were sitting in the living room. The curtains by Angelina were flapping lazily as a faint breeze wafted through an open window. She had her stockings rolled down around her ankles. Her housedress was hiked up and modestly shoved between her knees. Strands of graying hair were sticking to her face, and she was vigorously fanning herself with a magazine. Vincenzo was sitting in front of an electric fan that droned quietly as it swayed back and forth blowing wisps of curly hair that tickled his forehead. He was smoking a cigar and holding a glass of ice to his cheek when he turned to see Connie and Dominic enter the room. His relaxed expression turned sour, and Angelina felt a twinge of anxiety grip her stomach at the sight of them holding hands.

"Mama? Papa? Can we talk to you for a minute?" Connie asked. She pulled Dominic forward until he was standing by her side, and gave him a nod of encouragement.

Dominic cleared his throat and shifted his weight from one foot to the other. "Thank you, Mr. and Mrs. Borzanna…for letting me speak to you."

Vincenzo and Angelina sat quietly and waited for him to continue.

"Well, Connie and me, we been talkin' and we thought we might wanna get married, and I wanted to see if that was all right with you."

Seconds of silence seemed like hours. Vincenzo rose from his chair and started to pace. He rubbed his hand over the back of his nearly, baldhead. Angelina, out of respect to her husband, waited for him to speak first.

"So, you wan' marry my daughter?" It was more of an accusation than a question.

"Yeah, I do. I mean…yes, Mr. Borzanna, I do."

"I see," Vincenzo said, slowly. He rubbed his chin and looked at Dominic through squinted eyes. "You have a job?" He fired the question like a bullet.

"Yes sir."

"You have money?"

"A little."

"You have a house to give to my daughter?"

"Well, not yet but I plan to sir...at least an apartment for now but definitely a house one day. I'll build it myself," he added.

"Ha!" Vincenzo laughed.

Connie grimaced, and she could see Dominic's jaw muscle flex with tension.

"Conchetta!" Vincenzo said, turning to his daughter.

"Yes, Papa." She jumped, dropping her arms down to her sides. She was nose to nose with her father.

"You wan' to be married to *dis* man?" Vincenzo asked, as though the thought of it would be hard to believe.

"Now, wait a minute!" Dominic said, taking a step forward.

Vincenzo glared at him, his eyes daring Dominic to take another step.

"Now now, not to worry." Angelina quickly intervened. "Come, let's sit down." She looked at Vincenzo with pleading eyes. "Vincenzo... please, what're you doin'?" she whispered. "You makin' dem nervous."

Vincenzo threw up his hands in disgust. "Ach! Do watta you wan'," he said, bitterly. "Nobody listen to me anyway!" He turned abruptly and walked back to his chair but before sitting, turned and glared at Dominic. "You take care of my daughter, you hear me?" His tone was soft but threatening. "Or you will answer to me, *capice*?"

"Yes, I understand, sir. I didn't mean to get upset...I just..." He stopped talking when Connie squeezed his hand.

"You just..." Vincenzo mocked, then sat in his chair.

"You two go now. We talk later, okay?" Angelina said, shooing Connie and Dominic out of the room.

"Thank you, Papa," Connie said.

Angelina followed them to the door. "Conchetta? Please, don' leave the front porch, and Dominic...in two minutes...you go."

"Yes, Mrs. Borzanna." Dominic's face was glistening with sweat.

When her mother closed the door, Connie turned to Dominic and apologized, "I'm sorry about that. He's just..."

"I know, I know…protective of his daughters," he said, finishing her sentence.

"But, that went good, don't ya think?"

Dominic looked at her with raised eyebrows. "Good? I thought your father was gonna pull a gun on me or somethin'! If that means it went good, then, yeah...I guess so," he agreed while mopping sweat from his forehead.

That evening, Angelina came into Connie's bedroom. It was only nine o'clock, but Connie had to open the store the next morning and decided to go to bed early. Philomena was sitting on the floor, in front of the mirror putting curlers in her hair. *"Philomena? Per favore, fammi stare solo con Conchetta,"* Angelina asked, wanting time alone with Connie.

"All right, Mama," she groaned. "What now?"

"Das enough Philomena," Angelina scolded. "You come back in a few minutes."

Connie smiled and shook her head. Philomena had been giving her a hard time about Dominic since she started dating him again. It used to hurt her feelings, now she just ignored her.

"What is it, Mama?" Connie asked. She sat up in bed, and propped a pillow behind her head.

Her mother eased herself onto the edge of the bed, and paused before speaking. "Conchetta? You tell me you and Dominic wan' to marry next month, why is dat? Why so fast?"

"I don't know Mama. Dominic just didn't want to wait, I guess."

"Um-hm, I see," she said, slowly. A look of worry darkened her eyes. "Connie? You not…uh…you…gon' have a baby?"

"Mama!" Connie was horrified. "No, no, no, Mama!" She said, shaking her head. "I'm still…you know…innocent."

"Molto buono," Angelina let out a sigh of relief, and nodded while patting Connie's arm. "I so sorry to ask dat, Connie but it jus' seem you in such a hurry…"

"Mama, Dominic just thought there was no need to wait, you know?"

"It was his idea?" Angelina asked.

"Well, sort of. I mean, I agreed, but yes he wants to marry me right away."

"Ah, Conchetta." Angelina took a deep breath. "You sleep now." She kissed Connie and tucked the blanket around her. "Philomena! You can come in now."

Philomena came into the room as her mother was walking out. She kissed her goodnight, and flopped on the bed next to Connie. She turned to face her. "So...what's goin' on this time? What was that all about, as if I didn't know? Hey, shutup out there!" Philomena yelled as Bettina, Maria and Lourdes found something hysterical in the hallway. "We're tryin' to talk here!"

The girls quieted and Connie started to explain. "Dominic and me," she said, hesitantly, "Ma and I were talking about Dominic and me."

"Oh, what a shock," Philomena scoffed.

"Come on Phil, let me talk." She took a breath and suddenly blurted, "We're getting married." She squeezed her eyes shut tight, anticipating an explosion.

Philomena's eyes grew wide. "Are you serious?"

"Uh-huh."

"Oh Connie, I think you're making a big mistake."

"I know you do." Connie eyes filled with tears.

"You don't look very happy."

"I'm happy," she said, hugging her pillow to her chest.

Philomena wasn't angry. She felt sorry for her sister. "Hey, listen Connie...don't cry. I don't wanna upset you. You do what you think is right, okay? Come here." She reached for her, and Connie fell into her arms.

Chapter 8

It was the fifth of September, two days before Connie would have started eleventh grade but she was instead about to walk down the aisle to marry Dominic Preste. For lack of time, she happily accepted Violet's offer to use her wedding gown, and all the girls pulled their bridesmaid's dresses from the closet. The emotion in the Borzanna house could only be described as subdued excitement. Philomena continued to mope, while Carmella, as usual giggled excitedly as they prepared for the wedding.

"Come on everybody...heaven's to Betsy, this is Connie's wedding day. Let's have fun," she urged. She was placing the last hairpin into Connie's mass of curls. "Connie, you look like a doll," she said, looking at Connie's image in the mirror. "Doesn't she look like a doll, Phil?"

"Yep, a real doll," she replied, absently.

"Well, I could never look as beautiful as Violet," Connie said. "But the dress does look nice, doesn't it?" She placed her hands on her tiny waist and inhaled.

"Well, look at you!" Violet said, coming in the room followed by Giordana and Maria. "Connie, you look beautiful. Lourdes sweetie, you missed a button," she observed, pointing toward the neckline of the dress. Lourdes placed a dainty, satin button through the buttonhole.

In between pleadings with Vincenzo to finish getting himself ready for the wedding, Angelina checked on the girls' progress. She fixed a special family breakfast earlier that morning, and presented Connie with a lace tablecloth she had actually been crocheting as a gift to Giordana for her wedding in the fall. She wrapped the tablecloth in tissue paper, tied it with a pink bow and handed it to Connie.

With tearful eyes, Connie gently ran her hand over the tiny stitches her mother had so diligently worked on for months. "Thank you Mama but when did you have time to do this?" she asked, as she gently lifted the folds of lace, marveling at the intricate pattern. "I certainly didn't give you much notice about the wedding."

"Just you never mind…I work on t'ings for all my girls, so enjoy, my Conchetta. I pray for you to have much happiness." She embraced Connie, and quickly left the room.

Vincenzo sat slumped in his chair, impatiently tapping his foot as the girls made last minute adjustments before leaving for the church. He looked grumpy and uncomfortable, dressed in his Sunday suit and blue tie. A white handkerchief was stuffed into his breast pocket under a white carnation Connie had slipped into his lapel. He was holding a match to the end of a cigar when Angelina entered the room, tucking a stray hair into a tightly wrapped bun.

She glanced at him and frowned. "Vincenzo…please, you look like you goin' to a funeral."

"Ach…" he grumbled.

Angelina stood at the bottom of the stairs and called, "Girls! Is time to go." She adjusted the belt of her blue flowered dress, and ran her hand over the white buttons that closed the front of the dress just above a hint of cleavage. Standing in front of an oval-shaped mirror on the wall of the living room, she studied her image as she placed a pillbox hat toward the back of her head, securing it with a pearl-tipped hatpin. A cluster of white carnations was strapped to her wrist. "Girls…" she called again.

"Coming!" they answered, and descended the stairs in single-file. They lined up in front of her. Angelina raised her eyebrows, smiled playfully, striking a pose with one foot in front of the other, and her hand behind her head.

"Ooh…you look beautiful, Mama," Carmella said.

Lourdes grinned, and clasped her hands together placing them under her chin. "Yes, look at you, Mama. My, my…pretty as a picture."

Angelina laughed. "Let me look at my girls." She walked back and forth, reveling in the beauty of her daughters. "*Ah, guarda come sono belle le nostre figlie,"* she said, grinning with pride. "Vincenzo, come see our girls!"

"Angelina, please...I am right here," he said, "no bellow at me."

"Sorry, Vincenzo..." she covered her mouth, looking embarrassed. The girls laughed. "Vincenzo, look at our daughters...*si, bellissime*?"

"*Si,"* he answered with a quick smile, and went back to his chair.

They heard the rustling of Connie's skirts as she slowly descended the stairs. She seemed to float toward them. The gown fit her perfectly, hugging her tiny waist, and the white satin accentuated her olive-colored skin. Her hair was swept up in a cluster of ringlets, with sprigs of "baby's breath" tucked in each curl.

"Doesn't she look beautiful, Mama?" Maria whispered.

"*Si*," Angelina said, pulling a handkerchief from the sleeve of her dress, dabbing her eyes. When Connie reached the bottom of the stairs, Angelina pulled her to her bosom. "Connie," she whispered. "You don' haf to do dis, you know?"

"Mama...but I want to marry Dominic," she said, emphatically. "He's changed. You'll see...you'll all see."

"All right, we go den." Angelina turned to Vincenzo, who was leaning against the front door. "Papa, we ready now."

"Andiamo." He gave Connie an affectionate smile, took her hand and led her out the door.

Angelina held hands with Lourdes and Bettina, and they, along with the other girls followed the bride and her father to the church.

*

Antonio and Sergio Preste looked dashing in their military uniforms and cordially ushered guests to their seats, while Vittorio, who was the best man stood at the altar next to Dominic. Antonio greeted Angelina, and offered his arm to her. She smiled and allowed him to lead her to a pew in the front of the church where she sat with Mr. Leone, Pasqual and a few close neighbors. She placed her purse on the seat next to her to make room for Vincenzo, and folded her hands in her lap. The swell of music coming from the pipe organ filled the church. Angelina was barely in control of her emotions. She nodded to well-wishers as she sat, appearing stoic, trying desperately to ignore the lump in her throat. She lifted her head and glanced toward the altar where her eyes met with

Dominic's eyes. His grin was triumphant, and Angelina wondered if she would ever rest easy again. She hated to admit it, but he looked strikingly handsome in a gray striped suit. He wore a six-button vest over a stiffly, starched white shirt, and a black necktie was neatly knotted under the collar. He was charismatic, with a smile that portrayed charm and arrogance that some mistook for confidence but Angelina knew better. She could see why Connie was attracted to him but there was evil hiding below the surface, and that's what frightened her.

Vincenzo waited at the back of the church, Connie holding tightly to his arm. He was about to hand his precious Conchetta over to a man he loathed but, Angelina had convinced him that Connie would probably run away and marry Dominic if they tried to stop her. Connie swore Dominic had changed, and with great trepidation, her parents agreed to the marriage.

The ceremony was as it should be, emotional and spiritual but lacking a certain joyful atmosphere. Upon meeting friends and family for the first time, Dominic charmed them. He was relaxed and attentive to Connie. She was enjoying her wedding day but was reserved and careful not to draw too much attention to herself. Dominic liked it better when she was quiet, and all she wanted was to make him happy and live a peaceful life.

There was a small reception in the Borzanna home, and Angelina had a variety of food beautifully displayed on the dining room table. Everyone ate and enjoyed Jimmy Dorsey songs blaring from the horn of the Victrola that sat on a table in the corner of the living room. The rug had been taken up and Dominic and Connie did what they did best, and danced every dance. He twirled her and dipped her, the skirt of her wedding dress twisting and flowing. It was as though their dancing was choreographed, and the guests cheered for more.

"Let's sit for a minute, Dominic," she said, breathlessly.

Dominic complied and followed her to the corner of the room where Angelina had lined up folding chairs she had borrowed from the church. He sat, took his handkerchief from his pocket and wiped his forehead. "Whew…you're dancin' pretty good there, girl," Dominic said.

"Thanks but I'm exhausted."

"Ya wanna sneak out?" he asked, with a sheepish grin.

"Sneak out? Ya think that's okay?"

Her question seemed to irritate him, and he flopped back in the chair. "Oh for God's sake, Connie. What're ya worried about?"

"Nothin', I just don't wanna be rude."

"It's not rude. We're supposed to sneak out. People expect that."

"Okay but...I should tell my parents we're going, don't ya think? I mean they really gave us a beautiful wedding, and I wanna thank them, ya know?"

"All right," he groaned. "Let's go tell them now, so we can go."

Angelina was in the kitchen washing wine glasses and Vincenzo was sitting on the back porch with some friends, smoking cigars and sipping Chianti.

Connie wrapped her arms around her mother, and gave her an affectionate squeeze. "Hi, Ma."

"Ah, Conchetta, you have a good time?" She turned and hugged Connie, and gave Dominic a pleasant smile.

"Could you get Papa, and ask him to come in for a minute? Dominic and I are going to leave and we wanted to talk to both of you."

Angelina opened the back door. *"Eh, Vincenzo...lei potrebbe entrare un munito?"*

Vincenzo got up, teetered a bit, and came in the door. He groaned when he saw Connie standing with Dominic by her side.

"Havin' a good time, Papa?" Connie asked.

"*Si, si*...I, uh, just talk a leetle wit' *i miei amici*."

Connie watched as her father rocked back and forth. He had obviously had too much wine. He held onto the edge of the kitchen table to steady himself.

Connie took Dominic's hand. "We both want to thank you for giving us such a beautiful wedding." She took a step forward and embraced her father and mother. A tiny sob sounded in the back of her throat.

"Don' you worry, just go and be happy," Angelina said, standing back, gently smoothing Connie's hair. "You be good to my Conchetta, you hear Dominic?" She wagged her finger at him.

"I will, and thanks Mr. Borzanna." Dominic extended his hand and Vincenzo took it, giving it a brief shake.

Vincenzo brushed past Dominic, and took Connie by the shoulders. He paused and looked intently into her eyes, and smiled. He took her cheek between two fingers and gave it a twist, cleared his throat and walked back outside.

Dominic followed Connie as she made her way around the room saying goodbye to her sisters, Dominic's brothers and the rest of the guests. They ran from the house laughing, and dodging handfuls of rice as they hopped into a car they borrowed from Vittorio. Connie's sisters had covered it with paper carnations, and a sign that read *Just Married* hung from the back bumper.

Connie was disappointed that they were not going on a honeymoon. But she understood that they didn't have the money, and that Dominic couldn't get off work.

"It was nice of Vittorio and Tessa to let us use their house," she said, when Dominic pulled up to the curb. She looked at the small bungalow with its peeling paint and dangling shutters. A rusted ringer washing machine was tossed in the alley on the side of the house. It wasn't much of a honeymoon destination but she didn't want to complain or sound ungrateful. "Where are they staying, anyway?"

"They went to Antonio's for a couple of days. Said we could stay as long as we want, though."

"When they come back, where are we gonna go, Dominic...are we looking for a place?"

"Connie, we have plenty of time. We'll find something. In the meantime, this'll be fine."

Connie agreed, not wanting to make him upset. "Yes, this is fine for now."

He found the key under the mat, put it in the lock and opened the door. Dominic flipped a light switch and a single overhead bulb lit up the room. It felt strange being there without Vittorio and Tessa being home, and Connie wasn't quite sure what to do. The rooms were small, sparsely furnished but clean and tidy. There was a two-cushioned, gray sofa trimmed with dark wood. It was placed under a double window that was draped with heavy maroon curtains that gave the room a gloomy feeling. A lace doily was placed over a torn spot on the sofa's arm. An antique, round-topped table with a tripod base sat in the corner of the room with a picture of Vittorio and Tessa sitting in the center. Tessa was holding a small bouquet of flowers, and both stared into the camera lens with somber expressions on their faces. Connie figured it must have been taken the day they got married.

Dominic took Connie's valise and placed it in the spare bedroom, then came back into the living room. She was still standing by the front door, her jacket buttoned over her wedding dress, and her purse draped over her shoulder. She felt shy and uncomfortable, and found it hard to make eye contact with Dominic. He was suddenly a stranger to her.

"I know this isn't much of a honeymoon, Connie but I have to work tomorrow. You know that, right?"

"I know Dominic, it's okay." She was distracted. She couldn't stop thinking about what was to happen that night. The wedding night… the sound of it made her shiver. She was still a virgin, and even though Dominic had tried many times to convince her that she was being stupid for not wanting to make love, he never forced her. She was curious but scared.

"Are you as tired as I am?" he asked, stretching and yawning.

"I am a little tired. It's been a long day."

"Why don't we just relax a little, before…well, you know…just relax a little." He took her by the hand and led her toward the bedroom he had been occupying for the past several months. Connie sat down on the edge of the bed and folded her hands in her lap.

"Hey, Connie, you know we'll only be staying with Vittorio for a little while, right?"

"I know."

"We're gonna get our own place as soon as I can save a little money."

"I know." Her body was tense. She looked up at him, and her lips quivered when she attempted a smile.

"Relax, will ya, Connie?" He said. "Take your shoes off…get comfortable. God, you act like you're scared to death. You're even shivering."

"I'm not scared," Connie said, defensively. "I'm just…resting a second." She slipped off her shoes, and put them neatly by the side of the bed. "Gosh, my feet *are* killing me." She leaned back, lifted her feet and wriggled her toes. Connie looked around the tiny room. Her attention was drawn to a small accordion sitting on the top of Dominic's dresser. "What's that?" she asked.

"What's what?" He looked toward the dresser. "Oh that. That's a concertina...was my father's," he said, quietly. He walked over to the dresser, put his hands on his hips and looked at the instrument for a few seconds. He reached out and caressed it before taking it in his hands, and then sat down next to Connie. He rested the concertina on his lap, and his obvious reverence for the instrument kept her from touching it.

"It's beautiful," she said, leaning forward to get a better look at the hand painted figures on the front of the miniature accordian.

He slipped his hand, ceremoniously through the frayed strap and placed his fingers on the wooden keys. "Ya wanna hear me play it?"

"Sure."

"My father used to play it all the time," he said, softly. His eyes turned warm as he spoke of his father, his smile wistful. He suddenly seemed to be in a place where *he* was the only one invited. He moved the bellows back and forth, his fingers moving over the keys creating an "oom-pa" sound along with a melody. He turned his head toward her as he played but was far away in his thoughts. The song ended.

"What was that song...it was beautiful," Connie asked.

"It's called *Gli Evviva Alla Sposa*...means cheers to the bride."

"Dominic..." she whispered, and placed her hand over her heart. "Did you play that 'specially for me?"

"Well...sure, okay." He had only at that moment realized the coincidence. He looked at her and nodded. "But it just happens to be the only song my father taught me. He used to play it at weddings... back in Italy."

"Oh..." She smiled with embarrassment. "Did he used to sing that to your mother?"

The rare softness of his expression suddenly turned ugly. He looked away, and without responding stood up and carried the concertina, placing it back on the dresser.

"Well anyway, that was wonderful, Dominic. You never told me you could play an instrument."

"Oh, it's just for fun...parties and things, you know."

"Well, I liked it."

Dominic took off his jacket and shirt and draped them over a chair in the corner of the room. He kept his trousers on and pulled his suspenders up over his undershirt. Connie watched him out of the corner of her eye as he placed her valise by the bedroom door. She smiled, remembering how her mother so carefully packed for her, folding her new white, cotton nightgown and bed jacket. Angelina had also packed a dress she had sewn for Connie. It was a form fitting rayon dress with black satin trim, and a delicate lace collar. She had made the dress especially for Connie's first day of marriage. She folded it and covered it with tissue paper, and placed it in the suitcase.

Connie smiled as she thought about the day before, and how her mother struggled to explain what she should expect on her wedding night.

"Are you going to bed in your wedding gown, Connie?" Dominic teased. "Why don't you get undressed, too? Come on. We'll lie down together, okay?"

"Okay, Dominic," she said, feeling awkward. "I'll get changed now. Where's the bathroom?" She was hoping he didn't hear the quiver in her voice as she spoke.

"Down the hall...don't you remember? You've been here before, Connie," he said. He pointed. "Right down the hall, see?"

"Oh yeah, that's right, I forgot." With her valise in her hand, she squeezed past him as he stood in the doorway, and she could smell the remains of his aftershave. She picked up her skirts and tiptoed down the hall. Once inside the bathroom, she shut the door, turned the lock and leaned against it, and stared at her image in the mirror. She stood at the sink and swiped at the dark circles under her eyes, and splashed cool water on her cheeks. She struggled with the buttons on the back of her dress but cringed at the thought of asking Dominic for help, so she sucked in her stomach and reached for the last three buttons and finally managed to undo them. She carefully lowered the dress, stepped out of it and hung it on a hook on the back of the bathroom door. She made a mental note to bring the dress back to her mother for proper storage, sure to be used again. She removed her slip but left on her bra and panties. She filled the sink with warm water and washed her hands and face and brushed the curls out of her hair. After taking off her underwear, she stood naked on the cold tile floor, and quickly slipped her nightgown over her head. She looked in the mirror again, shrugged, and walked barefoot back to the bedroom.

Dominic was lying in bed, on his side with his head propped up in his hand. He was waiting for her, and she blushed when she saw that he was bare-chested. *Did he take off his underpants too? I could just die!* She stood in the doorway as if waiting to be invited.

"Connie…come on, get in bed," he urged, looking at her hungrily.

She went to the opposite side of the bed and lifted the covers. She took a quick peek at his lower half and was happy to see that he had not yet removed his underwear. She lay on her back looking up at the ceiling, and stayed as far to the edge of the bed as she could without spilling off the side onto the floor. She pulled the covers up over her nose, her eyes peering over the top of the sheet.

"Come here Connie." Dominic patted the mattress next to him. "For God's sake, come over here by me." He extended his arm, inviting her to lay next to him, and she inched her way over, resting her head on his chest. He gently cradled her and she was beginning to feel more comfortable. They lay there in that position for a while, when Dominic leaned over to kiss her. His mouth felt moist and hot as it covered hers. He parted her lips with his tongue. He reached under her nightgown and skimmed his hand lightly over the soft skin of her belly, and she stiffened as he began to groan with pleasure. Cupping her tiny breasts in his hand, he ran his fingers over the hardness of her nipples. He tugged at her nightgown, pulling it above her waist, and stared at her body. He seemed hypnotized; his eyes were glazed and hungry. With his mouth open, he licked his lips and edged his body closer to hers, and Connie began to shiver. Dominic stopped. "Are you okay? What's the matter?" His voice sounded deep and raspy.

"I'm okay…I'm just a little nervous, I guess. I'm sorry, Dominic," she said, sounding like a child.

"Okay…well, just relax. I'll help you. There's nothing to be afraid of, Connie. I won't hurt you, you know that."

As hard as she tried to relax and clear her mind, she felt panicked. She wanted to be a good wife and didn't want to disappoint him, so she lay quietly and let him do what he needed to do. Her breath escaped with a grunt when the weight of his body rested on hers. She felt the hardness of him, feverish and throbbing, touching her legs, probing between her thighs. He pushed her legs apart with his hips, and when a sudden, searing pain gripped her, she let out a strangled cry. He thrust himself inside of her and she gritted her teeth, squeezed her eyes shut. She balled her hands into tight fists as his body rose and fell in frantic rhythm. He moved slowly at first, then fast and hard; a scream was trapped in the back of her throat. Her insides felt stabs of pain, and the dampness she felt, was sure to be blood. Guttural groans came from deep within his chest, and the primal sound of it frightened her. His motion, breathing, and moaning became more intense when suddenly, he whimpered like a child. She could see the whites of his eyes as his gaze rolled toward the ceiling. The weight of his body collapsed on top of hers, taking her breath away. *Oh God, please let it be over,* she prayed.

Dominic rolled his body off of hers and lay on his back, smiling and panting. Beads of sweat trickled down the sides of his temples. His bare chest glistened. "That was good, Connie…real good." He pursed his lips and let out a long breath of air.

Connie lay motionless but slowly turned her head toward him. "Uh-huh," was all she could mutter. There was a strange pulsing throb between her legs, and she felt wet and sticky.

"I'm some lover, ain't I Connie?" He asked, sounding proud.

Connie smiled and nodded.

"You could move a little more, though," he added. "You know what I mean?" He made a grinding motion with his hips. "But, hey listen, you'll get better. Don't worry, I'll teach you. By the time I'm done with you, you'll be like a whore in bed, right?" He laughed and pinched her playfully on the nipple.

She gasped and put her hand over her breast. She looked away when she felt tears filling her eyes.

Dominic lit up a Lucky Strike, and blew smoke rings as he lay back on his pillow. "How 'bout you make us somethin' to eat?" He snuffed out the cigarette in a tin ashtray. "Go see what Tessa's got in the icebox, okay, Mrs. Preste?" He winked and made a clicking sound with his mouth.

"Okay." She turned her back to him and sat on the edge of the bed and pulled her nightgown back down from where he had pulled it above her breasts.

Dominic stayed in bed, making no attempt to cover his nakedness. He was relaxed, lolling happily with his hands behind his head. His legs were crossed and his exhausted penis lay limply to one side. Connie thought it was the strangest thing she'd ever seen. She scurried barefoot into the kitchen to see what she could fix for him, and her legs quivered as she explored the tiny icebox. She groaned when she felt the twinge of a migraine starting in her temple. She found a ham, wrapped in brown paper, sliced it and simmered it in a cast iron skillet that she found in the stove. She broke two eggs into the pan and fried them along with the ham. The thought of eating sickened her, so she only made enough for Dominic. She looked in the cabinets and found a plate and some silverware in a drawer by the sink and placed them on the small kitchen table that was covered with a red and white checked oilcloth.

"Dominic…it's ready," she called.

"Comin'." Dominic sauntered into the kitchen stretching and yawning, and Connie was relieved to see that he had put his underwear back on. He looked at the table and seemed pleased with what she had prepared and ate hungrily, dipping pieces of ham into the egg yolk. "Not bad, Connie."

"Thanks." She sat across, with her chin in her hands and her elbows resting on the edge of the table. Her eyes were burning and felt puffy, and the migraine was now hammering at the top of her head.

"You're not eating?" Dominic asked, as he wiped egg yolk from his chin. "I was starved."

Connie picked up a napkin and handed it to him. "No, I'm not hungry. I'm really tired Dominic, do you mind if I go to bed now?" She was swallowing back nausea.

"After I eat, sure. Wait for me and I'll go with you."

"Okay." It was close to midnight, and she obediently waited for him to finish eating. She cleared his plates and washed them in the sink, and by one o'clock in the morning, she was finally back in bed. Dominic proceeded to have sex with her two more times. He finally fell asleep and Connie turned on her side, buried her face in her pillow and cried herself to sleep.

*

Connie woke before the sun came up, and quietly slipped out of bed and sat in a chair by a window that overlooked the alley at the back of the house. There was a row of rusty, dented, garbage cans surrounded by alley cats, and they were rummaging through scraps that had spilled out onto the ground. She sat for a while watching the cats, when she remembered that Dominic had asked her to wake him at six o'clock to get ready for work. She looked at the clock on the dresser and saw that she still had ten minutes, so she tiptoed into the kitchen where she filled a percolator with water and coffee. She fired up the stove, and after a few minutes, the coffee started to bubble into the glass dome of the pot, and the aroma of fresh coffee wafted throughout the house.

"Coffee smells good, Connie." Dominic came into the kitchen wearing green overalls, work boots, and a long-sleeved, undershirt. He was carrying his tool belt and after placing it on the floor by the table, he waited for his breakfast.

Connie placed a steamy bowl of oatmeal on the table in front of him. He sniffed at the oatmeal, drizzled it with milk and a spoonful of sugar. "So what are you gonna do today?"

"I dunno, maybe go visit Violet," she shrugged. "It feels kinda funny not going to work. I hope Mr. Leone makes out okay without me."

"Yeah, I been meanin' to talk to you 'bout that," he said, casually.

"About what?"

"No, nothin', we'll talk later." He finished eating, quickly downed the coffee, and gave Connie a peck on the forehead. He gathered up his tools and went out the door. Forgetting to ask whether to expect Vittorio and Tessa, Connie ran to the back door. "Dominic..." she called but he was already halfway down the block. She came back into the kitchen, washed the dishes and put everything back where she found it. She made the bed, took a quick bath, got dressed and decided to walk to her parents' house.

*

Connie found her mother home alone. She was in the kitchen and Connie called to her. "Mornin', Mama."

"Conchetta? Dat you?" Angelina's face showed concern and surprise. She was at the stove stirring a pot of polenta when Connie came in the room.

"Where is everyone?"

"Conchetta, I surprise to see you." Angelina turned, wiped her hands on her apron and greeted Connie with a kiss. "Nobody home, just me. Why you here, Conchetta? What has happened?"

"Nothing, Mama." Connie sat at the table and started to cry.

Her mother took her into her arms and cradled her, stroking her hair. "What is it, Connie? Tell you mama. Why you come home?" Angelina gently pushed Connie back and looked at her again. She sat in a chair across the table and waited for Connie to speak.

"Oh, Mama, it was horrible. I mean last night...you know what I mean?" She shuddered and a sob made her shoulders rise.

Angelina reached across the table and took Connie's hand. "What ees horrible? Did he hurt you?" She asked, looking confused.

"No, Ma...not exactly, I mean not on purpose." She wiped her nose and continued. "Well, this is hard for me to talk to *you* about, Mama but..." Connie looked down at the table. "Well, I...I didn't like it," she stammered. She looked up and whispered, "Making love."

"*Oh, per amor di Dio,*" Angelina couldn't help but smile.

"What I mean is...well, it hurt! There, I said it!"

"Oh, Conchetta."

"Dominic seemed happy but I was miserable. I didn't like it, Mama! What am I gonna do...I mean, I'm married now, and I didn't like him touching me! Is there something wrong with me?"

"Ah...my Conchetta," Angelina sighed heavily, and sat back in her chair. She thought before she spoke. "Is you first time, eh? Yes, you are married now, and it is...how you say... you duty, you know... " She struggled to find the right words. "Maybe you just scared. You scared, *bella?"* Angelina asked, searching Connie's face for answers.

"I don't know," she whined. "I'm so tired, Mama. I had to cook for him in the middle of the night and then..." she would rather die then tell her mother they had sex two more times. "Well, I'm just tired, that's all. And Dominic wants for us to live there with his brother and Tessa for a while. I don't want to live there with them," she cried harder, verging on a tantrum. "And I don't want to stay in that little room. I think Vittorio and Tessa will be coming home later today and...oh, Mama, what am I gonna do?" She buried her face in her hands. "What have I done?"

"Listen to you mama. Your place is wit' you husband but he did not tell the truth when he promise Papa dat he have a place for you to live." She sat quiet for a moment. "I gonna talk to Papa, and he will tell Dominic...you gonna stay home... here wit' us, and when you husband find a place for you to live...den you go be wit' him, eh? How would dat be?"

"Oh Mama, I don't know. I don't wanna make Dominic mad. I already told him it would be okay to stay with Vittorio and Tessa for a while."

"Don' you worry, *bella*...Papa will take care of everyt'ing." Angelina sent Connie upstairs to rest.

Vincenzo came home later that morning, and Angelina explained the situation, pleading with him to stay calm. "He hurt her?" He asked angrily, pushing back his chair as he stood up.

"No, Vincenzo...he no do not'ing. She's not happy living in dat leetle house with Dominic's brother and his wife, das all."

"They get married yesterday! Now she no wanna be married?"

"Oh yes, she wan' to be married," she quickly made clear. "She's jus' a leetle...scared."

"Too late now, Angelina."

"I know but you talk nice to him, eh? Tell him Connie stay wit' us till he find dem a home. Make him understand."

"Ha!" He scoffed. "He's a liar, dat Dominic! He tol' me he had a place for dem to live!"

"Vincenzo, please keep you voice down. Let's not upset Conchetta."

"He tol' me 'fore dey marry, he buy her a house, no? He promise me! He don' have nothin'! He's a bum!"

Angelina wrung her hands while Vincenzo vented his anger.

"I tell you what! *He* notta stayin' here!" He puffed up his chest and pointed at the floor. "Ah, no, no, no, just Conchetta, *capice*?"

"But Vincenzo, if she wan' him to stay here...he's her husband."

"I don' care! He don' give my daughter a place to live...I don' give *him* a place to live!"

Angelina threw her hands in the air, realizing he had made up his mind. She went back into the kitchen, sat at the table and prayed.

Later that morning, Vincenzo drove to a building site where several men he knew worked at Phillip's Construction. Some were standing at the opened end of a flatbed truck and some were sitting on the back of the truck sharing a laugh and finishing their cigarettes before starting work. Vincenzo parked his car and walked over to where he spotted his old friend, Alonzo.

"Eh, Vincenzo! *Como stai*? What are you doin' way out here?" Alonzo shouted when he spotted his old friend walking toward him.

"*Alonzo come stai? Lo sto bene.*" Vincenzo greeted his friend and reached out to shake his hand. "Eh, let me ask you somethin', Alonzo."

"Anything, Vincenzo. What can I help you with?"

"I look for the *stupido* husband of my daughter…Dominic Preste. He here?"

Alonzo laughed. "Stupid, you say. Well, I'm sorry my good friend… but he didn't come to work today. Told me he was gettin' married and took the day off."

"Zat so?" Vincenzo cocked his head. "Well, if he show up, I wan' you to tell him somethin' for me."

"Sure, what's that?"

"Tell him to come and see me if he wan' to see his wife again."

"I will do this for you, Vincenzo." Alonzo recognized Vincenzo's threatening mood. "Hey, Vincenzo…just so you know…the boy's a hard worker when he's here. Knows what he's doin'…smart…good with his hands."

Vincenzo nodded, shook his friend's hand and walked back to his car, and arrived home in time for lunch.

When Connie heard her father come in the door, she rushed downstairs. "Papa? Mama said you went to see Dominic. Did you see him? You didn't fight, did you?"

"I go to his work but, Dominic…he no work today."

"What?" Connie said, looking alarmed. "Well, what does that mean? Where do you think he is?"

"Conchetta, I don' know where he is, but I don' like what go on here. You just get married yesterday, for God's sake!" It was rare for Vincenzo to raise his voice.

"I know, I know…please, Papa, don't get upset," she pleaded. "Listen, Papa, thank you for trying…I'll be back. I have to go out now." Connie grabbed her sweater and headed for the front door.

Angelina called after her. "Conchetta, where you go? We eat first!"

Connie was already out the door. She walked several blocks back to Vittorio's house. The kitchen door was open, and she saw Tessa at the stove. Tessa turned when she heard a knock, and beamed when she saw Connie standing there.

"Conchetta! Ah...*ciao mia sorella*!" She said, greeting her new sister. She opened the screen door and held open her arms. "I so happy to look to you!"

"Thank you Tessa, you're very sweet." Connie sat down at the table and Tessa sat across from her, her expression turning to concern.

"Sometin' wrong, eh?" Tessa asked.

Connie paused, and leaned forward. "Tessa, have you seen Dominic? He left for work this morning but they said he wasn't there."

"No, I not see him, Conchetta. Oh, I so sorry...sometin' wrong, *si*?"

"Well, yes and no." She leaned against the back of the chair, shook her head and smiled. "I don't really know." Understanding Tessa's confusion, she simply requested, "Listen, if you see him, please tell him I'm staying with my parents, all right? *Mio mama e papa casa, capice?*" She repeated. "Would you do that for me?"

"*Si, si,* I tell heem. You stay here...wit' Vittorio and me, no? I like dat, Connie. Dominic no tell you dat? You stay here, *si*?"

"Yes he told me, Tessa but he said just for the weekend. He hasn't really told me much of anything else, and my father...well, he's kind of mad that Dominic doesn't really have a place for us to live. Our own place," she said, hoping Tessa understood. "You know what I mean? And it's so sweet of you to want us to stay here, but we're probably going to work something else out, all right?" Connie's eyebrows turned down with sadness when she looked at Tessa's disappointed expression.

"All right, Conchetta."

Connie stood up and put her arms around Tessa, kissing her on one cheek, then the other. "I have to go, Tess." She wanted to talk to her father again, and considering it was just past lunchtime, she knew he would be at D'Amo's Saloon. She was more angry than worried but if he wasn't working that day, then why wasn't he with her?

Half a block from D'Amo's Connie noticed a commotion in front of the bar. As she got closer, she could see some men trying to break up a fight. But many onlookers were cheering them on. She felt a sudden chill. Pushing her way through the crowd, she was horrified upon seeing her father straddling someone that was lying in a heap at his feet. She gasped when she recognized Dominic's green overalls. Her father's sleeves were rolled up, his hands balled into tight fists, and his knuckles bleeding. His chest heaved as he sucked air between gritted teeth. Sweat was running down the sides of his face. Two men were holding Vincenzo's shoulders but with a jerk, he pulled himself free.

Connie looked down at Dominic. Blood trickled from his nose, and a walnut-sized welt was swelling below his left eye. He was struggling to get to his feet, and Connie didn't know whether to help him up or to stand by her father.

"Papa, what happened? What did you do?"

Vincenzo jerked his head and glared at her. "What did *I* do?" he asked, indignantly. His face was red with rage. "Ask him what *he* do!" he growled. He pointed toward the ground where Dominic had temporarily given up trying to get to his feet. Only the upper part of his body was raised and resting on one elbow. "And let me say to you, my daughter! If you stay wit' dis, dis *padrone di puttana*...you are a fool, you hear me...a fool!" He stormed off in the direction of his car, flailing his arms, pushing people out of the way.

As the crowd disbursed and passed by her, some looked away, and some patted her sympathetically on the shoulder. She stood facing Dominic, who finally got to his feet, clinging to the side of the building.

"What did you do to my father?" She asked.

He looked at her, pulled a handkerchief from his pocket, and held it to his nose. He ran his fingers through his hair, flecked with dirt. "Leave me alone, Connie...ya hear me? Just leave me alone."

"No, I won't leave you alone, Dominic. I'm your wife and I have a right to know what you did to make my father so mad that he would want to beat you!"

Connie looked up when she heard the saloon's door opening. A girl, with platinum hair looked down at Dominic. Her breasts spilled over the top of her red floral dress, and with one hand placed jauntily on her hip asked, "You all right Dom, baby?" A dimple dented her cheek as she vigorously chewed a wad of gum. "Ha," she laughed in a gutteral cackle. "Dat wittle, bad man beat the shit outta you, baby?" She shrieked with laughter. "What did ya do, sleep with his wife, or somethin'?"

"Go to hell, Dottie!"

"Hey, watch it, buster!" She threatened, suddenly sounding tough. "Don't talk to me like that! Whatd'ya think I am, anyhow?" She waited for him to respond. "Well, ya comin' back in or what? Your beer's getting' warm." She shifted her gaze toward Connie. "Who da hell is that?"

"None of your business! And I said shut-up, Dottie, just shut-up!" He waved his hand at her and moaned, the movement seeming to cause him pain.

"Well, to hell with you!" She straightened her back, stamped her foot and slammed the door. Connie could still hear her yelling, "That's a helluva way to talk to a lady!"

"Well, I think I know what you were doing." Connie said, her face red with rage. "You couldn't even make it one day being married without cheating on me. That's nice. That's real nice, Dominic. Well, I'm glad my father hit you! He should have killed you! I hate you, I hate you!" She turned and ran down the street, leaving Dominic slumped over and bleeding.

"Connie...wait! Let's talk..."

Chapter 9

A month had passed, and Connie was back in her old room in her parent's house. Her feelings for Dominic had turned to regret and embarrassment, and she felt bad for the upset she had caused her family. Her father never spoke of that day, and there was an uncomfortable avoidance of eye contact between her and her father for quite some time. One day though, Vincenzo simply patted Connie on the back as she helped her mother in the kitchen, and she knew everything would be all right.

"Mama?"

"Yes, Conchetta."

"I'm thinking about going back to work at the bakery. I'm sure Mr. Leone will have me, don't you think?"

"I t'ink dat sounds like a good idea, Conchetta." Angelina was delighted to see her daughter smiling again. It had been a long time. "You go to see Mr. Leone today?"

"I think I will. Do you think Papa will drive me over there? It's a little chilly and I think it's going to rain."

"Sure, you go ask." She kissed Connie's forehead and gave her a motherly tap on the bottom.

*

Connie did go back to work, and she worked as much as Mr. Leone needed her and even begged for more hours. She was beginning to feel happy and content again. She liked being alone in the back of the store surrounded by the supplies of her work, the heat of the oven and the aroma of her baked goods. When she wasn't working, she spent time with her sisters. Life was simple again; just the way she liked it, going to the park and sitting by the pond roasting potatoes on an open fire, or eating watermelon and laughing at corny jokes. She was comfortable and safe. This was where she belonged, in Wickhaven, with her family.

*

It was a Tuesday morning and Connie asked her mother to please send Lourdes over to the bakery to tell Mr. Leone she was sorry but she wouldn't be able to work that day.

"Connie, what's a matter, you sick?" Angelina came into the room and sat on the side of the bed where Connie lay holding her stomach. Angelina placed her cool hand on Connie's cheek.

"I don't know, Mama, I feel like I'm going to throw up." Beads of sweat had formed on her forehead and her face was ashen.

Angelina went to get some castor oil, and Connie lay in bed, clutching her knees to her chest. Her mother came back with a large brown bottle and a tablespoon and told Connie to hold her nose and open her mouth. When the medicine trickled down Connie's throat, she scrunched up her face in a grimace and swallowed with a loud gulp.

"There, dat should make you feel better." Angelina recapped the bottle and placed it on the table by Connie's bed. She placed her lips to Connie's forehead and Connie started to moan.

"Uh-oh." She kicked off the covers, leapt out of bed and ran to the bathroom at the end of the hall and threw up. Her mother scurried after her and applied pressure to Connie's head as she threw up again. When Connie assured her mother she was finished, Angelina got her settled back into bed, washed her face and placed the basin on the floor beside the bed. Connie continued to throw up for another two hours, and finally fell asleep, waking later that afternoon, feeling fine.

When the same thing happened each morning for the next four days, Angelina sat on the side of the bed, and looked at Connie with concern. "Connie, when is the last time you had you monthly?"

Connie looked surprised by the question. "What?"

"You know, you time of da month," she repeated.

"I remember finishing right before the wedding, why?"

Angelina took a deep breath and said softly, "I t'ink you gonna have a baby."

*

Connie paused before she approached the front door of Vittorio and Tessa's house, and took a deep breath before knocking at the door. "Hello Tessa," she said, when Tessa opened the door.

"Conchetta!" Tessa clapped her hands with delight when she saw Connie standing on the stoop. "Oh Connie, how you been?" She embraced her, and pulled her into the house.

"I'm fine." Connie noticed that Tessa was wearing the same black dress she wore the last time she saw her. Her hair was loosely pulled back in a bun, but most of it was hanging in strings on the sides of her face. She looked tired. They sat together on the sofa. "Are you all right, Tessa?" Connie asked, gently lifting a strand of Tessa's hair away from her face.

"I okay."

"You look tired."

"Oh…yes, I a leetle tired. I cook and do wash, you know…in the cellar. Vittorio...he like me to use da stove down in da cellar." She laughed but Connie had the feeling it was more than that. "How are you, Connie? You look-a so skeeny! You sick?"

"Sort of," Connie said, with a faint smile. She glanced toward the hallway. "Tessa, is Dominic here?"

"*Si,* he ees here," she said. "You wan' to see him?"

"Yes, I do."

Tessa got up and started for the hall. "I get him for you."

"Thank you, Tessa." Connie leaned up against the back of the sofa and looked around the room. She placed her hands on her belly and smiled. She had mixed emotions since finding out she was going to have a baby, and didn't have a clue as to how Dominic would react. She thought about it, long and hard and decided he had a right to know but also realized, quite some time ago that she didn't know him at all.

Her father was going to be upset with her for telling Dominic but she had to do what was right.

"Connie," Dominic said, surprised to see her. "What are you *doing* here?" He stood in the doorway of the living room. His hair was still damp from a bath and he wore black trousers and a red flannel shirt that he was still in the process of buttoning.

"Hello Dominic, how are you?" Her voice sounded soft and steady.

"I'm all right…I guess." He looked puzzled.

"I need to talk to you about something," she said, feeling a pang of anxiety tickle her stomach.

Dominic didn't move from where he was standing and continued to stare at her.

"Come…sit down, Dominic." She patted the seat next to her.

He hesitated, then slowly walked over to the sofa and sat by her side. "What is it?"

"I'm not sure what you're gonna say, but…I, uh…I'm gonna to have a baby," she finally said.

Dominic turned his body toward her, his jaw dropping. He was visibly shaken. Connie stared back and breathed a sigh of relief when she saw a grin suddenly spread across his face. "Connie," he spoke almost reverently. She had never heard him say her name like that before. "I don't believe it!" He looked from her eyes to her stomach, then back to her eyes again. "Are you sure?"

"Yes, I'm sure. It's only been a few weeks but Dr. Ingram said it's for sure."

"It's mine, right?" He asked, stupidly.

Connie's head jerked, she blinked and let out a breath of air. "Oh my God, Dominic!"

"I didn't mean that, I didn't mean that…" he said, quickly.

"God, I hope not or you don't know me at all."

"I know you…I just…just forget I said that, okay?"

"Well…" her voice softened and she looked down at her lap. "It happened that first night. Our wedding night," she added.

"God, I can't believe it. I'm so proud, Connie. I'm gonna be a father." He looked away from her and shook his head. "How 'bout that?" He whispered.

"Well, I'm glad you're happy, Dominic. I felt you had a right to know."

"A right to know?" He asked, looking back at her. "I am the father!"

"Of course, Dominic but the way things have been…I wasn't sure what to do, ya know, 'bout you and me…"

"Well, this changes everything." He stood up and started pacing in front of her.

"What'dya mean?"

"Well, we're gonna go back together, that's what I mean."

"You really want that?"

"Don't you?" He asked, with surprise.

"Well, yeah. I mean, I want our baby to have both of us but…"

"Well okay then." Dominic sat down again. "Can I…touch…?"

"Yes," she said, allowing him to put his hand on her still flat belly.

He seemed in awe and slowly withdrew his hand and leaned back on the sofa. "Listen, Connie. About that day…with your father…it wasn't what you think or what your father thought…"

"Dominic," she interrupted and placed her finger to his lips to quiet him. "I don't want to know but I'll tell you one thing…I'll never forget how you hurt me."

With his arm over the back of the sofa, he looked out the window as she spoke.

"I forgive you, Dominic. I have to forgive you if we're getting back together for the baby's sake but Dominic, I can't live in that little room with you and a baby. I need for us to have our own place."

"I know," he said. "Hey, listen, why don't you go and stay with your family until I can figure things out. I'll find us a place."

Connie's expression turned optimistic. "Really?"

"Sure…" Dominic suddenly looked concerned. "Wait a minute, Connie. What about your father? He wanted to kill me, and I don't think he'd ever agree to us getting back together."

"Dominic, I'm going to have a baby. He'll understand that we want to try and make this work. His honor is at stake here, too. How would it look, his daughter living at home with a belly as big as a house, ready to have a baby and no husband?"

"Right." He nodded as he pondered the thought. "All right, well, that's settled," he said, slapping his hands on his knees before standing up. "I'll start looking for a place tomorrow. You'll handle your father, right?"

She nodded and moved forward to the edge of the sofa. "Well, I'd better be going."

"Okay." He stood up, took her by the hand and helped her to her feet, then followed her to the front door. "Hey...good to see ya," he said, sounding awkward. "And thanks for tellin' me about the baby," he added.

Connie smiled and stepped out the front door and turned to look at him. "Are you still working at the same place?"

"No, I got fired. My boss, it turns out, is a friend of your father's, so..."

"Oh, that's right." Connie winced. "Too bad."

"S'okay...I'm talkin' to a guy tomorrow who's the big boss with Tacoma Construction, and it looks pretty good that I'll get the job. My brother Antonio dates the guy's daughter...you know how that works. It's not what you know, it's who you know."

"Yeah, I guess so. Well, that sounds good. I hope you get it," she hesitated, and asked. "Good money?"

"Not bad."

"Okay. Why don't you stop by the house and we'll talk more."

"Are you sure?" He looked at her skeptically.

"I'll fix things with my father," she said, understanding his concern.

Dominic raised his hand to say goodbye, then closed the door.

Connie walked home, and later that evening, broke the news to her parents that she told Dominic about the baby, and that she and Dominic were getting back together. Vincenzo promptly but quietly, got up and left the room.

Connie and her mother watched him leave, and turning to her mother, Connie shrugged. Angelina took her daughter's hand and said, "He be okay, Conchetta. I talk to him, don' you worry but are you sure you do da right t'ing?"

"No, I'm not sure, Mama but I don't want to raise this baby alone. I want a nice family...like Violet, and a happy family like we have here."

"I see." Angelina looked sympathetic. "I pray for you, Conchetta."

*

In the following weeks, Dominic slowly eased his way back into the Borzanna house for brief visits to check on Connie but unfortunately, still did not have enough money to get them a place to live. Vincenzo usually got angry and went to D'Amo's the nights he knew Dominic was going to visit Connie, and the guilt and stress resulted in a painful, itchy rash on Connie's neck and stomach. Her mother sponged her in cornstarch baths and rubbed her with homemade remedies but not until Vincenzo agreed to curb his anger did the rash go away.

Connie finally had a ray of hope when Dominic told her he had gotten the job he wanted with Tacoma Construction Company, and that he was saving money while he lived with his brother. That pleased her. Even with winter setting in, work was plentiful because Tacoma Construction was involved with the development of some large office buildings in Uniontown.

One evening, as the Borzanna family gathered together to decorate for the coming Christmas holiday, Angelina managed to get everyone to the table for dinner. Lourdes heard a knock at the door and finding Dominic standing there, she looked back toward her father, who was seated at the table. She reluctantly invited him into the house. He had just finished work and before going home to change, decided to stop by Connie's to give her some news. He wore a fleece-lined jacket over his flannel shirt and overalls, and he wiped the bottoms of his work boots on a mat before stepping over the threshold. A knit cap was pulled down over his ears. His face was red, and with lips that seemed paralyzed from the cold, he mumbled hello. He rushed toward the fireplace where an inviting fire crackled. He took off his gloves and was rubbing his hands together near the flames when Connie turned and saw him.

"Dominic! I didn't know you were here." She gave her father a quick glance, her eyes pleading with him to behave.

"Oh yeah, I hope that's okay." Dominic gulped when he saw everyone at the table. He wasn't expecting to see all of them together and now he was embarrassed as they stared at him. "I just have some news...but it can wait. I'll come back another time." He started slipping his hands back into his gloves.

Connie got up and went to him. "No, no, don't be silly. Come, sit," she said, pulling a chair out for him. We're all glad to have you, right everyone?" Connie asked, giving her family an encouraging look. They responded with a collective grumble.

Angelina handed Dominic a plate. "*Venire, ha qualcosa per mangiare,*" Angelina said, inviting him to eat.

He smiled and thanked her, helping himself to a plateful of ravioli and meatballs. Philomena eyed him coldly but Vincenzo surprised everyone by offering him a glass of wine. He was being cordial for his daughter's sake and Connie almost cried at the gesture.

"So, what's the news?" Connie asked.

"Oh, yeah." Dominic swallowed a mouthful of bread. He took a swig of wine to wash it down, and Connie pulled her chair closer to his.

"Come on, Dominic, what is it?" She asked again.

"Well, you know I'm doin' really good at work. I mean, I'm learnin' a lot and I'm really good with my hands." He looked around the table, then back at Connie. "And my boss… Mr. Shisler? Well, he said I may even be able to get into the union soon."

"The union! Oh my…that's great, Dominic." Connie said, giving him a conciliatory pat on the back. Tension was still dominating the room but she noticed her family seemed interested in what he had to say.

"That's not all. They have this big…and I mean huge, construction job starting in Cleveland Heights, Ohio and Mr. Shisler wants to put me as foreman on the job! It pays almost double what I'm makin' now," he added, with a proud grin. "And Connie…they're gonna give me ten dollars a month toward the rent on an apartment there! And that's besides my pay!" The *ching* of silverware abruptly quieted.

"Cleveland Heights, Ohio?" Connie said slowly. "Gosh, I don't know, Dominic. That's so far from Wickhaven."

"Yeah, but it's a good thing, Connie. A good job, with good money, and I can take care of you and the baby proper, you know?"

Angelina dabbed at the sweat that had suddenly appeared on her upper lip. She glanced at Vincenzo who was staring at his plate. Connie saw that Dominic was disappointed with everyone's reaction, so she spoke quickly. "Well, that's great, Dominic. I'm very proud of you."

She flashed her mother a desperate look, and Angelina said, "Das very good, Dominic, very good. You been workin' hard, we know dat. I guess we knew one day Conchetta would move away."

"Ebry-body!" Vincenzo said, his voice bold and firm. "Is time for you to go." His command resounded like a clap of thunder.

The girls looked at each other and without protest, got up from their seats and carried their plates into the kitchen.

"Violet, you go home to you husband and child! Philomena… Lourdes, you go help you mama in da kitchen! The rest of you girls… go to you room!"

"But, Papa…" Maria pleaded.

"I said, go to you room."

"Yes, Papa." Carmella took Maria by the hand and the two girls climbed the stairs. "He talks to us like we're little children," Maria complained. Carmella batted at the hem of her sister's skirt as she walked behind her up the stairs.

"Conchetta and *Signor Preste*, you stay here."

The room was empty but for Vincenzo, Dominic and Connie. Vincenzo sat for a few minutes with his elbows on the table, his hands folded. "Dominic?" He said, without looking up.

"Yes sir?"

"Don' speak!" Vincenzo commanded, slamming his fist on the table, making the remaining glasses teeter.

Dominic jumped, closed his mouth, and sat up straight in his chair.

"You hurt my daughter, and amma show you what I can do to you, eh? Let me say dis to you, Meester Preste. You hurt my daughter again, I won't hurt you…I will kill you. You hear my words, Meester Preste?" Vincenzo cocked his head to one side and with eyes dark like the color of steel, glared at Dominic. His eyes were slits, and his mouth was turned down in a menacing snarl.

Dominic lowered his eyes and nodded in silence.

"You take Conchetta away from her family…das okay. She is you wife and is her duty to be by you side but you…you treat her like a saint, you hear me?" He pointed a gnarled finger at him. "Because if you don'…she's comin' home with her mama and me, and God help you…"

"I will, Mr. Borzanna. I'll treat her good, I promise."

Vincenzo snorted in response and nodded his head one time, signifying that the conversation was over. Then with a wave of his hand, he ordered them to leave the table. Connie went behind her father and kissed him on top of the head. He glanced up at her with sad eyes and shook his finger at her.

"Thank you, Papa," she said, and took Dominic by the hand, leading him toward the kitchen.

"We're going now, Mama," Connie said.

"Where you go?" Angelina asked, looking concerned.

"Oh well, ha…that's a good question," she laughed, looking at Dominic. "I guess I'm going home with Dominic. That's what you wanted to do, right Dominic?"

"Yeah, that would be great…if you want to, and if it's okay with your parents. You come home with me and we'll talk about the move and all…you know," he added, nervously.

"We do have a lot to talk about, Mama. Thanks for everything. I'll stop by tomorrow and we'll talk more, okay?" Connie kissed her mother and ran up to her room to grab a suitcase from under her bed. Her sisters stood silently in the bedroom looking confused. Carmella helped Connie pull clothes from the dresser and closet, and threw them into a suitcase.

"For the life of me, I can't understand why you're doin' this, Connie," Philomena said. She was sitting on the edge of the bed, folding Connie's nightgowns and underwear.

"I'm going to have a baby, Phil." Connie grabbed hair curlers, a brush and a tube of lipstick and threw them in with her clothes. Philomena and Maria closed the lid and sat on it while Connie and Giordana snapped it shut. "I love you all…I really do," Connie quickly said. Running down the stairs, she saw Dominic waiting for her by the front door, already bundled in his cap and coat. He helped her with her coat, wrapped a scarf around her neck, and rushed out the door.

Vincenzo sat in his chair. Angelina stood next to him. "What da hell we gonna do, Angelina?"

Chapter 10

It was 1943, and Connie was in the sixth month of her pregnancy. The winter had been particularly cold that year, and Connie was constantly wrapped in heavy sweaters and layers of socks. Vittorio was a bit stingy about putting extra coal in the furnace and the house stayed cold enough to see your breath in a cloud of vapor. She and Dominic loaded his old Studebaker with their belongings, along with gifts for the baby from her mother, and a fistful of dollar bills from her father.

Angelina had invited the entire family to dinner the previous Sunday to say their goodbyes, and she also invited Vittorio and Tessa. The dinner was wonderful as usual, and the atmosphere was relaxed and festive until it was time for Connie to leave. It was the longest "goodbye" in history, Dominic complained. Connie started with one sister, hugging and kissing until she got to the last sister, then started back at the beginning again. She had never been so overwhelmed with sadness in her life and didn't know how she was going to be able to live without seeing them and her parents whenever she wanted. She also felt guilty about leaving Mr. Leone at the bakery but he was very understanding when she explained. She would miss him *and* her job. She was hoping that maybe one day, she could open her own bakery, but that dream seemed out of reach, now.

Connie's father pulled her aside to tell her once again, that if she ever needed to come home, he would take care of her and the baby. She fell into his arms and held him tightly until he gently pushed her away.

"Is time to go, Conchetta. Go…we see you soon. Don' you worry, you Papa is here for you, eh?" He turned his back, and Connie knew he was choking back tears. It was the hardest thing she ever had to do; leave while seeing her family huddled together and weeping as they watched her and Dominic walk out the door.

*

Connie went to bed early on Sunday evening while Dominic sat in the kitchen with Vittorio discussing the prospect of him and Tessa moving to Ohio too. Sleep did not come easy to Connie that night, and it didn't help that she was suffering from terrible heartburn. By four o'clock in the morning, she couldn't stay in bed any longer, and she took it upon herself to wake Dominic. They decided to head out earlier than planned.

"Connie, did you pack some food for the car?" Dominic asked as he drove toward the outskirts of Wickhaven. He was fooling with the dials on the dashboard, trying to get some heat.

"Yes, I have cookies, crackers and some cheese. I have a bottle of fresh milk too. Is that okay for you, Dominic?"

"Yeah, that's good." They had left the house without waking Vittorio and Tessa since they said goodbye the night before. It was still dark, and the frigid morning air stung Connie's nose and lips. Billowing puffs of steam came from her mouth as she blew her warm breath on her hands. Tessa had placed a blanket in the backseat, and Connie gratefully wrapped it around her legs, and pulled it up tight under her nose. She felt her eyes go heavy as the car's motor droned, and by the time they approached the outskirts of her beloved Wickhaven, she had already drifted off to sleep.

"Hey…Connie! Wake up!" Dominic said, jabbing her in the arm.

"Wha…what's the matter?" Connie woke with a start.

"I don't want you to sleep when I'm driving, you hear me? Get me something to eat, will ya? Some crackers and cheese."

"Okay." She was fighting to stay awake, and stifled a yawn. She broke off a few chunks of cheese and placed them on top of the crackers. She held everything in the palm of her hand while Dominic ate, and when Connie offered to prepare some more, he held up his hand.

"That's enough but I'll take a sip of that milk."

She peeled the cap from the bottle and handed it to him. He put it to his lips, taking several swallows, then handed the bottle back to her. He wiped his mouth with the back of his hand and slipped it back into his glove.

"Feel better, Mister Cranky?" Connie teased.

"I'm fine, why? Watta ya mean, cranky?"

"No nothing Dominic, I was kidding. I was just asking if you felt better since you ate, that's all."

"Don't smart mouth me, Connie," Dominic threatened, and without warning, raised his arm and slammed the back of his hand into her jaw.

She gasped. Her hand flew to the side of her face, and her eyes were wide with shock.

"Dominic!" His name sprang from her lips in a garble. "What did you do that for?" She asked, rubbing at the sting in her jaw.

"Don't mock me, Connie. I told you that before. Don't ever mock me!"

"Mock you! What are you…?"

He reached over and covered her mouth with his hand. He was pressing with such force that her teeth cut into her lip. "You gonna shut up…huh? Are ya?"

She nodded. Her eyes strained to look at him. He removed his hand from her mouth, and then placed both hands back on the steering wheel.

Connie sat, resting her head on the back of the seat, staring out the window as she quietly wept. Her head was throbbing, her hands tightly squeezed together under the blanket.

They drove for a long time in silence and Dominic took occasional glances in her direction as she continued to stare out the window.

"You awake?" He asked, casually.

"Mm-hmm."

"What are you so quiet about?"

Forcing herself to look at him, she dared to speak. She couldn't believe he was asking her why she was quiet. "Dominic, you promised you weren't going to hit me anymore. You promised my father. I try never to do anything to make you mad but you still hit me."

"Ha! Your father," he scoffed. "He thinks he's so tough. You're my *wife* now, not *his* daughter. I don't like being put down, Connie. It makes me mad and I told you never to do that, didn't I? My mother used to do that to my father, and I swore no wife of mine would ever do that to me."

"If I don't know that I'm doing that, then how am I supposed to know?" Connie asked, defensively.

"Just don't put me down, that's all. I'm the boss and you don't put me down."

"All right, Dominic." Out of frustration, Connie decided to drop the subject. "Let's just forget it...I don't like fighting with you." She turned her face toward the window again and remained silent for several miles.

"I'm kinda stiffening up here, Connie. Rub the back of my neck, would ya?"

*

Feeling nauseous for most of the trip, Connie thought they would never reach Cleveland. Her fingers and toes were numb from the cold, and when they finally saw signs for Cleveland Heights, she referred to the directions that Dominic had gotten from his boss. They were looking for Cedar Road, where the Cedar Glen Apartments were located, and after making a few wrong turns, they happened to turn onto the street where the apartment building suddenly appeared before them.

The Cedar Glen Apartments was an old, but stately eight-story building with a crisscross pattern in its brickwork, and there were tall windows framed with wood. Cedar Road was a main thoroughfare littered with parked cars, and Dominic carefully maneuvered his car as he looked for an open space. Children, dressed in bulky snowsuits and woolen mufflers wrapped around their heads, darted between parked cars and screamed as they pelted each other with snowballs they had made from the leftover snow that had been plowed in a pile by the curb.

Dominic parked half a block from the apartment building, and told Connie to wait while he made sure they were at the right place. She nodded and gathered the blanket up around her neck. She looked up and down the street and noticed a small grocery store at the end of the block with a bank next-door and what looked to be streetcar tracks at the top of the hill. A furniture store, called Stern Brothers, was across the street and she was admiring a green velvet sofa in the display window when a little girl ran by the car with a snowball clutched in her mittened hand. A boy was running ahead of her. She peered in the window and smiled, and Connie raised her hand and smiled back.

Connie grunted when she shifted in the seat. She was suddenly aware of her aching back and throbbing jaw. She rested her head on the back of the seat and closed her eyes, and was just beginning to doze when Dominic opened the car door. "This is the place. Come on in, Connie, the landlord has some papers for us to sign."

They cautiously climbed the ice-covered steps and entered the front doors of the building where two women sat at the base of a stairway just inside the door. They were warming their feet and rubbing their hands together by a vent in the floor. Looking up when Connie and Dominic entered the building, the two women stopped talking. One of them wore a wool-pleated skirt, a brown sweater and rubber boots with fur at the top. Her hair was cut in the new bobbed style that all the girls were wearing, and Connie thought she was pretty. The girl returned Connie's smile. The other was painfully thin, with a pale complexion, and heavily rouged cheeks. Her cherry red lipstick looked grotesque and overdone. She wore a sweater unbuttoned enough to reveal cleavage, and sat with her legs splayed in front of her, her skirt tucked between her knees.

"Hi there, movin' in?" The skinny one asked.

"Yes." Connie smiled pleasantly, excused herself, and stepped over the woman's legs.

"Welcome to skid row." The skinny woman spoke again, laughing.

The other woman gave her a shove. "She's just kidding. It's not so bad here." She reached up and thrust her hand toward Connie. "Clara Keesport. This here's Dixie Tarkington."

"Hello, my name's Connie…this is Dominic."

"Howdy-do," Dixie said, reaching for Connie's hand but keeping her eyes on Dominic. She looked back at Connie again, focusing on the bulge under her coat. "Looks like ya got a little bun in the oven," she said, and clicked out of the side of her mouth.

"Oh Dixie, the things you say." Clara poked her friend again.

Connie smiled and rubbed her hand over her belly. "Just a few months to go."

Dixie leaned back, resting her elbows on the step behind her. The position made her breasts point toward the ceiling. "That's just what we need around here; another kid running up and down the halls."

"Dixie...for God's sake," Clara scolded.

"I'm just foolin'," Dixie laughed. "Well, hope ya don't freeze to death. The ol' girl's a little lax on the heat here." She took her thumb and gestured toward a door labeled with brass letters that read *OFFICE.* "That's her place, right there."

Dominic smiled and took Connie by the arm. "Thanks. Nice to meet ya."

"Likewise, I'm sure." Dixie said, and lit up a cigarette. Clara stood up and smoothed her skirt and started up the stairs. "Talk to ya later, Dix...gotta go feed my ol' man."

The aroma of cooking wafted through the halls, and Connie's stomach growled, reminding her that she had not eaten since the night before. Dominic knocked at the door of the office, and a voice called for them to come inside. They entered a living room crowded with antique furniture and vases of various colored glass. An elderly woman hobbled into the room leaning on a wooden cane. She was heavy, with thick ankles and feet that swelled over the top of her carpet slippers. The sleeves of her faded housedress barely covered flabby arms that swayed like wings as she made her way across the room. When she reached the door, she placed both hands on her cane to steady herself. "Well, well, well," she said, panting heavily. "You must be the Prestes. How'd ja do?"

"Hello, Maam," Connie said shyly.

"Well aren't you the cutest little thing?" She reached out a puffy hand and caressed Connie's cheek. "I'm Mrs. Lanin, and this is my buildin' and I'm the landlord too, so if you need anything, it'll be me ya come ta." She stopped to catch her breath. "Mr. Shisler called me and said you'd be arriving any day now. And look! Here you are." She smiled at Connie again. "Aw, you must be awfully tired, you poor dears. Can I get you something?" She took Connie by the hand and led her to a sofa by the front window. "Here, child, you sit down right here, you look exhausted." Connie sat and Mrs. Lanin slowly labored to a chair next to the sofa. It creaked loudly as she squeezed her sizable backside between the arms. She crossed her ankles and wiped sweat from her forehead. "Now, Mr. Preste," she said, looking at Dominic, "I'm puttin' the two of you in apartment 7A. It's all the way in the back of the building, but the good thing is it's on this floor. No steps for Mrs. Preste…no, no, no. Not in her condition." She reached back, smoothed her gray hair and tugged at the polka-dotted scarf that was knotted around her ponytail.

"No steps," Connie said, looking at Dominic with a grateful grin. "Thank you for that, Mrs. Lanin."

"Mr. Preste, I'll tell ya what. Why don't you take this key and go down the hall and take a look at the apartment while I get your little wife something to drink." She reached into her pocket, retrieved a key and handed it to him.

"Thanks," he said politely, and took the key from her. He walked into the hall. Mrs. Lanin struggled to raise herself from her chair and started toward the kitchen.

"I don't want you to go to any trouble, Mrs. Lanin," Connie said, noticing how difficult it was for the woman to move around.

"You want something hot to drink, or cold, my dear?" Mrs. Lanin asked, obviously not hearing what Connie said.

"Hot would be wonderful, if it won't be too much trouble."

"I've had this buildin' for twenty-three years," she shouted from the other room. "My late husband, Calvin…everybody called him Cal… he left it to me when he passed on, bless his heart, and I'm happy to say I ain't never had a tenant I didn't like. They're all like my children, ya know what I mean?" When Connie saw Mrs. Lanin coming back into the living room juggling a mug of something hot, along with her cane, Connie jumped to her feet and took the cup from her.

"Thank you, dear. I have a little trouble getting around as you can see. Damned legs. Used to be pretty decent lookin' gams, if I do say so myself," she laughed.

"Well, you seem to get around just fine." Connie sat back on the sofa and wrapped her hands around the warm mug and sipped the chocolaty foam from the top. "Mmm, that's really good."

"Good girl. Now you drink that down. Ah looky here, your hubby's back already. So, what'dya think…apartment okay?"

"It's fine," he said.

"Well then, how 'bout you two getting settled. I'll have my son, Hubie help you bring your things in. He's up in 4B fixin' a toilet right now. I'll send him to your place when he gets here. All right? All right." She stayed in her chair and waved her arm. "Scoot, you two! Get some rest."

The hallway was dark and smelled of mothballs. The floor was covered with a faded, floral carpet runner, and someone was cooking cabbage. When they reached 7A, Dominic took Connie by surprise and lifted her into his arms, carrying her into the apartment.

"Gosh, where did that come from? I didn't think you could even lift me," she joked.

"What do you mean? I can lift you," he said, defensively.

"No. I didn't mean that you couldn't lift me, I thought maybe I was too heavy."

"Oh," he said, quietly. He put Connie down and they stood side by side, studying the room. "What do you think?"

The furniture was old and patched. A burgundy, cloth-covered loveseat hugged the wall under a small, shaded window. A chair, with frayed brocade fabric and well-knicked legs of cherry wood sat opposite. An army blanket was tossed over the back of the loveseat, and a wooden coffee table, with a paperback book shoved under one leg was placed between the sofa and chair.

Connie nodded. "Nice…very nice," she said, turning to Dominic, giving him a reassuring smile. She wandered over to a window on the east side of the room and pulled back the shade. "Oh my," she exclaimed, when she looked directly into the window of an apartment in the building next door. She followed Dominic into the kitchen, which was so small they had to turn sideways to pass each other. Dominic was holding a match to the pilot light of the stove. It ignited with a quick explosion that made Connie jump. He opened the door of the icebox, thrust his hand inside and turned to Connie and smiled, "It's working," he said, "It's all working." A rust-stained, porcelain sink sat below a single wooden cabinet that contained two plates, two bowls, and two coffee cups. Dominic squeezed past Connie and left the kitchen. She followed him into the bedroom, and strangely enough the bedroom was larger than the living room. A double bed with a wooden headboard was up against the wall opposite the window. It was covered with a bedspread of a non-descript material. A night table sat next to the bed, with a lamp that had a wooden base that looked like the steering wheel of a ship. The single window in the room had a cloth shade and faced the street. A silver-painted radiator clanked and hissed, filling the room with steamy heat.

"It's nice, Dominic. I don't know what that girl was talking about; it feels like plenty of heat to me." Connie rubbed her hands together, holding them over the coils of the radiator.

"Yeah, I think so too. This'll be good, right?"

"It's fine. Dominic, come see." She took him by the hand, and pulled him to the side of the bed. "We'll put a crib right here by the bed, and the sun can shine in on the baby. See how it's shining right in that corner? And I'll make some nice curtains for the window."

"Okay, but we can't afford a crib right now. You know that, right?"

"I know but, we still have some time, we'll get one later." Connie spoke reluctantly. "Dominic, we'll be happy here, right? We'll be a real family."

"Sure we will."

There was a loud knock, and Dominic went to the door. A tall, heavy-set man in overalls stood in the doorway. A leather cap with woolen earflaps was perched on his head, and with a childish grin, he spoke in a deep voice. "Hello, I'm Hubert." He thrust a beefy hand toward Dominic.

Dominic took hold of the man's hand, wincing as his knuckles were ground together.

"Oh sorry," Hubert apologized with an embarrassed laugh. "Did I hurt ya? Ma's always tellin' me I don't know my own strength."

"S'okay. You must be Mrs. Lanin's son," Dominic said, "nice to meet ya."

"That's me," he grinned again, and puffed out his chest. "I'm the one ya call when somthin' needs to be done 'round here. Ma said you need some help bringing some stuff in from your car."

"We do, thanks…Hubert, was it?" Dominic smiled as the young man nodded. "Hey, Connie…Hubert is here. I'm goin' with him to get the stuff from the car."

"All right," she called back.

After several trips, Dominic and Hubert brought the last of the luggage into the apartment, and after handing Hubert two quarters, Dominic saw the young man to the door. Connie rummaged through the bags, pulling out what they needed for the night. She decided to save the rest of the unpacking for the following day. She laid out long underwear for Dominic and a flannel nightgown for herself, along with a pair of trousers and a white shirt that she hung in the closet for Dominic's first day at work. When she went into the bathroom to put shampoo by the tub, she found a fresh bar of soap by the sink and two towels draped over the side of a claw-footed tub.

While Dominic was making a quick trip to the grocery store to get something to eat, Connie decided to take a bath. She started running the water and hoped the hot bath would give her aching head some relief but the water came out a rusty brown. After letting it run a few minutes, the water cleared, and Connie plugged the drain, filling the tub midway. She slowly lowered her plump body into the warm water and layed back, closing her eyes, letting her arms float just below the water's surface. She was relaxed and the ache in her neck, that had been plagueing her throughout the day was slowing easing. For fear of falling asleep, she got out of the tub, dried herself and pulled her nightgown over her head. She rushed into the bedroom and slipped under the cold sheets. The bedsprings screeched as she shifted her body, trying to find a comfortable position, and after settling on her side and drawing up her knees, she fell into a deep sleep. Dominic had come back later that night but she never heard him. When she woke the next morning, he had already left for work. She went into the kitchen, and saw a hamburger, wrapped in paper, sitting on the kitchen counter. Next to it was a paper cup filled with cold coffee. He must have brought it home to her the night before.

*

Several weeks passed and Dominic was working six days a week, seeming to enjoy his new position. He was the project supervisor, and being in control suited him. Connie did what she could to make a nice home for him but ended up spending most of her day sitting in a chair by the radiator, trying to keep warm. Dominic was gone most of the time, and when at home, he seemed bored. When they did, on rare occasions go out together, he seemed embarrassed to be seen with her. Connie cleaned the apartment, did laundry in the tub, prepared nice dinners and listened, intently to the details of his day but for some reason, seemed annoyed by her most of the time. She started feeling lonely and depressed. When she asked for money to buy things in preparation for the baby, he ordered her to stop nagging and told her that they had plenty of time. He didn't allow her to handle any money. He paid the rent, and accompanied her to the grocery store every Sunday afternoon. She felt like a hostage, and missed her family desperately. She snuck change from Dominic's pant's pockets to call her parents on the payphone at the end of the hall, and just hearing their voices helped her get through the week.

One evening, while Dominic was eating his dinner from a snack tray in the living room, Connie asked, "Dominic, can I talk to you about something?"

"What about?" He asked, leaning back on the sofa. He wiped gravy from his chin and belched.

"Well, I know the baby will be here soon but I thought maybe I'd get a part-time job, ya know, here in the neighborhood. I need something to do. I'm so bored sitting here all day. It takes me no time to clean the house, and the rest of the time, I don't have anything to do."

"So?"

"Well, I thought a little extra money would be good, don't ya think? I could buy things for the baby." She nervously scratched at her arms while she waited for what she thought would be anger but surprisingly, he seemed to consider the idea.

"Go ahead," he said, casually.

"Really, Dominic? You don't mind?"

"I don't care…but where the hell are you gonna get a job?" His eyes lowered to her belly. "I mean look at you. Who's gonna hire you lookin' like that?"

"Thanks a lot," she pouted.

"Well, come on! People can see you're ready to have a kid."

Without responding, she put the last of the dishes in the sink, and waddled into the bedroom. She slipped loafers onto her swollen feet, and a sweater over her shoulders. When she came back into the kitchen, she finished washing the dishes, dried her hands, and turned to Dominic, who was standing at the counter polishing his dress shoes.

"I'll be right back, I'm going to Mrs. Lanin's. She seems to know everybody in town, and maybe she can help me find a job."

He continued polishing his shoes. "Ya got a lotta guts, Connie. I gotta give ya that. You don't care what ya look like and ya still go out there. You're somthin'."

"Yeah, well…I'll be back."

*

Connie was feeling optimistic since Mrs. Lanin told her about a local bakery, called Krasmeir's. The owners were old friends, and she told Connie to mention her name. The next morning, after Dominic left for work, Connie went to the bakery, and after hearing about her experience, Mrs. Krasmeir hired her immediately.

She started the following Monday and worked from nine in the morning to twelve-thirty in the afternoon, and her three-day a week schedule was perfect for her condition. She was always home in time to make Dominic's supper, and each week, when she received her pay, she proudly handed it over to him, after removing a handful of change for herself. She kept the change hidden in the kitchen drawer under the silverware tray and used it to call her parents every week.

Dominic bristled whenever Connie talked about her job, and didn't approve of her making friends. He laughed out loud when she handed over her pay, calling it "chump change," but she didn't care. She was happier than she'd been in a long time.

"The funniest thing happened today Dominic… you woulda laughed," Connie said, while they sat together at the dinner table. "This guy came into the store and he had his dog with him and..."

"Would you shut up about your job, for God's sake!" he snapped. "Your job is stupid, Connie. It's for stupid people. Don't you know that? Nobody wants to hear about your job! What do you think, that I can't support you with my job? I only let you work so's you'd stop nagging me!"

Connie took a deep breath and closed her eyes. "I'm sorry."

"God! You've ruined my dinner again!" He said, slamming his fork on the table, and storming out of the apartment.

*

For the next several weeks, Dominic hardly spoke to Connie. When he seemed to be in one of his dark moods, Connie apologized for things she didn't even do, in order to keep peace. She was relieved when he left for work, and looked forward to the days she worked at the bakery. Everyone liked her at Krasmier's, and thought she was fun. They appreciated her talent as a baker, and Connie decided that without her job, life would be like a prison.

One Friday evening, Connie prepared dinner, and placed it on the table at six o'clock prompt, as she did every night. When Dominic wasn't home by six forty-five, she put it back in the oven to keep it warm. She wasn't concerned about him coming in late, because there were some nights he worked overtime but by eight o'clock, she was exhausted and decided to lie down in the bedroom, falling asleep within minutes. She awoke to the sound of metal hangers being moved around in the closet. Dominic was rifling through his clothes. He was standing in his underwear, pulling on one of his new shirts. He had bathed, and his hair was freshly oiled and slicked back. The smell of his cologne permeated the air.

"Dominic?" Connie said, sleepily. She rubbed her eyes, and grunted as she struggled to raise her bloated body into a sitting position on the edge of the bed.

"Go back to sleep Connie."

"Your dinner is in the oven...you want me to put it on the table for you?" She looked at him as he zipped up his trousers. "Where are you going?" She asked, looking puzzled. "Why are you dressing up?"

"I'm going out."

"Out where?"

"Connie, why don't you just go back to sleep?"

"Well, where're you going? What's going on?" She sounded more alarmed than angry.

"I told you, I'm just going out. It's none of your damned business where I'm going, ya hear me?"

"I'm just asking," she said, defensively.

"Well...don't ask." He shrugged on his jacket.

Sniffing his cologne, Connie became suspicious and asked, "What... do you have a date or something?"

Dominic stepped to the side of the bed where Connie was sitting, and slapped her hard enough to knock her back onto the headboard. "I told you, it's none of your business!" He swung at her again but she covered her face with her hands. He stopped, turned and casually gazed at his reflection in the mirror above the dresser, smoothing his hair, and straightening his tie. She lay on the bed, her face still buried in her hands. She felt pressure behind her eye and knew it had begun to swell. Dominic took a wad of money from his dresser drawer, shoved a pack of cigarettes into his shirt pocket, grabbed his car keys and turned to look at her. "Goddamnit! Now see what you made me do? Go look at your eye, you fat..." he stopped himself. He walked toward the bedroom door. "You better not tell anyone where ya got that, I swear..."

"I won't," she quickly assured him, as she cowered on the bed.

When Connie heard the apartment door close, she sat up and gently touched her swollen eye. She dabbed at her bleeding lip. She winced and sucked air between her teeth as she rubbed her throbbing temples. "Sonofabitch." It was the first time she ever cursed.

She went to the kitchen and wrapped ice cubes in a towel and held it to her lips. She lay on the living room sofa, tears stinging her eyes, and after staring at the ceiling for what seemed like hours, she drifted off to sleep.

Connie awoke a little before midnight to find Dominic still not home. Wanting to get back to the bedroom, she raised her head from the arm of the sofa, lowered her feet to the floor and moaned. Her head was pounding. She closed her eyes, and breathed deeply before standing up. Finally steady on her feet, she staggered to the bedroom, got into her nightgown and looked in the mirror to examine the damage to her face. It looked worse than it felt. Her lips were swollen, and a trickle of blood had dried at the corner of her mouth. A deep purple bruise was still forming on her cheekbone, and her eyes looked dark and hollow. She touched a cool washcloth to her face; gently patting the sorest areas, drank a glass of water, and got into bed. She couldn't sleep.

Later that night, when Dominic came into the bedroom, she pretended to be asleep. He stripped off his clothes and fell into bed next to her, and Connie winced at the sour odor of beer, and cigarettes. Her nostrils also took in the scent of cheap perfume.

"You awake, Connie?" He asked.

"Not really." She stayed facing the wall. "Why?"

"Just wondering," he said, seeming to want her to ask where he'd been. When she didn't, he let out a long satisfied sigh, turned over and fell asleep.

"Whoremaster," Connie whispered.

The following Friday night, Connie prepared Dominic's dinner as usual but this time she didn't wait for him to show up at six o'clock. She put the dinner in the oven, and went to the corner of the living room, sat by a window and thumbed through a magazine. She didn't care if he had plans to go out or not. In fact, she hoped he would; she liked it better when he wasn't home. She was so physically and emotionally drained that nothing mattered to her except for the baby she was carrying.

Connie awoke in the middle of the night, wandered into the kitchen and saw that Dominic's dinner was still sitting in the oven. He had never come home that night, and she shook her head with disgust, threw the plate of food into the garbage and went back to bed. She lay on her back with her hands resting on her belly, feeling the activity of her precious baby inside. Her sleep was sporadic. Suddenly, a sharp cramp gripped her right side, and was piercing enough to frighten her. She panicked when she realized the sheets were soaked. "Oh my God, my water broke! Dominic?" She called. "Are you here?" Silence. She was alone and her baby was coming.

She sat up on the side of the bed and cradled her stomach as though it would drop to the floor if she didn't. She managed to get to her feet, and her face contorted when she felt the start of another contraction. "Everything's going to be all right little baby, just hang on."

Barefoot, she inched her way down the hallway to Mrs. Lanin's door. She knocked frantically three or four times before she heard movement within the apartment.

"Coming, coming!" Mrs. Lanin called, her voice sounding thick and heavy with sleep. "Just hold your horses!" The door opened, and Mrs. Lanin gasped when she saw Connie standing there, hunched over and moaning. "What happened? Are you all right my little angel?" Mrs. Lanin enveloped Connie in her arms and led her to the sofa.

"No," Connie groaned. "Ooh, Mrs. Lanin, it hurts. The baby's coming and Dominic's not home and I don't know what to do!"

"Now now, not to worry…here, you sit here. I'll be right back." Leaving the room, Mrs. Lanin shouted for Hubert. "Get in here, Son! Oh, saints preserve us," she said, as she hobbled back to Connie. Hubert followed seconds later, frantically zipping up his pants, barefoot and still in his pajama top. Mrs. Lanin wrapped a blanket around Connie's shoulders while Hubert stared at Connie as though she were about to explode. There was confusion in his eyes but he listened intently as his mother barked orders at him.

"Hubert, go start the car. I'll get Mrs. Preste outside and you get her into the car and take her over to Mercy General, you hear?"

"Okay, Ma." He slipped on his shoes without tying them and lumbered toward the door. Mrs. Lanin helped Connie to her feet, and the two women hobbled out of the building. Connie clung to Mrs. Lanin's arm as they walked down the steps, and Hubert, sitting in his mother's car, was gripping the steering wheel, revving the motor. When he saw them approaching, he jumped out and ran around to open the door for Connie, and after getting her into the car, he jumped into the driver's seat and floored the gas pedal.

Mercy General was just blocks away, and the car came to a screeching halt in front of the building. Connie's feet barely touched the ground as Hubert nearly carried her through the door. A nurse quickly fetched a wheelchair.

"Come dear, sit down," she said, helping Connie into the chair. "Are you the father?" she asked, looking up at Hubert.

"What…me? Oh, no, no, no. I just drove her here!" Hubert's fleshy cheeks turned red.

"Hubert," Connie said, touching his arm. "Thank you for bringing me here, and listen… if you see my husband, would you tell him where I am?"

"I sure will, Mrs. Preste. Don't you worry, you can always count on me." He smiled and waved as the nurse whisked Connie away.

She wheeled her down a narrow hallway to the labor room and helped her to her feet. There was a green cotton gown neatly folded at the foot of the bed.

"Put on that gown dear, and get into bed. I'll be back as soon as I can."

"Okay." Connie doubled over with another contraction.

The nurse pointed to a clock on the wall. "See that clock, honey?"

Connie nodded.

"When the contractions are three minutes apart, press this little button on the side of the bed, and I'll be back to check on you." She patted Connie's arm, and left the room.

Connie held her belly with one hand and undressed herself with the other. She wrapped the gown around her, and climbed into the bed. She curled up on her side as another contraction rippled across her stomach. She forgot about looking at the clock, and after what seemed like hours, the nurse came back, and started pressing Connie's contorting middle.

"I think you're about ready, dear…I'll call for the doctor."

The last thing Connie remembered was intense pain as the doctor's fingers probed inside of her. She passed out with the bed sheet clenched between her teeth.

Connie opened her eyes. A bright light hung above her, and she could hear the doctor's voice but could only see the top of his baldhead. Her knees were wide apart and he was peering between her legs. She felt the urge to bear down, and the doctor calmly said, "Push."

She closed her eyes, held her breath and pushed.

"It's only going to take one more try, Mrs. Preste."

She gulped in air, and bore down as hard as she could. The baby suddenly burst from her body into the doctor's hands. Connie promptly passed out again.

This time, when she awoke she was in a ward with three other new mothers who were apparently sleeping. Connie pulled up the covers, felt the jiggly flatness of her belly and smiled. She wanted to see her baby. Sunlight had just begun to spill through a window on the opposite side of the room, and it shown brightly on the gray concrete floor. She wondered what day it was.

"Mrs. Preste, are you up to seeing a visitor?" A nurse, with a sweet smile peeked around the corner of the door, and came to her with a tiny bundle. Connie's baby boy was wrapped in a blue blanket, and when he was placed in her arms, Connie giggled. She traced her finger around his heart-shaped mouth. His hands were clenched into tiny fists, and a mop of dark, curly hair framed his pudgy face. Connie cried as she cradled him, and suddenly didn't feel alone anymore.

*

Dominic sauntered into the hospital late that afternoon, stopping at the nurse's station to get directions to the nursery. He pressed his nose to the glass and looked for the name Preste. The baby boy was sleeping peacefully, and Dominic beamed with pride at the sight of his new son. He watched him for several minutes, then left to find Connie.

Connie's eyes were closed but she wasn't sleeping; just resting. Her hands were folded over her chest. Dominic stood quietly by her side, and sensing his presence, opened her eyes just as he was leaning over to kiss her on the forehead.

"Oh sorry…did I wake you?" He asked. "How do you feel?"

"I'm fine," she said, quietly, and turned away from him.

"I saw the baby. He's a good-lookin' boy, Connie."

Connie remained quiet.

"For God's sake, Connie…what's the matter?" He asked, sounding impatient. "Why aren't ya talkin' to me?"

"I don't know…I guess I'm just a little tired."

"Well, I guess that's to be expected," he pouted.

"So, what do you want to name him?" Connie asked, trying to lighten the mood. The last thing she wanted was to argue.

"I don't know," he shrugged. "What about Phillippe, you like that?"

"That was your father's name, right?"

"Yeah, we can call him Phillip…or Phil. Just so we don't name him Vincenzo," he added, with a smirk.

"Phillip is fine. Yes…Phillip Preste. I like the way that sounds," she said, ignoring his snide remark.

Dominic looked around the room, spotted a chair in the corner, and pulled it to the side of her bed.

"So, how did you find out I was here…and that the baby came?" Connie asked.

"I got home late last night." He looked down at the floor. "And when I walked in the front door, Mrs. Lanin told me what happened… so I came right over."

Came right over, Connie thought to herself. *Sure, eight hours later.*

"So, was it hard? I mean the pain and stuff?"

"Well, it lasted all night but I managed."

"That's good." Their conversation was awkward. They seemed to have nothing to say to each other, and Dominic shifted in his chair as he looked around the room. "Well listen, Connie…ya did good, real good." He got up and patted her on the top of the head, like a dog. "Don't get mad but I gotta go. I met this guy at work, and he wants me to come over to his place and help him with some kind of repair job on his bathroom sink. I don't know what the story is but I said I'd help him."

Connie closed her eyes and sighed. "Okay. Well, it was nice seein' ya. Drop by anytime," she said, sarcastically.

"Come on, Connie. You know I'm not comfortable in hospitals; they give me the creeps."

"Well, we wouldn't want you to be uncomfortable, now would we?" Connie flipped onto her side, turning her back to him. She really didn't care if he left but she wanted him to feel guilty for not being there for her.

"Connie…Jesus Christ, what'dya want from me, I'm here ain't I?" He waited and when she didn't answer, he changed his tone and asked, "When they springin' you and the boy outta here?"

"The baby and I can come home Thursday. You'll come pick us up, won't you…or do you have other plans?"

"Very funny. Come on Connie, you know I'll pick you up. I'll be here first thing Thursday morning."

"Okay. Go ahead if you have to, I'll be fine." As Dominic turned to leave, he noticed the patient in the bed next to Connie looking their way. He nodded cordially, and as an afterthought turned back and kissed Connie on the cheek. Connie looked surprised, until she followed his eyes to the woman, realizing the kiss was just for show. "You don't hafta do that."

"What're talkin' about…I wanted to," he said.

"Dear God," Connie said, quietly. "Dominic, please call my family and let them know about the baby?"

"I will."

"Thanks."

"I'll come visit ya tomorrow," he said, and walked out of the room.

"Is that your husband?" The girl in the next bed asked.

"Yes."

"I saw him when he first came in; he looks like a nice guy."

"Oh yeah…he's a real nice guy, all right. What's your name?"

"Agnes, what's yours?"

"Connie."

"Hello Connie."

"Did you have a boy or a girl? I had a boy," Connie said, proudly.

"I know. I saw him when they brought him to you this morning. He's beautiful. I had a little girl. I named her Barbara Jean."

"Barbara Jean…that's pretty."

"Thanks. My husband's coming for me in a little while, so I think I'll grab one more nap before they bring the baby in. It was nice meetin' ya, Connie."

"Thanks…you too."

Connie was tired but anxious to hold her baby again. This was a new beginning for her, and she prayed that the baby would bring out a softer side in Dominic; bring them closer together, like a real family.

"There's someone who wants to see you," the nurse said, as if she were singing. She handed the baby to Connie, and she cradled his head as his tiny mouth searched for her breast. As he suckled, she realized how strongly she had already bonded with her son. She gazed at his face, and watched as his eyelids, as delicate as gossamer, fluttered while he slept. He was content, and his perfectly shaped eyebrows furrowed as he continued to nurse. Connie knew she would never let anyone or anything come between them.

*

Connie loved taking care of Phillip. He was growing fast, keeping her busy from early morning until his bedtime, which was usually seven o'clock. She giggled as he splashed in the kitchen sink, where she bathed him each morning, and sang to him while she did her household chores. She delighted in listening to him gurgle as he lay on his blue blanket, waving his arms and kicking his pudgy feet.

Dominic was rarely home. He was either at work, out with friends or early to bed, and he still insisted that they didn't have enough money to buy furniture for the baby. Connie made a makeshift crib out of one of the dresser drawers, padded it with blankets, and set it on the floor by her side of the bed, and Phillip seemed perfectly happy.

She was thrilled when she got the mail and found letters from her parents, and there was always a five- dollar bill folded inside. In their latest letter, they said how wonderful it was seeing her and the baby. Phillip was only a few weeks old when Dominic surprised her by driving her and the baby back to Wickhaven for Giordana's wedding. A month after that, they drove back for Carmella's wedding. Philomena had gotten married two days after Phillip was born so unfortunately Connie missed the wedding.

Philomena and her new husband, Butch visited every few weeks and during one visit surprised Connie with the news that they were moving to the Cleveland area. They bought a liquor store in South Newburg. Dominic grumbled about the news and was always in a terrible mood after their visits but Connie didn't care; it was the best news she could get.

Philomena and Butch visited often, and the girls would steal away to the bedroom to catch up on family news, while Dominic and Butch sat in the kitchen sipping Sambucca and eating roasted peppers. Dominic usually talked about work, while Butch told dirty jokes.

"Tell me about Giordana's husband," Connie asked. "He seems nice."

"He *is* nice," Philomena agreed. "I don't know him that well but Giordana seems happy."

Giordana's new husband was Harold Bishop. They had started dating in high school and after a two year engagement married. Harold ran a small gas station he inherited when his father suddenly died from a heart attack.

"Carmella says hello, by the way."

"How is she?"

"You know Carmella. Everything's a riot."

After finding out she was pregnant, Carmella married the navy lieutenant she had been dating for several months. His name was Charles Ellington, and they moved to New Jersey where they lived in a small tract home with a white picket fence, and a beagle named Henry.

*

After putting Phillip down for a nap, Connie made her usual Monday afternoon phonecall to her parents. They always asked about Dominic, and she always lied and told them things were fine. She had fallen into a comfortable routine for her and Phillip, with morning baths and daily afternoon walks. One particular day, Connie had run out of flour. She dressed Phillip in overalls, wrapped him in a blanket and carried him to the corner grocery store. She picked up a bag of flour, and with Phillip straddled on her hip, placed the flour on the counter. Ida Schultz was at the register that day. She owned the store with her husband, Clyde, and Connie had idly chatted with her many times before but only knew Clyde by the sound of his voice coming from the stock room in the back. Ida was in her thirties, pretty, with soft features, and wavy, shoulder-length hair. She was kind to Connie, and always took time to fuss over the baby.

"Good morning, young Mrs. Preste, how are you today? Ooh…and look at little Phillip…he's getting so big," she cooed, playfully pinching his chubby cheek.

"Hello Mrs. Schultz, it's nice to see you," Connie said, placing some change on the counter.

"Now, what are you going to make with this big bag of flour?" Mrs. Schultz asked.

"I make my own bread every couple of days."

"You do?" She seemed fascinated. "You know I've never made bread in my life, isn't that awful? My mother used to but I never tried it."

"I'll show you, if you like," Connie offered.

"Oh, aren't you sweet? I'd like that, Mrs. Preste."

"Could you please call me Connie? I'll never get used to being called Mrs. Preste."

"All right Connie, and you can call me Ida."

"I'm going home to make bread now…you're welcome to come up to the apartment."

"Really? Hey, Clyde," she shouted. "I'm taking my break. I'll be back in a little bit. Can you watch the register?"

"All right." His muffled voice bellowed from the back of the store.

She turned to Connie and teased, "Come on, let's get goin' while the gettin's good?"

Ida winked at Connie, took off her apron and threw it behind the counter. She grabbed the bag of flour and followed Connie out the door. When they got to the apartment, Connie put Phillip in the bedroom for a nap. He had fallen asleep during the walk back, and had his face nestled in Connie's neck. She tiptoed from the room, leaving the door ajar, and joined Ida in the kitchen.

Connie showed Ida how to prepare the yeast, and added the rest of the ingredients, and before long, the two women were up to their elbows in dough. After placing the loaves of dough in a warm oven to rise, Ida went into the bathroom to wash up.

"Connie! What's all this in the tub?"

"Oh, sorry…that's our laundry. I'm soaking it in hot water."

"You mean you don't send it to the laundry?"

"No, they aren't taking any new customers, and besides I'm afraid we can't afford it."

"Oh, that's ridiculous for you to have to do your laundry this way. I have an idea. I send my laundry out every Wednesday, so why don't you put your laundry in a pillowcase and give it to me. I'll add it to our laundry."

"Oh, I couldn't ask you to do that! Wouldn't they charge you a lot more?" Connie asked.

"What are ya talkin' about? They'll never notice. It's no problem. So bring me your laundry on Tuesday. I'll see that it gets done."

"Thank you so much, Ida. That's so sweet of you."

"Well, for God's sake, you're takin' care of a new baby and the apartment; the last thing you need, is to be doin' laundry in the bathtub! Anyway, I owe you one. I get a loaf of bread outta this, don't I?" She laughed.

"You sure do! I'll bring it to the store tomorrow. Gee Ida, this was really fun. Come over any time."

"It *was* fun, wasn't it? Don't forget…Tuesday…laundry, all right?"

"Tuesday it is."

"Gotta go, Clyde's probably wonderin' where I went."

Connie heard Phillip's cry. "There's *my* boss," she laughed.

Ida spent many afternoons at Connie's, chatting over lunch, playing with the baby, folding laundry, and when there was time, baking in

Connie's tiny kitchen. It was a friendship that became very important to Connie.

One afternoon, when Ida was about to leave, Connie looked out the window and saw a blackened sky, and ferocious winds that were sending trashcans rolling down the street.

"Ida, I think you should wait until this storm passes. It looks nasty out there."

Ida agreed and they settled back on the sofa when Dominic came in the door.

"Dominic…hi," Connie said, surprised to see him. "Are you home because of the storm?"

Ida noticed a sudden change in Connie's mood. She felt a palpable tension.

"The lightening got pretty bad," he said, shaking the rain from his jacket, tossing it over a chair. "So I sent everybody home." He gave Ida a curious look. "Who do we have here?"

"Oh, I'm sorry. This is Ida. Remember, I told you about her?"

"Hello Dominic, it's nice to finally meet you," Ida said, cheerfully. "Connie's told me so much about you."

"She has, huh?" He glanced at Connie. "Nice to meet you too… Ida, is it?"

"Right, it's Ida. You have a sweet wife and a beautiful son, Dominic. You should be proud of them both."

"Oh, I am. He's a good boy, that Phillip," he said, looking down at his son. Phillip was lying on a blanket with most of the toes of his right foot shoved in his mouth.

Connie looked out the window, wishing the storm to pass quickly. "It doesn't look as bad out there now. What do you think, Ida?"

She stood at the window next to Connie and peered out. "Yeah, I think it's clearing.

I can certainly make a run for it." She put a scarf over her head and grabbed her purse.

"Thanks for coming, Ida," Connie said, taking her by the elbow as they walked toward the door.

"Oh sure…uh… I had a good time," Ida said, looking bewildered as Connie rushed her toward the door. "I'll see you later, and it was nice meeting you, Dominic," she added, looking back over her shoulder.

"Yeah, you too."

As Connie was closing the door, Ida stopped her, whispering, "Connie, is everything okay? You seem…"

"I'm fine, really."

"Okay," Ida said, sounding skeptical.

Connie closed the door, and picked Phillip up from the floor. She carried him into the bedroom, and handed him a bottle of milk. He greedily plunged the nipple into his mouth and held the bottle with his hands and feet.

"That was some storm," Connie commented, as she strolled into the kitchen.

"Hmm. Sure was," he agreed. "Nice lady…Ida was it?"

"Mm-hm…Ida. Yes, she is nice. I like her."

"I don't want her here anymore."

Connie stopped peeling potatoes, and looked at him. "Why?"

"I just don't," he said, casually. His expression dared her to question him. "You have no business talking about me with anyone, Connie. What goes on in this house is my business."

"Dominic, when she said I told her about you, all she meant was…"

"I said, no one comes in here unless I invite them, you hear me?"

"I hear you," Connie conceded. "I'll see to it she doesn't come over anymore."

"Good."

Chapter 11

When Phillip was eleven months old, Connie was in a panic because she was almost positive she was pregnant again. By now, Dominic was so distant from her and the baby, she was afraid of what his reaction would be. Connie told him she was going for a checkup, and since the doctor's office was on the other side of town, it would probably take her most of the day. He didn't question her, and before he left for work, he gave her enough money for the trolley. She got the baby ready, put extra diapers, and a bottle of milk in a bag, and scooped Phillip into her arms, and walked to the trolley stop at the top of the hill.

The clinic was busy, and there were several people ahead of her. She signed in and took a seat, and within a half hour a nurse called her name. She carried Phillip into the examining room, placed him in a chair, and took a cookie from her purse. He took it in his pudgy hand, broke off a piece and plunged it into his mouth. Connie slipped out of her clothes, and into the gown that hung by the door, and climbed onto the table, covering herself with a sheet. Phillip was still busy with the cookie when the doctor came into the room carrying a green folder.

He was reading Connie's chart. He took his time before looking up, then peered at her over the top of his wire-rimmed glasses. "Hello, Mrs. Preste."

"Hello, Doctor Finley," Connie said, sounding shy. She pulled the sheet around her waist.

"And who do we have here? This can't be Phillip!" The doctor straightened his back, put down the chart and placed his hands on his hips. Phillip looked up at him and smiled.

"He got big, didn't he?" Connie said, proudly.

"He's a fine looking boy! Can he have a lollipop, mama?"

"Sure."

The doctor slipped out the door, and came back with a cherry red lollipop. He peeled off the paper and handed it to Phillip. Cherry-colored slobber dribbled down his chin but he was behaving, and that was all Connie cared about at the moment.

"What seems to be the problem, Mrs. Preste?" The doctor asked.

"I'm not sure but I think I'm pregnant…again," she added. "I haven't had my…you know," she whispered, "period in a couple of months."

"Okay, well let's take a look." The doctor put on rubber gloves and had Connie lay back. She squeezed her eyes shut as the doctor pushed gently on her stomach while probing her insides. "Well, Mrs. Preste," he said, as he snapped the rubber glove from his hand, tossing it into a receptacle. "In my estimation, you may be pregnant but I won't know for sure until we take some blood." He sat in a chair next to Phillip, and looked at Connie with the expression of a loving grandfather. "Might I ask how old you are, dear?"

"Almost nineteen," she answered, looking at him curiously. "Why?"

"I was just wondering. You look very young but you also look very tired. Are you feeling all right? Are you getting enough rest?"

"I am…it's just…you know, with the baby and all."

"Babies are a lot of work, I agree but you must get as much rest as you can." He patted her arm.

"I'll try, doctor."

"Good. Now," he said, pushing himself to a standing position. "Why don't you take this little guy home? I'll give you a call with the results of your blood test. Miss Quinlin?" He called. "We need a little blood from Mrs. Preste."

Nurse Quinlin entered the room and gave Connie a pleasant smile. She tied a rubber strip around Connie's arm, tapped a vein and inserted a syringe, drawing back the plunger. With swiftness and expertise, she withdrew the syringe, held a piece of cotton to the tiny puncture, and covered it with a band aide. "That's it, you can get dressed now."

Connie slipped on her dress, picked up Phillip and stopped by the front desk.

"That'll be two dollars, today."

Connie got two dollars worth of quarters from the bottom of her bag and handed it to the girl.

"Your phone number, please."

"We don't have a phone," Connie told her. "Would it be okay if I call you for the blood test results?"

"That's fine. We should have the results in a few days."

"Thank you."

She walked to the trolly, sat next to a window and clutched a sleeping Phillip to her chest. She would be home much earlier than expected, and hoped Phillip would finish his nap so she could prepare Dominic's dinner.

It was one o'clock, and after digging her keys from the bottom of her purse, she entered the apartment. She stopped short when she heard voices coming from the bedroom. *Why is Dominic home?* She asked herself. *And why is he laughing?* A wave of nausea suddenly weakened her when she heard a woman's voice. The door was slightly ajar. Connie felt the blood drain from her face when she looked inside. A woman, naked and sitting upright was thrusting her body up and down. Dominic was below her, panting, his eyes rolling back in his head.

"Dominic! Oh my God!" Her reflex was to cover Phillip's eyes.

Dominic lifted his head from the pillow and looked toward the door. "Connie! What are you doing here?" He jumped up, nearly tossing the woman to the floor.

The woman turned around, and Connie recognized Dixie Tarkington, who jumped to her feet, grabbed a sheet and wrapped it around her naked body. She snatched her clothes from the floor and quickly got dressed.

Connie stared at Dominic. She couldn't speak, and found it unconscionable that he actually looked smug, even amused. With the baby still in her arms, she backed away from the door, finding it hard to breath. She also felt capable of killing them both.

"Connie, wait!" Dominic called after her.

Connie placed the baby in a laundry basket with some of his favorite toys. She walked back to the bedroom. "Put your clothes on and get the hell out of my house, you whore!" She hissed at Dixie. "If you so much as ever look at my husband again, I'll kill you with my bare hands!" She picked up Dixie's shoes from the floor and threw them, hitting Dixie in the back as she slipped her dress over her head.

"For God's sake," Dixie said. "Relax, why don't ya. We was just havin' a little fun." She picked up her shoes and casually sauntered, barefoot out the door.

Connie turned to Dominic and stared. Her eyes were red with rage.

He held up his hand. "I don't want to hear it, Connie," he warned. "It didn't mean nothin'. She was flirtin' with me and," he shrugged. "I mean, what was I supposed to do?"

Connie stood by the side of the bed. "You make me sick!" She felt the burn of bile in her throat, and started for the door. Dominic grabbed her arm, and in her struggle to pull away from him, got tangled in the sheet Dixie had left on the floor, and with a sickening thud, fell face down onto the floor.

Dominic stood over her, rolling his eyes. "Here, give me your hand, I'll help you up." He stopped short when he noticed a pool of blood spreading on the back of Connie's skirt. "What the..."

Connie moaned.

"What's happening? Why are you bleeding?" Dominic asked, with alarm. "I never touched you. I didn't do this."

"Dominic, please help me. I'm losing the baby..."

"Baby? What baby?"

"Just go get...aahh!" Connie screamed in pain and passed out.

Chapter 12

It was late September, and a crisp fifty degrees. Physically, Connie was feeling better but emotionally, she was barely coping. She lost the child she was carrying, and asked God to forgive her for thinking it a blessing.

Dominic had rushed Connie to the hospital that day, all the while warning her to keep it to herself how it happened. He never apologized for cheating with Dixie Tarkington but as hard as he tried, he couldn't hide the fact that loosing the baby had affected him. He refused to admit his guilt; he blamed Connie for coming home when she did.

During that difficult time in Connie's life, Philomena came to take care of her. She doted on Phillip, and seemed to enjoy bossing Dominic around. She ordered him to get his own dinner, and to iron his own shirts. Connie thought it was hilarious, and wished she could be more like her sister. Philomena made Connie stay in bed, and served her pasta fragioli, and sweet tea while Dominic sat in the kitchen grumbling over the pork and beans he poured from a can.

When Philomena was sure Connie was feeling stronger, she packed her things and went home to Butch.

"You better never get sick again, Connie!" Dominic warned. "You're sister's worse than my boss. God, I hate that woman!"

"Dominic, she was only here to help."

"Yeah, well…I don't know…I think I was the one doin' all the work!" He complained.

"Come on, Dominic, it wasn't that bad."

He left the apartment, slamming the door behind him.

*

Connie was used to Dominic coming home from work on Friday nights, changing his clothes, and going out but one particular Friday, she wasn't feeling well. She got up with a sore throat, and by afternoon, had a raging fever.

Dominic came home at six, and Connie was in the bedroom changing Phillip's diaper.

"Hi, Dominic," Connie said, her voice scratchy and thick.

"Hi." He came into the bedroom while unbuttoning his shirt. "What's the matter with you? You sick or something?"

"Uh-huh."

"Sick with what?"

"I have a cold."

"Well, stay away from *me."* He was facing the bedroom closet, going through a neatly arranged row of dress pants.

"Dominic? I was wondering...could you stay home and help me for a while? I mean, just 'till Phillip goes to sleep."

"Help you out with what?" He asked, suddenly agitated.

"I'm really sick, Dominic." She lifted Phillip from the bed and sat him on the floor. "Uh, I'm so stiff," she groaned, placing her hands on the small of her back. "I hope I don't make the baby sick."

"The baby...what about me? I gotta work, ya know."

Connie looked at him with pleading eyes.

"Connie, come on...you know I go out on Fridays," he whined, childishly. "Why tonight?"

"Sorry I didn't pick a more convenient day to get sick!" She was irritable, and knew she'd regret her sarcasm.

"Don't get smart with me!"

She flinched when he raised his hand but instead of hitting her, he put his hand on her chest, shoving her into the dresser. She quickly regained her balance and warned him, "Don't start with me, Dominic! Not in front of the baby...you promised!"

He snatched the baby from the floor and tossed him onto the bed. Connie gasped as the baby bounced, hitting the back of his head on the headboard. When she reached for Phillip, Dominic warned, "Don't you pick him up! You're gonna turn him into a queer if you keep babying him the way you do!"

"Dominic…listen, I'm sorry," she pleaded, suddenly frightened he would hurt the baby. "I didn't mean to say anything…I'm not feeling well, and I guess I'm a little cranky. You go out…have fun. Really." She reached for Phillip again.

"I said, don't pick him up!" His jaw muscles clenched, and he grabbed her by the wrist, and pulled her into the living room. "Okay, we're not in front of the baby now. What do you want to say to me, huh?"

"Nothing."

"Nothing?" He was gritting his teeth. "Come on, Connie. Tell me," he goaded her. "Somethin' on your mind, huh? Tell me! I'm a bad father? Is that what you wanted to say?"

"No, I didn't say that."

"Yeah, you're sayin' that. I'm a bad father, right? I'm a baby killer, right?"

"Stop it, Dominic…please," she pleaded.

"You know why I go out? Huh? I can't stand bein' here with you. Look at you! Who would wanna be here with you?"

"Who *do* you wanna be with, Dominic? You think I don't know you have a girlfriend?"

"You don't know shit, Connie."

"I know plenty!"

"Watch what you're sayin' Connie…I'm warnin' ya."

"Tell me Dominic…you think you can screw your whore girlfriend, then bring that dirty thing home, and stick it in me? Is she so good that you can't even stay home one night to watch your own son?"

Dominic's eyes were fixed on hers. He was panting with rage. His body stiffened. Reaching back, he thrust his hand toward her so quickly that she didn't have time to defend herself. He connected with her face, knocking her to the floor, the back of her head slamming into the corner of the coffee table. A chair flipped on top of her. He kicked at the chair, forcing one of its wooden legs to jab at her ribs.

"Dominic, please," she begged. "Stop, I'm sorry, I'm sorry!"

"I warned you, Connie! You don't tell me what to do, you hear me? You don't question me!" He kicked the chair again. She was pinned on the floor. Phillip was screaming in the bedroom. "Shut up!" Dominic roared. He grabbed his hat and keys, and left the apartment.

Connie was trembling uncontrollably. She felt her chest, hoping nothing was broken. She could hear Phillip sobbing. Pushing the chair off to the side, she leaned on the sofa and got to her feet. When Phillip saw her, he reached out his arms. She held him tight to her chest, and cradled the back of his head. He buried his face into the softness between her neck and shoulder. She sat on the edge of the bed, and rocked him until he was calm, and at that moment, she made the decision to pack their things and leave as quickly as possible. She lay Phillp down, and gave him a bottle, then pulled a valise from out of the closet, and started filling it with everything she could grab. There was a small amount of cash hidden in the silverware drawer, and she shoved the wad of bills into her purse. She prayed it would be enough for a train ticket to Wickhaven. It was already eight o'clock in the evening, and she was getting sicker by the minute. Her head was hot, and she was finding it hard to swallow. She picked up Phillip, slung her purse and the strap of the valise over her shoulder, and walked out the door.

It was several long blocks to the train station, and Connie's fever seemed to be breaking. Sweat soaked through her clothes as she walked briskly past stores, and crowds of people gathered outside of restaurants. The thought of being home with her family and in her beloved Wickhaven seemed to give her the strength to keep walking. A strained smile crossed her lips when the train station was within sight.

She ran to the ticket booth, and to her horror, all the windows were closed. She looked at the schedule on the wall, and saw that the last train to Unionville Station was due to arrive at nine forty-five. The clock on the wall above the terminal entrance said ten after nine. Deciding to take a chance and board the train without a ticket was better than going back to Dominic, so she and Phillip sat and waited.

The station was quiet. Some folks waited by the tracks, and businessmen were heading for home at the end of their workday. Connie sat on a bench, with Phillip perched on her lap. She dared to close her eyes but needed to pray. She didn't know what to say to God. Everything seemed so hopeless.

The train pulled into the station with a sluggish hiss, and after coming to a stop, the doors opened. A conductor leaned out the door and shouted, '*all aboard!*' Connie climbed the steps, found an empty car and flopped down in a seat by a window. Phillip giggled, now seeming to enjoy their adventure. Connie smiled and shook her head, grateful for his innocence. She wrapped her arms around his waist, laid her head on the back of the seat and gazed sleepily out the window as the lights of the station slowly disappeared. Phillip was wide-eyed until the rhythmic clacking of the train's wheels began to glide along the rails. He laid his head on his mother's chest, and clutched her finger in his hand. The train was at full speed, swaying from side to side, thankfully rocking Phillip to sleep. Connie dozed but woke when the conductor tapped her on the shoulder.

"Miss? I'm sorry to wake you," he said, in a deep voice. "Do you have your ticket?"

"Oh no, sir. I was hoping I could buy a ticket from you...the ticket booth was closed and…I, I'm not sure I have enough money." She felt silly when she started to cry.

"What's the matter, young lady? Are you in trouble?" He noticed a red, swollen area under her right eye. He gave her a concerned look, and frowned.

"I'm okay but I only have about four dollars, sir. Is that enough?" She reached in her pocket and pulled out the money.

He took two dollars, and put the rest of the money back in her hand. "There's no charge for the baby, Miss."

Phillip peered sleepily at the strange man standing next to his mother. He held his empty baby bottle to his chest.

"Miss, do you need some milk for the baby? I have some in the back."

Connie looked down at the empty bottle. "Oh, yes…that's very nice of you."

"Not to worry." He had a kind face, and his smile comforted Connie. Phillip giggled as the man reached down and tousled his hair. "I have a little grandson just about his age, and I know how much they can eat." Connie handed the bottle to the man, and within minutes he returned with the bottle filled with milk.

"Thank you so much. You're so kind," Connie said, looking up at him with appreciation.

"That's all right, little lady. Just take care of yourself and that little baby of yours."

"I will." Connie lay Phillip back and rested his head in the crook of her arm, as he drank the milk. She gave him a weary smile, and thought about how easy it was to please him.

Chapter 13

"Oh Connie, Phillip is getting so big!" Philomena cooed as she gently pinched his cheeks. She and Butch had just arrived in Wickhaven a few days before. They made the trip every couple of months but had no idea Connie would be coming with the baby. "Connie, why didn't you let me know you were coming? You and the baby could have driven with us." She sat on the edge of the bed, bouncing Phillip on her lap.

"I didn't know until the last second, Phil." Connie's tone was somber, and she looked exhausted.

"You're really having a rough time, aren't you kid?"

"Yeah, you could say that."

"I'm sorry, and I promise not to say I told you so."

"You just did," Connie managed to laugh.

"Didn't mean to."

"I know."

Lourdes came into the room and flopped down on the bed next to Philomena. "Connie, he is so adorable," she said, sweetly. "Can I hold him, please, oh please? I wanna kiss his fat little cheeks!"

Connie rested her head on a pillow, and watched as Philomena handed Phillip over to Lourdes. She felt a comfort and warmth she hadn't felt in a very long time. She was home…in Wickhaven.

*

Violet and Pasqual still lived nearby in a small three-bedroom house, two blocks away from Hazel Street. They were expecting another baby in a few months, and were a great help to Angelina and Vincenzo. Connie was anxious to see her. She missed her most of all. She didn't say it out loud but she was a little jealous hearing that Violet was working at Leone's Bakery again.

Besides Lourdes, Maria and Bettina still lived at home. Maria had graduated high school, and Bettina was to graduate in the spring. Beautiful and olive-skinned with brown eyes and voluptuous figures, there was no shortage of suitors following the two sisters. They still liked to dress alike and wore their chestnut-colored hair in long ringlets. Maria still loved roller-skating and playing basketball, while Bettina preferred staying home. Like their mother, Bettina liked to crochet and cook.

"Are you feeling better, Conchetta?" Her mother asked, prepared to give her another dose of cough medicine. Her sisters were taking turns tickling Phillip. He was on the floor shrieking with laughter.

"I'm feeling a lot better, Mama."

"Das goo, Conchetta. Philomena, take Phillip downstairs for a while, and Lourdes, why don' you go too? Connie needs to rest."

"Okay, Mama." Philomena picked up Phillip, and spun him around. He threw his head back and laughed.

Angelina leaned over and touched her lips to Connie's forehead, pleased with the coolness she now felt.

"I'm much better, Ma. It must have been a touch of the grip. Gosh, I've been home for three days and all I've done is sleep." She stretched, and settled back on her pillow.

"Well, you need sleep, *bella*," Angelina said, tucking Connie's hair behind her ear. "You got color in you cheeks. I didn't like da way you look when you come in da door."

"I'm sorry I scared you, Mama."

"Das okay, Conchetta." She patted her arm and straightened the covers. "You home now. We talk later, eh? I wan' to know why you home."

"Yes Mama," Connie said, lowering her eyes. "I think I feel well enough to come downstairs for dinner tonight. We can talk then."

"Okay, we talk. But right now...you rest."

*

After dinner that evening, Connie sat with her mother and father. She wanted to be honest with them, and tell them what was going on in her marriage. After hearing her story, Vincenzo was enraged. He wanted to drive to Ohio and shoot Dominic between the eyes but Angelina begged him to calm down.

"Papa, please," Connie implored. "Listen to me. I know I made a mistake marrying Dominic. I know that now." She held up her hand when she saw both her parents about to speak. "I know. I know…you warned me. You don't have to tell me. I've been so stupid."

"Conchetta, you notta stupid. You jus' t'ink you were in love," Angelina said, shrugging her shoulders.

"Oh, in God's good-a name, Angelina! In love? Bull sheeta!" Vincenzo bellowed. "In love wit'da devil?"

"Vincenzo please," she pleaded. "Connie, you listen to you mama now, eh…you hear me?" Angelina said, taking Connie's face in her hands. "Don' say you sorry to marry dis man…you have a beautiful baby. Dis is what God want, eh?" She turned to Vincenzo. "Eh?"

"Dis is true, Angelina." He closed his eyes and nodded.

Angelina continued. "Conchetta, you stay here…wit' you family, eh? We take good care of you and little Philly, *capice*?"

"Thank you, Mama but it's hard. I mean, we have a son, and a son needs his father."

Vincenzo sat forward in his chair, and pounded his fist in the palm of his hand. "If dat piece-a sheeta come to my door, I break botta his leg, you hear me, Conchetta?"

Connie closed her eyes and nodded.

"Hey, Connie!" Philomena called. She bounded down the stairs with Maria on her heels. "Oops, excuse us…were you all finished talking… didn't mean to interrupt."

"No, that's okay Phil, we're finished. I was going up to put Phillip to bed. I might go to bed myself. I'm still feeling tired."

"Too late…he's asleep already. We put him in our room and we put pillows on both sides of him so he won't roll out of bed."

"Thanks…he's a good baby, isn't he?"

"The best!" Philomena said. "Don't tell Violet I said that!" She started laughing. "Phillip's a good boy because he has you for his mama."

"Thanks Phil." She raised her arms over her head and stretched. "I'm so happy to be home." She took Philomena and Maria in her arms and hugged them. "Hey, where's Butch? You two are driving back tomorrow, right?"

"Butch is driving back. I decided to stay. He'll come back for me next week."

"God, you're so lucky to have a guy like Butch."

"What are you talking about?" Philomena put her hands on her hips. "He's lucky to have a girl like me!"

"Oh, excuse me," Connie laughed.

"Listen Con, there's a dance Friday night at St. Francis. Remember how much fun we used to have at the dances? How 'bout a Borzanna sister's reunion?"

"A reunion…sounds like fun."

"Violet and Pasqual are goin' too," Philomena added. "And I think some of the old gang will be there. You'll come with us, won't you? You should be feeling better by then."

"Oh, I don't don't think I should go, Phil," Connie said. "What if Dominic found out? I mean…I'm married."

"Well I'm married, and I'm goin'. Anyway, who cares? You're just goin' with us to have a little fun."

"Conchetta," Angelina urged. "Why don' you go? Papa and I will watch leetle Phil. Violet's boy will be here too."

"Should I?" Connie asked, feeling guilty but excited.

"Yes, you should," Maria said.

"Okay, I'll go! It'll be fun being with Violet too."

"Oh goody, we'll have a ball!" Philomena clapped her hands. "Gee Connie, it's great being home, isn't it? Too bad Carm and Giordana couldn't be here."

The girls said goodnight, and went up to bed.

The next morning, Connie had Phillip sitting on the edge of the kitchen table happily gnawing a biscotti cookie. Connie listened to her mother humming and watched as she spooned ricotta cheese onto a sheet of dough that she would make into ravioli.

"You look happy, Mama," Connie observed.

"I am happy." She touched Connie's chin, leaving smudges of flour behind.

"I spoke with Violet on the phone. Gee, she sounds wonderful. Who watches Anthony while Violet works?"

"Pasqual."

"Anthony's really a cute little boy, isn't he?"

"Ah…Anthony." Her mother smiled. "*Bel ragazzo*." She kissed the tips of her fingers. Bot' my boys are beautiful, eh?" She caressed Phillip's cheek. "And many more beautiful boys and girls on da way…" she laughed.

"I think I'll go see Violet at the store, and maybe Mr. Leone will be there. Have you heard anything about Mrs. Leone? How has she been since the stroke?"

"Oh, I don' know, Connie. I know she's at home."

"I'll have to stop by and visit."

Angelina stirred a pot of sauce, waving her hand over the pot, sniffing the aroma of garlic. "Eh, Connie…why don' you go dere now? Give *me* da baby…you go, okay?" Angelina lifted Phillip from the table and held him in the air. "Whee…we have a good time, you and you grandmamma, eh?"

"Are you sure, Mama? He can be quite a handful."

"Eh Connie, whatta you talk? I gotta eight babies. How you t'ink I take care of eight babies and cook-a macaroni for you Papa? Like magic?" They both laughed, and Connie hugged her mother and gave Phillip a kiss.

*

Violet was behind the counter when Connie came in the door. She looked up when she heard the tinkle of the bell, and her face lit up when she saw her Connie. She finished giving change to a customer, and when they were alone, Violet ran around the corner of the counter. "Connie, I'm so happy to see you." She wrapped her arms around her, squeezing her tightly. "I'm glad you're feeling better," she said, putting her hands on Connie's shoulders, and pushing her back so she could look at her face. "I didn't think I'd get to see you until dinner tonight." Her expression turned curious. "Hey Connie, wait a minute. What's going on? I can tell by your eyes that something's wrong."

"Come on Violet, not now. I just wanted to see you and find out how you're doing. Another baby on the way," Connie said, patting Violet's belly.

"Yeah, number two on the way," she said. "But enough about me...I want to know about you. This isn't just a family visit, is it?"

"No but I wanna talk about babies," Connie insisted.

"Okay, but you *will* tell me what's goin' on, right?"

"Yes, I will," she agreed.

"By the way, when you were sick in bed, I got a glimpse of that kid of yours...he's adorable."

"Isn't he great? And you know what? We're fine now that we're home. God, how I love Wickhaven," she said, hugging herself. "I didn't realize how much until I was away from it."

"Yeah, I can imagine. But Connie, I really do wanna know what's going on?"

"I didn't want to get into it now, Violet," Connie protested. "I came home because things haven't been too good between Dominic and me. He, uh...he's been beatin' me up pretty bad."

"Oh dear God, you're kidding!"

"It's been rough. He's jealous, he's mean...you name it. And the night I decided to leave..." she stopped and shook her head.

"Is he cheating on you?"

"Oh yeah," Connie said. "I caught him."

"Bastard!"

"I think he has a girlfriend, and I said some things I shouldn't have, so it was partly my fault. I started questioning him, and he went crazy. So, I grabbed Phillip and we got outta there."

"Oh Connie, I'm so sorry...what are ya gonna do? Are you staying here?"

"I don't know, Violet. I'm just waiting to see what happens. I don't know what to do."

Violet embraced her, and spoke softly. "Anything Pasqual and I can do, just let us know, okay?"

"Thanks."

"First of all, I don't care what you said to him, he has no right to put his hands on you...you hear me, Connie? I mean it, damn it!"

"I know." Connie pulled back. "Violet, would it be awful of me to change the subject?"

"No, what did you want to talk about?"

"Mr. Leone. How is he? Is he here?"

"No, he's at home. It's been slow, so sometimes it's just me. Do you miss working here, Connie?"

"You know something? I do. I learned so much here. How 'bout Mrs. Leone? I think about her so often."

"She's about the same. She's home but I don't think she's gotten much better, so Mr. Leone is home with her a lot."

"That's a shame."

"Yeah, I feel bad for them."

"Well listen, I just wanted to stop and say hello. I don't want to saddle Ma with Philly for too long. She's cooking and all."

"Philly." Violet giggled. "That's so cute. I like that. Philly," she repeated.

"Yeah…cute, huh? He's really somethin'. Hey, I'll see you tonight."

"Sure."

"I can't wait to see Anthony and Phillip together," Connie laughed.

"Oh, that Anthony's a handful, I'll tell ya," she said, rolling her eyes and laughing.

*

When Connie got back to the house, her parents were sitting in the living room with Phillip sleeping between them. Connie looked at her mother and knew something was wrong. "Hi," she said slowly. "Is everything all right?"

"Conchetta, I don' t'ink you go to da dance wit' you sisters," her mother said.

"Why, what's the matter?"

"Papa's friend say Dominic been driving 'round to look for you. He's been down our street too. I don' like it Connie, so I t'ink you better stay here…yes, Papa?" She turned to Vincenzo, who was rubbing the gray stubble on his chin.

"You stay here, Conchetta," he said, quietly. He looked down at Phillip.

"All right, Papa," Connie agreed. She settled back in a chair and thought. She couldn't simply pretend that Dominic didn't exist. She looked at her father, and asked again, "He's been driving up and down this street?"

Without looking at her, Vincenzo nodded. He looked sad. "If he try to come here, Connie…I don' know what I do if he do dat." The thought seemed to distress him.

"Papa, he probably *is* going to come here. I mean…Phillip *is* his son." Connie looked away from her father's troubled gaze.

"Papa, they have to talk," Angelina said, and turned to Connie. "You talk, yes Conchetta? But…you stay here." She sounded frightened.

Vincenzo grunted as he pushed himself up from the sofa. He leaned over, placed his hands on the sides of Phillip's head, and kissed the top of his curly hair, then walked toward the front door. He lowered his head, looking weary and defeated. "I go out, Angelina," he said, placing his fedora on his head.

They watched him go out the door.

Connie told Philomena about Dominic being in town. She and the other girls understood why Connie decided not to go to the dance. They offered to stay home with her but Connie wouldn't hear of it. They stayed anyway.

She tried not to think about Dominic that night, and soon found herself laughing with her sisters. The joy of being together filled the room. She occasionally excused herself, and peered out the living room window into the darkness, looking for headlights. But the only light she saw was coming from a single street lamp that was casting a dull glow on the slick, rain-soaked road in front of the house.

Violet's little boy, Anthony loved Phillip, and assumed the job of being his protector. Connie and Violet laughed as Anthony marched through the house, pulling Phillip behind him on one of his grandmother's crocheted blankets.

The following morning, Connie was upstairs tending to Phillip. She froze when she heard a knock at the front door. She knew it was Dominic. She stood at the top of the stairs and listened.

"Mr. Borzanna," Dominic said, surprised to find Vincenzo home on a weekday. "I didn't expect to see you."

"Wha' you wan'?" Vincenzo asked, with a menacing snarl.

"I wanna see my wife."

"You do, eh?" Vincenzo's slight figure somehow seemed to fill the doorway.

"I do, Mr. Borzanna. I would like to talk to Connie, with your permission, of course."

"She no wanna talk to you!"

"Now, wait a minute," he said. Connie could hear that Dominic was losing his patience. "Look, I just wanna tell her I'm sorry."

"Hah! Now you sorry?" Vincenzo threw back his head and laughed.

"Look...Mr. Borzanna, would you please just ask her if she'll talk to me? That's my wife and son, and I want them to come home where they belong."

"Wait here!" Vincenzo growled, slamming the door in Dominic's face.

"Sonofabitch," Connie heard Dominic say.

Vincenzo heard him too, and he was about to open the door when Connie rushed down the stairs and stopped him. "It's all right, Papa. I'll talk to him." She gently placed her hand on her father's back, and urged him to go into the living room. She opened the door but didn't invite Dominic in. "What do you want, Dominic?" She asked, coldly.

"Can I come in, or do you wanna come outside to talk to me?"

"Neither."

"Look Connie, we need to talk, and I wanna talk to your parents, too."

"About what?"

"I want you to come home. I wanna forget all that stuff that happened. I want you and Phillip home with me."

"Wait a minute," Connie said, and slammed the door.

"Damn...she's as bad as the ol' man!"

She opened the door again. "I can hear you, ya know?" She closed the door again but not as hard.

After several minutes, she opened the door and said, "Okay, you can come in. My father says to sit over there." She pointed to a chair in the corner of the room. Angelina and Vincenzo sat rigid, and stone-faced on opposite ends of the sofa. With their arms crossed, they watched Dominic's every step as he walked across the living room, and sat. He lowered his head, and tucked his hands between his knees. The room was deadly silent, and if Dominic had learned anything, it was not to speak until Vincenzo spoke first. He lifted his head and looked in Vincenzo's direction. The old man's steel-gray eyes seemed to burn into Dominic's brain. They stared at each other like two boxers waiting for the bell to ring but it was Angelina who spoke first.

"Dominic Preste," she said, low and steady. "You are in our home because our daughter say she wan' to talk to you." She paused, and her eyes narrowed. "I see the eyes of da devil when I look to you. My husband…he would like to see you dead!"

Connie sat quietly, her eyes never leaving Dominic's face.

"You hurt my daughter!" Angelina continued. "I will never forgive you for dat. Conchetta's papa and I will not tell her what to do but if she say she go home wit' you, we have hearts dat will be broken."

"I understand," Dominic said, glancing at Connie.

"I warn you, Dominic Preste…" She waved her finger at him. "If you hurt my daughter again, I will kill you wit' *my* own hand, you hear?"

Dominic nodded, then lowered his head again, and looked at the floor.

Connie hoped she was wrong when she thought she saw a smirk on his face.

"I told Connie I was sorry, Mr. and Mrs. Borzanna."

"Dats not good enough!" Vincenzo finally spoke. He stood up and crossed the room to where Dominic sat on the edge of his chair.

I don't remember an apology, Connie thought.

"Well, I don't know what else you want me to do, Mr. Borzanna." Dominic sunk back in the chair, and looked up at Vincenzo. "I'm not the only husband that's ever made a mistake."

"You make a promise to Conchetta's mama and me, do you remember?" Vincenzo pounded his chest for emphasis. "You promise dat you never hurt Conchetta."

"I know."

"You lie!" Vincenzo put his finger in Dominic's face.

"I didn't mean to hurt her," Dominic said, defensively. "Honest to God, Mr. Borzanna, I didn't mean nothin' by what I did. I promise it'll never happen again but I wanna talk to Connie and have her and Phillip come home."

"*I miei occhi la guarderanno*," Vincenzo warned that he would be watching. He cocked his head to the side, and narrowed his eyes. "I tau't you know who I am. Don' you remember what I can do to you, boy?" As he spoke, he casually pulled back one side of his sweater, revealing a silver-handled pistol that was tucked snugly into the waistband of his trousers.

"Oh, dear God," Dominic said, shaking his head, almost feeling sorry for the old man.

"Listen to me! You treat my daughter wit' respect, *capice*? And you better treat my grandson good too...you...you..."

"Vincenzo, *vieni qua*...sit, sit," Angelina said, patting the sofa cushion next to her. "Now, what do you have to say for yourself, Dominic Preste?" She asked.

"I promise to take care of Connie and Phillip," he said, as though he were making an oath. "I do...honest to God. I promise you."

Vincenzo turned to look at Connie. "Conchetta, you do what you must do. I have no more to say. You marry him, and you now a mother," he shrugged, and raised his hands. "What amma gonna do? I am you papa but I can no tell you how to live you life." He slapped his hands down to his sides, as if at a loss. "So, if you go...you go," he shrugged. "If you stay, you mama and me...we take care of you and da baby." He nodded his head indicating he was finished speaking. Turning to Angelina he said, "Come, Angelina, we go...dey talk."

Angelina got up and followed her husband into the kitchen. Connie and Dominic sat quietly for a few minutes.

"Holy shit. Well, I see your father's still crazy."

"He means what he says, Dominic. At least he cares about me. That's more than I can say about you."

Dominic leaned over, caught Connie's eyes, and whispered, "You're coming home with me Connie, you know that, don't you?"

"I don't know that, Dominic," Connie answered. Her expression was determined. "I need to think about what I'm going to do. Phillip's taking a nap and I want to be with my family a little while longer.

So, I'll just stay here for tonight. Come back tomorrow and we'll talk again."

"No more talk!" he said, in a strained whisper, pounding his fist on his knee. "I need you to come home now…I gotta go back to work! I can't be hangin' around waitin' for Mr. and Mrs. Mafia to tell you what to do."

"Don't push me, Dominic," she snapped back, "and don't talk about my parents that way!"

"All right, all right," he said. He took a deep breath. "I'll come back tomorrow." He stood up quickly and placed his hands on his hips.

"Thank you," Connie said. She almost felt sorry for him. It was painful for him to compromise.

"God knows, I don't want your father to shoot me," he said, sarcastically.

Connie rolled her eyes, and walked behind him toward the front door.

*

Dominic came back the following day, and he and Connie sat in the dining room playing with Phillip. Dominic held the baby on his lap, and Phillip giggled while his father made funny faces but when the baby started to fuss, he handed him back to his mother.

"He's teething," Connie explained.

"Oh, thought maybe he didn't like me neither."

Hearing Phillip fussing, Lourdes came into the room. "You want me to take Phillip for a little while?"

"Would you, Lourdes? Thanks."

She took Phillip, put him in a stroller and wheeled him out of the room.

"Well?" Dominic said, glad they were alone.

"Well? Connie repeated, without looking at him.

"Did you come to any decisions? I'm ready to go home, if you are. If I don't get back soon, I'll lose my job, Connie."

"I know." She paused, and looked up at him. "Dominic? If I know that you're gonna change, then I'll come home but if things stay the same…well, I don't wanna come home to that. How am I ever gonna trust you again?"

"Everything will be fine but you gotta change too, Connie. You gotta stop pushin' me and makin' me lose my temper. You know," he raised his eyebrows for emphasis, "a lot of it's your fault, too. I mean, I didn't wanna say that to your parents but…I mean, I don't wanna get mad, but you start naggin' at me, and…"

"Sorry." Connie suddenly felt guilty. "I didn't know I was doing that. Being married is new for me too, Dominic. I'm doin' the best I can."

"I know but I mean…come on…a man can only be pushed so far and…"

"I know," she stopped him. "I shouldn't have said what I said."

He had won…she was now blaming herself, and Dominic found it hard not to grin with triumph.

"Well, now that that's settled…what'dya think? Are you ready to go today?"

"I guess so but I need to talk to my parents. Where have you been stayin'?"

"My bother's place."

"Can you go back there for a little while, so I can talk to my family? I need to get some things together."

"Yeah, I guess so." His mood seemed lighter. He had successfully manipulated her and he liked that.

"Thanks." Connie tried to break the ice, and leaned in to kiss him on the cheek.

"Oh," he said, seeming surprised. "Yeah…well, I'll see you later on." He smiled awkwardly, and headed for the door.

After he left, Connie closed the door. She turned and leaned against it, closing her eyes and praying, *"Dear God, please tell me he's not lying. Please tell me he's going to change.*

*

"Conchetta!" Angelina shouted up the stairs, after hearing a knock at the door.

"What, Ma?"

"He's here."

"I'll be right down!"

Angelina opened the door, looked at Dominic and waved her hand for him to come in.

"Mrs. Borzanna," Dominic acknowledged her.

Angelina walked back to the kitchen leaving Dominic standing in the middle of the living room by himself. Connie came down with Phillip in one arm, carrying the valise in the other. Dominic climbed the first few steps and took Phillip from her.

"I'll be right back," Connie said.

"I'll take the baby out to the car."

"No, Dominic. First, I want to take him in to say goodbye to his grandparents. Wait here." She went into the kitchen where she found her mother sitting at the kitchen table. She was crying, and Connie felt guilty knowing that she was breaking her mother's heart...again. "Ma, please don't cry. Everything will be all right now. I promise. Won't you say goodbye to Phillip?"

Angelina looked up and turned her tear-streaked face toward her precious grandson and reached for him. He giggled and fell into her embrace, wrapping his chubby arms around her neck. She held him tightly and kissed his face. Phillip gurgled happily, while his grandmother wept. Still holding Phillip, she walked into the living room, and handed the baby to Dominic. She turned toward Connie, and took her in her arms. "You go now but Conchetta... I wan' you to get a...how you say, *telefono*." Turning to Dominic, she said, "You hear me, Dominic? I wan' Conchetta to call me."

"Okay...we'll get a phone." Dominic rolled his eyes as he carried his son out the front door.

"I will, Mama. Please tell Papa I love him." Connie said, understanding why her father didn't want to be there to say goodbye to her again.

"I will. And he loves you too, Conchetta," she added.

"Bye, Connie." Lourdes, Maria and Bettina stood at the top of the stairs. Philomena had already gone home to Butch, and Violet said goodbye before going to work that morning.

"Bye." Connie said, as she ran to the car, crying.

Dominic had the motor running, and the baby was laying in the backseat covered with a blanket. Connie jumped into the car and stared straight ahead; she didn't dare look back.

*

Connie sat quietly while Dominic seemed to be concentrating on the road. She was non-chalantly watching the scenery out the window, still asking herself why she agreed to go home with him. *Is he going to punish me?* She couldn't help thinking. When they reached the outskirts of Wickhaven, he glanced several times toward the backseat to make sure Phillip had fallen asleep, and without warning, he lifted his foot from the gas pedal, raised it up and kicked Connie in the side of her leg with such force, she fell halfway off the seat. Before she knew what happened, he kicked her again, knocking her to the floor. He held one hand to the steering wheel, grabbing her hair with the other.

"Get back on the seat, you stupid bitch!" The car swerved as he struggled to steer with one hand. "You're really a piece of shit, you know that…to embarrass me that way."

"Dominic, please…"

"You make me drive all over town looking for you," he hissed. "And then I have to beg your parents for forgiveness?" He spit out an angry laugh. "Bullshit…I'll tell them all to go to hell and you can go with them!" He glanced back at Phillip when he heard him moan. Dominic calmly smiled, "Go to sleep, Son." He spoke in a controlled tone even though he was still clinging tightly to a fistful of Connie's hair. "Don't you ever…ever, walk out on me again, Conchetta," he mocked, as he said her name. "Ha…what a stupid name. I swear I'll come after you and I'll kill you if you ever leave me again…and I'll kill Phillip too!" He glared down at her. "Yeah! You heard me! I'll kill him too, you hear me? I will. Don't think I won't, cause I will."

"Okay, okay." Connie's head was laying back on the car seat. "I'll never leave again…I promise. Just, please stop…"

Dominic opened his fingers, and took his hand from her hair. She slowly slid her body up onto the seat and clung close to the door. She looked at him out of the corner of her eye, and rubbed her head. She felt the throb of a bruise forming on her leg. She couldn't think. Hopelessness gripped her. She was trapped. He had finally broken her… it was time to give up.

Chapter 14

Fourteen years later

Dominic and Connie had been living in a small house in Bay Village near Sagamore Hills for the past eleven years. As their family grew, so did Dominic's salary. He was now a senior member of the union, and in control of high profile building projects that afforded him the house in Sagamore Hills but now, even that house was beginning to close in on them.

Dominic and Connie had two sons and a daughter, and one on the way. Phillip was now fourteen, Lucinda, who they called Luci was eleven, and Vito was four.

Phillip was small for his age, thin and frail looking. His face was long and narrow, and just beginning to show signs of adolescence, with a small cluster of pimples on his cheeks. He had an engaging smile and sparkling, mischievous blue-green eyes, shaped like his father's. He wore glasses that he repeatedly lost or broke until his father refused to buy them anymore. He was an above average student for the first few years that he attended St. Mary's Catholic School for Boys. He was also an alter boy, and fantasized about being a priest one day, until his parents transferred him to public school where he discovered girls. He had a natural wit, a disregard for rules and a penchant for making his father angry.

Vito looked exactly the way Phillip did when he was five years old. He was Dominic's favorite and managed to stay out of trouble but seemed to constantly get Phillip *in* trouble. Vito was the only one able to make their father laugh, perhaps because Dominic recognized himself in Vito. Approaching his fifth birthday, Vito was already headstrong and temperamental, with a biting sense of humor.

Phillip was closest to Luci, four years his junior. She was a light haired, delicate girl, with her mother's regal nose, brown eyes and olive skin. She had a sweet disposition, always ready to help. Like Phillip, she was comical, and the two often got into trouble after falling into uncontrollable fits of laughter. Dominic bristled at the sound of laughter, especially at the dinner table, and especially when he thought the laughter might be about him. Punishing Phillip and Luci soon became a nightly ritual. Their father forced them to kneel on the cold, hard bricks of the fireplace hearth until they were willing to act serious again.

By observing and adopting her mother's behavior around her father, Luci feared her father and was obedient to his every demand. She was painfully aware of the consequences that followed disobedience. She learned from her mother that it was okay to lie; lying was a survival necessity that managed to appease situations that would normally push Dominic into a rage. When her father was home, Luci noted her mother's constant expression of panic, and along with her mother made sure she was busy; cleaning something, cooking something, it didn't matter. Being idle was sinful and punishable. Having fun was unforgivable, unless Dominic was the jokester, then nervous laughter was the result.

*

"Connie!" Dominic called, as he came in the door from work. "I need to talk to you."

"I'm in here," she answered from the boys' bedroom. She was sitting on the edge of the bed folding laundry when Dominic came into the room.

"Hi," she said, looking up as she continued folding. "What do you need to talk to me about?"

"My cousins, Gino and Fiona are coming to the United States to live, and I told them they could stay here with us until they get situated."

Connie dropped a pillowcase to her lap, and looked at Dominic. "What? Dominic, I don't know…I mean we're so crowded already, and with another baby coming and all...where would they sleep?"

"I don't know yet but we'll work it out," he said, and left the room. She stared at the empty doorway, and sighed.

She served dinner that night, sat down and cautiously asked, "When are your cousins coming?"

"I got a letter from my mother, and she said the fifth of July." He stabbed his fork into a plate of lettuce and shoved it into his mouth before continuing. "Salad's a little salty, Connie," he said, turning up his nose. "Remember I told you not to use so much salt. Not good for my blood. I gotta teach you how to cook, or what?" He teased.

"Sorry," she said. Phillip hated the way his mother apologized for everything.

"That's okay, it's not so bad if you're hungry. Real hungry, that is. Right kids?"

For some reason, that made Lucinda giggle. She kept her head down but peeked at Phillip. He looked back at her and snorted a laugh.

"Hey, stop it, now. You kids sit quiet and eat!" Dominic commanded, banging the end of his fork on the table.

"Sorry, Dad," they said, in unison. Forced frowns replaced their grins; they lowered their heads again but it was too late. Lucinda, no matter how hard she tried, couldn't control herself. She laughed and spewed a mouthful of milk across the table, nearly gagging.

Phillip's eyes grew wide with shock. "Oh, my God…" he muttered, his eyes darting from his father to his sister, anticipating the explosion that would be his father's temper.

Vito looked at his mother. "Is Daddy mad, Mommy?"

Dominic got up from the table, his chair flying backwards into the wall. He grabbed at the edge of the table, lifted it and flipped it on its side. Plates of food, and glasses of milk went crashing to the floor. "Go to your room!" He ordered. "Come on…lets go. Get in there. You too, Vito…git!" The thud of his work boots pounding across the floor warned them to cover their backsides, as well as the backs of their heads. Phillip and Vito ran into their room, and Lucinda scurried off to her room, and grabbed her favorite doll, clutching it tightly to her chest as she cowered on her bed. "Phillip, you go over to that corner and kneel down and stay there till I tell you to get up." Dominic stood in the hallway outside their rooms. "Vito, you get back in the kitchen with your mother. Luci…stay put!"

Dominic went back to the kitchen. Connie had already righted the table, cleaned the floor, and set a fresh plate of food at Dominic's place. He sat down and continued to eat while Connie finished picking up broken glass. As though nothing had happened he said, "A buddy of mine from work said he has an old sofa bed he's getting' rid of, so I thought I might take it, and put it in the living room for the boys to sleep on. That way Gino and Fiona can use the boy's twin beds. What'dya think?"

"Okay." Connie agreed, knowing she didn't have a choice.

"What's that face for?" He asked.

"What face?"

"I know what you're thinkin', and I don't wanna hear any shit about this Connie. I already told my mother they could stay here."

"Don't worry, Dominic…we'll manage just fine," she said, forcing a smile. *God forbid, he should ever say no to his mother,"* she thought.

Chapter 15

Gino Pescatori, and his sister Fiona arrived at the airport on a hot, muggy Sunday afternoon. Dominic was anxiously waiting for them. Connie stayed home and cleared out the boys' dresser drawers, and put the finishing touches on dinner. She was six months pregnant and dreaded taking on the responsibility of cooking and cleaning for two more people but as usual, she obeyed with a smile on her face. She stirred sauce that was bubbling on the stove, and laid the palm of her hand on a loaf of bread that was fresh from the oven.

Phillip and Vito were sitting at the kitchen table playing a game, while Luci played in her room. Connie, while standing in front of a fan was beginning to feel the heat of the day, and held a cold rag to her forehead. "Come on boys, let's move the game into the bedroom, I need to set the table."

"Aw Mom, come on…we're almost finished," Phillip whined.

Connie put her head down and smiled when Phillip's voice cracked.

"No, come on…let's go…scoot, scoot," she said, helping them pick up the game pieces.

"I don't know why Dad's stupid cousins have to stay here, anyway…"

"Phillip please, it's just temporary; it's what families do for each other."

"Stupid," he mumbled, as he and Vito carried the game into Luci's room.

Connie heard the front door opening. "Hey Connie, look who's here!" Dominic called out, sounding excited.

She smoothed her hair, took off her apron and walked into the living room.

"Gino…Fiona, this is my wife, Connie," he said, proudly presenting her with a wave of his hand.

"Ciao, Connie. Come lei e'? Lei e' cosi' bello. E' bella, Dominic!" Gino said, commenting on how beautiful he thought she was. He was holding his hand under her chin.

"Of course she's beautiful," Dominic said. "Would I marry someone ugly?" He laughed and clapped his cousin on the back.

Connie waited, leaned in to kiss Gino, then Fiona. She saw the boys standing in the hall and beckoned them forward.

"Oh, there're the boys," Dominic said. "Phillip, Vito come here," he urged, and they quickly went to stand by their father's side. "Where's your sister? Lucinda!"

Luci peered around the corner of the doorway. She walked, shy and pigeon-towed out of her room clutching at the hem of her skirt. She smiled and started twisting a strand of her curly hair as she stood behind her mother.

"Well anyway," Dominic said, seeming irritated by Luci's shyness. "That's Luci, this here is Vito, and this is my oldest boy, Phillip." He placed his hands on their heads as he introduced them.

"Ah, such big boys," Gino said, in perfect English. "Lucinda… beautiful, like her mother."

"Shake his hand, boys. Come on, don't be so shy," Dominic said, giving the boys a shove. "Luci come on, a nice hug for Fiona, huh?"

"What a beautiful family, Cousin Dominic," Fiona said, as the three children took turns accepting her hugs and noisy kisses. "And Connie… look at you…a baby on the way, and I know you went to a lot of trouble getting ready for us to come here. "

"Oh no, it was no trouble. We're happy to have you in our home."

Fiona wrapped her arms around Connie and gave her an affectionate squeeze. "I hope you let me help you," she offered. She held Connie by the shoulders and winked at her, giving her a reassuring smile. "May I?" Fiona asked, resting her hand on Connie's stomach.

"What…oh, sure," Connie laughed, and stuck out her belly.

Fiona seemed to go into a trance. She rubbed Connie's belly slowly and methodically in a circular motion. "Aha…it's gonna be another boy!" Fiona declared, throwing her hands up in the air.

"Hey…another boy, Dominic!" Gino said, patting him on the back.

"We'll see, we'll see," Dominic laughed, and noticed Connie's confused expression. "Fiona has a…sort of a gift," he explained. "She gets…what are they called, Fiona?"

"Visions," she said, mysteriously.

"Ah yes, visions," Dominic nodded.

Connie looked at Fiona who was giving her a playful grin.

*

Fiona was in her fifties, tall and slender, with a handsome face and dark eyes that crinkled at the corners when she smiled, and Connie noticed that she smiled a lot. She was playful and outgoing and Connie liked her. Her eyes were warm, and sincere, framed with thick black-penciled eyebrows. Her coal black hair was cut short and freshly permed. She had a motherly way about her and her colorful personality was a welcomed change. Connie was beginning to think having her and Gino in the house wouldn't be so bad. Fiona would be good company for her, and hopefully Dominic wouldn't be so likely to fight with her and the children.

"You both speak such perfect English. I was expecting to have to brush up on my Italian," Connie laughed.

"We both went to school here in the states," Fiona said, "then moved back to Italy to care for our parents. Now that they're gone, we both wanted to come back here. We love America."

Connie smiled as she watched Gino tease the children, and it was hard for her to believe that he was related to Dominic. He was much older than Fiona but just as nice. He was jovial, with a delightfully hearty laugh. He was short, like Dominic, and his well-fed stomach hung over the belt of his pants. He was balding but what hair he had was silvery white, as was the mustache that covered his upper lip.

Dominic brought their suitcases in from the front porch and set them on the living room floor. He proudly showed them around their tiny house until Connie called everyone to the dinner table.

"Connie, your house is very nice," Gino said. "I hope we're not putting you out."

"Oh no, Cousin Gino, we'll be just fine, don't you worry." She transferred several serving platters from the kitchen counter to the table. She had made homemade ravioli, topped with the tomato sauce she had canned the summer before. Another platter, with thick slices of roast turkey was placed in the table's center.

"*Mamma mio!*" Gino said, when he followed Dominic into the dining room. "It's like a feast!"

"I just hope it tastes good," Connie said. She called the children to the table and when everyone was seated, she and Dominic filled the plates.

As usual, Connie never sat down. She busied herself refilling plates, freshening water glasses and making sure wine glasses stayed full. Her plate sat empty while she rushed from the kitchen to the dining room table servicing everyone's needs. That was how Dominic liked it.

"Fiona please...have more," Dominic urged, shoving a spoonful of ravioli toward her. "Connie, give Fiona some more turkey."

"Oh, sorry," Connie said. "Please, Fiona, what can I get for you?" Connie jumped to her feet again.

"Oh no, no, no," Fiona insisted, holding her hands in the air. "Please, no more! My God, I feel like I'm going to burst! Connie, the dinner was wonderful, and for God's sake, Dominic, if I wanted more, I could get it myself...let your poor wife sit down and eat," she scolded.

Connie quickly changed the subject. "It was Dominic who taught me how to make ravioli," she said. "And the sauce...can you believe Dominic grew those tomatoes himself?"

"Really, I didn't know that," Fiona said. "Connie, don't you ever sit down?" She asked again, still concerned that she was doing too much.

"Ah...don't worry 'bout Connie," Dominic said. "She likes being busy. I always tell her to sit and relax but she never does."

"Well, I'd like to see her sit right now," Gino said.

"Okay, I'm sitting." Connie raised her hands in surrender and dropped down into her chair. She blew at a strand of hair that hung over her forehead. "I've been picking at the food all day, and by the time I sit down to eat, I'm already full!"

"Connie's a pretty good cook, huh Gino?"

"She sure is."

"Was the salad okay? Not too much vinegar, was there?"

"Nah…what're ya talkin' about? It was perfect!" He kissed the tips of his fingers.

"Good, good, just how I wanted to make it…perfect." He glanced over at Connie.

"Yes, Dominic makes good salad," she added, dutifully.

"Why don't you have some more, Gino? Connie, get Gino some more of the salad I made?"

"No, no," Gino protested. "Please, Dominic. No more. Connie, sit, sit," he said, batting his hand at her. "Too much food…my God! I'm too fat now!" He laughed, patting his belly.

"Connie, where's that bottle of Sambucca?" Dominic asked.

"I'll get it."

"You might as well put the coffee on too," he added. Turning back to his cousin, he asked, "You like Sambucca, Gino?"

"Yeah, sure."

"None for me, Connie." Fiona spoke loud enough for Connie to hear her in the kitchen. "I may have my coffee later but right now, I'm too full."

Connie came back into the dining room and suggested, "Why don't all of you go into the living room, and I'll bring coffee in there."

The boys eagerly followed the men and planted themselves on the floor by Gino's feet. They wanted to know everything about Italy, and what it was like to fly on a plane. Connie carried a tray of cups and saucers along with a fresh pot of coffee, and put it on the table in front of the men. "Fiona no, please…" she said, when she saw Fiona clearing the table. "You've had a very long day. Please, go sit and relax. Luci will help me, won'tcha honey?"

"Yes Ma," Luci droned, and slowly followed her mother into the kitchen.

Fiona joined Dominic and Gino in the living room, and the three cousins sat together speaking excitedly in Italian, reminiscing about their childhoods back in Italy. Dominic shooed the boys into the kitchen to help their mother.

They left, and quickly came back. "We're done, Dad," Vito and Luci said, as they ran back into the room. "Mom said we could come back in. Tell us again, cousin Gino," Lucinda begged, "how you carried a goat on your back!"

"Come on now kids, that's enough," Dominic said. "Let's go…all three of ya, go play in your rooms."

"Aw, Dad," Vito pouted.

"Don't *aw Dad* me, get goin'."

With the children out of the room, Dominic was full of questions about his mother and sisters, who still lived in Palermo. Connie finally finished up in the kitchen, looked at the clock on the wall, and was surprised to see how late it was. It was a school night, and time for the children to go to bed, so she went into the living room and politely asked Dominic if he, Gino and Fiona could move their conversation back into the dining room so the boys could go to bed.

"Of course Connie," Fiona said, looking apologetic. "See, we are putting you out."

"No, not at all Fiona, the boys will be fine. They're actually excited… it's like they're camping out."

Connie sent the boys to wash up and put on their pajamas while she opened the sofa bed, and covered it with a sheet and blanket. After getting them settled, she put Luci to bed and turned off the lights. She stood in the hallway and dug the heels of her hands into her lower back and stretched. She was exhausted and would have liked to go to bed but Dominic would never allow that. She went back into the dining room where Dominic and his cousins were polishing off a second bottle of red wine. They were laughing and telling funny stories about some woman, back in Palermo named Graziella, and how she chased after her cheating husband with the broken end of a water pump handle and ended up beating him to death. Connie didn't think the story was all that amusing but apparently you had to know Graziella to find the humor in it. It was eleven o'clock and Connie could barely keep her eyes opened. She stifled a yawn, and rested her chin in the palms of her hands, blinking and smiling at one story after another. When Fiona said she was tired and ready to go to bed, Connie excused herself and joined Fiona in the living room.

"Come Fiona, I'll show you where everything is."

"Connie," Dominic called after her. "Before you go, could you get Gino and me some of that cheese we got the other day? Wait'll you see this cheese, Gino. Just like back home. Got it in the city at the Italian market…and Connie, we got crackers too, don't we?"

"Yes, we have crackers. They're in that cabinet right next to you."

"Where?"

"Here, I'll get them for you." She turned to Fiona and shrugged. "Men," she whispered. She got the block of cheese from the refrigerator and set it on the table. Reaching behind Dominic, she pulled the box of crackers from the cabinet, along with two plates, a knife, and napkins that she folded neatly in front of them. "There we go. Are we all set now?"

"Yeah, we're good, thanks," Dominic turned to look at her. "Where you goin'? Why're you in such a hurry?"

"I'm not in a hurry, Dominic. I'm just helping Fiona get settled." She made a hasty retreat when Dominic went back to his conversation with Gino. When she passed through the living room, Fiona was carrying her suitcase, tiptoeing past the boys, toward the bedroom.

"Fiona, what can I get for you? Do you need anything?" Connie whispered.

"No, I'm fine, dear. You look exhausted. Why don't you go to bed, too?"

Connie smiled and nodded. "I'm going to." She took one last look at the boys and also checked on Lucinda, then went to say goodnight to Fiona. She poked her head around the corner of the bedroom door; Fiona, in her nightgown, was applying cold cream to her face. "Just wanted to say goodnight, Cousin Fiona."

Fiona rubbed her hands on a washcloth and smiled, "Connie dear, come in."

"I'm just checking to see if you need anything."

"No, I have everything I need. I feel bad though… the boys sleeping in the living room like that."

"Don't be silly. Those boys can sleep anywhere," Connie laughed.

Fiona returned her smile and moved to the edge of the bed and sat down. "Sit with me, Connie," Fiona said, and touched a spot on the bed next to her. "You know what?"

"What?"

"You, my dear, are overworked."

"Oh," Connie laughed. "Three kids'll do that to ya. I'm just a little tired, that's all."

"Oh no, you're more than just a little tired. You haven't stopped since we walked in the door. Don't think I didn't notice... and Dominic, well…I noticed that too. He's tough on you. I don't care if he is my cousin, that's not right!"

"Oh my God, Fiona…please, don't say that." Connie suddenly felt panicked. "If he thought I was talking about him…"

"Connie," Fiona said, gently, "calm down, dear." She paused and studied Connie's expression. "You're afraid of him, aren't you?"

"No…I just don't want …" Connie spoke hesitantly, and lowered her voice to a whisper, "I don't want him to hear me."

"Now, what's going on here?" Fiona pressed her.

"I shouldn't be talking to you about this, Fiona. Really, I shouldn't."

"Hey, it's just you and me…tell me, what's going on?"

"Dominic is…well, I don't know, very…" She struggled to find the right words. "Listen, I'm really not comfortable talking about this."

Fiona took Connie's hand. Her eyes were warm and sympathetic. "I understand. Listen, when you're ready to talk, you tell me, okay dear?"

Connie smiled and let out a breath of air, sounding relieved. "Thank you Fiona, you're very sweet to worry about me like that." She paused. "Huh," she laughed and shook her head, "It's hard to believe you're related to my husband."

Fiona leaned back on the bed. "Well, let me tell you something, my darling, we have a whole family full of secrets, and some of them not too pleasant."

"What do ya mean?" Connie's eyes widened with curiosity.

"Well," Fiona leaned in, looking toward the door, lowering her voice to a whisper, "first let me say thank God Gino and me are related to your late father-in-law's side of the family…not the old lady."

"The old lady?" Connie looked puzzled.

"Dominic's mother."

"Oh her," Connie said, and lowered her head. "I haven't even met her yet, and I don't like her. She has some sort of a sick hold over Dominic."

"Hmm, I bet she does..."

"What about her?"

"Just let me tell you, that if you knew her, it would answer a lot of questions about Dominic, that's for sure."

"Why...what'dya mean?"

"She's one of the meanest people *I've* ever known. When we were kids, I remember her beatin' the hell outta her kids but she used to beat the hell outta her husband too! Sad, very sad...he was a darling man. Loved his kids. The old lady...not a big woman, mind you. Just plain mean. Ooh, *Madonna*." She laid her hand on the side of her face, and rocked her head back and forth. "And whenever one of her kids tried to get close to her, she'd push them away like they made her sick or something. And if they, God forbid, did something wrong?" Fiona made the sign of the cross. "They'd pray for mercy, I tell ya. She'd even lock them away in the shed that was behind the house. They screamed until they lost their voices."

"Oh my God." Connie stared at Fiona in horrified disbelief.

"Now listen, I don't mean to scare you..." Fiona quickly said. "But I always wondered how Dominic and his brothers turned out." She looked off in the distance, then back to Connie again. "You know what I mean...being raised that way and all. I remember Dominic being really close with his father; idolized him." She looked away again, as though an old memory had just come to her. "Yes...he was heartbroken when his father died."

"What happened to his father? He talks about him a lot."

"There's a question for you...no one really knows. The old woman saw him lying in a pool of blood in the barn or something, I don't know, it was all very hush hush. Hit his head, maybe. I never really got the whole story but I'll tell you...Dominic was never the same again... finding his father laying there and all."

"Dominic saw his father when he was killed?" Connie asked, raising her hand to her mouth. "My God...he never told me that."

"Like I said, I don't know the whole story. It wasn't talked about… we were kids and not allowed to talk about things like that." Fiona leaned back on her hands again, and took a deep breath. "I've probably said too much but I thought you might wanna know… and well, I don't know, maybe then you'd understand why Dominic is the way he is."

"Well, it explains a little, I guess." Connie sat on the edge of the bed looking down at the floor. "But sometimes he's so cruel, Fiona. He can be like the devil himself…and it's like he hates me but then he doesn't want me out of his sight." Connie paused and thought for a second. "You know, I do notice when I ask about his mother, he becomes very defensive…like I'm saying something wrong about her, when I'm really not, ya know? It's like he's protecting her but punishing me."

"I don't know," Fiona said, shaking her head. "You sure do have your hands full. I'm sorry, honey." She covered Connie's hand with hers. "Listen, I know all the Preste's, and they're all kind of…different. Especially the sisters…dear God, they're worse than the mother."

"The sister's too?"

Fiona giggled, "Some of us named them *Significare e Brutto*…oh my God, don't tell that to Dominic!"

"I don't know what that means."

"Oh sorry. We called them…let's see…in English it would be, Mean and Nasty." She covered her mouth and laughed.

Connie leaned back on her elbows. "Oh my God, that's just great," she said, not seeming to find the humor. The two women were silent for a few seconds, alone in their own thoughts. "Well, you know what," Connie said, stretching and yawning. "I'm tired, and as far as I know, Gino and Dominic are still drinking and talking, so I'm sneaking off to bed."

"All right dear, get some sleep and we'll talk some more in the morning."

"Good night." Connie embraced Fiona, and kissed her on the cheek. She stopped at the door, turned to wave, and quietly stepped next door into her bedroom.

Chapter 16

After a long, painful labor, Connie gave birth to a baby boy, just as Fiona had predicted. Dominic reluctantly agreed to name the boy Vincent, after Connie's father, and when they brought the baby home from the hospital, Connie was grateful to have Fiona there to help.

Gino, like Dominic was a hard worker, putting extra hours in at the shipyard, and saving enough money to put a small down payment on an apartment building in Euclid Heights. He and Fiona kept one apartment for themselves.

Dominic still went out on Friday nights, and feeling that he could trust his cousin Gino to be discreet, he invited him to go along. Connie never questioned them about where they went. She actually looked forward to Friday nights when she could get some peace and quiet. Gino liked being with Dominic but he didn't understand his disrespect to Connie. After several nights of watching his cousin carouse with strange women, Gino couldn't take it any longer.

Connie answered a knock at the door and smiled when she saw Gino, dressed in his gray pinstriped suit and red tie. "Hello Gino, how are you?" She invited him into the house, and gestured for him to sit but he remained standing by the door. She sat on the sofa and went back to her mending. "Everything okay, Gino?"

"I'm good, Connie," he said, looking edgy. "I think I'll stand, though. Is cousin Dominic ready?"

Connie eyed him curiously. "He'll be ready in a minute," she said. "Can I get you anything?"

"Nah…I don't want nothin', I'm okay."

"How's Fiona doin' with her guy?" Connie asked, knowing that Fiona was seriously smitten with an older gentleman she had met. He was widowed and looking for an apartment, and happened to move into Gino and Fiona's building. His name was Edward, and the two had been dating for several weeks.

"She's fine," Gino said, casually. "They're talkin' 'bout getting married."

"No…" Connie let the shirt she was mending drop to her lap. She looked at Gino and smiled. "Married?"

"Yeah…too soon if you ask me but she's a grown woman…" he shrugged.

"Yes she is, and she's very smart too, so don't worry…I'm sure she knows what she's doing."

Dominic came into the room. He was wearing one of his best suits, and new leather shoes. "Oh Gino, I didn't hear you come in," he said, as he finished knotting his tie, "how ya doin?"

"Dominic," Gino said, quietly acknowledging his cousin.

"Hey, Connie," Dominic said, turning to her, "me and Gino have a meeting tonight at the Italian American Club, so I won't be home til late…so, don't wait up."

"I never do," she said, without looking up.

Gino turned his back and swore under his breath.

Dominic looked at his cousin curiously. "Hey Gino, what's the matter with *you*?"

"Nothin'," Gino answered. "Listen Dominic, I been thinkin'…why don't you go by yourself tonight. I don't wanna be no part of this no more, know what I mean?"

"What?" Dominic's eyes widened, and Connie noticed a look of panic on her husband's face. "Part of what? What're you talkin' about?" Dominic laughed nervously. He turned to Connie and shrugged. "What's with this guy?"

Connie knew what Gino was upset about. There was no meeting… Dominic was seeing a woman. She had known for a long time what

Friday nights were about. What Gino didn't know was that she didn't care anymore.

"I gotta go..." Gino said, turning toward the door. "You should talk to your wife. I'll see you, Connie." Gino nodded in her direction, and left the house without looking at his cousin.

Dominic stood staring at the front door. "Huh, what the hell..."

Is that a look of guilt on my dear husband's face, Connie thought, with a wistful smile. "Gee, I don't know, Dominic." She glanced at the clock on the wall. "Hey, you better get goin'...you don't wanna be late for your meeting."

Dominic eyed her suspiciously but didn't respond. "Night," he said, quietly and left the house.

*

On a Saturday morning in May, Fiona and Edward went to City Hall and got married. Connie was the only one who knew but was sworn to secrecy, and excitedly planned a special dinner for them following the quick ceremony. Not only would Fiona tell her brother and Dominic about the wedding but Connie and Dominic also planned on asking Fiona and Gino to be the Godparents for Vincent.

When dinner was over, Gino placed his elbows on the table and leaned forward. "Now...dinner is over. Why did you want to talk to us, Dominic?" Gino asked.

"Before Dominic speaks, dear brother, I have an announcement to make," Fiona interrupted. When she had everyone's attention, she proudly announced, "Edward and I got married yesterday!"

"Ah...how 'bout that," Gino said, giving Connie a wink, trying to sound surprised.

"You knew," Fiona said, pointing an accusing finger at her brother.

"Of course I knew. It's all you talked about for months, then you go out on a Saturday morning dressed in your best dress and wearing a hat, and acting like a schoolgirl...of course I knew..."

"Congratulations," Dominic said, rising from his chair. He kissed Fiona on the cheek, and shook Edward's hand. When he sat back in his place, he continued. "Now it's my turn. Connie and me wanna ask the two of you something...Fiona and Gino," he clarified. "We'd like to ask you to be Godmother and Godfather to Vincent. He's going to be baptized next week, and we would like you to stand up for him." Dominic turned to Edward. "Uh, listen Edward," he said, apologetically, "you understand…they're family..."

"Oh yes, yes of course," Edward said, raising his hand and nodding. He actually seemed relieved.

"Well, how 'bout that Fiona, isn't that nice?" Gino asked.

"So nice…we'd love to," Fiona said, giving Connie's hand an affectionate squeeze.

Later that evening, Connie and Fiona were in the kitchen putting the dishes away, when Connie overheard Dominic talking to Edward. She and Fiona stood by the door and listened.

"Hey Edward, you do what you want but I'm tellin' ya…don't show your wife too much love…I'm just sayin', ya know? And whatever you do, don't give her too much."

"I don't understand," Edward said.

"You don't know what I mean by too much? Too much…you know…buyin' her stuff. You know, shit like that. Because she'll walk all over you."

Edward stared, not knowing what to say.

"No, really," Dominic continued. "Take it from me…I mean, look at me, with my wife… I don't go 'round tellin' her how great she is and stuff, and she…well, she respects me." He thought for a second, and laughed. "It don't hurt that she's stupid too," he laughed again. "Seriously, if you show them too much love, they won't respect you, it's as simple as that. They *have* to be afraid of you, or they'll do bad to you, you know what I mean? And if your wife does bad, well then, you gotta teach her right." The sound of his fist hitting the palm of his hand made Connie jump. Her hands flew to her mouth. Fiona put her arm around Connie's shoulders and held her.

"Shh, I wanna hear what Edward says," Fiona said.

"I treat Fiona just fine," Edward said, "and she deserves to be treated that way. So, I think I'll stick to my way of doing things, if you don't mind."

Dominic gave Edward a quizzical look. "You're not Italian, are you?"

"No, why?"

"What are ya…Irish, or something?"

Edward laughed. "No, I'm of English dissent but I don't think that has anything to with how I treat Fiona. We'll be just fine…thanks anyway."

"Jesus…try to help a guy…" Dominic said, with an insolent grin.

Connie moved away from the door and stood in the kitchen hiding her face. "Oh my God…I'm so embarrassed."

"Don't worry about it, Connie." Fiona took Connie into her arms. "He's the idiot. I just feel bad for *you*."

"Me too," Connie agreed.

Dominic was a fool if he thought Connie respected him. It wasn't respect. It was fear. Any love she may have had for him was gone, and she was wedged so tightly into her life of abuse that she simply accepted it as her fate.

*

"Connie…that's all the milk we have?" Dominic asked, while standing in front of the open door of the refrigerator.

"I'm going to the market today, Dominic. I'll pick some up, okay?"

"No, that's not okay! You go get it now!"

"Dominic," she said, when she came into the kitchen with Vincent in her arms. "Please, calm down. There should be enough for you to have some cereal. Was it cereal you wanted this morning?"

"No, I don't want anything right now but I don't like it when we're this low on milk, that's all!"

"Okay, no problem," she said, calmly. "I'll go now." She took Vincent into Phillip who was sitting on his bed, reading a comic book. "I'm running to the market, Phillip…please watch the baby, okay?"

"Okay, Ma." He took Vincent from her. "Come here, squirt," he teased, and playfully tossed the baby on the bed.

Connie got her coat and purse, and made the quick drive to the corner supermarket. When she got home, she put the milk in the refrigerator, and saw that Dominic was in the back yard repairing a broken wheel on the lawnmower.

"Dominic, I'm home," she called.

"Okay. Did ya get the milk?"

"Yes, I got the milk. You want some cereal or something?"

"No, not now."

Connie shook her head, and wondered why he was so panicked about milk. "Okay, well let me know if you need anything."

"Hey Connie, come here. I'm working on this tire here," he said, when she approached his side. "I need ya to hold these pliers."

"Oh sure." She took the pliers and squeezed tightly around the bolt.

"You're not doin' it right, Connie," he complained, grabbing the pliers from her. "Here, let me do it," he snapped. "You can't even hold pliers the right way?"

"I'm sorry, Dominic, I thought that's the way you said to hold it."

"I'll do it…but stand here in case I need you."

"Okay." Connie obediently stood by his side while he reattached the wheel.

"There…that's done." He got up from a kneeling position, and turned the lawnmower upright. He glanced over at Connie who was still standing next to him, "You can go now," he said, dismissing her.

"Dominic? Why did you get so upset because we were low on milk?"

"What?" He looked at her curiously.

"You know, you got angry about the milk, why is that?"

"I don't know. Why are askin' me *that*? What do you care?"

"I was just curious…you know, like maybe from your childhood or something…"

"Jesus Christ, Connie. What are you sayin'? That my mother didn't take care of me? You puttin' my mother down?"

"No, I was just…oh, never mind. I didn't mean to upset you." She turned and started for the house.

"Sonofabitch," he said, with frustration, "I hate when you talk about my mother!"

Connie stopped, and attempting to quell an argument said, "I wasn't saying anything about your mother, Dominic. I didn't mean anything…sorry."

*

"Hello," Connie said, after picking up the phone. "Hi Violet, how are you?"

Violet had planned a family reunion, and wanted Connie and the children to come back to Wickhaven, and when Connie mentioned it to Dominic, he simply said, 'no.'

"Why, Dominic?"

"Because I said no, that's all."

"Dominic, that doesn't make any sense at all!" She said, fighting anger. "My God, I haven't seen my family in two years. What would be so wrong taking the kids for a visit?"

"I can't stand those people, Connie, you know that."

"Well, you don't have to go. I could go with the kids," she protested.

"It's just not a good time." He got up and walked out of the room and later that night, when she broached the subject again, she was given one of the worst beatings she ever had. The next day, she called Violet and said she was sorry but they couldn't come to the reunion. Connie refused to speak to Dominic for several days, and the next time Violet called was to tell Connie that their father had died in his sleep.

Chapter 17

Dominic continued to impress the executive department at Tocoma Construction and was now a respected, and highly paid member of the union. He had put away a substantial amount of money over the years, and decided it was time to build a house for his family, so along with Vittorio, he went to buy a piece of ground.

"I want to drive over to Euclid Heights tomorrow," he told Connie. "Vittorio bought a house there and Antonio's buying one too, and they were telling me the ground is really at a good price right now."

"Euclid Heights…where Gino's apartment building is?"

"Yeah, a lot of big houses goin' up there."

"Okay, what time do you wanna go?"

"Early."

"Very good, I'll have the kids ready."

"Connie, make me some eggs, would ya?"

"Sure."

"And a little toast…not too much butter, though. My stomach's been bothering me a little. I hope there's nothin' wrong."

"I'm sure you're fine," Connie assured him.

"Oh, and Connie…a little of that ham, okay? And fry it up just enough to heat it, not brown. I hate when you make it dry." He grimaced and rubbed his stomach. "My stomach don't feel too good…I don't know, maybe I'm just hungry. What do you think, Connie? Think I'm okay?"

"I'm sure you are, Dominic," she said. *You should only drop dead now, you pain in the ass,* she thought. "No problem." His breakfast was on the table within minutes, and when he sat down, she placed a napkin by his plate.

"Ech, you know what Connie? My stomach still don't feel too good today. Just give me a little oatmeal instead."

She took the plate away, and from past experience, had already made the oatmeal. It was sitting in a pot on the back burner. "No problem."

Phillip sat at the other end of table. He was thumbing through a magazine about cars, but listening to the conversation between his parents. He looked up and caught his mother's attention, and rolled his eyes.

She frowned, and shook her head.

"You got a little coffee there, Connie?" Dominic asked.

"Mm-hm." She reached for the pot and poured coffee into a china cup.

"You didn't make it too strong, did ya?" He asked the same question every morning. "Don't forget to put water in my juice too…the acid kills me," he said, with a pained expression. He ate the oatmeal, sipped some coffee and drank down the juice. His cheeks puffed out as he belched, and he pushed back from the table. "I'll be home around six."

"All right, Dominic, you have a good day, now." Connie cleared the table and started breakfast for the kids.

"Thank God, he's gone," Phillip grumbled, tossing the magazine on the table.

"Phil please, don't start," Connie said, as she put bowls of cereal on the table. "Where're your brother and sister?"

"Vito! Luci!" He bellowed. "Hurry up…we're gonna be late for school!"

"Hush, Phillip! The baby is still sleeping."

"Sorry."

Connie sat down and ate Dominic's plate of ham and eggs. Vito came bounding into the kitchen, plopping himself into a chair, and scooting close to the table. "Is Dad still here?"

"No, he left for work."

"Good!"

"Vito! You and your brother have got to stop that! That's your father; you should show him respect."

"Oh my God, Ma! Are you kidding?" Phillip laughed. "Respect him? All he does is yell at us, and beat the crap out of us. And he beats you too, Ma. You think we don't know that?"

"Yeah Ma," Vito agreed in his little boy voice. "I heard him call you a dirty name." He snickered and shoved a spoonful of cereal into his mouth.

"That's enough," Connie scolded. "If you behave yourselves and do what you're told, you'll stay out of trouble."

"Mornin' Mom," Lucinda mumbled, sounding sleepy.

"Mornin' Luci, didn't you sleep good?" Connie asked. She pushed Luci's hair back from her face.

"I guess so."

"Good, now eat your toast. It's almost time to leave for school. We're going to look at some property tomorrow, so I want all of you to be ready early, you hear me?" Connie said.

"Property? For what?" Phillip asked.

"Your father wants to build a house for us."

"Why do *we* have to go?" He objected, vehemently.

"Because your father said you have to go, that's why."

"Aw, man," Vito whined, looking at his older brother to show his alliance.

"That'll be enough of that. Now get your books together and get going."

*

The following morning Connie, Dominic and the four children piled into Dominic's Buick and drove the short distance to Euclid Heights. They met with Vittorio and Antonio who had told Dominic about a piece of ground for sale on the corner of Hyatt Street and Liberty Avenue.

"This is nice…huh?" Dominic said, after getting out of the car. He walked to where his brothers were standing in the middle of a large corner lot, thick with overgrown weeds. "What do ya think, Connie… nice?"

"It's big," Connie observed, holding her hand up to her forehead to shield the sun from her eyes. She was carrying Vito in the other arm, balancing him on her hip.

"We can build the house facing toward Liberty Avenue, and build a garage on the back of the house. What do you think, Antonio?"

"Yeah, I think that's good, Dom," he agreed, looking around the property with his hands on his hips, nodding his approval. "But I think you should put the garage on the back of the lot. It's dangerous having it attached to the house."

"I don't know..." Dominic said.

"That would be a long walk from the garage to the house, wouldn't it?" Connie asked.

"Too dangerous," Antonio repeated, shaking his head.

"How much do they want for the lot, Dominic?" Connie asked.

"Four thousand, but I'll offer him three thousand."

They continued to walk around the lot, and the kids were busy scaling an oak tree at the corner of the property.

"Connie, I'm gonna to drop you off at Vittorio's, and you and the kids can visit with Tessa. We'll go make a deal with Mr..." he turned to Vittorio, "what was his name?"

"Hadden or Hayden, somethin' like dat."

"Okay, let's go."

Later that night, Dominic and his brothers came back to Vittorio's house, slapping each other on the back, laughing and celebrating the good deal they had just made. Connie shushed them as they drunkenly tripped their way into the living room.

"The baby's sleeping." She scolded, waving her hand at them. "So... what happened?"

"Are you ready to start building a house, Connie?" Dominic asked, looking at her with a lopsided grin?

"Yeah, I guess so. Did you get a good deal?"

"I gave him a thousand cash, and we have to give him another two thousand tomorrow. So, yeah, I think we got a good deal, right Vittorio?"

"Yeah, yeah, ya gotta a good deal." Vittorio nodded.

"Come...everybody, is time to eat." Tessa said, wiping her hands on her apron.

*

The building of the house was a yearlong process, and Dominic was determined to build it himself. Connie stood obediently by his side while he hammered nails, mixed cement, installed plumbing and electrical work. She carried stone from the back of a truck to the front of the house where Dominic was building a wall around the property, and handed him tools, held ladders and stirred cement in a galvanized tub.

Phillip hated the whole process. He worked by his father's side, after school and on weekends but the day usually ended with a fight and a beating. Phillip did his best to follow his father's instructions but never seemed to get it right. His father enjoyed belittling him in front of everyone, and he called him "stupid" so many times, that Phillip seethed to the point of fantasizing about his father drowning in a vat of cement.

"Look at you…what a baby," his father taunted. "Now, don't go runnin' to your Mommy, tellin' her, boohoo…daddy's so mean," he mocked. "Be a man, for Christ sake! How ya ever gonna make it in this world if ya go around actin' stupid."

By the time the house was finished, Phillip had developed a terrible rash on his feet, and under his arms that caused him pain and embarrassment. Connie took him to a doctor, who told her that Phillip was suffering from bad nerves. She told Phillip the doctor was wrong, and all she needed to do was change laundry detergent.

*

The family finally moved into the house on Liberty Avenue on the second day of May 1956. It was a grand house and Dominic was proud. There were spacious rooms for the boys, a room for Luci and a large bedroom at the end of the hall for Dominic and Connie. A stately living room, with a gray, stone fireplace and bay window took up most of the main floor but sat empty for several months. The family gathered mostly in the kitchen and den, where the children watched television, and where Dominic took his naps after work.

Connie loved the house, and had hopes to fill it with happy memories. It was a little formal for her taste but she spent most of her time in the kitchen anyway. The window above the sink had café curtains and looked out over the backyard where she could watch the children play. She picked out a handsome, crystal chandelier for the dining room but Dominic chose the custom furniture for the living room, as a surprise for her. Upon delivery, she complimented his choice but was horrified at the gaudy, ornate gold pieces with brocade fabric he insisted stay covered with plastic. Heavy marble tables held gold lamp bases with white satin shades, also wrapped in plastic. For years the room sat like a mausoleum, only used when Dominic wanted to impress visitors. His father's concertina sat in a special spot atop a mahogany table he had imported from Italy, and when he played it for family gatherings, Connie thought of the first time he played for her. She remembered the emotion and love in his eyes that day. It was such a long time ago. That love she saw was for his father. She wasn't even sure now if he was capable of loving.

The children were settled in their new school, and Dominic was running the operation at a new job site. Connie was happy at home, taking care of Vinnie. She had made friends with her next-door neighbor, May Binder, and often chatted with her in the backyard. May was divorced, with two teenaged daughters, and a son a couple years older than Vinnie. After getting to know each other, the two women felt confident enough to share details about their lives. They supported each other emotionally, and formed a bond that would last for years.

Phillip, like most teenaged boys started dating. He had grown from being a skinny, pimple-faced boy from Catholic school, to a handsome, olive-skinned young man that charmed the girls in his new public school. With his sleepy, blue green eyes and dimpled smile, there was no shortage of interested girls. He used his sense of humor to mask deep insecurities.

Phillip's dating was a nightmare for Connie. She lied to Dominic and made excuses so Phillip could sneak out of the house. When Phillip first started to date, his father always caught him before he left the house and quickly made up a reason why he couldn't go out; or simply said no. Connie was sickened when she realized it was because he was jealous of his own son being with young girls. "I could get those young girls to go out with me," he'd say. "I just don't want to. So don't think you're better than me, Phillip...cause you're not. You'll never be the man I am."

One Friday night, Connie waited until Dominic fell asleep on the sofa, then shooed Phillip out the door to meet his new girlfriend. Dominic usually slept until nine o'clock, and then would go up to bed but that night, he slept until nine but instead of going to bed, he looked for Phillip. Connie played dumb but Dominic knew his son was out for the evening. Phillip, not asking for his father's permission to go out was an unforgivable rule-breaker. Dominic was seething. Connie sat in the den, praying while Dominic waited in the kitchen. At eleven o'clock Phillip came in the door, his father ambushing him from behind. He pummeled him with his fists, and kicked him as he lay on the floor writhing in pain. "Who are you to go out of this house without telling me?"

"You can't hurt me," Phillip groaned, defiantly.

"Oh yeah?" Dominic whipped his belt from around his waist, and raised it above his head, bringing it down with a sickening *crack* into the back of Phillip's head.

"Dominic! Don't do that!" Connie cried, desperately. She ran into the room and grabbed his arm, raised and ready to strike Phillip again.

Dominic gripped her shoulder, his fingernails sinking into her skin. "You want some too, Connie. Huh? Is that what you want?"

"Dad, leave her alone, Goddamnit!" Phillip cried, forcing himself between his mother and father.

Dominic bit his lower lip and smiled. "You a tough guy?" He let go of Connie and turned his attention toward Phillip again, and with a thrust of his hands on Phillip's chest, pushed him to the floor. He drew back his foot and kicked Phillip in the crotch. Phillip's body curled into the fetal position where he stayed for several minutes, moaning and choking.

"Dominic, please..." Connie pleaded, breathlessly. "Please stop."

Dominic stood firm, his feet spread apart, and his hands balled into tight fists. He was panting and glaring down at his son. His expression was one of triumph.

Phillip's pain turned to numbness. He felt the burning, bitter taste of bile rise up in his throat and at that moment, he just wanted to die.

"You stupid piece of shit, get up. Get up, I said! Be a man, for Christ's sake!" Dominic hissed through gritted teeth, and kicked his son in the backside.

Connie moved toward Phillip but Dominic blocked her with his arm.

"He can get up on his own, Connie…right, Son?"

Phillip struggled to get to his feet.

"You're almost a man now, aren't ya? You wanna fuck all the girls, right? You can take a little kick in the balls once in a while, can't ya?"

Phillip was standing, hunched over, looking down at the floor. Tears were falling and landing on the tops of his shoes. Saliva dripped from the corner of his mouth.

"There ya go...see? You're okay. Look Connie, he's okay," he said, slapping Phillip on the back. "He's a man, like his dad; he can take it, right, Son?" He was smiling. He sat at the kitchen table, put his arms up in the air, stretched and yawned. "I'll tell ya what… I think I'd like you to go outside and wash my car."

Connie stared at him but said nothing. She looked at Phillip, her eyes pleading. She gave him a slight nod, telling him to please do as his father ordered. It was dark outside but Phillip obeyed, put on his jacket, and quietly walked out the back door.

"I'll come check the car later, Son…to see the job you did."

Phillip was glad he didn't have a gun because if he did, he would have shot his father that night. Connie stood in the middle of the room shaking and fighting nausea, while Dominic went back to the sofa to lie down. She wanted to go out and talk to Phillip but knew that Dominic would stop her. "*Goddamned sonofabitch,*" she cried, quietly. *"Why don't you drop dead, you bastard*?"

Phillip had finished washing the car, and came into the house, shivering violently, not from the cold but from pain. His father had gone up to bed and his mother was waiting for him. She was sitting at the table, in the dark, sipping coffee. Phillip hadn't noticed her when he hung his jacket.

"Phillip? Are you okay?" She whispered.

"Ma! Jesus Christ, you scared me."

"I'm sorry, Son. I wanted to wait for you…make sure you were all right."

"I'll be okay," he said, flopping in a chair opposite her. He looked at his mother. "I hate his guts, Ma. I swear to God, I do. I wish he was dead!"

"I know," Connie said, wringing her hands, looking shattered. She understood because she hated him too.

"He hurt you?" Phillip asked, as an afterthought.

"No."

"You sure?"

"Yeah," she said. "*You* okay?"

"Are you kidding?" He smirked.

Connie found it hard to look at him.

"I'm goin' up to bed, Ma." He stood up and leaned over to kiss her on the cheek. "How sick is it that I can only give my mother a kiss when he's not around?"

*

Phillip's body was aching so badly, he could hardly climb the stairs. His brothers were asleep, so he took a pack of Kent cigarettes from under his mattress, climbed out the bedroom window, onto the roof, and leaned up against the cool bricks. He clenched a cigarette between his teeth and lit it, drawing deeply, letting a thick puff of smoke travel to his lungs. He blew the smoke skyward, watching it disappear into the night air. He held the cigarette between his finger and thumb, looked at it with a sideways glance and said to himself, "*If I can suck on this cigarette and smoke it all the way down in one puff, my father will drop dead!*

Chapter 18

Dominic received a letter from his mother informing him that she was coming to the states, along with his two sisters. After vigorous arguments with his brothers, Dominic convinced them that their mother would be better off living with him, and that they were welcome to have the sisters.

It was the summer of 1959 when Ottavia Giovanna Preste and her daughters Gia and Annette had arrived in the states. Connie, with Phillip and Luci's help had been cleaning the house for days. She moved Vinnie out of the room that was the nursery, and into the room Phillip shared with Vito. Dominic bought a new bed for his mother, and Connie decorated the room with a new spread and matching curtains. This was a day of celebration for Dominic, a day to show off his family, his house and his success. His entire family was coming to dinner, and Connie had been cooking for three days. She checked and rechecked pots that were simmering on the stove, and after Luci came downstairs with Vinnie in her arms, she joined her brothers, who were standing in line to be inspected by their mother. Connie fussed over them, licking her fingers and smoothing stray hairs. She straightened the boys' shirt collars, and ran a brush through Luci's hair for the third time.

"Ma, stop it," Vito said, irritably pushing her hand away as she pressed at the stubborn cowlick on the top of his head. "What're ya so nervous about?"

"Shut up, Vito. Don't give me any shit right now!" Connie warned.

"God…what's with Ma?" Vito grumbled, looking up at Phillip. "She hafta cuss at me like that?"

"Shut up Vito," Phillip echoed his mother's words, and poked him in the ribs.

"Just stop it you two," Connie said. "I just want everything to go right, that's all." She grabbed the dishtowel she had tucked into the waistband of her skirt and flung it over the edge of the kitchen sink. She moved to the backdoor and watched the driveway. The kids went into the den. "Don't get dirty," she hollered. She placed both hands on her fluttering stomach when she saw Dominic's car pull into the driveway, followed by Vittorio and Antonio. Sergio and his family got out of the back of Antonio's station wagon. Vittorio and Tessa's two girls, dressed in pink, ruffled taffeta reminded Connie of birthday cakes. They looked like twins, though a year apart. They wore their jet-black hair in perfect ringlets that cascaded down their backs. Sergio and his wife, Anna had two sons, one younger than Vito and one older. They were wearing their Sunday suits, and their hair was freshly oiled and combed to the side. Antonio and his wife, Gemma had a boy the same age as Luci, and he stood at the back of the car, alone, looking completely disgusted with having to be there.

Connie, of course was closer with Tessa that her other sisters-in-law but got along fine with Anna as well. Gemma however had a tendency to talk behind people's backs, especially Connie's.

Still standing in the doorway, Connie watched as the Preste family rushed to Dominic's car. They pushed and shoved each other to help the old lady out of the front seat, and she angrily slapped to leave her alone. The two sisters were the last to get out of the backseat. Thinking back to her conversations with Fiona, Connie shivered. The old lady looked frail, and walked slowly. Her back was slightly curved, causing her to look at the ground as she walked toward the house. She was dressed in black with a black, cotton scarf on her head, tied under her chin. A black, button-down sweater was wrapped around her shoulders. As she approached the house, she lifted her head, and Connie was stunned at the remarkable resemblance between Dominic and his mother. The woman looked sad; troubled but there was coldness in her eyes. Connie had seen that look in Dominic's eyes so many times before.

"Kids come on, they're here!" Connie shouted. Phillip, Luci and Vito came running, and stood by their mother. Luci held Vinnie in her arms. Connie watched as Dominic took his mother by the elbow and helped her up the back steps and in the back door.

"*Il benvenuto alla nostra casa, Preste di Madre,*" Connie said, in perfect Italian, welcoming Dominic's mother to their home. Connie leaned down to embrace her but the old woman stood rigid, her arms down to her sides. Connie stood back and clasped her hands behind her back, and gave Dominic a nervous smile.

Dominic took his mother by the arm and led her to a chair in the corner of the kitchen, where she sat, stone-faced with her hands folded in her lap. Before he walked away from her, she reached and took hold of the sleeve of his jacket. "*Che e' il suo nome*?" Asking what was Connie's name.

"Conchetta...her name is Conchetta, Ma. Remember...I told you that," Dominic said, looking annoyed. His mother nodded slowly, and shifted her gaze toward the children who stood obediently by Connie's side.

"Give your grandmother a hug boys...go on," Connie urged, "Luci, you too." Luci sat Vinnie down on the floor. He latched onto Connie's skirt and cowered, burying his face into the back of her legs. "He's a little shy. Come, Vinnie...say hello to your grandmother."

Mother Preste looked at him with her coal black eyes, and thin lips turned down in a grimace. Vinnie's eyes widened and his lower lip started to quiver as he grabbed a tighter handful of his mother's skirt. Connie quickly picked him up and handed him to Luci who swept him off to the den. *"Midispiace. Deve conoscerti,"* she apologized, explaining that Vinnie needed to get to know his grandmother.

Without expression, Mother Preste nodded.

"Can I take...oh sorry...*posso portare la sua sciarpa e la sua borsa?"* she asked, offering to take her scarf and purse for her.

"Nah."

Connie smiled, turned and joined Dominic and the rest of his family.

*

Annette was the younger of the two sisters. She was tall and thin with coal black hair that she wore in a pile of heavily sprayed curls on top of her head. She had an attractive face that Connie thought was ruined with an orange-colored makeup. Her black-penciled brows were thin and severe, and her full lips were tinted with a mauve-colored lipstick. She wore a white, silk blouse tucked neatly into the waistband of a black pleated skirt. The blouse was unbuttoned to the crease of her bust line. Her voice was husky and loud but Connie thought her to have a colorful personality, flirty and a bit bawdy. Connie remembered a story Tessa had told her about Annette being an embarrassment to her mother. She was still single, and out of control, and it was rumored that she had at least two abortions, and could smoke and drink any man under the table. Annette was one of the reasons Mrs. Preste wanted to come to the United States. She wanted Annette's brothers to find her a suitable husband, and apparently they already had. Connie didn't know who the man was but Annette agreed to meet him because he supposedly had money. His name was John Finnochio and he worked at the same oil refinery plant as Vittorio. He was tough and old fashioned, and came from a hardworking family back in Italy, and after coming to the United State, he saved almost every dollar he ever made. He owned a home in Dellhaven, a two year-old car, had a bank account, and most important of all, agreed to court Annette.

*

Gia was in her thirties, and married to Masto Costanza, who was due to join her in the states the following month. She was fashionably dressed in a navy-blue suit, and a double-strand of pearls that were draped elegantly under her collar. Connie eyed Gia enviously as she sat away from the table, her legs crossed, showing off open-toed, designer shoes. Her hair was dark and cut short, finger waves perfectly sculpted around her tastefully made-up face. She had a constant smirk and a demanding tone to her voice, as she talked over her brothers in rapid-fire Italian.

Everyone was gathered at the kitchen table while Connie continued to work. She listened to their conversation while filling water glasses and preparing the salad. No one seemed interested in her or what she was doing. Gia occasionally covered her mouth with her hand, and spoke softly to Dominic, then stole brief glimpses at Connie.

"Dominic come, take me for a tour of your house," Gia said, with a thick Italian accent. "I wan' to see everyt'ing you build." She followed him from one room to the next, nodding approval. "Very nice, Dominic...you did a good job." She casually swiped a finger across the coffee table, and closely inspected it. Dominic's expression was that of a child waiting for approval.

Sauntering back into the kitchen, Gia's designer heels clicked across the tile floor. She stood next to Connie. "Well Conchetta, my brother... he build you a beautiful home, eh? I hope you're good to him," she smiled, and looked back at Dominic. "Look what he has done for you... my God," she added, standing with her arms folded.

"Yes, he built us a beautiful house," Connie agreed, suddenly feeling embarrassed with everyone watching for her.

"Gia," Dominic said, "why don't you sit here." He pulled out a chair, and poured her a glass of wine, setting it on the table. Gia walked slowly over to Dominic. She smoothed her skirt before easing back in the chair, almost regally, seeming to enjoy the attention.

The family was soon engaged in vigorous conversation again, and when Dominic saw that Connie was having difficulty working around them suggested, "Listen, why don't we move into the living room so Connie can finish getting dinner on the table?" He picked up his glass of wine and walked out of the kitchen, the rest followed but Mother Preste sat quietly in the corner watching Connie work.

Gia stood in the middle of the ornate living room. "My God Dominic, why in the world would you get furniture like this?" She asked, sliding onto the plastic covered wingchair that sat by the fireplace.

"What'dya mean?" Dominic asked, sounding offended.

"No...I just mean it's so, so...I don't know, just nothing I would like. But if you like it..."

Connie was listening, and stole a glance at Dominic. He stood up and laughed the kind of laugh that meant he was getting mad; about to explode. "Well, Connie liked it, so I got it for her. That's the kind of husband I am."

"Oh...I didn't think you'd pick this style."

"Now listen, Gia…most people can't afford furniture like this. It's all imported, ya know."

The plastic made a crunching sound as Gia sat back in the chair. "Why are you taking that tone with me, Dominic?" She asked. "If your wife likes this kind of thing, what do I care…I was just asking."

Connie rolled her eyes, turned and went to the kitchen window to check on the kids. She walked over to her mother-in-law. "Mother Preste…can I get you anything?" She asked, feeling sorry for the old woman. She looked lonely and no one was bothering with her.

"Nah," Mother Preste looked up and waved her hand.

"Connie!" Dominic called.

Connie left the old woman and stepped into the living room. "What is it, Dominic?"

"Go get Ma and bring her in here with us."

Connie went back into the kitchen, gently placing her hand on the old woman's shoulder. "You want to go into the other room with the rest of the family?" Connie asked, pointing toward the living room.

"Nah."

"Okay." Connie straightened, rubbed her aching back and sighed. She went back to Dominic. "She wants to stay in the kitchen."

"So leave her there," he said, "whatever she wants."

Connie was putting the finishing touches on the dining table when she heard the familiar sound of the "oom-pa" coming from Dominic's concertina. She stood at the entrance of the living room and watched as Dominic's sisters and brothers did the '*tarantella*', linking their arms and spinning around the room. When he finished playing, they clutched their chests, laughing and flopping onto the sofa. The music of the concertina, once again, brought a warm smile to Dominic's face, and a rare sense of joy to the house. She went back into the kitchen, and noticed Dominic's mother sitting with her fingers in her ears. Tears were streaming down her face. Connie walked over and put her hand on the old woman's shoulder. "Are you okay?" She asked.

She jumped at Connie's touch. "Ach," the old woman said, turning her head, wiping tears from under her eyes.

Connie called Luci into the house. "Luci, would you tell everybody that dinner is on the table?"

After Luci did as her mother asked, Dominic came into the kitchen and told his mother, "Mama, come on…time to eat, *mangiamo*."

She flapped her hand at him, and stood up on her own. *"Posso camminare da mie,"* she told him, explaining she could walk by herself. She took tiny steps into the dining room where Antonio pulled out a chair for her at the head of the table.

"Ain't this nice, Ma?" Dominic asked, proud of the food Connie had displayed on the table.

Hot, steaming bowls of pasta fragioli were at each place along with plates of fresh green salad. A meat platter was piled high with sliced turkey and cornbread stuffing. A large, hand painted bowl was filled with ravioli, and another with meatballs. There was a plate of pork that was used to flavor the tomato sauce, and a bowl of fresh grated cheese. Dominic stood up to slice bread. "Help yourself everyone. *Mangiamo!"*

"Here, Ma," Annette said, placing a ravioli and one meatball on her mother's plate.

Connie filled the children's plates, and got them situated at the picnic table on the back patio, where they ate and giggled as the older ones teased the younger ones.

"Gia, what the hell…you're not eating?" Dominic asked, while chewing on a mouthful of bread.

"Don't worry 'bout me, Dominic. I'm not hungry."

"Not hungry…how do you come into someone's home and not eat?" Dominic's temper was rising again.

"It's cause she's too fat," Vittorio laughed.

"You better not say that," Gia warned.

Connie was standing behind Dominic's chair. She leaned over and quietly whispered in his ear, "Dominic, it's all right, don't get upset… maybe I can get Gia something else."

"Well, that's just stupid. No, Connie! You don't get her nothin' else! I gotta tell ya, Gia, I'm a little mad here."

Gia waved her hand, looking smug. "Calm down, Dominic. I'll eat another time…just not right now."

Dominic grumbled under his breath a minute or two then dropped the subject. Connie found the whole thing extremely odd.

Vittorio tapped Tessa on the shoulder and gestured for her to help Connie, who still hadn't sat down to eat.

"Oh yes, yes…let me go help her," Tessa said, getting up from the table.

"Connie's all right, Vittorio," Dominic said. "Don't make Tessa get up."

"Dominic," Vittorio said. "For God's sake, your wife's been running around ever since we got here. She's gotta eat too, eh? Come on Connie, sit down." Vittorio wedged a chair between Tessa and Annette.

Connie glanced at Dominic, wiped her face with a dishtowel and sat down. She took a few bites, and pushed the food around on her plate feeling Dominic's eyes on her. "Can I get anybody anything?" She quickly asked.

"I could use another glass of wine, Conchetta," Gia said, holding her empty wineglass above her head.

Tessa put her hand on Connie's shoulder. "Sit Connie…I'll get it." As she walked into the kitchen, Tessa turned and flashed Gia a look of disgust.

"So Connie, where are you from?" Annette asked.

"Upstate Pennsylvania. A little town called Wickhaven."

"That's where you and my brother met, right?" Gia asked.

"That's right."

"Dominic tells me your father was a *contrabbandier* or what was it you said, Dominic?"

"A bootlegger," he answered, casually.

"Bootlegger…" Gia repeated. "Huh."

"Yup, he was mean too. I'll tell ya what, he was a little guy but he was tough! Sonofabitch carried a gun!" He laughed and slapped the table, nearly toppling the glasses. "I'd like to know some of the shit that went on with his little group of mafia pals."

They all laughed and looked at Connie for her reaction. She lowered her head and forced a smile, looking at Dominic out of the corner of her eye.

Noticing her annoyance, Dominic put her on the spot. "What Connie? You know it's true. He was mafia, for Christ sake, you know that."

"I know," she said, quietly. "I wasn't saying anything." She got up from the table, pretended to clear some dishes but mainly wanted to get out of the room.

Annette followed her into the kitchen, got her purse and pulled out a Polaroid camera.

"Come on, let's go into the living room. I want to take a family picture. Ma, you come sit in the middle. Vittorio, eh…help Ma up," she ordered.

Dominic gathered everyone on the sofa around their mother, and Annette suddenly thrust the camera toward Connie. "Here Connie, you take the picture." She nestled herself between Antonio and Sergio and asked, "You know the right button to push, don't you?"

"I think so."

"Okay everybody, smile," Annette said.

"Don't you want a picture with Connie too?" Tessa asked.

"No…we just want family," Gia said. The comment hurt Connie's feelings but she was more hurt that Dominic didn't defend her. She handed the camera back to Annette, and went into the kitchen.

"Connie, did you put the coffee on?" Dominic asked, poking his head in the kitchen door.

"I'm doing it right now."

"Okay." He turned, and then stopped. "Hey Connie, how 'bout my sister, Gia? Watta bitch. Do you believe she wouldn't eat nothin'?"

"I know," Connie said, as she continued to work. "Is she always like that or is she mad about something?"

"Huh," he laughed. "Mad? She's not mad…just jealous. She's so jealous that she'd starve to death before she'd eat our food."

Connie looked at him, "Jealous...because the food we made is good? My God…"

"She's weird, all right. By the way, I tried to change her mind but I think she hates you."

Connie spun around, and stared at him. "What?"

"I'm just sayin'…" he shrugged. "I told her you're a good wife and all…she's like that, though…doesn't like anybody having better than her."

"Hey, Dominic," Vittorio called from the other room. "We're gonna go sit out in the backyard."

"All right, I'll be right there." Turning to Connie he asked, "Ya want me to send Luci in to help you clean up?"

"Sure," she said, absently. She was stunned by what he said. *She doesn't even know me. Why would she hate me?"*

Dominic followed his brothers and sisters out the back door. The children were playing on one side of the yard while the grownups seated themselves at a cedar picnic table nestled between two fig trees. Dominic beamed as his brothers admired his vegetable garden, and he picked one of his blood red Beefsteak tomatoes and displayed it proudly on the table. "What do ya think of that? Bet ya never saw a tomato like that." Inside the house, Mother Preste sat, once again in the far corner of the kitchen, watching Connie and Luci work.

"Mom," Luci whispered as she dried the dishes. "Why is she staring at us like that? What's wrong with her?"

"Shh, Luci please," Connie scolded. "Nothing's wrong with her, now be quiet."

"Well, I don't like her. She looks mean," Luci pouted.

Connie placed her finger to her lips.

Tessa came back into the house, and pulled a chair alongside her mother-in-law.

"Connie, what a beautiful dinner…my God, you cook for days, eh? *'Che un Connie di cena piacevole non era fatto*?" Tessa said, asking if Mother Preste enjoyed the dinner. The old woman nodded slowly. Tessa sat with her legs open, her skirt draped between her knees. "Ees hot in da kitchen, Connie." She fanned herself with a magazine. "You gonna be so tired tonight."

"I'll be all right, Tessa. You know all about it…you work like this too…I've seen ya."

"Eh…" Tessa nodded, in agreement.

"You still goin' down the basement to cook, and to do your canning?" Connie asked.

"Oh yeah, I still do dat."

"How 'bout hanging the clothes…still not using that dryer Vittorio bought you?"

"Ha," Tess laughed. "You *know* me, huh Connie?"

"Yes I do, so don't talk to me about too much work," Connie smiled. She placed the last plate in the cabinet, filled china cups with fresh coffee, and carried them outside, along with a large bowl of fruit. When she came back into the house, Tessa had gotten Mother Preste settled in Dominic's easy chair.

"She sleep now," Tessa whispered.

"Good, now sit down with me. So, Tessa, how have you been, really?"

"Amma okay."

"Good, good. Your girls are beautiful, Tessa."

"T'ank you, Conchetta. Dey good girls." She paused, and looked in Connie's eyes. "Connie? You gonna be okay with *Preste de Madre*?"

Connie smiled. "If I can handle Dominic, I can handle anybody. I'll do the best I can, ya know?"

"*Credermi, capisco*," Tessa said, in understanding.

"I mean it's only for a while. I think the plan is for her to move in with Gia and her husband. Dominic doesn't really tell me that much but I did hear him fighting with Gia on the phone. Jesus, they're even jealous over who takes care of their mother!" She shook her head.

Chapter 19

Shortly after Dominic's mother moved in, his union went on strike, and what they thought would be a brief layoff, turned into months of negotiations. Money, for the first time in years was tight, and unemployment checks were small. Connie was eventually forced to start paying bills from their savings. She waited until Dominic was out of the house before paying bills because seeing her in the act of writing a check seemed to send him into a rage.

Late one evening, the scent of coffee brought Dominic downstairs where he found Connie sitting in the dark, her hands wrapped around a mug.

"What're you doin' up?" he asked. He ran his fingers through his hair and yawned.

"Sorry, did I wake you?"

"Yeah sort of, I smelled coffee. What's the matter?" He asked again.

"Just couldn't sleep, that's all. I *was* thinking though."

"Yeah, 'bout what?"

"We didn't think the union strike would last this long, so maybe I should get a job to hold us over."

Before she finished, Dominic had already started waving his hand and shaking his head. "No, don't start that."

"Wait a minute Dominic. Listen, please. Come sit, I'll get you a cup of coffee." She continued talking as she grabbed a cup from the cabinet and poured the coffee. "May told me about this little bakery on 6th Avenue, you know the one…Franco's. Well, she said they were hiring, and I'd really like to help out Dominic, ya know…while money's a little tight right now."

"Ah…God." The thought of her getting a job seemed to distress him. His head dropped in resignation.

"It's a nice little bakery Dominic," she continued. "Right around the corner from Dr. Mendleman's office."

"Yeah, I know the one," he said, looking up at the ceiling. He let out an audible sigh, and Connie knew he realized it was a good idea. She almost felt sorry for him.

"I…called them today, and they said they need someone from noon to five a few days a week."

"You called them already?"

"Just outta curiosity, Dominic," she quickly added. "I'm pretty sure I could get the job, and the money would help, don't ya think?"

"What about the kids? Who's gonna look after 'em? I won't be here. I have these shitin' side jobs, and when I'm not working, I'm on the picket line.

"I'm sure that I could work something out. Do you think your mother could watch Vinnie for a few hours? It's only four days a week."

"Are you nuts? No way..."

"Why not? I mean it would just be for a few hours."

"I said *no*, Connie." He said firmly. "Dear God, could you see my sisters now if I had my mother baby-sit. You don't understand, Connie… that's just not gonna happen. "

"Okay, I was just asking. *My* mother used to baby-sit all the time. I didn't think it would be a problem."

"Yeah, well…not *my* mother, okay?"

"Okay, I understand." Now that she thought about it, she really *did* understand. As long as Mother Preste had been with them, she never helped Connie with anything; never even picked up her own dish, so the thought of her babysitting *was* a bad idea.

"If you can't find someone to watch Vinnie, then you just stay at home, Connie. I don't care…we'll make out somehow. The union will probably call me back to work soon. Besides, I don't like the idea of you working." He slid his chair back, stood up, and placed his hands on the small of his back and stretched. "I'm gonna lay down in the den."

Connie poured herself another cup of coffee and couldn't help but feel excited at the prospect of working in a bakery again.

*

"Hello," May answered.

"Hi May, it's Connie."

"Hi Connie, everything okay?"

"I'm fine but I have a favor to ask you."

"Sure, what is it?"

"You know the union's been on strike."

"Yeah, I heard."

"Well, it looks like I have to go to work for a little while."

"Okay."

"Maybe a few weeks or so," Connie continued. "I called about that job at the bakery you told me about, and they said they'd hire me if I wanted the job."

"Oh, good. So what'dya need from me?"

"I need ya to watch Vinnie. I'll pay you," she added, quickly.

"Oh come on Connie, don't be silly. I don't want no pay. It would actually help keep Dennis outta my hair for a couple of hours," she laughed.

"You're a doll, May."

"That's what they tell me," she teased. "Hey listen, you never know, *I* may need a favor one day."

"Well, you know I'm here for you."

"Hey, is your mother-in-law still living with you?"

"Yes, and I know what you're thinking. Why can't *she* baby-sit, right?"

"No Connie, I didn't mean that…I was just curious."

"If you *did* ask me that, I wouldn't blame you. It's the weirdest thing, May… Dominic acts like it would be horrifying to ask her to do anything. She just sits and watches me. And believe me, she does nothing."

"Dear God, I don't envy you. You've got it tough, I know."

"Yeah, well…better days are comin', my mother used to say."

"Well anyway, I can watch Vinnie. Do you know what days you'll be workin'?"

"Not yet. I'm going to the bakery tomorrow morning to find out. And May…I can't thank you enough."

"Forget it honey, anytime."

Connie hung up the phone, and it rang before she had a chance to take her hand from the receiver. "Hello," she answered, thinking May must have forgotten to ask her something.

"'Hello, Connie?"

Connie recognized Vittorio's gravely voice. He always cleared his throat before speaking. "Oh, hello Vittorio. How are you?"

"Good, good. Eh, let me talk to my brother…he dere?"

"He's taking a nap, Vittorio. Can I have him call you later?"

Before Vittorio responded, Dominic wandered into the hallway. "Who is it?" He was squinting from the light of the kitchen, and his hair was pushed up on the side of his head.

"It's Vittorio." She handed him the phone. Connie suddenly felt nervous. Phillip slipped out while his father napped but was supposed to be back in the house within an hour.

Dominic took the phone from Connie's hand, and fumbled with it before putting it to his ear. "Hey, Vittorio," he said, and then paused to listen. "Yeah, good, good, I'm good. What? Oh yeah, okay. We'll be right over." He hung up the phone. "We're goin' over to Vittorio's… just a visit."

"Oh, okay." Connie tried to look casual, giving him a pleasant smile as he headed out of the room. Dominic would expect Phillip to watch the kids or to go with them, and he wasn't home.

"Who you callin'?" Dominic asked, coming back into the kitchen.

"I was just callin' to see if Phillip was down at Doug's."

"Phillip's not home yet?"

"No but I'm sure he'll be home soon. The kids'll be okay with Luci."

"I'll be right back." He grabbed the car keys, and walked out the kitchen door.

Connie watched as he pulled out of the driveway. "Damn it, Phillip," she cried with frustration.

Dominic drove around the neighborhood looking for his son, and the longer he drove, the madder he got. He drove down Liberty Avenue, past the Amoco station where Phillip's friend, Doug pumped gas but he, nor Phillip were there. McEnery Boulevard was bright with storefront lights, and when Dominic finally spotted Phillip, he slowly pulled his car to the curb. Phillip was standing with friends in front of Piasano's Pizza. He was drawing a long toke on a cigarette, and laughing until he spotted his father's car. His face suddenly went pale. He dropped the cigarette and crushed it with the toe of his shoe.

"Hey guys, I gotta go. It's my ol' man." With his head, he gestured toward his father's car.

"Cool," Doug said. "See ya tomorrow?"

"We'll see." Phillip walked to the car, opened the passenger side door and got in. "Hi Dad, what's up?" When his father didn't answer, he knew he was in deep trouble. *Oh, well,* he thought, *here we go again.* He got beatings whether he was home or not, so it didn't much matter anymore. *So, bring it on, ol' man.* He turned his head and stared out the passenger side window, waiting for the first blow. Phillip was defiant and lately seemed to get satisfaction from pushing his father over the edge. Phillip's anger was so intense that sometimes he felt he could put his fist through a brick wall without feeling a thing.

"Do you know what time it is?" His father asked, in a steady, controlled voice.

Phillip looked at the clock on the dashboard. "Eight-thirty."

"And what time are you supposed to be home?"

"Six-thirty but nothin' was goin' on at home so I thought it was okay to stay out."

Dominic turned right on Liberty Avenue, and pulled over to the curb and put the car in park. He shifted his body to face Phillip, and like the speed of a jackhammer, he slammed his fist into the back of Phillip's head. Phillip's face hit the dashboard, breaking the corners of his two front teeth. Phillip's hand flew to his mouth. Blood trickled over his bottom lip. With eyes wide, he turned his head slowly, and looked at his father with blazing rage.

Dominic calmly turned on the ignition, pulled away from the curb and drove home.

After pulling into the driveway, he said, "Now, go run to your Mommy."

Phillip was on the verge of vomiting. He got out of the car, ran into the house, past his mother, and up to his room.

"What happened?" Connie asked, unable to grab him as he ran by.

"Leave the boy alone, he's all right," Dominic said, coming in the door. "I found him down on the boulevard. Smokin' too," he added. "How do ya like that? That's your fault, Connie…you know that, don't you? You're too easy on him. You treat him like a baby."

"I'm gonna go check on him," Connie said, starting for the stairs.

"No you're not," he objected. "Vittorio's waiting for us. You go get my mother ready, and tell her we're goin' out."

*

The following morning Connie sent Luci and Vito off to school. She dressed Vinnie and left him in the den to watch cartoons while she made breakfast for Dominic and his mother. She handed Dominic his lunch pail, and saw him out the door to the picket line. Connie got her mother-in-law settled in front of the television, and went to check on Phillip. He was sitting on the side of the bed, resting his elbows on his knees, looking out the window.

"Phillip?"

He turned around and looked at her. His lips were purple and swollen.

"Oh, Jesus, Joseph and Mary, what did he do to you?" She walked across the room and sat next to him. She felt the sting of tears in her eyes as she placed the palms of her hands on either side of his face.

"Look Ma," Phillip said, gently lifting his upper lip, "he broke my teeth."

"Sonofabitch."

"I hate him, Ma. I really do. I hate his guts!"

"I know. I'm sorry, I'm so sorry. Listen, don't talk too loud; your grandmother's downstairs. If she hears you, she'll go right to your father."

"Oh my God," he said, dropping his head in his hands. "This family is so messed up."

"Listen, Phillip, I'm seeing about a job today. I don't know how long your father's going to be out… is there somewhere you can go? I mean, I'm not gonna make you go to school."

"Yeah, don't worry 'bout it. Believe me, I'm outta here."

Connie stood up, smoothed Phillip's hair, and put her hand to her mouth, "Oh my God," she cried, "look at your face…" She left his room, went into the bathroom and ran a washcloth under cold water and brought it to him. "Hold this on your mouth, it'll take down the swelling.

She left Phillip and went to her room where she put on slacks, a turtleneck sweater and sneakers. She dressed Vinnie in a t-shirt and jumper while he finished watching Romper Room, and then made sure Mother Preste was comfortable before leaving. Connie grabbed a handful of quarters for the bus to 6th Avenue.

*

When Connie arrived at Franco's Bakery, it was crowded with the early morning rush. She waited until the woman behind the counter was free, then asked, "Is Tony Salino here? I'm here to see about a job."

"Over there, honey," the woman directed with her head, as she filled empty bins with fresh doughnuts.

Connie saw a young man dressed in black trousers, a wrinkled dress shirt and a red vest emblazoned with the Franco's logo. A nametag read, *Tony Salino – Mgr.* and was pinned to his lapel. He was filling napkin holders when Connie approached him.

"Mr. Salino?" .

"Yeah, can I help you?" He asked, without looking at her.

"You're the manager, right?"

"That's me." He turned and smiled.

"We spoke on the phone…I'm Connie Preste. I don't know if you remem…"

"Oh yeah, I remember. How ya doin'?" He shook her hand, and looked down at Vinnie. "'Zis your kid?"

"Yeah, my youngest but I have someone to watch him when I work," Connie made sure to say.

"No problem…got three of my own. Come on, follow me." He walked toward a door marked EMPLOYEES ONLY, and Connie followed, with Vinnie still clutching her hand, his little shoes slapping on the floor as he ran to keep up with them. Mr. Salino nodded toward a chair across from a cluttered desk, inviting Connie to sit. "Scuz the mess," he said, as he shoved papers to one side. He sat down, leaned back and folded his hands over his stomach. "So, you say you got experience, huh?"

"I do. It's been a while but I remember everything. I even ran a bakery for a while. It was some time ago but like I said, I remember everything. It was called Leone's," she added, "in Wickhaven, Pennsylvania..." she stopped, realizing she was probably giving more information than he wanted. "Well, never mind...I'm sure you never heard of it."

"Well, I need someone on the ovens, so if you want the job, you can have it."

"Oh thanks, Mr. Salino." She reached to shake his hand. "Um, remember I said I can't work fulltime, I mean I got four kids, ya know?" She looked down at Vinnie who was wedged in the chair along side of her.

"I know," he nodded, "you told me. So how's about three days a week, eleven to three? Peak hours."

"Oh, that's perfect, when do you want me to start?"

"Monday okay for you?"

"That's fine," Connie said, eagerly. "I'll be here." She lifted Vinnie to the floor and headed toward the office door.

His chair squealed as he spun around. "Hey, don't ya wanna know what it pays?"

"Oh sure."

"Three fifty an hour, and I won't take out no taxes or nothin'."

"Okay. Thanks."

*

"Connie, Ma's not feeling too good tonight, so she's gonna go to bed early. I told her you'd bring her dinner upstairs." His tone was strangely cool and flat. Something was on his mind but Connie kept a smile pasted on her face as she served his dinner.

"Okay," Connie said, politely. "What's the matter with her?"

Dominic was sitting at the table with the children. He cut off a pat of butter and slathered it onto a piece of bread. "Don't know," he shrugged. "She's upset about something."

"Upset? About what?"

He stopped what he was doing and looked up at her with annoyance. "I don't know, Connie," he responded, sharply, "why don't *you* ask her." He looked at Vito and Luci, shook his head and laughed; his "evil laugh" Connie called it and it always sent shivers down her spine. "Kids, do you believe how stupid your mother is? I said I don't know what's wrong with your grandmother, and she asks me again. Hoo hoo..." he mocked as he laughed. He leaned in, smiled and whispered, "maybe your mother's deaf!"

Phillip looked down at his plate. Vito and Luci appeased him with a smile.

Dominic sat back, sipped red wine and turned toward Connie. "So, did you see about that job you wanted so bad?"

So there it was, Connie thought to herself. The job. The taunting, the coldness; it was about the job. She had wanted to wait until they were alone but since he brought it up, she answered quietly, "Yeah, I got the job."

"Well, look at you," he said, grinning, "the new bread winner of the family. Pretty proud of yourself, right?"

"Dominic, please...not now...the children. Besides, it's not like that, I just wanna help."

"Hmm...help, huh?" He was nodding, and thinking of what to say. "So," he paused, then fired a question at her, "who's watching Vinnie?"

"May Painter." Connie was leaning over the sink washing dishes. She felt a familiar throb begin between her eyes.

"She knows about this?"

"Yes, Dominic. She's the one that told me about the job."

"Great. Don't like people knowin' our business, Connie."

"She's just helping, Dominic."

"Helping...another one that's helping. That's just great. What time do you get done?"

"Three o'clock."

Dominic looked at her and raised his eyebrows. "My mother's not goin' to like this."

Connie cocked her head but didn't respond. She stared after Dominic as he got up and left the room. *What does his mother have to do with it?* She thought to herself. She looked at the children and held a finger to her lips to quiet them. She stood in the doorway and listened as Dominic sat by his mother, asking for her permission to let Connie go to work.

"Here, Ma," Luci said, holding a pile of dirty dishes. "Want me to wash 'em?"

"What?" The sound of Luci's voice brought Connie back to attention, and she went to the sink, feeling confused and angry.

"I cleared the table for ya," Luci said, proudly.

"Oh, thanks honey. You're a good girl." Connie took the plates from her, and placed them in the sink of soapy water. "Now you kids go to your rooms...and quietly, ya hear? Your Dad is tired, so don't bother him, okay?"

"Yeah yeah, we hear ya," Phillip mumbled. "I'm not goin' to my room, though. I'm goin' out back." He pulled a cigarette from his shirt pocket, gave his mother a defiant look and placed the cigarette in his mouth.

"Phillip! Goddamnit!" She gritted her teeth. "Don't let your father see you with that cigarette."

"Christ, Ma. You think he cares that I smoke?" Phillip said, with a smirk. "You're so..." he stopped himself, flapped his hand at her and walked out the door, into the yard.

Connie was too tired and too busy to worry about Phillip's anger toward her. The fact was, she understood his anger. What she didn't understand was why she put up with Dominic. Was it fear? Was it money? With four kids, where would she go? Dominic had threatened her many times that if she ever left him, she would end up with nothing. *And, by God, whatever we have now belongs to me, too,* she told herself. She watched as Phillip sat on the edge of the picnic table. He held the cigarette tightly between his thumb and index finger, and placed the filter between his lips, taking one, long drag until the cigarette was nothing more than a butt. "Dear God," she muttered, and dropped her head.

Later that evening, she prepared a tray for her mother-in-law and took it up to the old woman's room. Her door was closed, and Connie balanced the tray on her left arm, as she knocked softly with her free hand.

"Entrare," Mother Preste said, in a weak, gravely voice.

Connie came into the darkened room and placed the tray on the bed. "Are you all right, Mother Preste?"

"*Si, si,* sure," she responded, dismissing Connie.

Connie sat on the edge of the bed anyway. The woman eyed the tray of food, and wrinkled her nose as though she smelled something rotten. Her face was gaunt and creased with deep lines. Her skin was sallow, and dark circles framed her hooded eyes. Her salt and pepper hair hadn't been brushed in days and hung, like graying weeds around her face.

"Mother Preste," Connie said, again, "I'm worried about you. Are you happy here with us...because you seem so sad all the time?"

Mother Preste looked at Connie, "Eh?" she said, shaking her head, looking puzzled.

Connie knew the old woman understood her the first time, but indulged her and asked the same question again in Italian.

"Ees okay," she nodded. Her eyes were moist and looked like black marbles.

"Okay, well...there's your dinner. I want you to eat, okay? *Mangiare,*" Connie said, motioning as though she were putting food in her mouth. "If you need anything else, just tell the kids. They're in their rooms, and they'll come and get me if you need me." Connie waited for a response, and when there was none, she sighed and got up to leave the room.

"Conchetta," the old woman said.

"Yes, Mother Preste?"

Connie could tell she wanted to say something to her; maybe even thank her for bringing dinner to her but she simply stared, looking sad. "Dominic..."

"What about Dominic, Mother Preste?"

"Dominic...he is wrong," she said. The letter "r" rolled from her tongue.

"Wrong about what?"

"Please-a...you go."

Connie closed the door. She went into her room, leaned her hands on the dresser, and gazed at her image in the mirror. She thought back to when she was young, vibrant and funny. Now all she saw was worry. Deep wrinkles crept like cracks in the ice from the corners of her eyes, and lines feathered the edge of her lips. Her head was throbbing as it did the day before, and the day before that, and sleepless nights had caused deep, haunting circles under her eyes. She looked as old as Dominic's mother but without the gray hair. She closed her eyes and languished in a few rare seconds of quiet. She took a deep breath, rubbed her weary eyes, and went downstairs.

Dominic was still asleep on the sofa, and the boys were in the basement listening to records. Connie walked halfway down the basement stairs, "Boys, I want you upstairs now, let's go," she ordered. "And be quiet about it, your father's sleeping." She followed them upstairs where she found Luci sitting by her bedroom window, staring out into the darkness. She had a blanket wrapped around her shoulders. "Time for bed, Luci, let's go. Vinnie, you too, all of you to bed, and don't come downstairs, you hear?" After the boys went into their room, Connie glanced in at Luci again. "Luci?" she whispered. "You all right, honey?"

Luci turned and looked at her mother. Her eyes were vacant and troubled. "Uh-huh."

"What's the matter?"

"Nothin'."

"Something's wrong...what is it, Luci?"

"Nothin', Ma. Stop askin' me, please."

Connie paused. She leaned up against the doorway, folded her arms and studied her daughter's expression. "Well, when you feel like talking to me, just let me know."

Luci looked at her mother again and managed a weak smile. "Okay, I will...night." She lay back on her pillow and pulled the covers up under her nose. Connie flipped off the light and shut the door halfway. She stood for a minute in the hallway, and turned when she heard Luci close her door all the way, turning the lock.

Connie went back to the boys' room. She poked her head in the door and was relieved to see that Phillip had come back into the house. She beckoned him to come into the hall. "Phillip, do you know what's wrong with your sister?"

"What'dya mean?"

"Something's bothering her...she seems upset about something but won't talk to me."

"Oh yeah. I asked her too but she won't talk to me neither...almost bit my head off."

"Hmm, seems odd. She's not herself lately." Connie put her hand to the side of her face.

Phillip looked at his mother. He seemed to want to say something but stopped himself.

"What is it, Phillip."

"I don't know...all's I know is, I saw Dad standing here last night," he pointed to a spot just outside Mother Preste's room. "I had to go to the bathroom and I saw him just standin' there, kinda weird like...like he was still sleepin' or somethin'. He looked like he was gonna cry, and it really creeped me out. I said to him, *Dad*...but he didn't answer, so I left him alone and went back to bed. I could still see him standin' there... he went into Luci's room and shut the door. I thought maybe he heard her say somethin', I don't know. Then, I guess I fell asleep."

Connie felt the blood drain from her face, and her knees go weak. When she found her voice again, she said, "Okay Phillip, go to bed."

"You okay, Ma?"

"Yes, yes...go to bed, Son."

Did that bastard touch his own daughter? She asked herself. The thought made her run to the bathroom and vomit.

*

She knew Dominic too well. Her pounding temples told her that her night was not over. She came downstairs to find Dominic sitting at the kitchen table.

"Where have *you* been?" He asked.

"Just getting the kids situated, and I took your mother's dinner up to her."

"What's wrong with her?"

"I don't know...she seems sad. Are you sure it's the best thing for her to be living here, Dominic?"

"Well, now wouldn't your life just be perfect. A new job, getting rid of my mother...what's next, Connie? A boyfriend?"

"For God's sake, Dominic, I'm just thinking of your mother."

Dominic was quiet.

"Can I get you some coffee, or something?" Connie asked, hoping to change the subject. "You didn't eat much dinner; I could heat something up for you."

"Nah…what I ate made me sick anyway." He started to leave the kitchen but Connie stopped him.

"Dominic?"

"What is it, Connie…I'm tired."

"Have you noticed that Luci's been acting troubled…kind of quiet?"

"No, why?"

"Nothin'," she said, waving her hand. "I was just wondering if you noticed anything."

"Why are you askin' me? You're her mother." He started walking out of the room again, then suddenly stopped. "Hey, wait a minute. What are you sayin', that I'm the reason somethin's wrong?" He sounded alarmed but defensive.

"No Dominic, I was just curious if you knew…never mind, I'll handle it."

Dominic stood for a second, ran his fingers through his hair and left the room.

You sonofabitch…if you touched my daughter, I'll kill ya…

Chapter 20

Connie enjoyed the few days a week she worked at Franco's Bakery. She liked the other women and Mr. Salino treated her with respect, and it made her feel good to bring home a paycheck. She cashed her check on Fridays, kept five dollars for herself, and handed the rest to Dominic. His reaction was usually one of indifference.

At the end of each workday, Connie usually found Dominic's mother sitting in the den watching game shows. The sink was usually filled with the dirty dishes from whoever came to visit the old woman that day, and remnants of whatever they ate were left on the table. Laundry sat piled by the basement door.

Connie found a note on the kitchen table that said that Vittorio had picked up his mother and taken her back to his house. "God bless Tessa," Connie smiled, knowing it was probably Tessa's idea to give Connie a break.

"Connie, I'm home," Dominic called, as he came in the back door.

"Hi, Dominic" she said, holding the note in her hand. Dominic slipped off his jacket and draped it over the back of a chair. "You look like you had a good day," she said. "Can I get you anything?"

"How's Ma?" He asked, craning his neck to look toward the den.

"Vittorio and Tessa took her to their house for a visit. That's okay, right?"

"Yeah, s'okay. Jesus Christ, she's been so grouchy lately. What's wrong with her?"

"I don't know if it's grouchy, Dominic. I think it's more like sad."

"There you go again, Connie. What are you sayin'…that she's sad to be with me? You think she's happier with Vittorio?"

"No Dominic, I'm not saying that. Let's not have that argument again. Haven't you noticed that she's been that way ever since she arrived in this country?"

"I'm doin' the best I can, Connie! What do you want from me?"

"Dominic, please calm down. I didn't mean that you were doin' anything wrong. You're taking good care of her…maybe she's just an unhappy person."

"If my father was here…" he uttered.

"What? What about your father?" Connie asked

"I didn't say nothin' about my father. God, Connie, do you constantly have to be grillin' me?"

"I thought you said…oh, never mind. I guess I misunderstood."

Seeming exhausted, Dominic sat down heavily in a chair, and dropped his head into his hands. He was quiet for several minutes, when he looked up and asked, "Where's Phillip? I want him to clean out the garage, and Vito can help him."

"Phillip's at basketball practice, Dominic. Remember…Tuesday afternoons?"

"Basketball! Je-sus Christ! Basketball…of all the dumb..." he angrily replied.

Connie closed her eyes and took a deep breath. She fixed a smile on her face as she poured a cup of coffee, then turned around to face him. "When he comes home I'll send him out to clean the garage, all right, Dominic? Here, why don't you take this coffee and lay down? You'll feel better."

"Don't be rushing me outta the room, Connie. God, you're always pushing me outta the room. Why do you do that?"

"I'm sorry, Dominic. I just thought maybe you wanted to rest."

He took the cup from her and started out of the kitchen, and as an afterthought, said, "I forgot to tell you…the strike is over."

"What? You're kidding! That's great!" *Thank you, sweet Jesus,* she thought.

"Yeah, I start a job tomorrow." He slurped a mouthful of coffee. "The money's good, Connie, real good. It'll probably be long term, so you can quick your job."

"Oh, my job… you want me to quit my job?"

"Yeah, you can quit tomorrow."

*

Connie did quit her job that day and had to admit, she was glad to be able to stay home and catch up on her housework. Dominic even came home in a good mood that night. Working suited him and money made him even happier.

"Did you have a good day?" She asked.

He sat on the edge of a chair and pulled off his work boots. "Yeah, it was okay. Ya got anything to eat?"

"Here, have some soup. Dinner won't be ready for a little bit."

Wearing just his work pants and t-shirt, he pulled himself up to the table. Connie put a bowl of chicken soup in front of him, and he broke off a piece of bread, and dipped it into the broth. "So, did you quit your job today?"

"Yes."

"Good," he simply said.

Luci came into the kitchen, and stopped short when she saw her father. "Oh…hi dad," she said, quietly. "Mom? I'm supposed to go to a student council meeting at the school tonight at six o'clock. It's about the bake sale on Saturday. Can you take me?"

"I'll take you over," Dominic offered. "I gotta get my tires checked over at Mel's anyway. I'll drop you off."

"No!" Connie snapped, looking panicked. "I'll take her," she quickly volunteered. She stopped, regained her composure, and uttered a nervous laugh. "You're still eating, Dominic. I don't want you to rush. I'll run her over to the school." She dried her hands and picked up the keys from the table. "Come on Luci."

"What the hell's the matter with you?" Dominic asked, watching her as she hurried Luci toward the door.

"Nothing, I just figured you just got home from work and all…" She had barely slept through the night since Phillip told her about his father going into Luci's room that night. She hoped her imagination was running away with her, and that her fears would be unfounded but she didn't want to take any chances.

Dominic shook his head. "Woman's nuts."

Vito and Vinnie joined their father at the table. They ate soup, and mumbled one-word answers to their father's questions about school. A few minutes later, Connie came back into the house, and the boys were just putting their dishes into the sink. They went to watch television.

"Dominic? Let me ask you something."

"What's that?"

"Well, I've got a problem. I need to take your mother to doctor's appointments, and the boys to their games…you know? And I need to go to the market…and just like Luci right now, needing to go to school…"

"What're ya gettin' at, Connie?" Dominic said, impatiently.

"Well, what if you weren't here?"

"Yeah, so?"

"I know we can't afford it right now but maybe after you've been back to work for a while, we could get a second car."

"A second car? Ha! I can see it now…you'll never be home. You'll be out to lunch, and shopping…nah," he said, shaking his head. "You can use my car when it's here, and when its not, take the bus. You'll just have to run your errands when I'm home."

"Dominic, that doesn't even make sense. You don't get home until five o'clock. How am I supposed to make appointments for your mother after five? And I don't like to drive after dark, so when do I do the marketing?" She thought for a second before continuing. "Vittorio bought Tessa a car, and she says it's so much better now that she doesn't have to depend on Vittorio to drive her around." *That was a good one,* Connie thought to herself.

Dominic looked at her. "I know he bought her a car, I was with him when he got it." He thought about the car his brother bought. Dominic told him he was crazy to buy such an expensive thing for his wife but he'd be damned if his brother would have two cars to his one. "Damn it, Connie! I hate when you start bitchin' at me!" He went back to sipping his coffee; making slurping sounds that made her skin crawl. "Well, let me think about it, will ya? Christ," he grumbled. "I just get home and I can't even relax."

"I'm sorry, Dominic. We'll talk about it some other time."

He sat quietly for a while, then said, "I think that was a '58' Ford he got, wasn't it? Maybe I'll go look at the '59's. But that doesn't mean I'm gonna buy nothin'," he warned.

"I know. You do what you want," Connie said, turning her back to him, smiling sheepishly.

Phillip came in the back door. "Hi, Ma." He glanced at his father, and the tone of his voice turned somber, "Oh…hi Dad."

"Where were you?" Dominic asked, without looking up.

"Basketball practice."

"Huh, they let little runts like you on the team?"

"Yeah Dad, they let little runts like me play basketball too," he replied, sounding too tired to deal his father.

"Yeah, well…I think you should spend more time helping out at home, instead of running around playing basketball. That'll never teach ya nothin'."

"Dad, I do help out at home. Basketball is just a fun thing, and I like being on the team."

"Here ya go, Phil," Connie said, handing him a bowl of soup, rushing him out of the kitchen. "Take this and go sit in front of the television. Let your Daddy relax."

"Thanks, Mom." He walked past his father, and thought, *Daddy… I hate when she says that.*

Vinnie skipped into the kitchen, and landed with a hop next to his father. "Hi, dad…whatcha doin'?"

Dominic looked at his youngest son, and squinted his eyes. "Hey, Vinnie, what are you up to today?"

"I went over to Bobby's house, and we made turkeys outta paper. Mommy, can I have more soup?"

"Turkeys out of paper, huh?" Dominic laughed. "Where is it? Let me see."

"I'll go get it!"

"He's a weird little kid, ain't he, Connie?"

"Weird? No, why do you say that?"

"I dunno…he acts like such a baby."

"He *is* a baby, Dominic. He's only five!"

"Yeah well, I dunno…kid gives me the creeps some times."

"Here it is, Dad!" Vinnie was carrying orange construction paper that he had cut into the shape of a turkey. He colored the tail with red and blue crayon. "See, I made it with a outline of my own hand. Bobby's mom said I made one of the bestest ones she ever seen!"

"She did, huh? Listen, why don't you go in the other room with your brother. Take your soup with ya."

"Okay." Vinnie held the paper turkey in both hands, and rocked it back and forth. "Hey dad, know what?"

"What."

"When I go to school next year, Luci told me I could prob'ly be in the Thanksgivin' show!"

"Oh, yeah? And what are you gonna play, the turkey?" Dominic laughed.

"No Daddy, I wanna be a Indian. And I get to wear a costume and everything!"

"Well, now ain't that a kick in the ass?"

"Yup…it's a kick in the ass, daddy," Vinnie said, in his tiny voice.

"Vinnie!" Connie scolded.

"Daddy said it," he pouted.

Dominic laughed again. "Shut up, Son. Go eat your soup. Daddy's tired."

Vinnie walked slowly carrying his bowl of soup, staring at it to keep from spilling.

"I thought maybe I'd go pick up a second car this weekend," Dominic said, casually.

"Okay." Connie had no problem letting him take the credit for the car idea. "Then I won't have to bother you for your car."

"Well, I thought I had a pretty good idea".

"Did you want me to go with you?" Connie asked. "No, no…I'll pick the car. And, Connie, it's not gonna be just *your* car, you know? It's for taking my mother to the doctor…stuff like that, and I'll use it too."

"I know that, Dominic."

*

The following Saturday, Dominic pulled into the driveway with a 1959 yellow Volkswagen, and tooted the horn. Connie went to the kitchen door, dried her hands, and watched as Dominic stood proudly next to the car, his foot resting on the bumper. He waved his hand for her to come outside.

"Well, you like it?" He asked.

"It's cute."

"Cute? Well, it might be cute but it's paid for… fifteen hundred, cash." He pulled a handkerchief from his back pocket and rubbed the hood of the car. "I think I'm gonna like this car."

Connie was beginning to regret suggesting the car at all. He reiterated that the car wasn't just for her, and after again explaining the different buttons and pedals; he slipped the keys into his pocket. "I'm sure the car is going to come in handy," she said, flatly. She turned and walked toward the house.

"Wait, stay here. I wanna go get Ma and show it to her." He ran into the house like a little boy wanting to show his mother a new toy. Connie leaned against the garage, and waited. *What a jackass,* she thought. Dominic came down the patio steps, holding his mother by the arm. Mother Preste shielded her eyes from the sun, and tightly clutched her black shawl around her neck.

"I bought this car so Connie can take you to your doctor's appointments, Ma. What do ya think of that…ain't that nice? Nobody else is gonna do that for ya, huh?"

"*Si*, eez nice," she nodded. "*Quanda costa*?"

"Don't worry 'bout that, Ma. I paid cash."

"Ah," Mother Preste nodded with approval. "I go, now," she said, turning to go back into the house. Connie followed her, and while Mother Preste settled in a chair in front of the television, Connie started dinner. Dominic poked his head in the door, and yelled for Philllip and Vito to help him wash the new car. Phillip grumbled as he trailed out the door behind Vito.

Dominic soon discovered that the gas mileage on the little car was much better than his Buick, so he started taking the Volkswagen to work. That would have been fine but he took the keys to both cars with him. Once again, Connie was stuck at home.

*

"Dominic, Sunday is your mother's birthday, remember?"

"Yeah, so?"

"Gia called and asked if we could do something here. I told her that would be okay, so I need to go to the store. Can you leave the car for me tomorrow?"

"Why don't you go now?"

"Where, to the market? Now?"

"Yeah. The car's here...go now."

"But it's already seven o'clock..." she stopped herself. She was tired, and in the middle of cleaning up the dinner dishes. She was not in the mood for an argument, especially in front of Mother Preste. "Okay, I'll go now," she sighed.

"Don't be long." He glanced at his mother. She was sipping a cup of tea. "You want Connie to get you anything, Ma?"

She waved her hand.

"I won't take long, Dominic. I'll go get my purse." When she walked out of the kitchen, she paused in the hallway. Mother Preste was whispering to Dominic.

"Ma...she said she'd come right back," Dominic said, defensively. "She's not doin' nothin'...just goin' to the market." There was more whispering. "Why, what do think she's doin'?"

Connie waited and listened.

"Non si fidi di sue moglie," Mother Preste said, telling him he shouldn't trust his wife.

Connie closed her eyes and took a deep breath to calm herself, then went upstairs to the bedroom. She cursed under her breath, and sat on the edge of the bed. After slipping on her shoes, Connie picked up her purse and went downstairs. *What did I ever do to make this woman hate me so much?*

Before entering the kitchen, Connie put on her phony smile. Dominic and his mother were still sitting at the table.

"Here, you need some money." Dominic reached into his pocket. He pulled out a stack of bills, peeled off two twenties and handed them to her. "Get something good for the dinner. Is that enough money?"

"That should be fine." She shoved the bills into her purse where she always kept a crumpled mess of tens and twenties hidden in the bottom of her bag.

"What're ya gonna to get?"

"What would *you* like for me to get?" She asked turning to Mother Preste. "Is there anything special you'd like?" Connie felt her head beginning to pound.

"How 'bout gnocchi?" Dominic suggested. "And maybe a turkey."

"Okay, that sounds good," Connie agreed.

"How's that sound to you, Ma?" Dominic asked.

"Heh?

"Gnocchi and turkey...for your birthday dinner? How's that sound?" He repeated. She raised her hands and shrugged.

"We'll make it real nice for you" Connie said, fighting the urge to scream.

She grabbed the Volkswagen keys, and headed for the door when Dominic said, "Here, gimme the keys." He reached out his hand, wiggling his fingers as he got up from the table. "I'll start the car for ya."

"That's okay Dominic, I can do it."

"Gimme the keys," he repeated. She gave him the keys, and followed him to the car where he made her stand while he checked the oil, radiator and fan belt. As the minutes ticked by, frustration gripped her stomach.

After finally handing Connie the keys, she got behind the wheel and felt an exhilarating sense of freedom by simply pulling out of the driveway. Sweet escape. She looked in the rearview mirror. Dominic stood in the driveway watching her as she disappeared down the street. She drove the few blocks to the market, parked the car, and as she walked through the automatic doors, it felt as though she were entering Disneyland. She smiled as she walked up and down the aisles, stopping to chat with the girl that worked behind the deli counter.

Connie was checking the prices on Butterball turkeys, when she felt someone grab the back of her arm. She spun around to find Dominic glaring at her. "Dear God, Dominic, you scared me. What're you doing here?"

"What are you doing?"

"What'dya mean what am I doing? I'm shopping."

"You've been gone for forty-five fuckin' minutes," he said, in a sinister whisper. "My mother said you were gone too long for just picking up a few things at the market. Is there a reason for that, huh?"

"What?"

"Where did you go before you got to the market, huh? Tell me, Connie! Foolin' around, are ya? Think you're big shit cause ya gotta car now?"

"I didn't go anywhere," she said, defensively. "My God…I've been here getting the stuff for Sunday."

"Oh yeah? Well, you're gonna finish up now, cause I'm watchin' ya. Come on, let's go." He shoved her from behind. "I swear to God…you can't do anything right. Stupid bitch," he mumbled, angrily.

Her hands were shaking, and the migraine that had started earlier that night was attacking her temple with a ferocious throb.

"Huh, I don't know what I'm so worried about, for Christ sake… no man would ever want *you*."

Connie ignored him, and that made him angrier.

He suddenly broke into laughter. "Ya know what you look like? That Butterball turkey!" He continued laughing. "I think I'll call ya Butterball. How'd ya like that? Hi, Butterball," he mocked.

Connie chewed at her lower lip and thought, *How 'bout I call you motherfucker…hi motherfucker!* She finished picking up the things she needed, and felt a familiar wave of nausea that usually accompanied a migraine. *I wish you'd drop dead.* Hateful words were bouncing inside her head like ping-pong balls. The migraine was so bad now that her eyes could only focus on what was directly in front of her. Everything else was black. When they reached the checkout line, Dominic went ahead of her and the pretty, young cashier was obviously uncomfortable when Dominic made flirtatious remarks. Connie loaded the groceries on the counter, and returned a nervous smile to the girl.

"Here…let me do that for you, dear," Dominic said to the girl, lifting the bags and loading them into the cart.

"*Bastard,"* Connie said, under her breath. She pushed the cart into the parking lot while Dominic walked close behind. The nausea was intense, and she scurried between two parked cars and vomited.

Dominic took the cart from her, and pushed it the rest of the way to the car, loaded the bags into the trunk, and waited for her. "Are you finished?" He asked, when Connie walked toward him. She was holding her hand to her head.

"I don't feel too well right now."

"Let me get my car. I'll follow you home."

She got into the Volkswagen and waited. Sweat trickled down the center of her back, and she gripped the wheel to keep her hands from shaking. When she saw his car in the rearview mirror, she pulled out of the parking lot and drove home. Without any further discussion, they each carried two bags of groceries into the house.

Connie felt faint and was about to get sick again. She prayed he would leave her alone. Anger and hopelessness brought bile to her throat, and she ran for the bathroom. She heard Dominic laugh. She came back into the kitchen, and braced herself by holding onto the counter. She said a prayer as she put the groceries away. *Better days are coming...better days are coming,* she repeated inside her throbbing head.

"I guess my mother went up to bed already," Dominic said, as though nothing had happened.

"Probably." Phlegm caught in the back of her throat. She cleared her throat, and poured herself a glass of water.

"What's the matter with *you*? Ya got another one of your headaches?"

"I'm fine," she lied, and finished washing the dishes that were left in the sink.

"I'm gonna go lay down on the sofa. I got a bit of a headache myself." He started out of the kitchen. "I'll take a couple of aspirin when you get a second."

The house was quiet. Luci had put Vinnie to bed and the boys were in the basement playing records. Dominic was asleep in the den. Connie tiptoed into the room, past Dominic and lowered the volume on the television, then went halfway down the basement stairs and ordered Phillip and Vito to their rooms.

"Just go upstairs, boys. Your father's sleeping and I need to lie down."

"N'kay," Vito mumbled. He grabbed a popsicle out of the freezer before heading for the stairs. Phillip put on his jacket.

"Phillip? Where are you going?" Connie asked.

"Outside. He won't even know I'm gone...I got a key. Go to bed, Ma."

"Stay outta trouble, Phillip." She was too tired, and in too much pain to argue, so she locked the back door, and went upstairs. She went into the bathroom and gave herself an enema in hopes it would relieve pressure that was now causing pain in her legs. She held a washcloth under the spigot and soaked it in cool water, and when she got into bed, she placed the rag over her eyes. She never heard Dominic come to bed but she awoke in the middle of the night with him lying on top of her, forcing her legs apart. He had sex with her, and when he was through, Connie went to the bathroom and vomited again.

"You're a cold woman, Connie," he said, when she climbed back under the covers. "A cold, cold woman."

"I am what you made me, Dominic," she said, quietly as she turned her back to him.

"What I made you, huh?"

The next morning, he got up early, dressed, and left the house. Connie heard him pull the Volkswagen out of the garage. She went to the bedroom window, and watched as he drove down the street. Later that day, Vittorio dropped him off at the house, and Dominic simply told Connie that he had sold the car.

Chapter 21

It was the 1980's and all four Preste children were grown and out of the house.

Connie and Dominic were alone. Many years before, Mother Preste had died shortly after moving in with Gia and her husband and only three months later, Dominic's brother, Antonio died from a sudden heart attack. Dominic cried like a baby, and as the weeks and months passed, he became more paranoid and insecure, and talked about visions of his father; even conversations. Connie tried to get him to talk to her but he refused. His behavior was becoming more cruel and irrational. Even though he continued to be abusive toward Connie, he had become uncharacteristically dependant on her. When Connie swore she would leave if he didn't leave her alone, he threatened her life, then clung to her, like a child when he realized she was serious. This abnormal vulnerability confused and frightened her. She always ended up appeasing him, promising to stay. Their relationship was sick and out of control. Connie thought him pathetic, and found that he needed her to be more of a mother than a wife. She felt hate for him for such a long time. He needed her but she certainly did not need him. The only thing she wanted was her house and their money. She would die before she would let him leave her with nothing. They had scrimped and saved themselves into a small fortune, and Connie refused to jeopardize losing it; or even worse, lose it to another woman.

*

Vittorio was the only one of Dominic's brothers to still live nearby, and the two visited each other every Sunday. Vittorio was retired, and he and Tessa were very dedicated to caring for their grandchildren, unlike Dominic, who thought his own grandchildren a nusiance. He forbade Connie to baby-sit because it took time away from him, and it broke Connie's heart. Among their five grandchildren, six-year old Jamie was closest to Dominic. He was the result of a brief marriage between Vinnie and a girl he dated in high school. They were both involved in drugs and when the marriage ended, the girl left town, leaving Jamie with Vinnie. A court judge declaired Vinnie unfit to care for the child, and to prevent him from being put into foster care, Connie and Dominic were morally forced to take the child in. Dominic had no choice; this was his blood.

*

Phillip and Beth had been married for twenty years. They were happy, well suited for each other and in a new phase of their lives being without children at home. Their marriage was in a comfort zone but found that the only time they were short with each other was when they were anticipating a visit with Phillip's parents. The tension in Dominic and Connie's house exhausted Phillip. Visits brought back memories of secrets, deceit and violence. It seemed to seep from the very walls. He hated the pain he saw in his mother's eyes. The cynical grin on his father's face still gave Phillip chills. The visits always started out fine, with his mother inviting family, and with all his favorite foods. But the mood always ended up taking a dark turn when Dominic reverted to sarcasm and blame. Even though it had been twenty years, he still blamed Beth for taking Phillip away from his family. Tension always escalated when he talked down to Beth like she was an outsider. Phillip seethed while Beth calmly smiled and excused herself from the room. She managed to cope but insisted the visits be kept short. Phillip was happy to oblige. When they finally walked out the door, they both felt the relief that one must feel when escaping a traumatic experience.

*

In the summer of 1965, seventeen-year old Luci eloped with Raymond O'Grady, the epitome of everything Dominic hated. He was Irish, a high school dropout, and no stranger to the local beer halls in town. Raymond O'Grady had a mutual disdain for Luci's parents, and had no problem when Luci told him that he was not welcome in their home. Connie accused Luci of marrying Raymond to get back at her father, and sadly watched as her daughter's self-esteem slowly dwindled, just as hers did so many years before. Luci and Ray's relationship was tumultuous. After many a fight, Luci was locked out of her own home and sent packing to her parents, and calling the police was useless since Ray's closest friends, and drinking buddies *were* the police.

Now, after twenty years of marriage, and three children Luci was a mere shadow of who she used to be. Sadly, she had become her mother. She made excuses for Ray's behavior and often blamed herself.

Connie felt guilty that her daughter had fallen into her footsteps, and she made up for her mistakes by giving money to Luci whenever she asked for it. Luci took advantage of her mother's vulnerability, and habitually went to her mother for everything. Connie started hiding bank statements from Dominic, and intercepting phone calls from the bank when they inquired about large withdraws. Ray thought the situation ideal, and eventually quit his job, leaving him more time to spend at the bar.

*

Vito and his wife, Barbara had their first child in the spring of nineteen ninety-three, and Connie and Dominic made the one-hour drive to the hospital to see the new baby.

"Hello," Connie sang, as she peered around the door that led into Barbara's room. She was sitting in a chair sipping an apple juice, and watching television.

"Oh…hi." Her puffy feet were propped on a chair. "Did you see the baby yet?"

"No, we stopped here first," Connie answered, leaning in to give Barbara a hug. "How do you feel?"

"I feel pretty good now. I went into labor yesterday afternoon and then had the baby around two this morning."

"I know, Vito told us."

Dominic stood in the doorway. "How ya doin' there, uh Barbara?" He asked, sounding uncomfortable. "Feelin' okay, are ya?"

"I'm good now," she laughed. "You okay?"

"I'm okay."

Barbara smiled. Her father-in-law's idiosyncrasies didn't seem to bother her. "Why don't you get another chair and sit down."

"No, I'm good," he said, waving his hand. "Where's Vito?"

"He had to go back to the house...he'll be back later."

Dominic sat and watched television while the two women talked. "Okay Connie," he finally said, "why don't we let her rest and we'll go see the baby."

She turned to Barbara. "You don't mind if we go see the baby, do you?"

"She doesn't mind if we go see the baby," Dominic interrupted, shaking his head. "What a stupid question."

"Dominic, please..."

"Connie, please..." he mocked.

Barbara ignored the sudden tension. "No, that's okay. You two go see the baby...I'm going to get back in bed anyway.

"You take care now," Dominic said. "You look good."

"Thanks. Do you know how to get to the nursery?"

"We'll find our way," Connie said, getting up and leaning in the kiss Barbara. "We'll probably stop back to see Vito."

They walked down the hall and stopped at the nurse's station.

"How do we get to the nursery?" Dominic asked.

"Make a right at the end of the hall," a nurse told them, slowly taking her eyes from the chart she was reading. She looked up briefly and smiled. "That way," she pointed.

They came to a large glass window where several babies were sleeping, snuggled tightly in blue blankets for the boys and pink blankets for the girls, each wearing a matching, knit cap. Connie cooed when she looked at two of the babies with their eyes shut tight and their mouths puckered like little rosebuds. She read the nametags at the foot of each crib, and when she saw *Baby Preste,* she quickly pointed him out to Dominic. He was sleeping peacefully. Dark curls peeked out around the edge of his cap, and a tiny, beaded bracelet dangled from his chubby wrist.

"Oh, he's beautiful." Connie dabbed at her eyes with a tissue. "Ah, look Dominic…he's got that same little indentation in his ear, just like yours." She reached up and touched the edge of Dominic's ear. "Isn't that something?"

"Don't say that Connie," he snapped. "What's the matter with you?" He looked from side to side making sure no one was listening.

"What? What do you mean, Dominic? I was just…"

"Let's go." He grabbed her arm, pulling her toward the elevator.

"Aren't we gonna wait and see Vito?"

"No." He walked briskly through the lobby, and out of the main doors, with Connie running to keep up with him. Dominic didn't speak during the drive home, and when they walked in the back door, he slammed it hard enough to make the glass rattle.

"Dominic, what's wrong? Why are you so mad?"

"You're sick Connie, ya know that?" He yelled, turning to face her. "What are you gonna do now? Tell people that I'm the father of that baby?"

"What?" Connie's eyes bulged; her mouth flew open with shock.

"Are you saying that I fucked my own daughter-in-law?"

"Oh, my God!" Connie put her hand to her mouth. "Why are you saying that?"

"You stay away from me. You're sick, Connie," he repeated, vehemently. "You've accused me of a lot of things but this is the worst!" When he tried to leave the room, Connie blocked the doorway.

"Dominic, I…I…" she stammered, unable to comprehend what would make him think such a thing.

"I said get away from me!" He warned. He grabbed her by the back of the hair, yanking her head to the side. She fell into the table, and held the table's edge to steady herself. She stared up at him with stunned disbelief. He stood over her for a second, then turned and left the room. When she got back on her feet, she looked toward the den and saw him sitting, his face in his hands. She waited. He was crying and mumbling unintelligibly.

She dared to go into the room but needed to find out what was wrong. "Dominic, please…tell me what's wrong? Something seems very wrong here. We got to get to the bottom of this, and fix it…whatever it is…"

"Shut up! You don't get to the bottom of nothin'! You're nothin', Connie. You don't deserve nothin'." He was still crying, and a spray of spittle flew from his mouth. "Just leave me alone, woman." He buried his face in his hands again. "Leave me alone, Mama..."

"Mama?" Connie repeated, "You just called me...*Mama*."

Dominic slowly stood up, his face contorted in a horrifying grimace. His eyes were like fire as he walked toward her.

Connie feared him her whole life but this was different. He seemed in a trance, unpenatratable. She walked slowly into the living room. He methodically followed. As he got closer, she picked up a heavy brass lamp, and hurled it at him, just missing his head. It crashed into the wall behind him, and a large chunk of the plaster fell to the floor. He seemed unphased.

"I don't care anymore, Dominic!" She screamed. She stood in a defensive position, ready to run. "Ya know what, Dominic? Even if you kill me, it would be a blessing! You've made me hate you!" Her mouth was dry. She was panting.

Dominic continued to stare, an eerie smile crossing his lips.

"I can't take this anymore, Dominic...I'm too old. I'm tellin' ya right now, either you're gonna have to kill me or you're never gonna hit me again. Because I just don't care anymore. You've ruined me."

"You're such a bitch." He growled, barely moving his lips.

"I am what you made me, Dominic," she responded defiantly. "If I'm a bitch, it's because you made me that way.

"What kind of mother would do what you did?"

"Do what? What are you talking about? What did I do?"

He stared, as though hypnotized. "No mother does what you did."

"Dominic...please, I'm tired," Connie said, running her hand over her hair. She sidled over to a chair and sat down. "I know you're tired too. I want to go upstairs. Let this be over," she pleaded. "The beatings are going to stop now... or I'm leaving. I mean it this time...I will leave."

He was leaning up against the wall but looking at the floor. "Leaving?" He said, absently. Suddenly, he looked up and seemed aware of her presence. "Where you gonna go? You might wanna think about that, Connie cause you're not gettin' no money from me," he added.

"You know that don't cha? You wanna go…then go," he said, with a smirk. "I'll give you ten thousand dollars…that's it. And with the money I got, I can get any woman I want."

"Dominic, you have to stop. I don't even know why you're so mad. Dear God in heaven…half the time, I don't even know who you're talking to."

"No man will have *you*, that's for sure. You're an old woman, Connie. It's over for you." He laughed but the laugh was forced. When he looked up, and caught the pain in her eyes, he quickly looked away.

Connie cleared her throat, and spoke softly. "I don't want a man, Dominic. You see…men actually make me sick. You've seen to that, haven't you? You know what I want Dominic? I wanna be left alone. Alone," she repeated. "You're a whore master, Dominic. I'll tell you what…I'll make a deal with you. From now on, you don't bother me… and I don't bother you. I'm done Dominic." She stood up and walked past him. She was too tired to be afraid, and without looking at him, walked up the stairs.

"Sonofabitch," he laughed. "You really think you're somethin', don't cha?"

She kept walking, and calmly entered their bedroom, undressed, put on her nightgown and got into bed.

Chapter 22

Connie was feeling the heat of an August afternoon, and mopped her forehead as she went down to the basement to throw a load of clothes in the washer. Another load was finished, so she stood by the dryer and folded the clothes, stacking them neatly in the clothesbasket. She could hear the radio reporting that the heat wave that had been hovering over Cleveland Heights was going to stick around for another couple of days.

She stopped what she was doing, cocked her head and listened when she noticed the radio had been turned off. She picked up the basket, climbed the basement stairs and found Dominic in the kitchen, hanging up the phone. "Dominic, I thought you were out in the garage."

"I came in for a glass of water. Connie…listen, that was Philomena on the phone…your mother's in the hospital."

"She is?"

"She's pretty bad, Philomena said."

Connie sat down, looked up at Dominic and said, "I want to go see her."

"Okay, we'll drive up today."

"Thank you, Dominic," she said, surprised by a rare sign of compassion.

"What?"

"Well, it's just nice that you're being so understanding."

"It's your mother, Connie. Jesus, I'm not a monster."

*

As they approached Wickhaven, Connie gazed out the window at her beloved childhood home, and was overcome with emotion. She smiled at the thought of the memories she left behind so many years before, memories of her mother and father, her sisters and Leone's Bakery.

Dominic pulled the car in front of Violet's house, where they were going to stay the night, and after entering the house, Dominic stood back while the two sisters embraced and cried. Hearing the commotion, Pasqual came into the room with the aid of a walker. Even though he had broken his hip the year before, he and Violet both had taken care of Vincenzo until he died, and were doing the same for Angelina.

"Eh, Dominic...*come lei e', il mio amico*? Good to see you," he said, smiling broadly.

"Pasqual, how are you?" Dominic reached for his hand.

"I do the best I can Dominic," Pasqual laughed.

They settled in the living room. "How's Mom doin' today," Connie asked.

"No good, Connie. We'll go see her in a little bit. Sometimes she recognizes and sometimes not. I think she's ready to go."

"Oh, don't say that, Vi."

"No, in a good way Conchetta...she wants to go...maybe to be with Papa, I don't know."

"Maybe."

Violet's once long, raven-black hair was now blue- gray, cut short, with the remnants of a permanent curling the hair that was combed away from her face. Her spine was curved from arthritis, and Connie felt sad as she watched her sister walk across the room toward the dining room table. The two couples sat together, eating ham sandwiches and sipping root beer. Connie's food sat on her plate, untouched. After lunch, Connie helped Violet clean up, while Dominic and Pasqual went back to the living room.

*

The hospital where Angelina was, was more than one hundred years old but clean and modernized with electronic doors and smooth tile floors. Connie saw Philomena and Carmella coming out of their mother's room, and the three women raced toward each other and embraced.

"Connie!" Carmella said, with a catch in her voice. "I'm so happy you're here. I think Mom is waiting for you…honest to God, I think she wants to see you before she goes. Now, for gosh sakes…don't let her see you crying." She took a tissue and wiped tears from Connie's cheeks.

"I know, I know… I'm fine. Dominic, do you want to come in with me?"

"No, you go first…I'll be there in a minute."

Connie walked into the room. Her mother looked comfortable, peaceful but tiny in the bed. She had gotten painfully thin, and had lost most of her hair. Connie walked up to the side of the bed and rested her hand, gently on her mother's hand. Angelina's eyelids fluttered. "Mama?" Connie said, quietly. *Ciao mamma, sono Conchetta. Lo sono qui con te.* She hoped her mother knew that she was there. "I'll be right outside, Ma." She patted her hand and left the room. Maria and Lourdes were waiting in the hall, and rushed toward Connie.

Seven sisters sat together that night, in the parlor of Violet's house. The only sister unable to be there was Giordana. She lived in California, and her husband was too sick to be left alone. He had battled cancer for years, and she never left his side.

Even though they knew their mother's death was imminent, the sisters, now old and plagued with various ailments were able to laugh, reminisce and catch up on each other's lives. Pasqual, Butch, Dave and Dominic sat in the kitchen playing poker. The sisters talked about the tragic death of Maria's husband some years before in a boating accident, and Lourdes' divorce from her high school sweetheart. She was happy though, living with her oldest son, in New Jersey. They knew about Connie and her troubles with Dominic. They comforted her, and jokingly cursed Dominic, which led to fits of laughter. Connie wished she could stay there forever. They compared stories about their grandchildren, bragged about their grown children's successes, showed pictures and cried about how they missed their father.

Nearing one o'clock in the morning, most left, and went to the local Holiday Inn for the night. Dominic and Connie helped Violet clean up the kitchen, and then went to bed in the spare room. In the morning, they drove to the hospital for one last visit, and Connie knew it would be the last time she would see her mother alive. She was an old woman herself but with the thought of losing her mother, she couldn't help feeling like an orphan.

The next time Connie saw her mother was at her funeral, two weeks later.

Chapter 23

Connie woke up at four in the morning, pulled a sweater over her nightgown and slipped on a pair of socks, and went downstairs. Dominic was still sleeping and she decided it was a good time to get started on her baking. Phillip and Beth were flying in for a short visit and she felt more excited than she had in a long time. She wanted it to be a special occasion. Dominic had invited his family, and Carmella and her husband were driving from western Pennsylvania. She also expected Vito and Barbara, and Luci would probably stop by with her boys. Vinnie was ordered to stay away, and Connie hoped he would not do as usual, and just show up at the door. He was high on drugs most of the time, and she didn't want another incident between him and his father.

By the time Dominic got up, Connie had already made walnut cookies, pizzels, more than seventy ravioli, and had a twenty-two pound turkey in the oven.

"Want me to make the sauce, Connie?"

She turned to see Dominic standing in the doorway. "Oh Dominic, I didn't know you were up. You wanna make sauce? Sure, over there on the counter." Lifting her chin, she directed him to the counter where three jars of crushed tomatoes sat. "They're already seasoned, so all you have to do is pour them into that pot, and put in the sausage."

"I know what to do."

"I know you do…you taught me, remember?" She lied but she wanted to keep him in a good mood.

*

Luci picked Phillip and Beth up at the airport, took them to her parent's house, and went home, explaining she would be back later. When Connie greeted them at the door, they were both surprised to see how thin she was. She seemed more nervous than Phillip remembered, and was alarmed by her haggard appearance.

"Come in, come in," she said, excitedly. "How're the kids? Why didn't they come with you?"

"They were busy, Ma."

"Oh, okay…I don't know, youz do what you want."

"Ma…they're fine," Phillip said.

Dominic came as far as the doorway of the kitchen, stood back and waited for Phillip and Beth to come to him.

"Hi Dad, how are you?" Phillip wrapped his arm around his father's shoulders. Beth leaned in, giving him a kiss on the cheek. She remembered how he had always smelled of Aqua Velva but now he smelled of perspiration and dirty hair.

"I'm good…how was your trip?" Dominic asked, in a high-pitched voice that sounded like a shy child. He seemed distracted.

"Fine…no problem." Phillip pulled out a chair, and sat at the kitchen table alongside Beth. Connie was running around the kitchen, placing napkins in front of everyone, making coffee, and dishing up fresh fruit and Danish pastries.

"How long are ya stayin'," Dominic asked.

"Just for the weekend, Dad," Phillip smiled, "I told you, remember… we could only stay for the weekend," he repeated. "We have to go back on Monday."

"Oh, come on…Jesus Christ…just the weekend? You can probably make arrangements to stay longer," Dominic insisted. "Aren't you the big boss?"

Phillip shifted uneasily in his chair. "How're you two doin'?" He asked, changing the subject. "Feelin' okay?"

"Yeah, we're good," Dominic said, looking over at Connie. "I know what you're thinkin'...your mother don't look so good. S'pose it's my fault."

"Why, what happened?" Phillip asked, though he was already aware there was trouble between the two. Vito had called weeks before, warning him that something was going on, and when Phillip spoke to his mother on the phone, she was edgy and evasive. She constantly lied, saying everything was fine.

Connie stood at the stove shuffling pots and pans. "Oh come on Dominic, let's not talk about anything right now. We have a houseful of people coming."

Phillip looked at Beth. She shrugged, and raised her eyebrows. The tension was palpable. "We'll talk later," Phillip finally said. "Who all's comin'?"

Connie finally sat at the table. "Did your sister say she's comin' back to the house?"

"Said she was...by the way, what's goin' on with her? She looks terrible."

"Don't ask," Dominic said. "If I could, I'd shoot that bastard ol' man of hers right between his Goddamned eyes."

"Dominic," Connie said, sounding exasperated.

"Well I would, Goddamn it! Sits at the bar from morning to night with the sonofabitchin' cops around here...they're all asshole buddies. He could probably commit murder and they'd look the other way, then go have a beer!"

Phillip looked at Beth and rolled his eyes. "Okay, relax Dad...we don't have to get into that now."

"Anyway..." Connie reverted back to Phillip's earlier question, "your Aunt Carmella and Uncle Dave are comin' from Pennsylvania."

"Really?" Beth said. "I like her, she's so funny. She and Uncle Dave are a riot together."

"That sonofabitch," Dominic grumbled. "I can't stand the way she laughs at everything. And that laugh of his..." he mimicked Dave's deep, choppy laugh. He turned and pointed a finger at Connie. "He ain't smokin' in this house, Connie! I'm warnin' ya. I'll throw 'im out on his ass, like I did before!"

"Dad, my God...what's with you today?"

"Nothin'." He got up and opened the cabinet below the sink. "Here Beth…want some of my homemade wine? You like wine, right?" He poured her a glass.

It only took twenty minutes in their house for Beth to happily welcome a glass of wine. "Thank you, Dad." She took a sip and smiled uncomfortably as Dominic watched her.

"Whoa, look at her go," he laughed. "This girl can hold her liquor, can't she?"

"Okay, Dad." Phillip held up his hand. "That's enough." Memories of why he moved so far away were beginning to flood back. His father was doing what he did best; making everyone uncomfortable. When you think he's doing something nice, he's setting you up to make fun of you. Phillip was not going to allow him to do that to Beth again.

The phone rang and Dominic answered. He quickly hung up, and informed Connie that his sister Annette was not coming.

Thank God, Connie thought. "Oh, that's too bad."

Everyone's attention went to the door as Barbara followed Vito into the house, she standing back smiling while he proudly presented their new son. Phillip and Beth greeted them and took turns fussing over the baby. Connie continued preparing dinner, and smiled as she listened to the increased volume of jovial conversation. There was suddenly a conspicuous hush when Luci came in the back door followed by Vinnie. At nearly six feet tall, his entrance into the room was that of a bull; his chest thrust out, a demented grin revealing rotted teeth, and gaping holes where teeth used to be.

Phillip was the first to speak. "Hey, Vinnie…how're ya doin'?"

"I'm great," Vinnie replied, overconfidently. "What's up with you?" He looked over at Beth, and simply acknowledged her with a nod.

"Hi Vinnie." Beth said, quietly and got up to join Barbara in the den.

As the day progressed, Connie insisted upon waiting on everyone, even though no one needed anything. She held off dinner as long as she could, waiting for Gia and her husband but when they didn't show, Dominic ordered everyone to go ahead and eat. As the family was finishing dessert and enjoying a second cup of coffee, Gia and her husband casually sauntered in the door.

"Gia, where the hell ya been?" Dominic asked, angrily. "We're done eating!" He turned to Connie, "Connie, heat up the turkey and ravioli."

Gia raised her hand to stop Connie. "Don' do that, Connie…we ate already."

Dominic stood up. "What the hell…you ate already? You knew you were comin' here for dinner!"

"Dominic, it's okay." Connie attempted to calm him. She turned to Gia. "Well, at least come sit and have dessert."

"Oh no, Connie…your whole family is here…we don't wanna impose. We can't stay."

"What the...for Christ sake! Of course the whole family is here… that's why we invited you!" Dominic was about to explode.

"We come back anudder time," Gia's husband said, looking embarrassed. "*Ciao*, everybody."

They walked out the door leaving Dominic standing in the middle of the kitchen, his mouth open, and his hands clenched into fists. "Sonofabitch!"

"Don't worry about it, Dominic…come on, come sit with the kids." Connie laid her hand on his back, and urged him into the dining room.

"I'm never gonna forget that, Connie." he stated, before sitting down.

"I know. Let's calm down. You just sit with the kids and enjoy your dessert. I'll bring you some ice-cream."

"I don't think I can eat, Connie. That made my stomach a little sour."

"Well, just try." Connie went back to the kitchen and started dishing up bowls of ice cream when she heard the familiar sound of the concertina. She went to the dining room and watched Dominic, standing with his foot on a chair, the concertina resting on his knee. He pumped the bellows, and rocked methodically to a familiar melody. Phillip, Vito and Beth sang along. Luci got up and went into the kitchen while her mother stood in the corner of the dining room. Connie was once again bewildered by the peaceful expression on her husband's face. *What is it about that stupid little instrument?* She never knew Dominic's father but she felt love for him. Anyone that could have such a long-lasting effect on someone like Dominic must have been very special.

*

The following day, Phillip requested that his mother not invite anyone over for the rest of the weekend. He wanted to spend the day with his parents, and get to the bottom of what was going on between the two of them. He sat at the table with his father. They shared a pleasant breakfast, and Dominic talked about his retirement and how he spent his time.

"Golf and bowling…that's good," Phillip said, mopping up the last of his egg yolk. "Keep ya healthy, right?"

"Oh, I'm healthy as a horse," Dominic said, puffing out his chest. "Air's clean here. Better than Colorado, I bet ya. I hear the air's thin there…can't breath right."

Phillip laughed. "Whatever you say, Dad."

"Why don't ya stay longer, Phillip," he asked again. "Let Beth go home, and you stay for a few days."

"Dad…come on, I can't. Hey…at least I'm here now, right?"

"Bullshit. Three days…what's that?"

Phillip changed the subject. "Anyway, do you two need help with anything? How're your finances?"

"Our finances…they're good, why?" He bristled. "You kiddin' me...I got more money than you'll ever have. Don't you worry 'bout me."

"Vito tells me you bought Vinnie a house."

"Well, just the down payment…he pays the mortgage."

Connie nearly choked. She had been secretly paying Vinnie's mortgage from the beginning.

Phillip looked at her, and she returned a pleading look, shaking her head. "Uh…we can talk about that some other time," Phillip said, understanding that his mother was telling him to shut up.

"Well it was either buy him a house, or he'd be living on the street," Dominic said. "And he got custody of Jamie again…so…"

Phillip pushed back his chair, stood up and stretched. "I understand. Well, what'dya say we move to the den," he suggested. "We can sit and visit. That means you too, Ma."

*

The following morning, Dominic got up and went to church. Phillip came downstairs and sat with his mother, sipped coffee and happily allowed her fuss over him. "What was that about yesterday, Ma? You know, when we were talking about you guys buying Vinnie a house?"

"Nothin', Phillip. Don't worry yourself about it."

"I'm not worried Ma, just curious. I wanna make sure you and Dad are watching your money...you know, doin' the right thing."

"Well, what do you wanna know?" She could not look him in the eye.

"Is your money in the bank? Did you invest? What?"

"Most of it's in the bank. We have some money with Smith Barney, and ya know... we bought the apartment house."

"Right, well it *sounds* like you're doin' the right thing. Mind if I take a look at some of your statements?"

Connie looked at him curiously. "Why are you so interested?"

"Just let me take a look, Ma."

Connie went into the dining room, opened the drawer of the buffet, pulling out a handful of papers. She laid them on the table in front of him. He studied them for a while, and Connie waited.

"Ma? Why is there an eight hundred and ninety-five dollar withdraw every month that goes to CBA Bank. You don't have a mortgage on the apartment house, do you?"

"No," Connie answered, quietly.

"It's Vinnie's mortgage, isn't it?"

"You're father doesn't know, Phillip and you can't tell him, you hear?" She sounded fearful.

"Doesn't he look at the statements?"

"No. He doesn't understand that stuff, you know that?"

He looked back at the paperwork. "What are these withdraws...ten thousand in June, five thousand in September...another eight thousand back in August..." Phillip flipped through the pages and looked up at his mother. "Ma? What's goin' on?"

"Listen, Phillip," she said, sitting next to him, lowering her voice. "Some of that's bail for your brother, some went to Luci...I don't know." She was flustered. "But like I said, your father doesn't know. He'd kill me…" She laid her hand on Phillip's arm. "Listen Son, I've stopped sneaking money to them, so just leave it alone, okay?"

"I'm just trying to protect you, Mom. Hey, I'm trying to protect me and Vito too. It's not fair, Mom. There's thousands and thousands of dollars goin' to Vinnie and Luci and…well, Vito and me…I mean, don't get me wrong but one day we'll end up with nothing."

"I know. I understand, no more money going out, I promise."

"You have enough savings, Mom to live real comfortable, you know that, right? There's close to eight hundred thousand here, and that doesn't count the apartment house. You're doin' good but the way you're handin' out money…well, it won't last long."

"Okay, let's put this stuff away before your father comes home," Connie said, shuffling the papers into a messy pile. She put them back in the bottom of the buffet drawer, and sat down across from Phillip. She looked at him and smiled, seeming to be waiting for more questions.

"Okay, now what's goin' on with you and Dad? Why do you look so thin and why does Dad say it's his fault?"

"He's just been…oh, I don't know, he's your father. You know how he is. He's been givin' me some trouble but now that Vinnie and Luci are staying away, it's been a little easier."

"Well, that's good. If there's anything else I need to know, just tell me."

"No, that's it. Everything's fine."

"Hmm," Phillip groaned. "I think you're lying."

She stood up and walked to the kitchen sink. "So, did you and Beth get packed?"

"We're packed."

"Can't wait to leave, can ya?

Chapter 24

Connie and Dominic had temporary custody of Vinnie's son, Jamie again. But that ended when Vinnie took his parents to court. He lied, claiming to be clean and sober, and standing before the judge, he added that he was getting married. Connie found this revelation laughable but to her horror, found out it was a girl named Rochelle Collucci, a stripper who had been jailed several times for public drunkenness and drug possession.

Connie was convinced that Vinnie's long-time drug use had completely robbed him of his senses, and damaged his brain. He was irrational, his actions jerky and erratic. He never held a job for more than a couple of weeks, and had been arrested for everything from drug possession to lewd behavior. He hung out with drug addicts and ex-convicts, and his bullying and arrogance, landed him in the hospital more than once, most recently because of a drug dealer from downtown Cleveland. Vinnie ended up with a broken nose and three cracked ribs. While recuperating in the hospital, he pleaded with his mother to let him and Jamie move in.

Looking at Connie with an expression of disbelief, Dominic roared, "No! I don't want him here, Connie. He's a Goddamned drug addict!" He was vehemently shaking his head, and waving his hands in protest. "He's nothin' but trouble, and I've had it with him. I can't believe you want him here."

"But Dominic..."

"Let that whore take care of him!" He shouted. "Holy shit, Connie! I can't believe you!"

"She can't take care of him. She's as bad off as he is."

"Jesus Christ..." Dominic lowered his head, sounding exasperated.

"He can't go back to his house, Dominic. Whoever beat him up... well they know where he lives, and he's got Jamie to worry about."

Dominic stared at Connie a few seconds before responding. "Are you kidding me? You believe what he tells you? God, Connie...you *are* stupid. He's messed up 'cause he's a drug addict! What's the matter with you? I paid for his house, I bought him a truck, I took care of his kid, I've bailed him outta jail...God knows how many times. What do you want from me?"

"I know, I know," she cried. Suddenly, Connie turned with a jerk when she heard the back door open. It was Vinnie. He was using a cane, and his right eye was purple and swollen shut. Stitches ran from his cheekbone to his ear. "Hey," he mumbled, and limped to a chair. "What're you guys doin'? What're talkin' about? I bet it's about me... right?"

"How did ya get here, Vinnie," Connie asked.

"My buddy dropped me off." He shifted in his chair. His upper lip raised in an eerie grin, revealing red, puffy gums. Connie was repulsed. She had to look away from her own son. He wanted to talk to them about something, and slobbered as he bragged that he was about to get rich. Connie listened while he talked nonsence about suing somebody. She covered her face with her hands but peered at him through her fingers. His clothes were tattered and dirty and she wondered how he turned out this way? He had an arrest record that covered more than twenty years, and his driver's license had not just been suspended but taken away for good.

"Calm down, Vinnie," Dominic said, sounding weary. "What are you doin' here...you know we don't want you here."

"Hey man," Vinnie responded, indignantly. "I'm just hangin' out, s'all."

"Just hangin' out, huh? Well, where's your son?" Dominic asked.

"He's home with Rochelle."

"You let that whore watch your son?" Connie asked, banging her hands on the table.

"She ain't no whore, Ma," Vinnie barked, swiping at spit that escaped the corner of his mouth. He turned to look at his father, and laughed. "Nice mouth on your wife," he said, gesturing toward his mother with his thumb.

"Have a little respect, would ya?" Dominic said, looking at his son with disgust.

"Why should I? You don't respect her."

"That's enough, Vinnie…what is it you want?"

Vinnie ran his fingers through his thinning hair, and groaned when he tried to straighten his back. "Listen dad, I got some doctor bills, and me and Jamie need a place to stay for a little while…you know, till I get a job and get back on my feet. I got a couple people livin' at the house, so maybe they'll pay the mortgage while I'm gone."

"Holy shit," Dominic mumbled. "I can just imagine who's staying at your place." He paused and took a deep breath. "I'm only doin' this for Jamie, ya hear? You can stay here for a while…but just till you get a job. You need to take care of your own kid, ya hear?"

"I hear ya, I hear ya…das cool man."

"Yeah, that's cool man." Dominic mocked. He looked at Vinnie's face. "Thought you were pretty tough, huh? I guess you found out different."

Connie stiffened.

"Hey man, don't start on me."

"Vinnie, I think you'd better go," Connie quickly intervened. She got up and walked to where Vinnie was struggling to get to his feet. She grabbed him by the elbow, and urged him toward the back door.

*

Vinnie dropped Jamie off at his parent's that night, met some friends at a bar, got high and snuck into his parent's home the following day while they were out, stealing cash and bank cards from his father's dresser.

"That's it, Connie!" Dominic's face was purple with rage. "He's outta here and he can take the kid too. That's right," he said, noting Connie's expression. "Don't be givin' me no looks…I'm done. Vinnie's a grown man, and you know what? I think he's dangerous."

"Dangerous? You think he's dangerous?"

"You don't think he's dangerous, Connie? My God, he stole from me, right under my nose. He's a drug addict!"

"I know, I know." She buried her face in her hands, and sobbed.

Dominic went to the kitchen when he heard the phone ring. "Hello?" He was silent for a long time. "Well, how do'ya know it's my kid? Uh-huh, uh-huh…really?"

Connie froze. She walked into the kitchen and stood quietly, one hand covering her mouth, waiting for him to hang up. She knew it was bad news. "What's goin' on, Dominic? What's wrong?"

"Sonofabitch!" He said, banging the phone back on the wall. "Oh, you're gonna love this," he said, placing his hands on his hips. He was biting his lower lip. He sat down as though his legs could no longer support him. He placed the palms of his hands on the tabletop. "Vinnie, and one of his "druggie" friends just went to about eight different… what're them machines called…you know, outside the bank where you can get money?" he asked, looking up at her.

"I don't know what they're called but I know what you mean. What happened?"

"Well, it just so happens that you're precious son, Vinnie went to about six or eight of them machines from here to downtown Cleveland, and withdrew money from our account." He looked up and said, "He's so fuckin' stupid that he didn't know they have his picture at every bank! Jesus Christ…what an idiot!"

"Oh, dear God." Connie flopped down in and chair, closed her eyes, and blessed herself. "Goddamn him! Why is he doin' this to us?"

"They asked me if we wanna press charges," he said. "I'm callin' the police." Dominic seemed to make a last second decision.

"Dominic, no!" Connie jumped up and grabbed the phone from his hand. "You know what that police station is like. They'll beat him, Dominic…you know that!"

"Maybe, that's what he needs, Connie!"

"Dominic, please. This'll be the last time but please don't call the police. Let's wait and talk to him." She was nearly hysterical.

Dominic placed the phone back on the wall and sat down. "Mother fuckin', sonofabitch…why's he doin' this? What's wrong with him?"

"I don't know. Dear God…please help us."

"Stop cryin', Connie. This is what happens when you don't discipline your kids. You always babied 'em too much. All of 'em! Jesus Christ, Connie, how many times did I tell you that...stop babyin' 'em?"

It was the middle of the afternoon, and even though bright sunlight beamed through the windows, the house felt dark and depressing. Connie busied herself in the kitchen while Dominic sat in the den, occasionally walking to the back door, watching for cars in the driveway. He was waiting for Vinnie.

Jamie came home first. He had been at his friend's house doing homework, and was invited to stay for dinner, after which his friend's father drove him home.

"Hi, grandma...where's Pop pop?"

"Where have you been, Jamie," she asked. Her face was drawn, her hair disheveled and unwashed.

"At Buddy's, why?" Jamie was suddenly aware that something was wrong.

"No, nothing. Here sit, I'll get you something to eat."

"I already ate," he said, still looking at her with question in his eyes. He walked into the den and sat next to his grandfather.

"Hey, Pop pop," he said softly, his dark eyes troubled.

"Hi there, Jamie, you just get home?"

"Yeah."

"Were you with your father?"

"No. Haven't seen him since yesterday."

"Hmm."

"Somethin' goin' on?"

"Yeah, your dad did somethin' kinda bad. Why don't you go upstairs, Jamie?"

"N'kay." He obediently went to his room and waited. He was used to his father being in trouble but this time it felt different, and he was scared.

Vinnie sauntered into the house just before eleven o'clock. His oil-stained motorcycle boots scraped along the floor as he shuffled with an arrogant swagger. Dominic was in an uncontrollable rage. He walked into the kitchen and stood chest to chest with Vinnie.

"What's wrong with *you*?" Vinnie asked, looking down his nose at his father. "What're ya doin'?" He backed away.

"What am I doin'? What am I doin'?" Dominic repeated. "I'm gonna beat the livin' shit outta you if you don't get outta my house right now!"

"Why…what's wrong?"

"Thought you'd get away with it, huh?"

"Get away with what?" Vinnie asked, suddenly looking panicked.

"We know you took money from our bank account, Vinnie. God, you're so fuckin' stupid. Don't you know they have cameras, you idiot?" His voice boomed.

Connie stood in the corner of the kitchen holding her ears, squeezing her eyes shut tight.

"What?" Vinnie asked, suddenly scared. He eyes darted from his mother to his father. "Listen, I was gonna give it back to ya. Come on, I was only borrowin' it."

"For what?" Dominic challenged him.

"I don't know…I have some bills that need to be paid, s'all. Come on, gimme a break…you guys are loaded. You wouldn't even a missed it."

"You sonofabitch," Dominic growled, and lunged at Vinnie.

Connie jumped to her feet, and ran up behind Dominic, grabbing him by the arms.

"I want you outta here, Vinnie…now! And take your kid with ya!" Dominic was panting. Connie was afraid he was going to have a heart attack.

"Well, how am I supposed to take care of Jamie?" Vinnie was backing away from his father. "I don't have nothin'! Why don't you keep 'im?"

"I don't give a shit that you don't have nothin'! Just get your kid and get out!"

"You're actin' nuts, Dad. You're throwin' your own grandchild out?"

"Get out, Vinnie…honest to God, before I kill ya." Dominic's body was rigid, and as Connie held his arm, it felt like steel. "Jamie!" He yelled. "Come on, get down here and go with your father."

Jamie appeared in the doorway with his schoolbooks tucked under his arm, and a pillowcase slung over his shoulder filled with his clothes.

"Dominic, please?" Connie cried, "Don't hurt him."

"Shut the fuck up, Connie!" He turned and screamed at her, then glared at Vinnie. "You're nothin' but a shitin', drug addict thief, you sonofabitch! I don't want you in this house no more! You steal from your own father? What's the matter with you, and who was the piece of shit that was with you…no, don't answer…" he said, putting his hand in Vinnie's face to stop him from speaking, "I don't wanna know."

"Hurry up Vinnie," Connie pleaded. She positioned her body between him and his father. "Jamie honey, come on, it's time to go. Dominic? Can't Jamie stay here with us? He's got school…"

"If you don't shut up, Connie, I'm warning you…" he took Vinnie by the arm and shoved him toward the door.

"Don't push me, man!" Vinnie warned, and laid his hands on his father's chest, pushing him back.

"Oh yeah?" Dominic said, his voice challenging. He raised his eyebrows, his mouth twisting into a grotesque grin. "You wanna push me around, *maaan*?" He mocked, and stormed from the room.

"Dominic, what are you doing?" A wave of panic washed over Connie. She followed him to the hall closet where he kept a shotgun. "Vinnie!" She hollered, barely able to breath. "Get Jamie and go… please."

"Mother fucker's crazy!" Vinnie thrust out his chest, walked across the kitchen and looked back over his shoulder. "Come on, Jamie," Vinnie said, grabbing the boy by the back of the shirt. Connie pushed them both out the door.

Dominic, clutching his shotgun, pushed past Connie and nearly fell as he ran down the steps of the patio toward the driveway.

Vinnie saw his father approaching, the rifle raised and ready to shoot. He pushed Jamie into the truck, jumped into the drivers seat, gunned the motor, and sped down the street. Dominic aimed and fired, just missing the side of the truck.

Connie stood in the middle of the driveway, screaming. When Vinnie drove away, she ran back into the house expecting the police to show up at any moment. Dominic came back into the house, with the butt of the shotgun dragging on the floor. He glanced at Connie but didn't speak. His face was flushed, and sweat was running down his forehead. He put the gun back in the hall closet, went to the den, sat on the sofa and stared at the wall in front of him.

Connie gave him a few minutes to calm down, then quietly went into the room, and sat across from him. In a voice almost inaudible she asked, "Are you all right? Can I do anything for you?"

"You know what, Connie?" He asked, his voice quivering. "My mother warned me never to love my kids too much because they'd end up walking all over me." He paused. His eyes were sad when he looked at her. "But I talked to my father again," he smiled and nodded. "Did I tell you that, Connie?"

"No, Dominic…you didn't tell me." She spoke softly, and leaned forward.

"I told him what my mother said. And my father told me, *'you're mother is wrong, Dominic.'* Can you believe that, Connie? He said my mother was wrong. No one ever says my mother is wrong." He looked off in the distance, not talking to Connie anymore. The blue of his eyes intensified as they filled with tears. "Ma," he cried, in a long, moanful wail. "Why'd you take him away from me?"

"Oh, Dominic…what can I do to help you?" Connie started to get up from the chair but stopped. Dominic leaned against the back of the sofa, his eyes slowly turning toward the ceiling. He seemed to be focused on someone that was not there. In a controlled tone, he simply said, "I hate you for that, you know. No woman should do what you did, Ma." He leaned on his side, and rested his head on a pillow, and closed his eyes. He was asleep within seconds.

Connie sat for several minutes watching him. *What did his mother do, for God's sake?* She asked herself. She couldn't help but feel sorry for him. He was sick and she didn't know what to do.

*

Weeks passed and Jamie spent more time at his grandparent's than he did with his father. He showed up one day after school, sat at the kitchen table, and quietly did his homework. After eating a plate of spaghetti and meatballs, he went into the den, watched television, and went to bed in Luci's old room. Connie and Dominic never asked about Vinnie, and Connie was relieved that Dominic seemed all right with Jamie being there. He would never admit it but he felt guilty about the shotgun incident. He still worried that someone was going to report him to the police.

One morning, when Jamie sat at the table with his grandfather, eating oatmeal and toast, he casually asked, "Pop pop, why did you try to shoot my daddy and me?"

"What?" Dominic dropped his spoon, and looked at the boy. "Oh come on Jamie, I wasn't really shootin' atcha." He looked at Connie, then back to Jamie. "You know that, right?"

Jamie shrugged and continued to eat. "Guess so…" He wiped his mouth on his sleeve and pushed away from the table. "I'm gonna go watch television, okay?"

"Sure," Dominic said, and watched him leave the room. "Connie, did you tell him to ask me that?"

"What…no!" Connie said. "Why would I do that? I'm so embarrassed by what you did that day that I'm praying Jamie and Vinnie don't tell anyone! You could go to jail, for God's sake!"

"Shh…shut up, Connie." He looked toward the door. "I had a right to do what I did…you remember that, Connie."

The phone rang and Connie froze. She hated the sound of the phone because it was almost always bad news.

"Hello?" Dominic answered. "What do *you* want?" He listened. "Jamie's with us now." Another pause. "You want him to stay in that house you turned into a shit hole…with your druggie friends?"

"Pop pop? Is that my father?" Jamie appeared and stood next to Dominic.

"Yeah."

"Can I talk to him?"

Dominic reluctantly handed the phone to his grandson, and Jamie, stretching the coiled phone cord walked into the hallway, lowered his voice and spoke to his father.

Dominic looked at Connie, and she shrugged. Jamie walked back into the kitchen, reached up and put the phone back in its cradle and said, "My Dad's gonna pick me up, okay?"

"He's not supposed to be driving."

"I know but he said it's okay."

"Jamie…where's he takin' you?" Dominic asked, with genuine concern.

"Home…with him. Just for the weekend, I think." He went back to sitting in front of the television, after grabbing a handful of chocolate chip cookies.

"Now what?" Dominic asked. He rested his arms on the table and clasped his hands together.

"I guess we have to let him go," Connie said. "We don't have custody."

*

Jamie trailed behind his father as they walked up the sidewalk to Vinnie's house.

"We don't need nobody, Jamie," Vinnie told his son. He opened the door. "Come on in."

"Is this really *your* house, Dad?" Jamie asked. "Pop pop says he bought it." He wrinkled his nose when he stepped inside the foul smelling living room. Empty beer bottles cluttered the coffee table, some standing upright but most lying on their sides. Ashtrays were spilling over with cigarette butts, and piles of clothes were thrown in one corner of the room.

"*I* own this house, Jamie. And ya know what? Your ol' man's gonna be rich one day."

"How?"

"You'll see. Listen, I got a guy stayin' here, his name is Hurley…he's cool, he won't bother ya."

"Oh."

"We don't have nothin' to worry about, ya know? Your grandparents are rich, did ya know that?"

"They are?"

"Oh, yeah. They'll give me money." He stuck out his bottom lip and nodded. "They never use it. They ain't bought nothin' new in that house in thirty years," he laughed. "Anyway, they owe me."

"Why?"

"They just do, that's all…don't you worry 'bout it, okay?"

"Kay."

"That's where you'll sleep," Vinnie told him, pointing to a bare mattress laying on the floor by sliding glass doors that led to the tiny back yard. "I'd give ya a bedroom but Hurley's usin' it right now."

"That's okay." Jamie laid his schoolbooks on the floor, and sat Indian-style on the end of the mattress. "Got a blanket or somethin'?"

"Oh yeah, sure…here ya go." Vinnie grabbed a sheet that was draped over the sofa and threw it to Jamie. "Hey kid…I gotta go out for a while. You be okay?"

"I guess so. Hey dad…Pop pop says you're not s'posed to be drivin'."

"Don't worry 'bout it…I won't get caught. If Hurley comes in… well, just tell 'im who you are…he's cool. He don't care if you're here."

Vinnie left the house, and Jamie opened his spelling book and started on his homework.

*

That weekend, and every weekend that Jamie spent at the house, his father came home late at night and slept on the sofa. Sometimes he got up in the morning, and sometimes he slept until the following night. Jamie lived on microwaved macaroni and cheese, or settled for a bowl of cereal. He mostly watched television, or when Hurley was home, they'd sit on the sofa, and Jamie listened to Hurley talk about cars or watched in amazement as Hurley demonstrated the technique of blowing smoke rings.

Sometimes Vinnie came home so high, he'd wake up in the morning surprised to see Jamie. "Hey Jamie," he'd mumble, "what're you doin' here?"

"I've been here, Dad…don't'cha remember?'

"Oh yeah, sure…I remember."

"Can we go to Grandma's now?"

"Yeah, let's go."

*

The piercing sound of the phone cut through the silence of the house as Connie sat at the kitchen table. The room was dark, and she was sipping a cup of strong coffee in hopes of relieving the headache that woke her in the middle of the night. She snatched the phone from the wall on the first ring. "Hello?" She answered, tentatively. Her voice sounded thick and raspy.

"Ma, it's me...Vinnie."

"What's the matter? Where are you?"

"I got arrested Ma. I need ya to come down here and bail me out."

"Shit! Vinnie...sonofabitch!"

"Ma listen, will ya?"

"Jesus, Joseph and Mary...what did you do? Why'd ya get arrested, Vinnie?"

"They said drunk drivin' Ma but I swear, I wasn't drunk! I think it was cause I don't have a license. Listen to how I'm talkin' to ya! Do I sound drunk to you?"

"Goddamn it, Vinnie!"

"Ma! Will ya stop? Jesus Christ! You're such a..."

"Tell me where you are," Connie demanded, angrily. She could feel the pounding of her heart in her throat.

"The police station on Fourth and Unger. Get me outta here, Ma... please. You know what they'll do to me...the cops hate me here."

She hung up the phone and dialed Luci's number. She prayed that Luci's husband wouldn't pick up the phone, and after several rings Connie heard the sound of someone fumbling with the phone.

"Lo," Luci mumbled.

"Luci? It's Mom. Listen, I need your help."

"What's wrong?"

"Vinnie got arrested. He's at the police station on Fourth Street. You know where that is, right?"

"Yeah...oh God, you're gonna ask me to go there, aren't you?"

"Listen to me, Luci. Come pick me up and I'll go with you."

"Jesus God Ma, how long you gonna do this?"

"Get down here, Luci! I don't want to wake your father."

"All right," she groaned. "I'll be right there."

*

Connie and Luci went to the police station, and Vinnie was not only drunk but officers found PCP in his pocket. He had already been arraigned, thrown in the drunk tank and was sitting on a cot when his mother and sister walked in.

It was hot and muggy, the middle of summer, and Vinnie was dressed in jeans, motorcycle boots, a t-shirt and heavy leather jacket.

He was dirty, and several days' growth of beard made him look like a tramp.

"Where do I go to pay someone's bail?" Connie asked an officer.

"What's the prisoner's name, Maam?" The young officer asked without looking up from his paperwork.

"Vincent Preste."

At the sound of Vinnie's name, the officer lifted his head and asked. "You his mother?"

"Yes."

"Well, let me tell ya something…Mrs. Preste, is it?"

Connie nodded.

"If we arrest your son one more time, he may go away for good. This guy is trouble, Mrs. Preste. And we know he's dealing drugs," he added. "We just haven't been able to catch him yet. But we will."

"Jesus," Connie said, under her breath.

"You can go pay at that desk over there." He pointed to a desk where an older, white-haired officer was leaning back in his chair, talking on the phone. "Just give your son's name. He'll be notified of a hearing in a few days."

"Okay, thank you."

"Oh, Mrs. Preste?" The officer stopped her. "You seem like a real nice lady. You don't need to put up with the crap this guy is causing you."

Connie looked at him with tired eyes and said, "But he's my son."

*

Dominic never found out about the five thousand dollar check Connie wrote that night for Vinnie's bail. She had told him so many lies over the years, and taken thousands of dollars from their account that it sickened her to think what he would do if he found out.

Vinnie seemed to be staying out of trouble for the moment, and Jamie was spending most of his time with his grandparents. He was withdrawn, and didn't like talking about his father. He knew his father was always in trouble but loved him anyway. Dominic often questioned Jamie and asked, 'is your father working? Is he home at night? Is he doing drugs?' But Jamie just shrugged.

Weeks passed, and Vinnie slowly eased his way back into his parent's home for brief visits. He assured them that he was sober. He also told them he was working at a local gas station washing cars and saving his money.

"What are ya doin' with your life, Vinnie? Ya gotta start takin' responsibility for yourself and your son," Dominic said.

"I am, Dad. I told ya, I gotta job. I'm makin' money and I'm puttin' it away. I'm gonna buy the house from ya," Vinnie said.

Dominic stared at him, and shook his head. "Vinnie, you don't have a pot to piss in. What are ya talkin' about? Buyin' the house, for Christ sake." He got up from his chair and went to the refrigerator for a glass of orange juice. "Do you know how much it costs to buy that house?"

"Yeah, I know. I got money. I'm gonna have big bucks, you'll see."

"Big bucks, huh?" Dominic gave him a sideways glance. "What big bucks you got?"

"I don't have it yet. I'm gonna though. Some lady hit me with her car, and I'm suin' her. I got a lawyer and everything."

"Holy shit…you listenin' to this, Connie? Our boy here is gonna sue a lady for hittin' him with her car! What'd she hit, Vinnie…that piece of shit out there in the driveway? That truck with all the paint peeling off, and the dents and rotted fenders? That I bought?" He added.

"She hit me man, I'm tellin' ya!"

"You're fulla shit, Vinnie. You're gonna pay a lawyer, and you're gonna end up with nothin'! You know somethin'? You're the stupidest piece of shit…" Dominic threw up his hands and walked out of the kitchen.

"What's the matter with him?" Vinnie turned to his mother.

"Go home, Vinnie," Connie simply said.

"You'll see. I'm gonna be a millionaire, and you'll all wanna piece. And I ain't gonna give nobody nothin'. You'll see." He left the house, got into his truck, and slammed the door before driving away.

Connie leaned up against the doorjamb and watched him leave. *He has no license…look at him, God…he's driving and has no license.* She knew he was high by the way he slurred his words. His body movements were jerky and exaggerated. He was slipping away and she felt helpless.

Chapter 25

Dominic started spending more time golfing and bowling. Connie would have enjoyed spending time alone in the house but between juggling bank accounts, and keeping track of money she was secretly giving to Vinnie and Luci, she never got a free minute. The deceipt was exhausting her. The more money Connie gave, the more they asked for.

Dominic was usually gone a few hours a day but, soon started coming home hours later than usual. "I thought bowling was over at four o'clock," she asked. "It's past nine...is everything all right?"

"It *is* over at four. I went out...had me a little fun, you mind?"

"No, I don't mind. I just wondered."

"You mean you're not gonna ask where I go after bowling?"

"If you want to tell me, fine...if not, that's fine too." She was beginning to feel annoyed. She ladled a spoonful of soup into a bowl, and put it on the table in front of him.

"You're such a liar," he finally said. "You know you wanna know what I've been doing. You can't tell me you don't care."

"Oh, for God's sake, Dominic...I don't care."

Well into his sixties, Dominic still had a charismatic personality when around his friends, a magnetism that bewildered Connie. He was a shameless flirt, mostly to make Connie jealous. His affairs no longer bothered her but she did not like being made a fool of.

Dominic thought for a few seconds. "Nah…you don't need to know."

"Oh, Jesus, Joseph and Mary," Connie reacted angrily, slamming the soup ladle down on the kitchen counter. She stormed out of the kitchen.

Dominic calmly ate his soup, and smiled with satisfaction.

*

Connie was juggling two bags of groceries as she walked up the driveway toward the house. She noticed Dominic's car in the driveway, and after putting the bags on the counter, she stopped to listen when she heard voices coming from the living room. "Who in the world…?" She walked toward the living room. Dominic was sitting on the sofa next to a woman she didn't recognize. The woman jumped up when she saw Connie.

"Dominic? What's going on?" Connie asked.

"Oh, Connie." He calmly stood up, and rested his hand on the woman's shoulder. "This is Helen Karnicki. Helen, this is my wife."

The woman stared at Dominic. "Hello," she uttered, quietly. "I think I'd better go." She grabbed her sweater and purse, and started walking toward the front door. She stopped, and looked back at Dominic. "I need a ride home."

Connie stared at the two as they walked out the door together. They got into Dominic's car and drove away. *The bastard enjoyed that,* Connie thought. She went back into the kitchen, slamming cabinet doors as she put the groceries away. She was cooking when Dominic came back into the house a short time later.

"So, what do ya think, Connie?" He asked. "You said you don't care what I do, so I thought I'd bring her home. She's good lookin', ain't she?"

Connie was silent.

"That's how a woman is supposed to look."

"You sonofabitch!" Connie turned to face him. "How dare you bring that whore into my house!"

"What're ya so mad about? You said you didn't care." He was laughing at her.

"Don't give me that, Dominic. That's the lowest thing you could ever do, for God's sake. Bring your girlfriend home? My God, what's wrong with you? You're a whoremaster!"

Dominic's jaw started to flex as he ground his teeth together. He took a menacing step toward her.

Connie stood firm. "Go ahead, whoremaster! Beat the shit outta me. I don't care. You made me a bitter old woman, and I don't care if you kill me. How do ya like that? It would be the first peace I've had since I married you! Go ahead. Hit me!"

He slapped her hard, across the face.

She slapped him back. "You bastard!" She stood her ground and stared into his eyes.

Her reaction stunned him. A smile of satisfaction slowly crept across his face. "See, I said you were lyin' when you said you didn't care. Hoo-hoo..." he laughed, "You're jealous." He turned and walked out the back door. Connie was frozen in place, and found it hard to catch her breath. She grabbed her favorite pasta bowl, and hurled toward the door. It crashed and broke into a thousand pieces, and that was what made her cry. She left the shards of glass on the floor, and went into the den. *He can clean up the mess. He can make his own dinner too.*

*

Connie did not speak to Dominic for several days, and he found it amusing.

"Connie, aren't you ever gonna talk to me again," he smirked, "or are we just not gonna talk till they bury us in the ground?"

"I don't wanna be buried next to you," she finally said.

"Oh yeah, zat so?"

"Yeah, that's so..."

"Look, why don't you let me buy you something. I'll make it up to you...what'dya want? New furniture, a vacation...what? Tell me."

"I don't want anything, Dominic. Do you think that after all you've put me through, that new furniture or a vacation is gonna make up for it?"

"Well, what else do you want from me, Connie. I'm trying to make you happy here!"

She stopped what she was doing, sat down and dropped her head into her hands. She finally looked up, sighed and said, "You wanna do something for me, Dominic? I'll tell you what. I want for you to tell me that you believe me when I say I'm not afraid of you anymore. Numb is what I am. I don't feel anything anymore. After fifty years with you, I'm numb…empty."

"I know." He almost sounded remorseful.

"But you know what I want?"

"What?"

"I want you to go to a psychiatrist."

"A psychiatrist! Oh no…don't start that again." He slammed his fist on the table.

"Yes, a psychiatrist. There's something terribly wrong with you Dominic, and I know you say you don't care if I leave but I think you do. So, if you want me to stay here with you, you need to find out why you do what you do."

"Let me tell you something, Connie. You leave me, you die, ya hear me?"

"Ya see that, Dominic…the way you threaten me? That's not normal. I keep tellin' you…your threats don't bother me anymore." She sat calmly, and smiled.

"What're ya smilin' 'about? You're fuckin' nuts, you know that? You're crazy." He stood up, slammed his fist on the wall, and walked out of the room.

A few days later, while Connie was helping Jamie with his homework, Dominic came into the room. "Hey, Connie," he said. His tone was childlike, and it caught Connie off guard. "Find that doctor you were talkin' about and make an appointment…but for the two of us," he quickly added. "I ain't doin' this alone."

Chapter 26

"So tell me, Mrs. Preste, what seems to be the problem here?" Dominic and Connie sat side by side in front of a large walnut desk where Doctor Howard C. Robbins sat, his elbows resting on the edge of the desk, his hands clasped in front of him. His graying hair was thick and wavy, and with a condescending grin, he peered at Connie over wire-rimmed glasses that sat perched on the tip of his nose.

"Well, I really don't know where to start, doctor." She sat forward a little, her expression serious but nervous. Her eyes darted from the doctor to Dominic, and she cleared her throat a few times before continuing.

"It's okay, Mrs. Preste. Just slow down, and tell me what's on you mind." He smiled again and cocked his head, and for some reason, Connie had the urge to slap him.

"Well, I guess the thing that concerns me the most is my husband's temper. He gets violent and…he doesn't have any respect for me." She stopped, took a deep breath, looked at Dominic, and continued. "Over the years, I can't help but wonder if it has anything to do with his childhood…you know…maybe his mother?" She said, tentatively. She said it so quietly that the doctor asked her to repeat what she said. "I think it has something to do with his mother," she stated, and nodded her head. "There, I said it." She sat back in the chair, and looked at Dominic.

"Anything else, Mrs. Preste?"

"He's violent and…he goes out with other women, and I just can't take it anymore. My children are grown and I have no reason to stay and go through that anymore. I just want him to find out why he behaves like that."

"I see." The doctor nodded slowly. He turned and looked at Dominic. "What do you think about what your wife just said, Mr. Preste?"

"Well, I'll tell ya…I'm not comfortable with this," Dominic said, shifting anxiously in his chair, "I think I'd like to talk to you alone."

Connie turned to look at him. "Dominic…" she said, quietly.

"Do you have a problem with that, Mrs. Preste?"

"Uh, no…I guess not. But I want him to speak the truth."

"I will, Connie."

"Then, here's what we'll do," the doctor interjected. "This first session will be with your husband, alone. Then next week, Mrs. Preste, I'll meet with you, and we'll take it from there."

"Fine." Connie stood up, feeling uneasy. She chewed her lower lip and gave them each an icy stare before walking toward the door. "I'll wait in the other room." She knew what was going to happen. He was going to lie.

She sat for more than an hour before the doctor opened the door, walking side by side with Dominic into the waiting room. They appeared to have suddenly become pals.

"Okay Dominic, that was a good start," the doctor said, while patting Dominic on the back. "Ya got a good man here, Mrs. Preste, and I'll see *you* next Monday. Is that good for you?"

"That's fine," Connie said, resolutely. *A good man…ya got yourself a good man, Mrs. Preste. Dear God, what did he tell him?*

Connie stubbornly refused to ask Dominic what they talked about. In the beginning, he was smug but when she didn't ask him any questions, his mood turned dark.

The following Monday, Connie met with Doctor Robbins and decided to tell him everything. She emotionally drained herself. She talked about the beatings, the name-calling, the cheating, and her suspicions that he may have molested their daughter. Within that one session, she revealed more about her fifty years with Dominic than she had ever before. The more Connie talked, the more unbelievable she sounded. She described things that didn't seem possible; words continued to spill from her mouth. She suddenly stopped talking when she noticed the doctor staring at her with squinted eyes, and pursed lips. "Oh," she said, quietly. "I guess I've said enough."

"Are you finished, Mrs. Preste?"

"I think so."

"I've listened to you, and I've listened to your husband…" his patronizing tone made her want to get up and leave. "I'll go over my notes and we'll meet next Monday, all right? You're angry right now, and I think your thoughts may be a little…oh, let's say cloudy. Maybe even exaggerated. I think it just might be a matter of tweaking a few idiosyncrasies here and there."

"Tweaking a few…what?" Connie looked bewildered.

"Idiosyncrasies."

"Oh." A puff of breath escaped her throat in the form of a laugh. *A few idiosyncrasies? Was he kidding? Well, he can just tweak my ass,* she thought with disgust. *God, how I hate men!* She wanted to run from the office. It was all a waste of time. The doctor continued talking but she wasn't listening. "Uh-huh, uh-huh," she said, absently. She picked up her purse and walked toward the door. "Okay, bye." She waved at him with a quick raise of her hand, and slipped through the door into the waiting room.

Dominic was sitting, one leg crossed over the other with his black-rimmed glasses resting on the edge of his nose while he thumbed through a Popular Mechanic's magazine. He looked up, saw Connie's expression and laid the magazine on the table beside him.

Connie walked to the door. "Let's go, Dominic."

"What's the matter with you? What're you in such a hurry for?"

"Just take me home."

They went down the elevator in silence, out of the building, to the car. Connie was livid. She knew the doctor didn't believe her. Probably because of what Dominic told him. *Men…Goddamned whoremasters… they all stick together.* Seeing a doctor was her last hope…unless she could get Dominic to drop dead, and she was sure that wasn't going to happen anytime soon.

*

Connie was adamant that she was not going back to the doctor the following Monday but Dominic insisted they go. "Well, this is a change. Now you wanna go!" Connie said, angrily.

"Oh, we're goin' all right," he warned, with a sly laugh. "You started this and we're gonna finish."

"Why should we, Dominic? The only reason you want to go is to prove me wrong. Isn't that what it's about Dominic, you being right and me being wrong? You obviously lied and told him that I was a nut or something! You got a good man there, he tells me," she said in a mocking tone. "My God, what did you tell him, Dominic?"

"Maybe you are nuts, Connie. Did ya ever think about that? That the problem might be you?"

"Sonofabitch…" she hissed, and punched the palm of her hand with her fist.

"Ooh…listen to you." He laughed and pointed at her. "Maybe you're the one with a temper problem, huh?"

"I hate you, Dominic," she stated, as a matter of fact. "And I'm not going back to that quack!"

"Oh, yeah?"

"Leave me alone, Dominic…I'm warning you."

"You're warning *me*? Ha! Let me tell you something, Connie. I can get any woman I want. I don't need you, you hear me?"

"Shut up, Dominic!"

"Bitch…"

Connie grit her teeth, picked up a coffee mug and threw it at him. He ducked. The cup shattered when it hit the wall next to his head.

"Oh, you wanna play rough?" With lightening speed, he lunged toward her and grabbed her by the throat. Connie gagged and fell back against the kitchen counter, and swung at him with both hands. He laughed at her, and suddenly released his grip after shoving her backwards. "You're so stupid." He casually picked up his jacket and bowling bag and left the house.

Connie was hunched over, clutching at her throat. Tears streamed down her face as she slowly slid to the floor, where she hugged her knees to her chest and sobbed. "Die, you bastard…please…just die!"

*

To avoid another fight, Connie agreed to see Doctor Robbins. She felt defeated and knew she had already lost the battle. Dominic was in the bedroom standing in front of a full-length mirror, while Connie silently finished dressing. He, still thin and fit was wearing brown dress slacks, a freshly ironed shirt, and alligator shoes that matched his belt. Every hair was in place, and he smelled of Aqua Velva and hairspray. Connie sat on the edge of the bed pulling on her stockings, eying him with disgust.

"I'll meet you downstairs, Connie. Hurry up." He walked out of the bedroom.

There goes God's gift to women, Connie thought sarcastically. *Bastard...they can have him.* She pulled up her black slacks and tucked her black and white striped silk blouse into the waistband. She ran a brush through her hair, and touched a tube of pink lipstick to her lips and cheeks. She swiped her fingers under her eyes as if, by some miracle it would erase the dark circles embedded under her skin.

"Let's go, Connie!" Dominic yelled, from the bottom of the stairs.

She grabbed a handful of tissues, and a sweater and started down the stairs.

Dominic was waiting by the door, and turned to look at her. "You're wearing that again? I told you that getup makes you look fat."

"What would you like for me to wear?" She asked robotically.

"Forget it. Come on, there's not enough time for you to change now." He looked at her again. "Ya got something you could put around..." He gestured that he wanted her to cover up her neck.

"Okay, I'll be right back." She ran up the stairs, and grabbed a black scarf and draped it around her neck. "How's that, better?" She asked, meeting him at the back door. She patted at her neck. "This look better?"

"Yeah," he said, without looking at her.

*

"Well..." Doctor Robbins said. "I had a private session with Dominic and also with you, Connie...if I may call you Connie." He flashed the same idiotic grin that set her teeth on edge before. "And I've come to the conclusion, that it's obvious that you, Connie have a problem with...oh, what shall I call it...emotional exaggeration? Maybe its menopause...I don't know but I can tell you the accusations have brought a lot of tension to Dominic. And Connie...your jealousy will eventually drive your husband away, and it would be no wonder if he ended up in the arms of another woman. A man has needs, Connie and from what Dominic has told me...well, like I said, a man has needs. Clinical studies have proven..."

Connie could no longer hear his voice. She stared straight ahead, fighting the urge to take Dominic and the doctor by their throats, and slowly and methodically choke the life out of them both. The man's voice bounced within her head, not like words; more like the low drone of a machine.

"Now Dominic," Doctor Robbins continued, "let me turn to you. You have to reel in your temper." He motioned like he was using a fishing rod. "It's not going to do any good to react to Connie by yelling at her, so try and stay calm and communicate with your wife. Hear that word? Co-mune-a-cate," he repeated as if he was talking to a three year-old. "And when I see you again, I'm positive I'm going to be pleased with what I hear from you both."

"Thank you, Doctor." Dominic stood up and reached for the doctor's hand. "You ready, Connie?" He turned and gave her a sheepish grin.

It'll be a cold day in hell before I walk into this office again, Connie thought. She hoped she would find the strength to stand up. She gripped the arms of the chair and slowly pushed herself to her feet. She cleared her throat, fixed a smile on her face and slowly said, "Thank you, Doctor Robbins...goodnight."

Chapter 27

On Sundays, Dominic attended church by himself. A *dedicated catholic* the priests called him. He passed the collection plate and often shared a glass of wine with Father Finch after services. Connie stayed home. She couldn't bring herself to sit in church. She wondered if Father Finch knew that his favorite church member beat his wife after serving the Lord.

"You should be ashamed not going to church, Connie," Dominic scolded.

"I'm not ashamed, Dominic...I talk to God all day long. He forgives me for not going to church."

"Suit yourself but I know *I'm* goin' to heaven."

I'll see you in hell, you bastard, she silently responded.

*

"Hello?" Connie said, when the phone rang early one morning. "Oh hi, Celia." It was one of the women that bowled in Dominic's league. "I'm fine, how are you?" As she listened, she felt her cheeks flush.

"I didn't wanna say anything, Connie but you need to know... Dominic has been seeing someone...a woman from another league. Don't know her name but she's been goin' to the VFW with him on Friday nights, you know...for the dances."

Connie was too humiliated to speak.

"Connie...are you still there?"

"Yeah, I'm here. Thanks for letting me know, Celia."

"I'm sorry Connie. You don't deserve to be treated that way."

"Thanks...listen, I gotta go. Bye now."

Connie was already in bed when Dominic came home from bowling. She decided not to say anything about the phone call from Celia.

"You awake?" he asked.

Connie lay on her side, with her back to him. "Mm-hm, I'm awake. You want something to eat?"

"No, I don't want anything. I just wanted to remind you about the bowling banquet."

"I remember. It's this Friday, right?"

"Yeah, but you don't have to go if you don't want to."

"No, no...I'll go," she stated, firmly. "Why wouldn't I wanna go, Dominic? All the wives are goin', right?"

"Oh, well...yeah, I just didn't know if..." he stopped himself. "Fine, we'll go."

Go to hell, ol' man...ya can't get rid of me that easy. She wasn't going to let him make a bigger fool out of her than he already had. She would go to the banquet and hold her head up high.

*

Luci took her mother shopping at the mall where Connie bought a new suit. When she got home, she ran up to the bedroom, tried on the cream colored suit with her beige pumps and posed in the mirror. She put her hands on her hips, and turned from side to side. "Not bad, I guess." After hanging the suit in the closet, she took a bath, washed her hair and rolled it in curlers. She smoothed foundation on her face and dabbed a pale pink blush to her cheeks, and sat under the drier.

Dominic came home a short time later and took a shower. Connie covered herself with a robe, and went downstairs to perk a pot of coffee. She was second-guessing her decision to go to the banquet, and didn't look forward to the talk that would be going on behind her back. She went back up to the bedroom, and while Dominic finished in the bathroom, she brushed out her hair, put on her new suit, and stood in front of the mirror again.

"New outfit?" Dominic asked. A towel was wrapped around his waist.

"Mm-hm, got it today." She turned and posed. "Like it?"

"Yeah, it's nice." He gave her a familiar grin that always made her wonder if he was mocking her.

Dominic slipped on dress pants, and pulled on a navy blue jacket over a stiffly, starched white shirt. He neatly knotted a polka dot tie, and ran a comb through his hair. Connie followed him down the stairs and out to the car, where they rode in silence to the Holiday Inn. He parked the car, and turned off the ignition but didn't get out of the car.

"What's the matter?" Connie asked. "You ready to go in?"

"I just want you to know something. I'm probably not going to be dancing with you tonight."

She turned to look at him. "Fine," she said, calmly. "Why? Because your girlfriend will be there?"

His eyes narrowed. "Now look Connie, I don't want any trouble with you. These people are my friends. I just wanted ya to know, that's all. I told you, you didn't have to come tonight. I think I'm a pretty nice guy to let you know, don't ya think?"

"Thank you for letting me know, Dominic," she answered, in a snide tone. "You're such a thoughtful man."

"Get outta the car...let's go."

She trailed behind him as they approached the banquet room. Dominic put on his "game face", and acted as though he were running for mayor.

"Eh Dominic, there you are." A heavy-set man approached and gave Dominic a friendly clap on the back. "Come sit with us," he said, holding a bottle of beer in his free hand.

"I think we're sitting at table five, according to this card here," Dominic said.

"Oh, okay." He looked at Connie and smiled. "This the wife?"

"Yeah, this is Connie. Connie, this is Howard Berman. Runs the Dunkin Doughnuts on the boulevard.

"Oh, that's nice. Well, how do you do, Howard," Connie said, cordially.

"Nice to meet ya. Well, time for another brewsky..." he said, and went back to the bar.

"Charming," Connie said, sarcastically. She raised her head, and smiled as they entered the room.

"Better not embarrass me, Connie," he warned.

Connie laid her purse on table five, and smoothed the lap of her skirt while Dominic stopped to talk with friends. Connie watched as a blonde woman walked across the room toward him. The woman draped her arms around Dominic's neck and pulled him to the dance floor.

Dominic glanced at Connie, and shrugged. "Told ya…" he mouthed. He wrapped his arm around the woman's waist and started to jitterbug. Connie got up to go to the ladies room, and could feel eyes watching her. When she came back to the table, she was relieved to see Honey Keegan and her husband, Joe at their table. She liked Honey and thought maybe the evening wouldn't turn out to be a total loss.

"Hey Connie, how ya doin'?" Joe asked. He stood up and gave her a hug.

"Hi Joe."

Honey warmly embraced her. "Connie, you look fantastic!"

"Oh, I don't know how fantastic I look but I'm glad to see you," Connie laughed.

"It's good to see you too." Honey lowered her voice. "How are you really, Connie?"

Connie hated the way people asked that question. They looked at her with pity. Everyone knew about Dominic's cheating, Vinnie's drugs, and Luci's drunken husband.

"Fine," Connie responded.

"Connie? Can I ask you something?" Joe asked, hesitantly.

"What's that, Joe?"

"I wanted to ask you…how do you," he stammered, "I mean, Dominic's out there dancing…"

"Oh Joe, don't worry 'bout me. I'm not stupid. I know that I'm married to the biggest whoremaster there is."

"Oh my God…" he laughed. "Well yeah, I guess you're right. I mean, I like Dominic and all…but how he can do that…boy, I don't know."

"Seriously, it's fine, Joe. Nothing shocks me."

As the evening progressed, the only person Connie danced with was Honey. Toward the end of the evening, Dominic finally sat at the table next to Connie. The bandleader announced the last song of the night, when the blonde walked over to their table, leaning over to reveal a flabby, wrinkled cleavage that spilled over the top of her dress. "Come on Dominic, it's the last song."

Connie stood up and faced the woman. "Excuse me...but I'm his wife and you've danced with him all night. If you don't mind, I'd like to borrow him back from you for one dance...that's if you don't mind."

"Oh, I didn't even know you were here," she said. "Dominic...you bad boy!"

Connie moved closer to the woman. "Well, I'm here and I can be a first class sonofabitch," she said, putting her hand on her hip. "So, get your fat ass away from my husband or I'll flatten you so quick you won't know what hit ya."

The woman gasped. "Are you gonna let her talk to me like that?" She asked Dominic.

But before he could answer, Connie grabbed him by the jacket sleeve and nearly dragged him onto the dance floor. "You dance with *me,* or I'll choke you with my own bare hands in front of all your friends."

The last song was *In The Mood,* and Connie not only danced with Dominic but she kicked up her leg, twirled around him and wiggled her shoulders like a chorus girl.

"That Connie's somethin', ain't she?" Joe said to Honey. "I'll tell you what, she's got guts."

"She sure does," Honey said, and clapped her hands to the music.

*

Connie followed Dominic through the parking lot toward the car, when she heard a woman's voice behind them.

"Goodnight, baby." It was the blonde.

Connie kept walking. They drove home in silence, and when they finally walked in the back door, Dominic stupidly said, "I guess you're mad."

"Mad? Mad? I'll tell you how mad I am." She drew back her hand and with whatever energy she had, slapped Dominic across the face with such force he slammed into the wall. When he regained his balance, he stared at her, rubbed his cheek and laughed. He grabbed for her hair, pulling her forward, pushing her to the floor.

Jamie suddenly appeared in the doorway, and screamed, "Let her go Pop pop!"

Dominic ignored him and continued to struggle with Connie. Jamie ran out of the house, and soon returned with a pair of hedge clippers he got from the garage. He raised them above his head, and aimed at his grandfather's back.

"Jamie…no!" Connie screamed. She lunged toward Jamie, grabbing the shears.

Luci burst in the back door. "What the hell's goin' on?"

"Everything's all right." Connie was panting. "Go home, Luci, and take Jamie with you."

"I'm afraid to go," Luci said. She looked at her mother, then her father. Her mother's face was bruised, and her father was bleeding from his nose. "My God, look at you two."

"Luci, please," Connie pleaded.

"Are you sure, Ma?"

"I'm sure." Connie never took her eyes from Dominic.

"Dad? I mean it." Luci gave her father a look of warning. "You better leave Mom alone."

"Get out, Luci," he said, in a raspy voice.

"You two are gonna kill each other, aren't you?" She turned to Jamie. "Jamie, come on, I'll take ya home to your father's."

"Can't,"

"Why?"

"Dad's in jail."

"Jesus, Joseph and Mary." Connie couldn't help it. She laughed. She dropped her chin to her chest, and closed her eyes. "How much more can I take? Jamie, go home with Luci…I'll pick you up tomorrow."

"Okay, Grandma." He turned toward Dominic. "Pop pop? Please don't hurt Grandmom anymore." He followed Luci out the door.

Dominic left Connie standing in the kitchen. He went to the den, and turned on the television. Connie went upstairs, put on a nightgown, and crawled under the covers. She lay on her side and pulled up her knees, and softly wept.

*

"Ma, why do you let him do this to you?" Luci asked, as she walked around her mother's kitchen, spraying a bottle of Windex, wiping the counters with a paper towel. It was Monday morning and Dominic was in a bowling tournament that would last most of the day.

"I don't care what he does to me anymore."

"I don't believe that, Ma," Luci said, shaking her head. "He's gotta stop...I'm afraid he's gonna kill ya. Or you'll kill him. And ya know what, Ma...I gotta tell ya...I'm a little embarrassed. People come up to me all the time and say, '*Oh, I saw your Dad the other night with his girlfriend*.' Nice, huh? Everyone's laughing at ya, Ma!" Luci sat opposite her mother, reached in her purse and pulled out a pack of cigarettes.

"Don't smoke in the house, Luci. Your father will smell it...then I'll catch shit."

"Christ...nice life, Ma."

"What do you want me to do, Luci?"

"Confront him!"

"Confront him? That would get me nothing' but another beating."

"My God, Ma."

"Luci, I tried confronting him...didn't go too well," she said, pointing to the faded bruise on the side of her face.

"Mom?" Luci said quietly. "I know where Dad is right now."

"So do I, he's at the bowling alley." She looked at Luci. "Isn't he?"

"He's at the bowling alley all right, but he's there with...*her*."

"Sonofabitch!" Connie pounded her fist on the table. "How do you know that?"

"Ray told me. He just came from there. He left when he saw Dad... and the woman," she added, hesitantly.

Connie sat quietly for a minute, and then stood up. "Come on... drive me over there."

"To the bowling alley?"

"Yes."

"Oh, Jesus."

*

Luci pulled the car into the parking lot of the Greenside Lanes on 29th Street, and just by chance, Luci spotted her father getting into his car. Connie panicked when she saw a woman on the passenger side. "Let's go, Luci. Take me home."

"No, Mom. You have to stop this now. He's making a fool outta you…God, how I hate men."

Dominic looked up and when he recognized Luci's car, he looked confused. Connie stepped out of the car, and slowly walked toward him, her hands balled into tight fists. "You bastard," she hissed. "You're makin' a fool out of me, and I can't let you do that, Dominic. You can go be with your whore…I don't care but do you have to do it in front of everybody? Do you hate me that much?"

Go home, Connie," he simply said, and got in his car and drove away.

"Let's go Luci," Connie said, with frustration. "Take me home, please."

"Sorry Ma, maybe this *was* a bad idea," Luci apologized. "Are you okay?"

"Yeah, I'm fine. I just wanna go home."

*

Connie called Luci and asked her to take her shopping, and when Luci pulled into the driveway, Connie was waiting by the door. "What's goin' on, Ma? Where we goin'?"

"The new Strawbridge's. Is that okay?"

"Sure. Are we shopping for anything in particular?"

"Maybe…we'll see."

The store was busy with curious shoppers, and Connie was in the mood to take her frustrations out on Dominic's wallet. She and Luci walked into the main entrance, and Luci trailed behind her mother up the escalator to the second floor where racks of lavish furs were on display.

"Wow, look at these," Luci said, letting her hand gently glide down the sleeve of a mink coat. "God," she giggled, "I never saw nothin' like this before. Is this chinchilla?"

"Uh-huh," Connie said, distracted as she rifled through a group of fur capes.

Luci stood by her mother and whispered. "Ma? What are we doing here?"

"I'm buying myself a fur." She turned and winked at Luci. "I deserve it, don't ya think?"

"Oh my God," Luci said. "Are you kidding? What'll Dad say?"

Connie gave Luci a sheepish grin.

A saleslady approached and asked politely. "Can I help you?" She was tall and thin with perfectly coifed hair. Black-rimmed glasses, attached to a gold chain were resting on her chest. A measuring tape was draped over her shoulders, and she smiled as she eyed Luci from head to toe. Luci suddenly felt out of place in her jeans and sweatshirt.

"Yes," Connie answered, "I'd like to try some furs." She touched the soft fur of a white mink cape that had immediately caught her eye.

"That's a lovely choice, would you like to try it on?"

"Yes, thank you."

Luci was leaning on the glass counter by the register, watching her mother pose in a three-way mirror. Connie gathered the collar of the cape under her chin, and closed her eyes. "Ooh, I like this one."

"It looks lovely on you, Madam."

"It does look good, doesn't it?"

"Would you like me to ring it up for you?"

"How much is it?" Connie asked, still studying herself in the mirror.

"This particular cape is...let me see," She reached inside the collar, and pulled out a tag. "This one is nine hundred and fifty."

"Yes, I think this is the one I want."

"Very good choice." The woman took the cape from around Connie's shoulders, placed it on a hanger, and covered it with a plastic bag. She punched numbers into the register while Connie peeled nine hundred and fifty dollars from a fistful of bills she had in her purse. She grinned at Luci, and spoke out of the side of her mouth. "That'll show the sonofabitch."

"Excuse me, Madam?" the sales woman asked.

"Oh," Connie laughed. "I was just saying that I'm sure my husband will love the cape."

Chapter 28

Connie was lying in bed, clutching her side as another agonizing cramp gripped her. She held her breath, and suddenly felt a sticky wetness between her legs. She gasped when she lifted the sheets, and saw her nightgown soaked with blood. After shoving a handful of tissues between her legs, she ran to the bathroom. She was bleeding and in terrible trouble.

"Luci, please come and get me," she said, after getting to the phone. "I need to go to the emergency room."

"What's the matter?"

"I'm bleeding again, damn it. Listen, your Dad's at the bowling alley. We'll stop there, and he can take me over to the emergency room.

"I can take you, Ma."

"I know but I'm sure he's going to want to take me."

"Okay, Ma. Can you get up…can you walk?"

"I'm up, I'm standing in the kitchen with a towel between my legs."

"Oh God, I'll get there as quick as I can."

Luci helped her mother to the car, while her youngest son, Kevin sat in the backseat. They drove the short distance to the bowling alley, and before Luci ran into the building, poked her head in the window and asked, "Is it okay for me to leave you for a minute, Ma?"

"I'm okay. Just get your father."

Connie turned and smiled at her grandson. "How are you, Kevin?" She asked, calmly, trying not to alarm him.

"N'kay," he answered, as his fingers continued to manipulate the game he was playing. "You sick, Grandma?"

"I'll be fine, Kevin. I just need to go to the doctor's."

Luci returned within minutes, and jumped into the car. She lit up a cigarette. "Don't get upset Mom but Dad's in the middle of a game, and told me to take you…said he would check on you later."

"Bastard. Just take me to emergency, Luci."

That afternoon, Doctor Westenhouse performed an emergency hysterectomy on Connie, and after four days in the hospital, she was sent home. Alone most of the time, Connie recuperated, resting on a rollaway bed in the den. Luci checked on her mother as often as she could, while Dominic continued to bowl and play golf but grumbled angrily that she was taking too long to get better.

"Don't you think you'd be able to get up for a little while, Connie and maybe make somethin' to eat? You been sleeping all day, for God's sake."

"Dominic, please…I took a pain pill and I'm still kind of shakey on my feet. Can't you just heat something up from the refrigerator?"

"I don't feel like it Connie, I'm tired!"

"I'm sorry," Connie moaned. "I'll rest just a while longer. You can wait."

"But, what about me, Connie?" He whined. "You expect everybody to take care of you…but do you ever think about me?"

Just starting her second week of recovery, Connie was sleeping in the den when Dominic came home, stood by the side of the bed, and stared down at her. He purposely bumped the side of bed with his knee.

"Wha…?" Connie woke with a start. "What's the matter, Dominic?"

"No, nothin'," he pouted. "I didn't mean to wake ya…I just thought maybe you'd wanna get up… cause I can't take this much longer."

"Take what?"

"You…layin' here like this. You should be able to get up, don't ya think?"

"Sure, Dominic." She got to her feet, walked to the kitchen and prepared his dinner while he napped.

Chapter 29

Connie became an expert liar, skillfully cunning and secretive. She made withdraws, in small amounts from the joint account she had with Dominic, and deposited it into a secret account that was in her name alone. She had eventually accumulated a sizable amount of money. She felt guilty until she found out that Dominic had made an appointment with an attorney to prepare his will, requesting to not have Connie present. For all she knew, he planned on leaving all of his money to one or more of his girlfriends.

Dominic's demeaner changed rather quickly. He was tired most of the time, and his thoughts wandered. He often complained of feeling too sick to go out on Friday nights, and that really shocked Connie. Too tired to fight, the tone of his voice was weak, and he spent most of his time sleeping on the sofa. He went to one doctor after another complaining about everything from constipation to heart palpitations. Surgery to remove hemorrhoids kept him laid up for weeks. He developed shingles, and was diagnosed with diabetes. Connie went from fighting him to nursing him. She prepared special foods, kept track of his medications, and tested his blood. He spoke more often about seeing his long-deceased father, even having lengthy conversations with him. The hallucinations seemed to often occurr when Dominic was in his car. He told Connie how his father was sitting next to him. His sleep was restless, with bouts of panic. Connie comforted him as he whimpered like a baby. He would verbally berate his mother in Italian. *La mamma, il sangue, il sangue,* he cried, asking her about *the blood, the blood.*

Connie woke one night, horrified to find him clutching her breast, trying to nurse from her. He was asleep, crying for his mother. She placed her hands on the sides of his head, pushing him away from her. His mouth still puckered, was making a sucking sound that nauseated her. He cried like a child but continued to sleep, and after it happened again the following night, Connie started sleeping on the sofa downstairs. She was beginning to feel afraid to be in the house with him.

Connie wanted to remember the words he said during his nightmares, so with a pad and pencil in her hands, she stood in the hallway outside the bedroom. She jotted down the words he had spoken in Italian, and went downstairs to translate the words into English. Connie sat back and read the words. *The blood, the blood. So much blood. Mama, why did you take my father away from me? Look what you did. He's dead! I hate you Mama, I hate you!'*

"Dear God in heaven," Connie said, aloud. "How in the world could something like this be covered up and never talked about?" She wondered, did his brothers and sisters know? Did Dominic hate his mother so much that he wanted to hurt all women…even his own daughter? But he was so possessive of his mother, always needing to prove himself to her; making sure he was the best of all his brothers and sisters. Troubling memories flooded her thoughts. She was beginning to understand much of his anger, his insecurities and unimaginable acts of violence. She sat, quietly sipping coffee. She thought about talking to him but was afraid to bring up something that had happened more than sixty years ago, something that had affected his entire life.

*

"Connie." Dominic called, after returning from a doctor's appointment. "Can I talk to you?"

"What is it, Dominic?"

She followed him into the den and sat opposite him. His eyes told her that he was tired; troubled. He laid the palms of his hands on his knees, and leaned back on a pillow.

"Doctor Candafini gave me the results of my colonoscopy and said I have a cyst on my colon. He thinks I should get it removed but said it's up to me. It's not bad or anything," he assured her.

"Well, what do *you* think?"

"I think I should get it removed. He said it's a pretty simple operation."

"Then you should do it. When is he talking about?"

"Now, hold on Connie, don't rush me. I'm just askin' ya what you think."

"Dominic, do you want me to call the doctor and talk to him?"

"Yeah, call him…ya know, just to make sure."

Connie looked up the number and dialed the phone. "Hello, who's this?" Connie asked. "Hi, Sandy, this is Dominic Preste's wife. Is Doctor Candafini available? Thank you." She waited, and when the doctor came to the phone, she said, "Hello Doctor Candafini. This is Mrs. Preste, Dominic Preste's wife? I'm fine, thank you. Listen, I wanted to ask you, is it your opinion that my husband should have the cyst on his colon removed? Mm-hmm, mm-hmm, I see. Okay…well, thanks." She hung up the phone and turned to Dominic.

"Well, what'd he say?" He asked, anxiously.

"He said you should have it removed, Dominic.

"Okay." He sat quietly, nodding in agreement. "Well, I wanna get it over with, so I'll call tomorrow and see how quick they can do it."

"I think that's a good idea; get it overwith."

The next morning, Dominic called the doctor again and made arrangements to have the surgery the following Thursday. They instructed him to be at Falcon Crest hospital by seven in the morning, and assured him he'd be good as new within twenty-four hours.

For the next few days, Dominic came close to canceling the surgery but finally decided to go ahead with it. The day before the surgery, Dominic asked, "Connie, ya know what I want you to do?" He had been in the backyard clearing out the last of his vegetable garden.

"What is it you want, Dominic?"

"I want you to write a check for five hundred dollars to each one of the kids, including the grandchildren and mail it to them."

"Okay." She looked at him curiously.

"Connie?"

"Yes?"

"My concertina…you give it to Phillip if anything happens to me. He deserves it."

"Dominic…nothing's going to happen to you."

"If it does…"

"Of course, I'll give it to him."

"Now, look up Phillip's number for me, I wanna call him."

Connie pulled her address book from the drawer of the dining room buffet, thumbed through the pages and found Phillip's number. "Here ya go. It's right here."

He took the book from her, put on his glasses and dialed the number. "Hello Phillip? It's your father. Uh-huh, you too. How ya doin'? That's good. How's the weather? Uh-huh, well that's good." He was distracted; nervous. "Hey listen Son, I'm going in for some surgery tomorrow. Yeah well, I got a cyst on my colon and the doctor wants to take it off. Do ya think I'm doin' the right thing? Cause I don't think I'm gonna come through this."

Connie didn't understand his ominous tone, and she was sure that Phillip was confused by his father's need for advice.

Dominic nodded while he listened to his oldest son talk. "Well yeah, the doctor seemed to think it was a good idea but the reason I called is that if something happens to me, I have your mother sending you and each one of the kids five hundred dollars. No, no, I want to." He paused and listened. "I know I'll be fine but just in case, ya know? Well, say hello to Beth and the kids. Bye.

Chapter 30

A steady rain pelted a canopy of umbrellas that surrounded the gravesite. Mourners stood shoulder to shoulder around a bronze casket. Dominic was being laid to rest. Family and friends stood quietly as Father Finch, from St. Mary's Catholic Church spoke of Dominic's generosity to the church; his life as a family man, blessed with a wife, children and grandchildren who loved him dearly. Connie felt repulsed by the hypocrisy. The priest spoke of Dominic being a self-made man, uneducated but a hard worker, a financial success. Dominic would have relished in the moment.

"Ashes to ashes, dust to dust," Father Finch droned on, and threw a handful of, what was now mud on top of the casket. Connie was sitting on a chair surrounded by her sons and daughter. Someone was holding an umbrella over her head. *What are my children thinking?* She asked herself. *What are they feeling? Joy? Relief? It couldn't be sadness.* Dominic's sisters wept out loud, and his two remaining brothers stood expressionless; their hands folded in front of them. Connie was now a widow but did not feel grief. She wasn't ashamed. She felt sadness for Dominic's wasted life. She thought about his childhood and wondered if she had known sooner, could she have helped him? She loved him once, a long, long time ago. She had spent fifty-four years of her life with a man who never once experienced true joy. Because of him, she was a bitter, neurotic old woman consumed by fear and self-doubt. She never slept, and couldn't eat. Because of him, and because of what she allowed him to do to their children, her guilt was like a demon inside of her. She had plenty of money now but for some reason, it didn't matter. Peace and quiet was all she wanted. She smiled at Phillip who was seated to her right. He smiled back, and was wishing the entire event were over. He wanted to go home and take his mother with him so he could show her the way life was supposed to be but he knew she wouldn't go. She was attached to that house of horrors his father built so many years before. It held horrific memories for him but for some reason, it meant a lot to his mother. He also did not trust Luci or Vinnie. He knew they were thinking that money would be no problem now that their father was gone. They would not think twice about taking advantage of their mother's vulnerability.

The day before leaving for the hospital, Dominic sat with Connie and handed her pencil and paper, telling her to write down his very detailed instructions for his funeral. She vehemently objected but he insisted she list the clothing he wanted to be dressed in, the casket he wanted, and that no one was to touch his hair but her. If any gray was showing, she was to dye it. He even handpicked the guest list for the dinner party that would be held in his honor. Even in death, he wanted to look his best and show people he could afford the best.

*

Connie had known Jimmy and Albert Bonaventure since they were little boys, and remembered when they broke her patio window playing baseball in the backyard. She remembered catching them, with Phillip smoking in her basement. They grew up to be the top catering company in Falcon Heights but to Connie, they were still little Jimmy and Albie. When they heard of Dominic's death, they called Connie, offering their catering hall and dinner for the guests following the funeral. In Dominic's honor, they served dinner to more than one hundred guests.

Connie wore a black, silk dress with a black scarf tied around her neck fixed to the bodice with a diamond and pearl brooch. She was the perfect hostess, visiting from table to table, accepting condolences and embracing friends and family she had no desire to ever see again. *It'll be over soon*, she told herself. She wanted to go home, lock the door, and listen to her Sinatra tapes. She wanted to see what it would be like to do whatever she wanted, whenever she wanted, even if that meant doing nothing.

Connie saw Dominic's sisters and brothers sitting together at a table near the front of the room, and quickly looked away. She wasn't ready to deal with them now, or if ever. She wished Tessa and Vittorio were not sitting with them; she'd like to talk to them.

*

"Look at her," Gia said, jabbing an elbow into Annette's arm, "*E' tali rifiuti*", calling Connie trash. "Our brother made her a rich woman. I hope she's satisfied."

"*Gia, essere tranquillo*!" Masto chided. "Not now!"

Tessa sat quietly, her eyes cast down at the table.

Vittorio spoke up, "Eh Gia, why don' you shut up. Da woman jus' become a widow. Have a little respect."

"Well it makes me sick! Look at her kids over there. A bunch of losers and drug addicts," Gia continued her tirade, ignoring her brother's demand for quiet. "They'll probably go through Dominic's money in..."

"Das enough, Gia," Masto warned again. "Just eat and we go."

"I'm not going to eat this shit, are you kidding? I wouldn't give her the satisfaction." She turned up her nose and pushed the plate away.

"You know, Gia," Tessa interjected, "Dominic planned this whole thing. He even picked the food. Connie told me."

Gia was suddenly quiet, caught off guard. "Well, that figures. The woman can't even plan her own husband's funeral. Well, I don't know about you," she said, tossing her napkin over her plate, "but I'm ready to go, now. Come on, let's go." She pushed back her chair, stood up and smoothed her skirt. Masto glanced at the rest of the family, rolled his eyes, and wiped his mouth as he stood up. He followed Gia toward the exit, with Annette following close behind.

"Masto, are you leaving?" Connie asked, as they rushed past her.

"Conchetta, I am sorry but we mus' go," Masto lied. "Gia...she not feel too good. I t'ink she miss her brother."

Connie smiled and offered her hand. "Please Masto, tell her goodbye for me." *And I mean goodbye,* she thought to herself. She watched them walk out the door, knowing she would never have to see them again. The thought made her smile.

Connie went back to the table where Phillip and Vito were quietly chatting, and she suddenly realized how much she missed her sisters. Carmella and Dave were the only ones able to come to the funeral and that made her sad.

She eyed the plate of food in front of her, and pushed it away. Smiling, she accepted embraces from aquaintances that passed by. The noise in the room was swelling with chatter, silverware chinking on plates, and as the afternoon wore on, guests were feeling comfortable enough to share a laugh. Connie suddenly felt overwhelmed, excused herself and went to the ladies room. Once inside, she closed the door, enjoying the quiet. She held her hands under cool water, placed the palms of her hands to her cheeks, and closed her eyes. She dried her face and hands on a paper towel, and walked to a chair in the corner of the room. The chair was velvet, the color of a robin's egg, and Connie ran her hands along the soft fabric. It was a cozy nook next to a small circular table that was topped with an ornate lamp. A single, white rose was placed in a clear, long-necked vase. Next to it was a pile of prayer cards printed with the 23rd Psalm. Connie could have stayed there for the rest of the day. That tiny spot seemed to generate tranquility. She took a deep breath, closed her eyes and rested her head on the back of the chair. The air smelled of pine and perfume.

"Mrs. Preste?" A woman's voice, soft and timid broke the silence. Connie opened her eyes and looked at the woman standing before her. She had seen her before but couldn't place where. She was short, like Connie but heavier. She was well dressed, and attractive but overly made up. She had shoulder length hair, dyed a fiery red, heavily lacquered with spray. Connie thought her to be in her late fifties. Connie smiled at the woman, and suddenly felt the blood rush from her face. She had seen the woman before...with Dominic.

"Oh, Mrs. Preste, I hope you don't mind...I wanted to speak with you."

"What are you *doing* here?" Connie asked, trying to control her tone.

"Mrs. Preste, my name is Rita..." she extended her hand.

"I know who you are, and I think you should leave. Now."

"Please don't be angry, Mrs. Preste. I didn't come here out of respect to Dominic; I came here to see you. You see, I…I wanted to apologize to you for all the trouble…"

"Please stop, I don't want to hear your apology," Connie stopped her. "Like I said, I think you should leave now."

"But I need to explain," the woman pleaded.

"I think you have a lot of nerve coming here. This isn't some bowling tournament, this is my husband's funeral, for God's sake!"

"Please, Mrs. Preste. I'll go but not until I get a chance to explain," the woman said, more forcefully.

"Say what you have to say Mrs.…or is it Miss, or what?"

"Mrs., it's Mrs. Portman. You don't understand, Mrs. Preste. I lost my second husband three years ago and I was lonely. My girlfriend, Franny introduced me to Dominic. She was going out with him first, but didn't really like him that much, so she thought maybe I'd like him. She never told me he was married. Honest to God, I didn't know he was married. I never would have gone out with him, believe me. He told me he was separated for a long time. Some of the other girls at the bowling alley told me that he was married but…I was so stupid. I believed *him*. And that day when you came to the bowling alley, and I was in his car? Well, I was as shocked as you were when he told me you were his wife. I thought it was horrible. I told him so, too. I was so upset. I wanted to call you and apologize but I didn't want to cause you more problems." She paused, and looked down at the floor. "Dominic said he would kill me if I called you. And, by God, I believed him!" She started to cry. She took a tissue from her purse and blew her nose. "I told Dominic that night that I was really angry with him. He lied to me and I didn't like that. He took me back to my house, and when I told him to leave, he…" she stopped and looked away.

"What did he do?" Connie urged her to continue.

"He hit me…over and over. By the time he left, I was bloody and bruised. I went to the hospital and prayed my son wouldn't be on duty that night but he was. When he saw me, he was in a rage, and wanted to call the police. I begged him not to. I was afraid Dominic *would* kill me."

Connie looked confused. "Your son? He works at the hospital?"

"He's an emergency room doctor. His name is Candafini…Doctor Candafini," she explained.

"*Candafini*," Connie repeated the name to herself. "Doctor Candafini?" She asked, suddenly finding it hard to breathe. "Is he… your son? At Falcon Heights?"

"Yes," she smiled, though her expression was pained. "You know my son?" The woman placed her hand on Connie's arm when she saw her go pale. "Are you all right, Mrs. Preste?"

"Yes, yes…go on." Connie leaned back in the chair.

"Anyway, I had never seen my son so mad before. Oh my God, I was so nervous he would find out that it was Dominic who hurt me." She paused and shook her head. "He begged me to tell him who had done that to me but I wouldn't tell him. And I didn't tell him. I told him it was all over and to just forget about it. I had made a terrible mistake but it was over. I didn't want to go to the police, Mrs. Preste. I knew Dominic had kids and all…and a wife," she added, looking ashamed.

"Mother of God," Connie muttered.

"I just wanted you to know, Mrs. Preste that I'm not a bad person. I made a huge mistake with Dominic and I'm truly sorry."

Connie seemed dazed. "What? Oh, yes…it's all right, don't worry. Why don't you go now? It'll be all right." Connie said, absently. She just wanted the woman to leave her alone.

"You are a truly a wonderful person, Mrs. Preste. Dominic didn't know how lucky he was to have you."

"Thank you." Connie managed a smile.

The woman paused at the door. "Mrs. Preste? I have to ask you… why did you stay married to Dominic?"

Connie sighed. "Huh, that's a good question. Do you know how many people have asked me that over the years? There were reasons, I guess but I found out they were all the wrong reasons." She pondered the question. "Four children. Money. I don't know. If I left, he would've seen to it I had nothing, or he would have killed me." She shrugged. "Whatever…I stayed…but it doesn't matter now, does it?"

"I'm so sorry, Mrs. Preste. I think I should go, I've caused you enough problems." She opened the door, and turned back to Connie. "Can I ask you one more thing…if it's none of my business, I'll understand."

"What is it?"

"What did Dominic die from?"

"Oh..." Connie closed her eyes and took a deep breath. "Guilt, I think."

"Oh, I didn't know..."

Connie sat in the blue velvet chair and prayed. *Forgive me, Father but I ask you to bless Doctor Candafini and...maybe to forgive him.*

Chapter 31

Connie finally found peace…she thought. She was seventy-four years old, and considered herself healthy but was not aware of how seriously Dominic's abuse had affected her. Still unable to eat solid food, Phillip insisted she see a doctor but the doctor found nothing wrong. Her condition was psychological. She vomited daily, especially after encounters with Vinnie, or Luci. She developed a nervous cough, and battled rashes on her hands and face. She panicked at the sound of the phone. She had Vito call the phone company to have her number changed, and he also bought her an answering machine so she could screen her calls, making sure only to take calls from Vito and Phillip.

*

Vito and Barbara picked Connie up one evening and took her to dinner. She ordered her usual clear soup while Vito and Barbara dined on lobsters. Connie looked across the room and noticed one of her neighbors who lived just a few blocks from her. She had talked with her many times over the years, and Phillip used to go to school with her nephew, Scottie. Connie had always liked her. Dominic hated her and thought her loud and unladylike.

"Isn't that Valerie…what was her last name?" Connie asked. "Valerie Aldonno. Yeah, that's it. Valerie Aldonno. You remember Vito, the Vitale boy's Aunt Valerie, remember?"

"Oh yeah," Vito said, turning around to look at the woman.

"I'm gonna go and say hello." Connie got up from the table.

"Ma wait…talk to her later; your dinner is com…ah…okay, there she goes," he said, as he watched his mother saunter across the room. He turned to Barbara, and said, "Ya think she's a little hyper?"

"She's all right, Vito. Leave her go."

Connie walked over to where Valerie was sitting, and gently tapped her on the shoulder. "Valerie?"

Valerie looked up. She was sitting with a gray-haired gentleman, and they were sharing a dessert.

"Connie! Oh my God, how are you?"

"I'm okay."

"I was so sorry to hear about Dominic."

"Thanks. I saw you sitting here, and I just wanted to say hello."

"It's so good to see you." Valerie touched Connie's arm. "Hey, why don't we get together sometime?"

"Sure, that would be nice." Connie glanced at the gray-haired man.

"Oh, I'm sorry. I didn't introduce you. This is Lenny." Valerie said. "Lenny, this is Connie Preste…an old friend," she added, with a gentle smile.

"Hello Lenny." Connie offered her hand.

Lenny nodded and wiped his hand on his napkin before taking her hand. "Hello Connie."

"Valerie, why don't you come over the house for coffee some time. Just call me."

"I will. What's your number? I probably have it, but just in case…" Valerie rummaged through her purse for a pen. She wrote Connie's number on a napkin and shoved it into her purse.

"It's a private number, so don't give it to anyone."

"Okay, I understand. Hey, it's really good to see you looking so well, Connie. You okay?"

"Yeah, I'm much better now. It was tough for a while but you know…you've been there, right?"

"Yes, I have."

"Well, get back to your dessert. I'm here with my son and his wife." She turned and pointed toward the table where Vito and Barbara were sitting.

"Tell them hello."

"I will."

"Oh Connie," Valerie added. "How's Vinnie?"

"I really don't know, Valerie. He's living up in Bay Village. I don't see him very often, which is fine with me."

"You've really had a time with him."

For some reason, Connie didn't mind Valerie asking about Vinnie. Perhaps because Connie knew that Valerie had been through a similar situation with her own son.

Connie went back to her table and sat down. A bowl of chicken broth was sitting at her place, and she sniffed at the steam rising from the bowl. "Oh, this looks nice. How's your dinner, Vito? Good? Barbara? Your dinner looks good." She was rambling. "Yeah, that was Valerie. She's a nice lady, and I asked her over for coffee. That's okay, don't ya think?"

Vito looked at Barbara and rolled his eyes. "Ya okay, Ma? You're talkin' a mile a minute."

"I'm fine, why? Do I seem nervous to you? There's nothin' wrong with me havin' a friend over, is there?"

"Dear God...eat your soup, Ma."

*

A few days later, Valerie called and Connie invited her for coffee. Valerie asked if she would mind her bringing a couple of friends with her, and Connie thought that would be fine. Helen, Bootsie, and Valerie, all widows met at a senior dance club. After meeting Connie, the four women became friends, and Connie loved spending time with them. It reminded her of her youth, and the fun she had with her sisters. Connie was enjoying her freedom, and Vinnie and Luci, to her relief were leaving her alone.

Connie joined her friends at the senior dances, and they sat at the same table, every Saturday afternoon. They called themselves *The Golden Girls.* They did the foxtrot with ninety year-old men in orthopedic shoes and suits that smelled of mothballs. They shared Connie's homemade cookies, and laughed at Valerie's dirty jokes, and Connie felt more alive than she'd felt in years. To men over seventy, she was a real catch, attractive for a woman in her seventies, with a vibrant personality and a flair for dance. She made it clear that she had no interest in dating, and being with her girlfriends was as much fun as she needed.

*

Connie left for Colorado on a Sunday morning for a three-week visit with Phillip and Beth. She foolishly left Luci in charge of collecting the rent checks from the tenants at the apartment house, and when Connie arrived home, she was horrified to find that Luci had forged her name, cashed the checks and spent the money.

"Luci!" Connie cried. "Why did you do that? That's not your money, damn it!"

"God, Ma…what's your problem? Dad left you plenty of money. You would've given to me anyway, right?"

Connie sat down and groaned. "Dear God, Luci…that's not the point."

"What's the big deal?"

"That's it…I want you to leave."

"What?"

"I want you to leave. Don't come back until I tell you to. Do you understand?"

"You're kickin' me out? I bet you wouldn't do that to your precious Phillip," Luci replied angrily. She threw the strap of her purse over her shoulder. I'm leaving but I don't feel bad about what I did. You owe me, Mom!"

"Now, what does that mean, Luci? Is this about your father? Tell me, Luci…why do I owe you? How am I to understand unless I know what happened?"

"Like you care!" Luci ran out of the house.

*

After his father's death, Vinnie, with complete lack of reason thought he could take control of his mother's house and her life. He informed her that he was now head of the household and that she had to listen to him. If Connie didn't find him so pathetic, she would have laughed in his face. He told her she had no right to have *her* friends in *his* house, and that his father would be ashamed of her.

"What?" Connie's voice was shrill and piercing. Her body quivered with anger. "I have no right to what? You listen to me, you sonofabitch... this is *my* house. Not yours. And I don't give a shit if your father's doing back flips in his grave. I'm free, white and seventy-five and I'll do what I Goddamned want to! You hear me? Now get out!"

"Well, just to let you know mother dear...I'm movin' back in here. You need someone to keep you in line."

Connie's laugh sounded hysterical. "You must have shit for brains. You've got to be kidding me. First of all, you are not moving back in here. Second of all, I can take care of myself. You've been nothing but an embarrassment to me, Vinnie. Your father and I have spent thousands and thousands of dollars bailing you out of jail, paying your mortgage and paying off your debts! You look like you should be on Skid Row... and you think I need you to keep me in line?" She slapped her hand on her chest.

"God, what's the matter with you?" He stared with bloodshot eyes. "You talk like you're nuts!"

"Get out, Vinnie. Don't come here anymore, you hear me?"

Vinnie stood up straight, and puffed up his chest. His eyebrows were raised with a look of amused surprise. "All right, Ma. God, what are ya getting' so upset about? She's nuts," he said, under his breathe, and walked out the back door.

The phone rang. "Hello," Connie said, barely able to breathe.

"Hi Ma, it's Phillip. How are you?" he asked, casually.

"Hi Phil, I'm good. How 'bout you? How's the weather?"

"The weather's fine, Ma." Phillip smiled, and shook his head. *Always with the weather.* "I'm just checkin' on ya. Everything all right?"

"Oh, just fine. How's Beth? How're the kids?"

"Beth and the kids are great."

"Good. I'm feeling good too. I went out with Valerie this morning, and now I'm just gonna relax a little, you know."

"Uh huh." Phillip, hearing the tension in her voice was skeptical. "You sound nervous Ma, what's goin' on?"

"No, nothin'. Vinnie was giving me a little trouble, but I handled it."

"What'd he do?"

"Nothin', don't worry about it, okay? Well, you say hi to Beth and the kids for me."

"All right, Ma. Call me if you need me."

"Okay. Love ya. Bye-bye now." Connie hung up the phone, went upstairs and put on her nightgown. She came back downstairs, locked all the doors, closed the Venetian blinds, and heated up a mug of chicken broth. She sat in the den, and watched Wheel of Fortune.

*

It was the middle of winter when Luci showed up on her mother's doorstep. She and Craig were standing side by side in six inches of snow that had accumulated on Connie's porch. Luci held a suitcase at her side, and Craig had a stuffed pillowcase thrown over his shoulder. Kevin peered from behind his mother's back. He was carrying his schoolbooks.

"Luci? What's goin' on?" Connie asked, placing her hand on her stomach when she felt a familiar nervous rumble.

"He locked us out of the house, Ma." Luci stepped inside, and stomped snow from her boots. The boys followed, and Connie sighed as chunks of snow fell onto the rug. "Do you mind if we stay here for a while?"

"Well, what's a 'while', Luci? You know I'm getting pretty sick and tired of that bastard throwing you outta your own house. I can't have all of this craziness every time you guys have a fight!"

Luci gave her mother a look of warning, as if the boys didn't know what their father was like.

"I mean it Luci, I wanna live by myself now."

"Well, where am I supposed to go, Ma?"

Connie smelled beer. She didn't know if it was coming from Luci or Craig. The two boys went to the den, and switched on the television. Kevin sat on the floor, pulled his video game out of the pillowcase and hooked it to the television. Craig flopped down on the sofa, lit up a cigarette and amused himself by blowing smoke rings.

"Have you been drinkin', Luci?"

"Oh God…don't start, Ma. If anybody deserves to drink, it's me."

"Divorce the sonofabitch, Goddamn it! What's the matter with you?" Connie could feel her stomach tying in knots. Traces of a headache were creeping across her forehead. "You know you're gonna go back to that bastard. I don't understand you!"

"Ma, please…could you stop calling him a bastard?" Luci pointed toward the room where the boys were.

"Gimme a break, Luci. Do you think those boys don't know what's going on? They're not stupid." She pointed her finger in Luci's face and said, "You are, though!"

"Thanks," Luci pouted. She followed her mother into the kitchen, sat down, and lit up a cigarette. She put her head back and blew a stream of smoke toward the ceiling.

"Well, you *are* stupid. When you're father was livin', he offered to buy you a house, for God's sake. He even offered to pay for a lawyer! And what do you do? You go back to that drunkin' bastard."

"Oh God, Ma. I can't take this." Luci grabbed her coat and purse and stormed out of the house.

"Where the hell are you goin'? You just got here!"

Luci slammed the door and trudged through the snow to her car.

"Oh, I guess that means you're leavin' your kids with me again, right?" Connie watched as Luci got into her car, and drove away. "If you're goin' to the bar, don't come back here!" Connie shouted.

"What'dya got to eat, Grandma?" Craig asked. He was standing behind her.

Connie took a deep breath and composed herself. She turned slowly, and managed to smile. "What would you like, Craig?" She asked, calmly.

"Well, I don't want that shit you gave me the other night, that's for sure. What was that again…polotta…or somethin'?" He wrinkled his nose and stuck out his tongue.

"Polenta. It's called polenta, Craig. And I wish you wouldn't call it shit."

"Whatever, dude…I don't want it." He slurred his words so badly that half the time she couldn't understand a thing he said. He had dropped out of school in the eighth grade and his behavior was bad enough that Luci tried sending him to a special "boot camp" for troubled teens. He flunked that too. Too hard to handle, they said. His father was ashamed of him, and wanted him out of the house but agreed to let him sleep in the basement, like a dog. Luci's oldest son, Ray Jr. was married, and lived near by. He tried to help his mother by having Craig stay with him but that only lasted a week.

Connie put a ham sandwich on the table in front of him, and took one to Kevin. She returned to the kitchen and sat down at the far end of the table. Watching Craig, slouched in his chair, a knit cap pulled over his ears, Connie asked, "What happened at home, Craig? Did your parents have a fight?"

"I dunno. I think my dad was pissed cause I stole some tires."

"What? I don't understand. Why would he throw your mother out?"

"Dunno. Prolly cause she wrote a couple a bad checks to bail me out." He sounded like he had a mouthful of marbles. "Got any beer, Grandmaw," he said, with a smirk.

"No, and don't be fresh."

"Don't be fresh," he mocked.

Connie opened her mouth to speak but closed it again. She leaned her forehead on the palms of her hands. "Just finish your sandwich, Craig." She went back to the den. "Kevin honey, it's getting late." He was curled up on the floor, half asleep with his schoolbooks spread across the floor. "Why don't you go upstairs and get into bed, you have school tomorrow."

"Okay, Grandma," he responded, in a sweet, young boy voice.

He was a good boy, quiet and serious, an avid book reader. It was like he was born into the wrong family, Connie thought. He was a blessing, and Connie worried how he would turn out being raised by Ray and Luci.

"Where ya goin', asshole?" Craig asked as Kevin passed by. He laughed stupidly. Kevin ignored his brother and walked toward the stairs. "Idiot," Craig smirked. He finished eating and went to lay on the sofa. He lit up another cigarette, took a puff, and let it dangle from his fingers.

"Put that cigarette out, Craig." Connie snarled, and kicked him on the bottom of his boot.

"Hey! What's your problem, ol' woman?" He sat up with a jerk. He took another deep toke on the cigarette, snubbed it out on the bottom of his boot and lay back down.

"You know I don't want any smoking in this house."

"Yeah right, you let my mom smoke in here," he protested.

"Get upstairs Craig."

"God, you're such a bitch!" He jumped to his feet and stood over her but backed down when she gave him an icy stare. "I'm goin', I'm goin'. Don't get your tits in an uproar."

"Why, you little..." Connie reached her arm back, and swung to slap him but he ducked, laughing at her.

He turned and dragged his feet lazily across the floor toward the kitchen, and picked up the phone.

"Who are you callin' at this hour?" When he ignored her, she asked again, "Craig! Who are you callin', I asked you?"

"My mother! Okay?" He yelled angrily, thrusting his face inches from hers.

Connie went upstairs to her room, locked the door and checked under the mattress for the butcher knife she kept there since Dominic died. Not only did she fear Luci and Vinnie but now she feared Craig as well. Connie shuddered when she thought about the time Craig snuck one of his friends into the house. A strange teenaged boy had been sleeping under the bed in Luci's old room without Connie knowing. Craig laughed when he told his grandmother that the boy had been there for days. The boy simply strolled into the kitchen one morning, scaring her to death. Connie called the police, and Luci railed at her mother for overreacting. The boy was arrested for illegal entry, and Luci demanded money from her mother to bail the boy out of jail.

*

Without getting undressed, Connie climbed under the covers, prepared for another sleepless night. When the light of dawn peered through her bedroom window, she realized she had fallen asleep sometime after midnight. While the house was still quiet, she went down to the kitchen and started a pot of coffee when Luci came into the kitchen.

She laid a pack of cigarettes on the table, and ran her fingers through her disheveled hair. She wiped the sleep from her eyes and said, "Mornin' Ma, coffee ready yet?"

"What time did you come in?" Connie asked, unable to hide her anger.

"Late, okay? Don't start."

She placed a cup of coffee in front of Luci, and sat down. "I don't like what you're doin'."

Luci ignored her mother's comment, and sipped her coffee. "Ma," she finally said. "I need your help."

"Oh Luci…my God, what now? I can't keep doin' this," Connie whined.

"Relax, will ya Ma? Craig has to appear before a judge next Tuesday and I need to get that lawyer again. Remember Jordan Dooley?"

Connie dropped her head, and took a deep breath. "How much do you need?"

"God, Ma! Do you think I *like* asking you for money? I don't have money but you do! What am I supposed to do? Let my son go to jail?"

"Why don't you ask your husband for money? Craig's *his* son, not mine."

"Ha ha, very funny."

"Luci…how much do you need?"

"About five thousand."

"Oh, Jesus." Connie slapped the table in anger but went into the dining room, and got her checkbook. She sat down, wrote out a check and pushed it across the table toward Luci. "Here."

"Why're you so mad?"

Kevin came downstairs, took the bowl of Cheerios his mother poured for him and sat in front of the television. A few minutes later, he brought back the empty bowl and set it in the sink. "C'mon Mom, I gotta go to school."

Luci picked up her purse and followed Kevin out the door. "Thanks for the check, Ma," she said over her shoulder.

"Yeah, no problem," Connie answered, sounding defeated. She poured herself another cup of coffee, turned on her tape recorder and listened to Sinatra sing *Satin Doll.* She sat with her eyes closed, the corners of her mouth turned down as she swayed back and forth to the rhythm of the music. The silence was broken when Craig walked in the door.

"Wait out back, dudes." He mumbled to two boys that were standing on the patio.

"Craig?" Connie said, with surprise. "Where were you? I thought you were upstairs sleeping."

He ignored her and reached into her purse, pulling out a handful of crumpled up dollar bills.

"You *could* ask, Craig," she said, indignantly, and snatched the purse from his hands.

"I asked you a question, Goddamnit! Who are those boys?"

He continued to ignor her, grabbing cans of soda from the refrigerator.

Luci walked in. "What's goin' on?"

"First of all," Connie said, sarcastically, "Craig's just helping himself to money from my purse. He doesn't even try to hide it."

"Craig," Luci mildly scolded, giving him a disapproving look.

He laughed and blew smoke in her face.

"I don't want any smokin' in this house!" Connie repeated, attempting to grab the cigarette from his mouth.

"Shut up, ol' woman." He brushed past her, and flung open the refrigerator door, grabbing three more cans of soda.

"You little sonofabitch!" Connie slapped his face.

"Ma! Leave him alone!" Luci grabbed her mother's arm. "Craig, get outside."

Craig looked at his grandmother and smirked. "Fat ol' bitch." He kicked the door open with his foot.

Connie stared at her daughter. "You make me sick, Luci. You let him get away with that? My God, you've created a monster."

"You egg him on, Ma. You know you do. I told ya before not to make him mad. He's got problems, thanks to his father."

"Thanks to his father? Huh."

"What's that spose' to mean?"

Connie shook her head, and gave Luci an exasperated glance. "I think it's more like thanks to you." Without waiting for Luci to respond, she grabbed her coat and car keys, and walked out of the house, slamming the door behind her. She walked past the boys sprawled across her patio, got into the Cadillac and drove about a mile from the house to Forest Hill Park. She pulled into a parking spot but kept the car running, with the heater on full blast, blowing hot air in her face. She grabbed the steering wheel and squeezed until her nails dug into the leather, and let out a blood-curdling scream, not caring if anyone heard her. She cleared her burning throat, opened her eyes and spent the next few minutes staring out the windshield. She turned off the ignition, buttoned her coat to the collar, and stepped out of the car, and started walking along the pond's edge, when she found a bench by the water's edge. She sat down. Two squirrels were playfully chasing each other, chattering furiously, and stopping occasionally to look at her. When her hands and feet started to stiffen from the cold, she got back in the car and drove to Valerie's. She wanted to be anywhere but in her own house.

"Who is it?" Valerie asked, as she walked toward the door.

"It's me...Connie."

"Connie, hi. Is everything okay?" Connie came into the warmth of the living room and followed Valerie into the kitchen. Valerie listened to Connie talk while she put on a pot of coffee, and they talked well into evening and until Connie thought she felt calm enough to go home.

"Why don't you stay here tonight, Connie? I'm goin' out tonight but you're welcome to stay."

"Thanks but I think I'll be okay. I'm afraid of what they might do to the house."

"I understand. Call me if you need me, all right?"

"I will." Connie buttoned up her coat and went to the door. "Thanks for listening, Val...wish me luck." The two women hugged and Connie went to her car. She drove the few blocks home, pulled into the driveway and saw that Luci's car was not there. Connie had the key to the bottom lock of the kitchen door but not for the deadbolt, and when she tried to open the door, she discovered that the deadbolt was locked as well. She knocked. She cupped her hands and looked through the windowpane and saw the back of Craig's head as he lay on the sofa watching television. The room was filled with cigarette smoke.

"Craig! Let me in," she shouted, and knocked harder.

He raised his head, turned and looked toward the door then lay back down.

"Bastard!" *He's not going to let me in.* She started to shiver, and the wind was beginning to sting her skin. She kicked at the door and swore, and when she realized he was not going to open the door, she walked back to her car. She was angry enough to go to the police but decided against it. She couldn't call Valerie because she was out for the evening. Connie decided to sit and wait for Luci to come home. She started the car, turned on the heater and put her head back, quickly falling asleep. She never heard Luci come home that night. Luci had parked on the street when she saw her mother's car in the driveway. Connie spent the night in the car. When the sun came up, she shifted in the seat and rubbed the stiffness from her legs. Her feet were numb from the cold. She cringed while trying to flex her arthritic fingers, and her head throbbed. She got out of the car, and walked slowly toward her house. The back door was open, and Luci was sitting at the table smoking a cigarette.

"Ma! What the hell…where'd you come from? I thought you were still upstairs."

"No," Connie said, trying to stay in control. "Your bastard son locked me out of my own home last night."

"What?"

"Yes, Luci. You're precious Craig locked me out. And you know what? He knew I was knocking at the door. How do you like that? He knew I was at the door and he just laughed at me. He didn't care if I froze to death! I spent the night in my car, Luci!"

Luci cocked her head, as if not believing her mother's story. "Come on Ma, what did you do to him?"

Connie took off her coat and threw it over the back of a chair. "What did *I* do to *him*? Where is the little bastard, cause I wanna kill him!"

"Maybe he didn't here you knocking Ma, did ya ever think of that?"

"Didn't hear me knocking?" Connie asked. "He turned and looked at me, Luci! Then went right back to watching television!"

Luci looked away. "Well, I don't know…" she mumbled, and lit up another cigarette.

"Oh, that's good, Luci. Nothin' to say?"

"Wha'dya want me to say, Ma?" Luci snapped, unable to look her mother in the eye.

"Where is he? I wanna talk to him. This has gotta stop, Luci."

"He's out. I'll talk to him. Don't you say anything to him, let me handle it," Luci said.

Connie heated a can of tomato soup and poured it into a mug. She wrapped her hands around the cup. "My God, I'll never be able to get warm."

"Ma, listen…don't get mad but I need twenty dollars for Kevin's field trip today."

"Take it outta my purse," Connie said, wearily. She looked at the pile of dirty dishes in the sink. "Would it kill ya to clean up after your own kids?"

"What?" Luci asked, not really listening.

"Nothin'," Connie said, filling the sink with soapy water.

*

Valerie called Vito, telling him of his mother's troubles, and also got Phillip's number.

"Phillip, I'm tellin' ya, if they don't leave her alone, she's gonna have a stroke or a heart attack. I know you can't do anything way out there in Colorado but maybe you could talk to her. I try but she just can't seem to say *no* to any of them. They're like vultures."

"Okay, Valerie…thanks for keeping me posted. Did you talk to Vito?"

"Yeah…but I think he's busy right now. Said he'd look into it, though."

"Let me see what I can do, and like I said, thanks for calling. Listen, before we hang up, can I ask you to do me a favor?"

"Sure."

"Keep calling, because every time I call my mother, she says everything's fine and I know she's lying."

Valerie laughed. "I know. That's what she does…always says everything's okay. Don't worry…I'll let ya know what's goin' on."

"Thanks, Valerie. Bye."

Phillip called his mother, and Luci answered the phone. "Luci? Hey, how ya doin'?" He asked, trying to control his anger. "What're you doin' at Mom's?"

"I was havin' some problems at home, so I'm stayin' here for a while."

"You have the boys there too?

"Yeah, why?"

"Listen, you have to go back home, Luci. You guys are drivin' Ma nuts."

"Who told you that...and who are you to tell me what to do?"

"I'm tellin' ya, Luci. You have to leave Mom alone. I want you out by the end of the week."

"Who the hell made you boss?" She snapped.

"Somebody's gotta protect her!" Phillip could no longer contain his anger. "She can't keep supporting you, and she can't keep dealing with you and your problems. She's been through enough."

"Why don't ya talk to Vinnie, he's a bigger problem. He's bleeding Ma dry. Did ya know that?"

"I'm not talking about Vinnie right now, I'm talking about you."

"Where's all this comin' from, Phil? I take *care* of Mom, I'll have you know. I take her to the store and we go to lunch together..."

"Stop the bullshit, Luci. I'm telling you to move out of Mom's and that's that."

He hung up and dialed Vito's work number. "Vito?"

"Hey Phil, what's goin' on?"

"Sorry to call you at work but I'm concerned about Mom."

"Why, what's the matter?

"You know her friend, Valerie?"

"Yeah."

"She called me. Luci's living at Mom's again, and she's got Craig and Kevin there too."

"I know, Valerie called me too but I've been so busy..." he stopped. "Shit. What happened? Did Luci's ol' man kick her out again?"

"I don't know but Valerie said the situation's pretty bad. Somethin' about Mom sleeping in the car because Craig locked her out of the house."

"What?"

"Yeah, isn't that nice? And Luci acts like she doesn't know what I'm talkin' about."

"Well, what'dya wanna do?"

"I told Luci to move out by the end of the week. So, we'll see but in the meantime, I want you to go get Mom. Take her home to your house until Luci gets out. I think you should change all the locks too…keep Vinnie out, know what I mean? He's broken in two or three times and stole money. I'll fly up if you want me to."

"No, I can handle it."

"For now, go get Mom."

"Okay."

"Call me after, okay?"

"I will, Phil."

"We have to do something, Vito. Between Vinnie and Luci, Ma's gonna have a heart attack or something."

"I know," Vito agreed.

"And you know Mom's too weak to do it herself. God knows how much money she's given them."

"Yeah, I know."

"Well, keep me posted."

"I will. Talk to ya later."

*

Vito drove to his mother's house the following morning, and found her alone when he arrived. He was ready for a fight with Luci.

"Vito!" Connie said, with surprise. "What are *you* doing here?"

He was alarmed at his mother's appearance. Her eyes were sunken, and she was haggard and thinner than the last time he saw her. She coughed continuously, and considering it was past noon, it was not like her to still be in her pajamas. Vito trailed her as she picked up dirty towels and clothes from the floor. The house smelled like beer and cigarettes, and Vito felt a twinge of guilt that he didn't check on her sooner.

"Ma, what the hell is happening here?" The den and the kitchen table were littered with dirty plates and plastic lids filled with cigarette butts.

"I know," Connie said, sounding exhausted. She threw the armful of dirty clothes she was carrying back onto the floor, and sat down.

"Ma, I'm here to take you home with me, so how 'bout you go pack a bag."

"What? Pack a..." She was too tired to argue. "Okay. You're taking me to your house?" She seemed confused. "Vito, I'm afraid to leave the house. Luci's here...and so is..."

"I know, Ma," he interrupted her. "Phillip called me. He called Luci too, and told her she had to be out by the end of the week. In the meantime you're comin' home with me."

"How did he find out?"

"That doesn't matter, Mom. Come on, go pack your stuff so we can get outta here before Luci comes back. Where is she, anyway?"

"I think she went back to her house. I think that sonofabitchin' ol' man of hers called her about something. I don't know. He calls and she goes runnin'." Connie hung her head as though it was too heavy for her to hold up. "I'll be right back." She groaned as she stood up, and headed for the stairs. "Vito, I'm afraid they might wreck the house."

"Don't worry about it Ma."

Connie grabbed a few sweaters and slacks from her dresser drawer and threw them into a suitcase, and went downstairs. She checked the stove, left a note for Luci and got in the car with Vito, and rode with him to Lexington Estates. He and Barbara had recently built a new home, thanks to a two hundred thousand dollar check from Connie. There were six bedrooms in the house but for some reason, Barbara had set her mother-in-law up in the sewing room. A twin bed was made up with a blue comforter and a single lamp sat on a table by the bed. Connie didn't care; she just wanted to rest.

That night, Connie helped Barbara clean up the dinner dishes, and spent the next hour sitting with Vito while Barbara took the boys to soccer practice. "You know, your brother wants me to sell the house," she casually informed him.

"Phillip wants you to sell?"

"I don't know about selling, what do you think?"

Vito nodded. "I agree with Phil, Ma. It's the only way to stop Luci and Vinnie from drivin' ya nuts."

"I guess if I sell it, I could spend six months here and six months in Colorado."

"You could do that. I could find you a nice condo nearby, and I can take care of it when you're away…that would be a good plan."

Connie nodded but her expression turned to disappointment. *A condo*, she thought. *A six-bedroom house that I paid for, and he wants to put me in a condo.*

"You okay, Ma? You got quiet all of a sudden."

"Me? Oh yeah, I'm fine," she lied. "I'm just fine. I think I'll go to bed." She quickly stood up, and walked toward the stairs. "Night," she said.

Looking bewildered, Vito's eyes followed his mother. "Night, Ma."

Six days after Connie arrived, she was once again left alone in the house. Vito was at work, and the children were in school. Barbara was too busy with running errands and going on luncheon dates with her friends to have time for Connie, and Connie soon felt that she was in the way. After overhearing Barbara tell Vito that his mother's coughing was keeping her up at night, Connie had had enough. She picked up the phone and called Valerie.

*

Connie sat by the front window with her suitcase by her side. Barbara was in her bedroom all morning, and had no idea Connie was planning to leave. Connie looked out the window when she heard a car door close, and smiled when seeing Valerie and Honey walking toward the front door.

"Barbara?" Connie called.

Valerie knocked on the door and Connie invited them in. "I'm so happy to see you." She wrapped her arms around both women, and wept. Barbara came out of her room, and walked halfway down the staircase. She leaned against the banister, and crossed her arms. "Did you call me?"

"Oh, Barbara…these are my friends, Valerie and Honey."

"Hi," Barbara said, with a quick wave of her hand.

"Listen Barbara, I think I've stayed long enough. I'm just in the way here, so Valerie's gonna take me home."

"Oh…okay, you sure?"

"I'm sure…so, uh…well, goodbye." Connie stammered. She waited for Barbara to respond, and when there was none, said, "Thanks for everything."

"You're welcome."

"Tell Vito I'll call him later."

"I'll tell him," Barbara said, and started back up the stairs.

"What a bitch!" Honey said, following Connie to the car. "My God, I've never met anyone so cold! Wait, yes I have, now that I think about it. *My* daughter-in-law!"

"Listen, Connie," Valerie said. "I think you should stay with me for a while. I called your house, and Luci is still there but she said they're leaving soon. Then you can go home."

"Okay," Connie happily agreed. "You don't have to twist my arm."

*

Phillip called his mother every day. She was still staying with Valerie, and he was disappointed to hear her say that she added Vito and Barbara to her list of people that she was finished with. She swore she would never step foot in their house again, and he believed her.

The phone rang and Valerie answered, handing the phone to Connie. "It's for you, Connie, it's Phil."

"Hi Phil."

"Hi Ma, anything new?"

"No, not really. I told Vinnie he had to start making his own mortgage payments; he wasn't happy but what am I supposed to do?"

"I'll tell you what to do. If he doesn't start making the payments, I want you to sell the house," Phillip said, firmly. "You own that house and you've been paying the mortgage for him for almost twenty years, for God's sake."

"I know, I know." She was feeling pressured but knew he was right. "I'm livin' on a fixed income here, I can't afford to keep doin' this, and I don't wanna touch the money your father left. I need that for later, ya know what I mean?"

"I understand." He thought about the three hundred thousand dollars she gave to Vito, and could only imagine the hundreds of thousands of dollars given to Vinnie and Luci. "Mom, I wouldn't exactly call it a fixed income but that doesn't mean that Vito, Luci and Vinnie have a right to take all your money."

"Well, I'm not givin' anymore!" She stated, adamantly. I wanna sell that Goddamned house that Vinnie's in. I want him out. He's turned it into a shithouse with all his "druggie" friends stayin' there. Do I have to evict him first, or what?"

"No, you can just tell your lawyer to give him written notice that you're selling the house, and then get a realtor to put it on the market. You want me to make the calls for you?"

"Would you? I just don't feel up to it, Phil."

"Okay, I will. Do you know if Luci's out of the house?"

"She's supposed to be out."

"Well, I'm gonna call on Friday and make sure."

"Okay, Son. Thanks."

"And Ma, do me a favor, please? No more lying. Every time I call you, you say everything is fine, and I know that everything is not fine, so no more lying. I want the truth. And don't dare write any more checks to anyone, hear?"

"All right."

Phillip and Vito each got frantic phonecalls from Luci, begging them to let her stay at her mothers. They refused. Connie stopped paying her bills, stopped giving money to Kevin for school, and to Craig for beer and cigarettes. She refused to pay for Luci's dentist appointments, and her visits to the beauty salon. Luci was outraged. Ray O'Grady was in a rage as well. His meal ticket had suddenly been revoked.

It was all a sordid plan. Ray and Luci had long since made up, and they discovered that it was financially beneficial for Luci to live with her mother but unbeknownst to Connie, Luci snuck home daily to fix meals for Ray and to sexually satisfy him. They had used Connie for her money, and when there was no more money being handed out, Luci stopped calling her mother. Connie felt like a fool.

*

A notice to vacate was sent to Vinnie, and he promptly went to a lawyer. The lawyer advised him to sue his mother, which he did. In the interim, Connie received two very disturbing calls within a three-week period. One was from a woman who had hired Vinnie to clean out her basement, rake her leaves and clean her rain gutters. She had given him a check for one thousand dollars but Vinnie never returned to do the job. The woman was livid and threatened to have Vinnie arrested. The second call was from Mr. Amstead who owned a small television repair shop on the boulevard. He had hired Vinnie to sweep up in the evenings but, two days after Vinnie started the job, three televisions were missing. He too demanded payment and threatened to call the police. Connie was frantic. She paid the lady her thousand dollars and also wrote a check for five thousand to the storeowner. It continued to be one dilemma after another.

When the court date of Vinnie's lawsuit against his mother came up, Connie stood angry and stone-faced alongside her lawyer. Judge Francine Carol Burdini was residing. Vinnie was six feet away from her, looking smug while his lawyer shuffled papers. The judge read the transcripts, and glared at Vinnie, slowly shaking her head. Turning toward Connie, a sympathetic smile replaced her grimace. She leaned forward and said, "Mrs. Preste, I've seen your son in this courtroom more times than I care to remember, and I must tell you…I'm convinced that he is determined to not only destroy his own life but yours as well. He has abused the system and I'm sure you too, for far too long. As harsh as it may sound, I suggest you stop enabling your son, and move on with your life. Unfortunately, I have no doubt that I'll be seeing your son in here again but I don't want to see *you,* Mrs. Preste. Do you understand?"

"I understand, your honor," Connie answered, quietly.

"Mr. Preste," Judge Burdini turned toward Vinnie, giving him a cold stare, "you should be ashamed of yourself…dragging your mother into this courtroom. Your attorney, and I use the term loosely, was unable to supply me with one document that proves you own the house you've been living in all these years, nor was he able to give me one receipt that you ever paid a mortgage payment. Your mother has bailed you out time and time again and your attorney has given you some very poor legal advice. My determination is that your mother legally owns the house you've been living in, and has every right to sell it! So my ruling is in favor of the defendant." She slammed the gavel one time and said, "Next!"

Connie never saw Vinnie again. She went home, changed the locks again, and got a new phone number. Phillip still called everyday, and was pleased to hear a rare calm in his mother's voice. She was spending time with Valerie and Honey again, and back to attending the senior dances, but couldn't shake the feeling of doom that hung over her head like a black cloud.

*

"Hello?" Luci answered her mother's phone.

"Luci?" Phillip's said with surprise. His heart sank when he heard his sister's voice. "What are you doing at Mom's?'

"God…hello to you too," she said, indignantly. "Relax, will ya? I just came to take Ma to lunch."

Phillip could here mumbling in the background. Luci was covering the mouthpiece.

"Hello Phillip." It was suddenly his mother on the phone.

"Mom? What's going on?"

"No, nothin'." She sounded edgy and evasive. "Everything's fine. We're goin' out to lunch is all."

She was lying, and that angered him. He hung up the phone and called Valerie. His suspicions were right. Luci had moved back in but this time, only with Craig. Valerie said things were worse than ever because Vinnie had broken into the garage and stolen some lawn equipment, and Connie was again, handing out money. Phillip asked Bethany to pack a bag for him and he was on a flight to Cleveland the following morning. He was disappointed in his brothers and sister but even more disappointed in his mother.

*

Phillip sat in his mother's den, facing her, and watched as she fumbled with the wrapper on a piece of hard candy. She tossed one after another into her mouth to help quell a nagging tickle cough. Phillip hadn't seen his mother since her visit to Colorado, and was concerned by her appearance. She was thin and drawn, her hair uncharacteristically unkempt, and he hadn't seen her eat anything since he arrived.

"I'm really happy you're here, Phil but I feel bad that you had to make a trip here for all this shit goin' on. I wish it was just for a visit."

"I'm wanna fix things, Ma. You obviously aren't strong enough to do what you need to do to get your life in order, so I'm here to help." He was having trouble keeping his frustration in check.

"I know, you're right." She turned away from him, crossed her arms over her chest, and leaned back in her chair. "I feel like a fool letting things get this bad."

"Mom," Phillip leaned forward and rested his elbows on his knees, "you know this has to stop."

"I know." Connie covered her face with her hands, and shook her head. "Oh my God, those bastards are gonna kill me, aren't they?"

"Mom, why don't you sell the house and get away from here. Then they can't bother you. You can stay with Vito, and then you can come stay with Beth and me."

"Oh Phil, I can't. I promised your father I would never sell this house."

"Mom," he scolded, "you mean to tell me you're gonna let Dad control you from the grave? That doesn't make any sense."

"And I will *not* go and stay with Vito! Not the way they treated me that last time. No, no way." She stood up and started to pace. "They haven't even called me, not once! Cold…they're just plain cold."

"All right, calm down Ma. Come on…sit back down…relax."

She flopped down in the chair and crossed her legs.

"Selling the house is the answer, Ma, or Vinnie and Luci are gonna continue to take your money. Aren't you tired of cleaning up their messes?

"Ha, you're not kiddin'."

"Well then…"

"Listen Phillip, let me try for a while longer. Luci hasn't been here for while and I think she knows I'm serious this time. I have a restraining order on Vinnie, the locks are changed again and no one has my phone number, so if it starts up again, then we'll talk. Is that okay with you, Son?"

"Ahh, Ma. You're tough, ya know that?" He sat back, and smiled. "Oh, and while I'm thinking about it…you tell lies, Ma. You lie to me all the time and you've got to stop that."

"I do not lie," she said, indignantly. "When do I lie?"

"All the time, Ma."

"You want some more coffee, Phillip?"

"No, I've had enough, and you're changing the subject."

"Well then, let's go over to the lawyer's office so I can make a few changes. I want to take care of this today. I need to get some things off my mind."

*

For the first time in his life, Phillip felt uncomfortable being around his mother. He felt the heaviness of her depression. She was consumed with guilt and distrust, and was harboring hate for so many people that conversations with her were draining. He sat at the kitchen table and watched as she pulled reams of paperwork from the buffet drawer, and shoved it into her purse. She struggled with the papers because of severe arthritis that had gnarled her fingers. She was easily frustrated, and looked on the bad side of everything. Phillip understood but it made him sad.

"Good morning, Mrs. Preste." Albert Finster greeted Connie and Phillip at the door of his downtown office. He was dressed in jeans and a denim shirt. "Please excuse my casual attire but I'm in the office alone today, and you're my only appointment." He led into his office where they sat in front of his desk.

"This is my son, Phillip, and I want him to be here for this meeting," Connie stated firmly.

"Of course, how do you do, Phillip?" He shook Phillip's hand.

Phillip liked the man immediately. He was soft-spoken, with an engaging smile. He listened intently as Connie explained that she wanted her assets to be in Phillip's name, along with hers.

"Mom, are you sure you wanna do this?"

"Quiet Phillip, I've made up my mind. You see, Mr. Finster, I have three other children, and over the years I've given them hundreds of thousands of dollars, and they've given me nothing but heartache. But Phillip…" She turned to look at him, her voice trembling, "his father and I never gave him anything, and he never asked for anything, so I want to do that now. He's a good son, and it's obvious that *I* can't be trusted with the money, Mr. Finster. My other three would steal it from me in a heartbeat." She sat back, clapped her hands one time and nodded her head. "So that's what I wanna to do today."

"That's fine, Mrs. Preste."

"One more thing…I want your opinion on something. I'd like to give Phillip a gift of money before he goes back to Colorado. What do you think?"

"I think that's very wise. I'm a firm believer in giving gifts of money while you're still living."

"Well, good. That's what I'm gonna do then."

Phillip felt humbled and a bit embarrassed. "My God, Mom, what're ya doin'?" He looked at the lawyer, and shrugged.

"You're mother loves you very much Mr. Preste."

*

Phillip spent the rest of the week getting his mother's bank accounts in order. He spoke with Luci and repeated to her that she was not to move back into their mother's house again, and also to keep Craig away. Demands for money were to stop. He ordered her to pass the message along to Vinnie, since she was the only one to have contact with him. Phillip knew this would sever any ties he would have with his siblings but to protect his mother, it had to be done.

"What time's your flight, Phil?" Connie asked. They were sitting in the den, and he was finishing a plate of scrambled eggs, bacon and toast.

"Ten o'clock," he said, looking at his watch.

"That's what I told Valerie…said she'd be here around eight."

"That's fine." He took his plate into the kitchen, rinsed it off and placed it on the dish rack. "Ma listen, I really appreciate what you did but if you change your mind, you know you can put everything back the way it was."

"No way! Why would I do that? Look what you do for me, Phillip… you're all I've got."

"I don't know, I just feel funny."

"Phillip, please! Will you stop that? I have no doubts at all about what I did. But with the others…well, I don't trust myself, Phillip. From now on, when they ask me for money, I can honestly tell them that it's not up to me."

"Yeah, but I don't want any trouble from them, especially Vito...he doesn't know what's going on."

"I don't care." She raised her hand. "It's none of his Goddamned business! I've given him what...two, three hundred thousand dollars, and I'm not welcome in his house? That's bullshit!"

"All right Ma, don't get excited. We're past that now."

"I'm not getting excited and that's the last I want to hear about it. I hate having all that money. Look what it's done. I would have been better off poor! No...that's it, I want you to have it."

"Well...thanks, Mom." He wrapped his arms around her shoulders.

"Okay, enough about that." She gently pushed him away.

Connie spotted Valerie's car pulling into the driveway. "There's Valerie, Son. Get your bag."

Chapter 32

Phillip went home to Bethany, and she cried when Phillip handed her the check his mother had given him. She could hardly speak when she called to thank Connie, so she wrote a letter instead, and Connie carried the letter with her all the time.

Phillip unpacked but had an extra suitcase that he laid on the bed.

"What's in that suitcase?" Beth asked.

"You'll see." He opened the case and lifted out something wrapped in a blanket. He set it on the bed, and peeled back the blanket. Beth smiled when she saw her father-in-law's concertina.

"Your mom *gave* it to you?"

"Mmhm."

"I have just the place for it," she said, gently picking it up and leaving the room. She cleared a spot on the fireplace mantle.

"I like it there," Phillip said.

*

Valerie called on a Friday night, and Phillip was alarmed when he heard her voice.

"What's wrong, Valerie? Is Mom okay?"

She explained that Luci and Craig were back with Connie. Vinnie, somehow got his mother's telephone number, and was calling several times a day, blaming her for all his problems. He told her that because of her, he had nowhere to go. "Now, you know your mother Phil, she can't say no. They're driving her nuts."

*

When Vinnie showed up on his mother's doorstep, he was violating a restraining order, and to keep him from getting arrested, Connie gave him whatever money she had in her purse, and sent him away. She changed her number for a third time, and thankfully didn't hear from him for several days. After a ferocious argument with Luci, Connie sent her packing as well.

After a quiet, uneventful month, Connie thought it safe to leave the house and visit her sister, Carmella in New Jersey. Luci however, took advantage of her mother being out of the house, and moved back in. When Connie came home, Craig was sitting at the kitchen table with two of his friends. He dared to grin at her as she stared, in disbelief at her kitchen, strewn with empty beer bottles, the air reeking of cigarette smoke.

"What the hell is goin' on here?" Connie asked. She dropped her suitcase on the floor. "What're you doing here, Craig?"

"We're livin' here, grandmaw," he said, mocking her, as usual. "Take a chill pill, why don't ya."

"Where's your mother?"

"In here Ma," Luci called from the den. She was watching television, folding laundry.

"You two," Connie pointed to the two boys sitting with Craig. "Get out…yes, that's right Craig, I'm tellin' them to get out!"

"Bitch!" Craig snarled, and followed his friends out the door.

Luci sauntered into the kitchen, and snuffed out a cigarette. "Sorry 'bout the smoke," she said, casually. "Where ya been?"

"That's none of your business, Luci. What're you doing here?"

"The usual. My ol' man's got a bug up his ass about somethin', so me and Craig left. Kevin decided to stay with his father."

"This is insane," Connie said.

"What?" Luci asked, seeming to be completely unaware of why her mother was angry.

"Luci," Connie said, speaking slowly. "You're not supposed to be here. Anymore. Ever," she accentuated. "I told you…I can't help you anymore. No more money, no more living here.

"What are you talking about, Ma? You're tellin' me that all of a sudden you don't have any money?"

"I didn't say that. I can't touch my money anymore."

"Why?"

"I've turned the handling of my money over to Phillip, and I can't write any checks without getting his approval." Connie said. "There…I said it. That's the way it is, and I don't wanna hear another word about it!"

"You gave your money to Phillip?" Luci's face was red with rage.

"He's in control of everything now, Luci. I can't give you any more money. That's it! There's nothing's left that I can touch. Your brother's the only one looking out for *me*. For me!" she repeated, placing her hand on her chest.

"Oh really, so when did this happen?"

"I told you Luci, I don't wanna hear another word about it. You and Vinnie have bled me dry and I'm done! That's it! From now on, if you need money or if you need someone to get you outta trouble, go tell that bastard husband of yours!"

"This is bullshit!" Luci picked up the phone and started to dial.

"Who are you calling?"

"Phillip," Luci said, turning her back to her mother.

"Put that phone down!" Connie demanded. "I said put it down!" She grabbed the phone from Luci, and slammed it back on the receiver. "You're not calling him. He's just looking out for me. He's the *only* one looking out for me. I told you before, Luci that I couldn't afford to give you any more money. And you can't keep living here. You gotta get out!" She grabbed the sides of her head, and went to the den and sat down.

Luci followed and stood over her mother, her hands on her hips. "Well, where am I supposed to go, Ma? I mean, you're just gonna throw me out on the street? That's real nice. What kind of a mother are you?"

"Oh, don't give me that story again, Luci. I'm not falling for it anymore. You try to make me feel guilty, like I owe you or something."

"You *do* owe me, Ma!" Luci screamed.

"What do you mean, I owe you? I've given you more money…"

"I'm not talkin' about that…I'm talkin'…" Luci stopped short. "Never mind."

Luci walked back into the kitchen and lit up a cigarette.

Connie followed her. "You have to stop punishing me, Luci for whatever happened years ago. I'm not responsible for you anymore, Luci. Can't you understand that?" Connie couldn't hold back the tears. "For God's sake Luci, you're over fifty years old. You're married more than thirty years. When does it stop being my responsibility to take care of you? Whatever happened to you, I'm sorry…but I can't do any more. I'm an old woman now, and I've practically given all my money away to you and your kids, and to Vinnie and Vito…I mean, what's left for me? Social Security and your father's pension?" She looked up at Luci. Her face was stained with tears, her expression broken. She searched her daughter's face for a sign of compassion but there was none. "And one more thing, Luci, I'm gonna sell this house."

"Yeah, right," Luci scoffed.

"No, I'm going to sell it." Connie repeated. "You people are forcing me to sell the one thing that meant anything to me. I don't *wanna* sell it, but I have to. I can't live like this anymore." She swiped at the tears running down her cheeks.

"I know you Ma, you'll never sell this house," she said, with a cocky grin, "you're just upset." Luci went back to the kitchen, and grabbed her mother's car keys. "I gotta go pick up Kevin at school."

"Where's *your* car?" Connie asked.

"Ray's got it…won't gimme the keys. He's such a jerk off," she said, and walked out the door.

Connie rummaged through a drawer, and found the number of a real estate agent she got from Valerie. She put the card in her pocket as a reminder, and sat back down at the table. She was drained. Beads of sweat formed on her forehead yet her hands were cold as ice. She placed her hands on her temples when she heard a loud ringing in her ears. The room started to go black.

*

Connie opened her eyes. Blurry images hovered over her. She could hear her name being called, and she wanted to answer but her mouth wouldn't move.

"Connie? Can you hear me?" It was Valerie. She was stroking Connie's arm.

"Wha…where am I?" Connie said, finally finding her voice. She sounded hoarse, and her throat felt like sandpaper. "Valerie, is that you?"

"I'm here. You're in the hospital, Connie. I stopped by your house, and found you on the floor."

"Oh…" Connie murmured, not quite understanding what had happened to her. An IV needle, covered with surgical tape was inserted into the back of her hand.

"I called Vito, Connie. I hope that's okay. He'll be here tonight when he finishes work."

"That's okay. Don't call Phillip though. There's nothing he can do all the way out there, ya know?"

"I already called, Connie. He would've killed me if I didn't. I'm sorry."

"S'okay."

"Good evening, Mrs. Preste." A doctor came into the room wearing a white lab coat, and carrying Connie's chart. "I'm Dr. Weinman, from emergency. I'm a neurosurgeon, and I examined you when they brought you in."

A nurse fussed with Connie's blanket while the doctor continued. She had laid a tray of syringes and glass vials on the table.

The doctor wrote on the chart as he spoke. "You gave your friend quite a scare."

"I'm sorry," Connie said, quietly.

The doctor laughed. "You don't need to be sorry. I don't think you had a stroke on purpose."

"A stroke?"

"Just a mild one, Mrs. Preste but a warning, that's for sure."

"Oh dear God." Connie made the sign of the cross.

"No, don't worry. There's no visible sign of damage. And you're talking," he smiled. "That's always a good sign. You were lucky but you're going to have to make some major changes in your life. I understand you have a lot of stress right now." He ran a metal instrument down her arm, then down her leg. "Feel that?"

"Yes, I feel that."

"Good. Now for the stress...you're going to have to do something about that, and you're going to have to eat. I mean real food. I understand you pretty much live on soup?"

"Mmm," Connie shrugged.

"Well, that's not good enough. You need to take better care of yourself."

Connie closed her eyes. The nurse slipped the large black band of a blood pressure machine around Connie's arm, and hit a switch. Connie cringed when the band tightened on her arm. The nurse jotted numbers on the chart.

"Not too bad, sweetie," the nurse said. "Your blood pressure is creeping back to normal now." She drew four vials of blood, and left the room.

The doctor was waiting for the nurse to finish, then stood by Connie's bedside. "We're going to keep you in here for a couple of days for observation, and when we get you a little more nourished, we'll let you go home. Okay?"

Before Connie could answer he was on his way out the door.

"A stroke," Connie said, looking at Valerie.

"Just a mild one, Connie. Don't get upset. That's what they don't want you to do." Valerie pulled up a chair and sat next to her. "Listen Connie, if you don't do something drastic, those kids of yours *are* gonna kill you...for real next time. You know that, don't you? They're not gonna stop. They don't have any sympathy for you, and it might not be my place to say it but it's true."

"I know."

"Connie listen...since Dominic died, you have a second chance at life. You know what I mean?" Valerie asked. "Don't let your kids ruin that for you."

"I know," Connie nodded. "I really don't wanna sell my house, Valerie. It's all I have that belongs to me. But I know I have to," she added. "Those bastards! They're making me do it."

"It's a house, Connie. It's not as important as your life. Look, don't worry about it right now. Just rest and when you come home, we'll talk about it then, okay?" Valerie kissed Connie on the forehead. "I have to go but I'll come by again later. Vito will be here tonight. Call me if you wanna talk. There's a phone right here," she pointed out.

*

Connie was released from the hospital later that week. Valerie picked her up and drove her home, and Connie was visibly shaken when she got out of the car and saw a 'for sale' sign in her front yard.

"Phillip," Valerie said, noticing her friend's surprise. "He discussed it with Vito, and Vito agreed it was the best thing, so Phil called a realtor yesterday afternoon." She waited for Connie to respond. "You okay?"

"Yeah, I think so. Everything's happening pretty fast but I'm okay.

Chapter 33

Connie arrived in Steamboat Springs on a Friday morning, and when she saw Phillip and Bethany waiting for her at the gate, she fell into their arms and wept. She was exhausted and emotionally drained, and the three held tightly to each other for several minutes before saying a word.

"What would I do without the two of you?" she cried. "God has blessed me with a son and daughter like you."

Phillip took his mother's arm, and Beth took the other. They walked to baggage, picked her one suitcase from the carousel, and took her home.

Connie's house had sold two months before. She packed up the entire house herself, and what furniture she couldn't sell, she gave away. She offered her fur coats and fur cape to Barbara, but she declined. She used the excuse that she didn't have the closet space within her four thousand square foot home, and Connie could have kicked herself for offering the fur coats in the first place. The house that Vinnie lived in sold but only after it was gutted, fumigated and cleared of the equipment Vinnie used for raising marijuana plants in the basement. She had freed herself of any ties she ever had in Cleveland Heights.

*

Connie, living in Phillip and Beth's house was a difficult adjustment for everyone. She often secluded herself in her room, and though she was finally safe, she was not quite rid of the demons that had followed her through her life with Dominic. An ever-looming cloud of darkness seemed to create heaviness in the house. Connie knew it was because of her. Sleep came to Connie in two and three hour spurts. She was usually up for the day by three a.m., finishing her first pot of coffee by dawn. By noon, sadness and guilt sent her back into depression again. There were never phone calls from Vito, Vinnie or Luci, which didn't surprise Beth or Phillip. They considered it a blessing but it just reaffirmed to Connie that her three grown children didn't care about her at all; only money. When Connie gave in and allowed it, Beth and Phillip sat with her for hours, counseling her. They tried to convince her that her life was different now but the depression lingered. She refused to listen when they said she should be eating solid food. When she tried, she gagged herself and went back to eating soup. Her weight was dropping drastically and Phillip and Beth were at a loss. They could no longer handle the situation by themselves.

Phillip took a deep breath before approaching his mother one morning. "How're you doin' this morning, Mom?" he asked, casually.

"I'm fine, why?" Connie answered, clutching her chest, sounding alarmed.

"No, Ma…nothing's wrong. I was just asking how you are."

"Oh."

"Listen," he continued. He eased himself onto the sofa in her cozy sitting room, she in a chair by the window. "Beth and I were talking and I thought maybe you might want to go see someone," he spoke hesitantly. "You know, talk to someone about how you're feeling."

"What do you mean…like a psychiatrist? No!" She objected, vehemently. "I don't need a Goddamn doctor filling me up with pills. Just give me a little time…I'll be okay."

"Mom, first of all, please calm down. You don't need to cuss."

When she calmed, Phillip continued. "Listen Mom, you sit up in this room for days doing nothing. You don't eat…"

"Those sonofabitches…they don't even have the decency to call!" She cried. "They made me sell my house! Goddamnit!" She slammed her fist on her thigh. "I don't have nothin'! I'm like a bag lady!"

Phillip stood up, and glared down at her. "Don't say that! A bag lady? We brought you into our home, Mom. Beth takes care of you like you're her own mother! My children show you love and spend time with you. Everyone is trying to make up for everything that's happened to you. So, don't say that. You're going to have to try and put all that crap behind you and look forward." The last thing he wanted was to be angry with his mother but that seemed to be the only way to get her attention.

"I'm sorry, Phillip." She felt ashamed. "I know I say the wrong things all the time. I'm so stupid."

"And stop saying you're stupid!" Feeling frustrated, Phillip walked out of the room.

*

Over the next few months, when Connie showed no sign of improvement, she relented and agreed to see a doctor. Phillip took her to two or three different psychologists who unfortunately didn't offer much advice but prescribed medications that Connie was convinced were meant to kill her. She didn't trust anyone. There were two or three occasions where she passed out after taking a half dosage of a very mild sedative. Beth prayed for patience while she helped Connie through one episode after another. She told Phillip that his mother was worrying herself into panic attacks, and that the entire situation was beginning to take its toll on her too. Beth was a positive person and just beginning to enjoy what was supposed to be the best years of *her* life but she was feeling smothered by her mother-in-law's negativity. She found it difficult to be in the same house. Connie sensed Beth's discomfort, and tried to show how much she really appreciated what they were doing for her but she wasn't able to rid herself of the demons.

Time passed, and with faith and perseverance, Connie started to embrace the love that was surrounding her, and admitted that God truly had given her a second chance. She slowly conquered her depression, though there were days she sat in her room and had a good cry, thinking about her children that were no longer a part of her life. She felt the sting of guilt knowing they grew up to be selfish, greedy adults. She allowed them to be subjected to their father's distorted way of life. She felt guilt knowing she should have rescued them, and should have taught them to be loving and kind but it was too late now. The damage was done and she couldn't change that. She was too old and too tired. But Connie did need to make peace with God. She repented, read the Bible and prayed constantly.

For five years, Christmas, Easter and Mother's day was the only time she got a call from Vito. She almost wished he didn't call at all. It was hurtful to her that his calls seemed like a nuisance to him, or an unwelcome obligation. But the love she received in Phillip's home was stronger than her bitterness, and her anger was finally beginning to fade. Guilt reared its ugly head from time to time but Beth convinced Connie that God wasn't punishing her, He was blessing her, so why should she punish herself?

Beth was pleased with her mother-in-law's progress but couldn't help being frustrated over the food issue. She urged Connie to listen to the doctors that assured her that there was nothing physically wrong, but Connie stubbornly protested, "I can't eat and that's that". So soup and fruit juice were her daily diet. Beth accepted defeat.

It had been a long and difficult journey for everyone but Connie soon joined the fun and laughter that filled Phillip and Beth's house. Phillip's son, Andrew and his wife lived just a few blocks away. They, along with their two young sons visited often and Connie loved the happy commotion. Andrew's younger sister, Caroline, still lived at home and treated her grandmother like she was her best girlfriend. They developed a strong bond and relied on each other spiritually.

The family got together often, and there was always singing and goodhearted teasing. Connie hadn't seen that since she was a young girl back in Wickhaven. She didn't have to be afraid that someone would start a fight, no tables went flying across the room; she could hug anyone she wanted without worrying about the consequences. Andrew played his grandfather's concertina, and Connie sang in Italian and clapped her hands while the children danced. There were Sunday dinners together, and last minute plans out to lunch, movies and baseball games, school plays and church. It was a dream that Connie never thought she would experience.

Connie called Valerie every week and gave her a minute by minute report of the household's activities, and Valerie laughed as she listened to her friend sounding excited and happy. "They treat me like a queen, I tell ya!" Connie beamed.

Connie often called Carmella and Philomena. They kept her abreast of what was going on with the rest of their sisters. They were all widowed except for Violet who still had her beloved Pasqual. Sadly though, Violet as well as Maria were showing signs of Alzheimer's, and to everyone's shock, Bettina and Lourdes, now in their seventies, had been in and out of psychiatric hospitals for treatment of severe depression.

Connie sat for hours reminiscing about her childhood; she prayed for her sisters and wished them the happiness she had been blessed with so late in life.

Chapter 34

It was springtime, and the Colorado air was cool and crisp. Snow still draped the mountain tops like puffy white blankets. Connie was in her sitting room, enjoying a cup of hot chocolate when Phillip appeared in her doorway.

"Mornin', Ma."

Connie looked up and smiled, wonderfully relaxed and happy. "Good morning, Phil, come in. I was just looking out the window, enjoying the view of the mountains. Just look..." she said, turning to face the window again, "it takes my breath away."

Phillip leaned forward and looked. "Mmm, somthin' isn't it?" He sat on the canary yellow loveseat that was adjacent to where his mother sat in her favorite rocking chair. "This is such a nice room, isn't it?" Phillip said. Beth had painted the walls a soft, sage green and surrounded the room with pictures of the children and grandchildren. An aged, sepia shaded photo of Connie's mother and father hung in a special spot above her chair. Beth had also hung a picture of Connie's parent's and all eight girls above Connie's bed. Lace curtains were draped delicately in a picture window, and a mahogany wall unit housed her color television where you were sure to find her, every morning watching Joyce Meyer. Connie gave Joyce Meyer credit for helping her heal. The coffee table and end tables were cluttered with gifts from Andrew and Caroline and Andrew's children. Scented candles lined the windowsill.

"Oh, I love this room," she said, wrinkling her nose as she grinned. She ran her hands over the arms of her chair.

"Mom, can I ask you something…you don't have to answer me now," he said, raising his hand.

"Sure, what is it, Son?" Connie's expression turned to concern.

"Everything's fine," he assured her. "I was just wondering…if you really thought about it, what did you always want to do with you life? I mean is there something you always wanted to do but didn't get to do it?"

"Where is *this* coming from?" She asked, eyeing him curiously.

"Come on, Ma…indulge me."

"Well, can I think about it for a little while? I don't know where you're going with this." She gave him a sideways glance and squinted. "I don't wanna take any big trips or anything," she warned. "I'm not up to it."

"No, it's nothing like that. I'm just curious, that's all. You think about it and get back to me, okay?"

"Okay." She watched him leave, and tapped at her temple wondering what Phillip was planning.

Later that day, Connie found Phillip and Beth relaxing on the back patio sipping coffee from huge mugs labeled *World's Greatest Mom*, and *World's Greatest Dad*. They each held a section of the newspaper.

"Hi, kids." Connie sat on a lounge chair, and propped up her legs, feeling the heat of the afternoon sun on her skin.

Phillip lowered his paper. "Hi, Ma…what's up?"

"You two don't mind if I sit here a while, do you?" Connie asked.

"Of course not, Mom," Phillip couldn't help but laugh. "Sit, relax. That's what *we're* doing."

"Well, I don't wanna get in the way."

"You're not in the way, Mom." He smiled and shook his head. "It's nice and cool but the sun feels great, don't ya think?"

Beth slid her chair closer to her mother-in-law. "You're thinkin' about something, aren't you? Come on…" she teased, "Tell me what's on your mind."

"Well, Phillip asked me the strangest question this morning and I couldn't stop thinking about it."

"Well, what did you come up with?" Beth asked.

"Oh, he told you what he asked me?"

"Uh...yeah, Ma. He pretty much tells me everything," she laughed. "So, ya better be careful what you say!" She gave Connie a playful poke.

"Well, I thought about it. It kind of stretched me out, I hafta tell ya."

"Stressed, Mom," he corrected her.

"Stressed," she repeated. "Anyway, shut up and let me finish," she said, laughing.

"The only thing I could think of was that I always wanted to have my own little Italian bakery, you know, like when I was a kid back in Wickhaven."

"Really?" Phillip raised his eyebrows, pretending to be surprised.

Beth looked at Phillip, and smiled sheepishly. "How did I know you were going to say that?"

"An Italian bakery in Steamboat Springs. An interesting concept." Phil said, rubbing his chin thoughtfully.

"Oh, come on you two." Connie waved her hand. "You asked me, and I gave you an answer...it doesn't mean we can do it!"

"I think we should!" Phillip said, slapping his hands on his knees.

"We should do what?" Connie asked. She sat back and studied them both. She cocked her head and frowned. "We should do what?" She asked again.

"Hmm, I can see it now," Beth said. "*Connie's Little Italian Bakery.* What do you think Phil? Sound good?"

"Sounds good to me."

Epilogue

Connie stood on the sidewalk of Ski Time Square Drive. She couldn't hold back the grin that spread across her face as she admired the old English-style lettering that read, *Conchetta's Italiano Dolce.* Nestled between a used bookstore called Murphy's and Nehman's Ski Shoppe, Connie's bakery sat at the base of a mountain in the Torian Plaza. It was the most beautiful sight Connie had ever seen. She opened the door and smiled as she looked up, hearing the tinkle of the brass bell that hung from the doorframe. She closed her eyes and sniffed the sweet aroma of freshly baked bread.

Caroline and Andrew had been hard at work since opening the shop at six-thirty that morning. Connie sat down on one of the ice cream parlor-styled chairs and laid her purse on the table.

"Grandma!" Caroline called, running from behind the counter. She threw her arms around her grandmother's neck and kissed her noisily on the cheek. "What can I get for you? Coffee, tea...what?"

"Nothing, honey. Now, stop fussin' over me, and go take care of that customer," she said, giving Caroline a pat on the backside.

Caroline went back behind the counter and greeted the customer with her usual bubbly personality and contagious smile. She filled a pink paper sack with a variety of cookies and handed it to the woman. Andrew peered through the window of the kitchen, waved and blew his grandmother a kiss. Connie had spent months teaching him how to make her special pastries, and as fate would have it, Andrew had already graduated from culinary school the previous year, and had planned on being an executive chef but now wanted to master pastry making. The store had only been opened for six months, and already locals, as well as tourists were coming in and asking to meet Conchetta. She happily obliged. Donning her pink apron with the double set of ruffles that read *Grandma Conchetta,* she stepped from behind the counter and gave hugs, and posed for pictures. She placed warm cookies in the tiny hands of children that were wide-eyed as they studied the display cases filled with sweets. Connie was a local celebrity and she loved it.

The bakery was warm and inviting, just like she had always dreamed about. Folks came to sit and enjoy a cappuccino, share a piece of pie or a plate of cookies. Beth had decorated the shop to look like an old world Italian kitchen, with lace curtains, swept back and tied with white, satin ribbon. Antique chests, hand painted with colorful flowers were topped with cookie jars and antique coffee mugs. Jars of rock candy sticks, and biscotti were placed on small round tables that were covered with stiffly starched pink linen tablecloths, and topped with thin-necked vases filled with fresh flowers. Customers helped themselves to coffee from the coffee bar, and by eight o'clock in the morning, all the tables were usually full.

Andrew worked tirelessly to keep the display cases filled with lemon pastries, nut-filled cookies, cheesecakes, and a variety of breads that his grandmother taught him how to make. One special bread that Connie had learned to make some sixty years before was called Leone's Tuscany Cheese Bread. It was now Andrew's specialty.

Even though Connie was enjoying her life, embracing her family and putting forth an effort to find peace, September fifth somehow still enveloped her with sadness. It was the anniversary of the day she had wed Dominic; a day that she had so hoped would change him. She longed for those days in Wickhaven when she was just a young girl, in love and filled with hope for the future. She now sat by her window, gazing out at the mountains but she wasn't really seeing the beauty of the mountains that day. She saw Mama, standing at the wood-burning stove making dinner, Papa napping with his cigar clenched in his teeth. She could hear Carmella's laugh, and remembered the satin smoothness of Violet's wedding dress that later became hers. She thought about the first time Dominic put his lips to hers; how it made her stomach flutter, and the first time they danced, and how she knew every step he was going to take. Connie could hear the lilt of the concertina and pictured the warm smile that it brought to Dominic's lips. She wanted a home filled with love and laughter; the kind of home she grew up in. If she had only known the secrets...maybe she could have helped Dominic.

"Wickhaven," Connie whispered. "It was so long ago. I wish I could go back for just one day."

LaVergne, TN USA
30 August 2009
156368LV00001B/4/P

9 781449 007492